The LEGACY

THE LEGACY

A RIVERS WILDE NOVEL

DYLAN ALLEN

The Legacy
A Rivers Wilde Novel

Copyright © 2018 by Dylan Allen

ISBN: 978-1-968707-95-8

Published by Blue Box Press, an imprint of Evil Eye Concepts, Incorporated

V72021DA

Dedication

For my Day Dreamers…thank you for the inspiration.

Welcome to Rivers Wilde

Dear Reader,

Rivers Wilde is an ode to the city I grew up in; Houston, TX. I was inspired to create the series to show a side of Texas I knew well but hadn't seen portrayed in the romances I read.

The series celebrates the innovation, diversity, and abundance of opportunity that makes the city a beacon of prosperity for people across the globe.

As a result, it is a true American melting pot and I hope the series does that attribute justice.

The fictional enclave of Rivers Wilde is a small town within a very large city. It's also the result of a clash of titans.

The Rivers are old, Texas money. Sugar, oil, and natural gas are how they made their fortune. And with that bounty, they helped found the city they're the self proclaimed kings of.

In the 1980s, the oil markets were crashing and the Rivers found themselves hard up for cash. With no other viable options, they sold part of their precious land to the usurpers they'd previously refused to even acknowledge.

The Wildes are an immigrant family, one part Irish, one part Jamaican. They own restaurants, grocery stores and real estate and have made a fortune so large, it can't be ignored.

They bought the jewel in The Riverses crown, some of the most expensive property in all of Texas, and created an enclave that became home to the most sought after real estate in the city.

While the Wildes prosper, The Riverses seethed. Seeds of their resentment burrowed deep into the fertile soil of their dislike and grew tenacious roots.

Thirty years later, the rivalry continues. And it's got to do with a lot more than bruised egos.

Today, a new generation holds claim to the helms of power in both families. Will they put the past behind them and usher in a new era of cooperation between the two ruling families in Houston? Or will the sins of their fathers continue to cast a shadow over them?

I hope you enjoy finding out! And welcome to Rivers Wilde.

Prologue

HAYES

"You wanted to see me?" I duck my head through the heavy oak door of Swish's office.

I breathe a sigh of relief when I see that he's alone. Everyone else has met with me in pairs—mostly with their lawyer present. I haven't had a truly personal conversation in a whole week.

"Hello, son." Swish greets me in his swashbuckling East Texas twang that sixty years of living in Houston hasn't ridden him of. Despite the red-rimmed eyes and the disheveled, finger-mussed state of his normally perfectly styled, legendary silver hair, he's smiling at me. It's a beleaguered lift of the left corner of his mouth, but it's more of a smile than I've seen on his face in a month. It's sincere and warm, and when he says, "I'm glad to see you," I believe him.

He tugs his glasses off his nose, dangles, then drops them wearily onto one of the haphazard stacks of paper littering his desk.

"Come in, close the door." He gestures to it and then hefts his bulky frame out of his chair and strides over to sit in one of the tufted dark red leather seats in front of his desk.

He's had this office in Rivers House for as long as I've been alive and the smell of old books, aged leather, and coffee is comforting to my badly tattered nerves.

"Have a seat." He nods at the identical chair across from him. The warm smile is gone and what's replaced it is so grave, so grim, that my stomach clenches. I wipe my suddenly sweaty palms down the front of my jeans-covered leg and do as he asks.

He groans through a yawn, presses the heel of his hand to his bleary eyes and rubs them slowly.

He's oozing fatigue, and it's catching because I'm starting to feel weighed down by my own as I watch him. He looks old. And I'm very aware of the fact that time is not on his side…or any of ours, really. But he folds his gnarled, spotted hands over the middle of his infamously large beer belly and leans back in his chair.

"The last two weeks have been…difficult." His voice is weighed down by all the things we've faced this week.

Difficult.

Memorizing the first nineteen lines of *Chaucer's Canterbury Tales* in Olde English for class last month was *difficult*.

Having to live without someone you love and knowing you'll never hear their voice again isn't difficult.

The worst day of my life has already come and gone. The boulder of pain that has lodged itself into my chest is heavy and no other emotion has been able to find a foothold in it for weeks.

With each day that's passed since my father died, I've become more convinced that what I'm feeling is something bigger, less definable than simple pain.

Pain is a basic, localized thing.

What *I* feel is sophisticated, all-encompassing.

Pain has a remedy.

There's no cure for what has taken root inside of me.

I wish he would get to the point so I can go back to my room and put on some music and try to sleep. My father loved Elvis. I used to think it was such an odd thing for a boy from East Texas—who grew up sucking at the teat of Wednesday night Bible study, Friday night football, and Sunday morning service—to love music that my grandmother used to call the *Devil's seduction*. The night he died, I played one of his albums on repeat and fell asleep to "Can't Help Falling in Love." Now I can't sleep without listening to it.

"Your father was like a son to me. That I have outlived him *and* his father…" He shakes his head. "I don't know how to feel about it, Hayes. But the one thing I know is that I wouldn't wish it on anyone. I've had a real difficult time finding reasons to be grateful for my advanced age, son. But today, I'm glad I'm here—because you need someone," he says solemnly.

This time, his lips only quirk when he attempts to soften the grave-ness of everything.

"You don't have to smile. I don't even try," I say. We're familiar bedfellows when it comes to sitting across from each other with grim sadness between us.

When my father's brain tumor returned so aggressively—and within weeks of his surgery—it was Swish who told me it was time to get ready to say goodbye. He was dead two weeks later. In so many ways, my life feels like it's come to a screeching halt.

I haven't been to school. My stepmother has taken my brothers and gone to her parents' in College Station. And my uncle Thomas and his newest future ex-wife have camped out in the wing of the house that belonged to my father.

"You're so much like him," Swish remarks and draws me back to the present.

"Am I?"

"Yes, and your father, God rest his soul, was so much like his father, too." he adds,

"They weren't anything alike," I interject and lean forward because I want to see his agreement with my own eyes. All l I see is pity. "They weren't," I insist.

He sighs. "I know your grandfather was ruthless at times -"

"All the time," I mumble. People tell all sorts of stories about him. Your father didn't speak highly of him. Thomas only speaks of him in hushed tones of reverence.

"Whatever ill he's accused of, he was a brilliant businessman and investor. You've seen the reports about your father in *Forbes*?" he asks.

I roll my eyes and groan. "Yeah, but he said they exaggerate."

"No, they don't," he says, and my jaw drops.

"You mean, we're really worth twenty billion dollars?" I ask.

"There is no 'we.' It was your father's, and now it's yours."

"He left it *all* to me?" I ask, incredulous.

"90% of it, yes. The rest to Eliza and the boys," he says mirthlessly.

"Holy shit." I sigh and lean back.

"You are too young to step into your father's shoes. The will says that in the event of your father's demise before you're of age, the com-pany shall be lead by someone of the board's choosing."

I nod. "So, it's only until I'm thirty?"

"Yes. As long as you're deemed qualified."

"Are you taking over until then?"

He shakes his head. "Your Uncle Thomas will be stepping into your father's role."

I recoil at the suggestion. "What? How?"

He holds his hand up. "Let me finish and I'll answer your questions."

I nod.

"He and your father made an agreement and we rewrote the succession plan."

I scoff. "He turned his back on the company. He *can't* run Kingdom."

"Yes, he can. He has plenty of executive experience."

I shove out of my seat. "He's spent the last twenty years running every business he's been the head of into the ground."

Swish shakes his head in disagreement, but doesn't meet my eyes. "Hayes, that's not true. Your father trusted him to be a good steward until you're ready to take over."

I cross my arms over my chest and shake my head in disbelief. "How can you say this like it's not a terrible idea?"

"Because, it's done. But trust me, I wasn't happy about it, but I was overruled." He sighs. "Can you please sit down? I'm too old to be looking up at anyone while I'm trying to my best to help them."

I flush at the reproach in his voice and drop into my chair. "Sorry. Go on."

He shuffles the papers in front of him. "You're your father's only child. If you die before you turn thirty or before you have children, your uncle and his heirs will inherit everything. This will be a very powerful motivator for your uncle to undermine your return." he explains.

My jaw drops. "You think he wants me *dead?*" I ask in horror.

"Of *course* not," he says dismissively. "I'm just reminding you of what's at stake. If something happens to *you*, the entire family's future will be in his hands. And he is *not* fit to hold it," he says, slamming his palms on his desk in a rare display of temper.

"What can we do?"

"I'll be keeping an eye on him as long as I can. Whatever his business skills are, his personal ones don't inspire confidence. Since his last divorce, he's taken an advance on his income from the trust every month," he says sadly but with growing conviction in every word.

"What if he runs through it all?"

"Don't worry about that. I have discretion over what happens to your personal inheritance. It won't be tied to Kingdom's fortunes. You can't touch it until you're ready to assume the chairmanship."

"But your income payments will be held in trust for you by your Aunt Gigi."

"Who?" I ask sharply, sure I hadn't heard him correctly.

"Your father has an older sister, Georgiana, but everyone calls her Gigi," he says again, and I sit back. A cold weight spreads in my core as I look at Swish with eyes that go from wide with shock to narrowed in suspicion.

"No, he doesn't," I insist.

"Yes, Hayes, he does," he says softly. He watches me solemnly, and I realize, with real horror building in my chest, that he's telling the truth. But…my father wouldn't hide his sister. Would he?

"How come I've never even heard her name before?" I ask, the demand in my voice softened by the quaver in it. My entire *body* is shaking. My mind is whirling. I don't understand.

"She was disinherited before you were born," he says, and I blanch at the idea.

"Are you serious?" I ask rhetorically—the answer is obvious from the look on his face.

He just nods.

"But w-why?" I stutter on my question because I can't imagine that there's an answer that would help me understand.

"She chose a man over her family, and that was that. Your grandfather wrote her out of the will, out of the family Bible, out of the family tree, and for him, she hasn't existed in almost sixteen years," he says.

"His own daughter?" I ask. My grandfather was not a kind or loving man, but he behaved like family was paramount to everything. And he liked control. Over everything. I can't imagine him having a child out in the world whom he couldn't rule over with his iron fist.

"It was her choice. Your father stayed in touch with her—secretly. The week before he died, he asked her to be your guardian," he says.

"He did?" I ask dumbly. But I've stopped thinking. What else don't I know about my family? About my father? Part of me wants to know. The other part hopes I never find out.

"I would have rather he'd let me be your guardian, but he insisted. He wants you to live with her. And she agreed. So, she's coming to get you, Hayes." His big body heaves with his sigh like he's relieved to have said it.

"Coming from…where'd you say? Post what?" I ask. My head is spinning; I don't even recognize my own voice.

"Positano," he says with a weird accent.

"Where the hell is that?" I ask.

"Italy," he says.

"What's she doing there?"

"She lives there," he says slowly, his face contorted like he's bracing for a strong gust of wind.

"In *Italy*?" I ask.

"Yes. She got married and moved there with her husband. They're not married anymore, and she stayed after they got divorced."

"When is she moving here?" I ask

"She's not. You're going to live with her, in Positano," he says.

I look at him, confused and in denial about what he's saying and shake my head as it starts to settle.

"But—I live *here*. I just made the JV team. I have a girlfriend," I say and my life flashes before my eyes like a movie. But the reel is withered, burned, incomplete. My heart races as panic starts to set in.

I scramble to my feet. The chair scrapes against the floor as I push out of it.

"I'm in the middle of my freshman year. I just—"

"There are no options for you to stay here." He cuts me off brutally.

"But…" I shake my head helplessly.

In the span of two days, my life has gone from charmed to something completely foreign and terrifying. "I don't even know her. We've never even met," I say.

"You will get to know her. She's already here," he says.

"What?" I swivel in my chair, my eyes frantic as they scan the room.

"No, son," Swish raises his voice and I look back at him. "I meant that she's in Houston, at the St. Regis. Not here at Rivers House."

I let go the breath I was holding, the rush of oxygen to my brain makes me dizzy. I sag in my seat and drop my head into my hands, my eyes squeezed shut and focus on trying to make my heart slow down."

"I wouldn't do that to you, Hayes." Swish sounds sad that he has to remind me of that.

And he doesn't. If there's anyone in the whole world I trust implicitly, it's him.

I sink back down in my seat, disappointment ripe in my chest. The ache in my throat makes my neck throb. And my head is too heavy for it to hold up anymore.

This house, which has been passed on to from father to first born son, that has never truly felt like home. But with my father gone, it's a monument of memories that are the only things I have left. I can't fathom not even having that small piece of him anymore.

"It's what your father wanted," Swish says gently.

I raise my face just enough so he can see the glare in my eye. "That's emotional blackmail."

"Maybe," he shrugs, but his eyes are full of regret. "It's also true. So stop wasting time throwing a fit and start thinking about how you're going to make the next sixteen years of your life count."

I take a quick, fortifying breath and sit up to look him in the eye. My father raised me face obstacle head on and to find the opportunity in every challenge. I'm his heir and the guardian of his legacy. I'm going to make him proud.

Even if it hurts.

"Okay." I have a million questions and protests on the tip of my tongue, but I don't say them. What would be the point? "Tell me what's going to happen." I ask in a voice that's as hollow as my heart.

Swish does me the courtesy of not smiling and acknowledges my acceptance with a brisk nod. "You'll leave with her in two days. And you will take care of yourself and your name. As I said, she'll receive your income payment. She'll spend what she needs to for your upkeep and education. But the rest will be yours to spend as you wish."

"I understand," I mutter when in fact, absolutely nothing makes sense.

"One more thing," he says, and I nod.

One more thing—a million more things - it didn't matter when he'd taken everything I care about.

"By virtue of your last name, you'll find that people use you to get close to the money and power you'll have access to. Don't trust anyone without verifying, first, that you can."

This speech, at least, is familiar. My father drilled that into me from an early age. He encouraged me to make first, but never be at the expense of the family. *It* always comes first.

For him and now, for me.

"All of this is your legacy." Swish waves his arms around the vast room that's been his seat of power for the last forty years. "You have to come back and make sure the Rivers name, mission, values, and ethics remain intact. Your family isn't respected just because it's wealthy. It's because they use that money to do good, to create opportunity. They have been to Houston what the Medici were to Europe during the Renaissance. And you've got to remember everything your father taught you. Gigi will do a good job keeping your feet on the ground."

The calm in his voice is at odds with the chaos every single cell in my body is gripped by. My entire world has been ripped to shreds, and I'm being sent halfway across the world to live with a woman I don't know.

"What about my brothers?" I ask, even though I'm afraid for the answer.

"They'll stay with their mother. Here at Rivers House."

"I bet Eliza will be happy," I mumble to the floor. I normally hide my resentment toward her, but now that my dad's gone, so is my restraint.

"Sadly, I can't deny that's true."

He glances at his watch. "It's almost time to leave for church. Go put on your suit and be ready in half an hour. We'll ride over together."

"No, I want to ride with my brothers."

"And Eliza?" His salt and pepper eyebrows lift in surprise.

"I want to spend as much time with them as possible." I say in a voice laced with accusation.

He gives me a grim smile. "Of course. I'll see you there."

My father married Eliza when I was seven. She was a recent widow with three young sons.

But he married her because she was from an old family and had her own wealth to bring to the marriage.

Just like my biological mother had been.

He told me that the woman I chose had to be someone just like that. The thought terrified me. The only good things about my father's marriage were my three little brothers.

My heart tugs at the thought of them. Stone, the closest in age to me, is only ten. But we've always been close.

Their mother was an equal opportunity terrorist. She made them as miserable as she made me and we'd formed a real brotherhood in the trenches of Eliza's crazy.

My father adopted them, so we're not just brothers in spirit—the law says we are, too.

I've always looked out for them. Held their hands through everything. But today, they'll have to manage without me.

I'm not riding in a car with her. I'm not going to sit next to my

Swish and listen my uncle deliver a eulogy that should have come from me.

I need to be somewhere I'm safe and can think and cry the way I need to. I turn away from the stairs and toward the rear exit of the house.

The crunch of footsteps behind startles me, but not enough to make me turn around and see who's behind me.. I'm not supposed to be on this part of our property. I've been warned repeatedly that this part of our property is off-limits.

But I'm not worried about getting in trouble. I've already been kicked out of my house, what else could happen.

"Yo! What are you doing here?" a man's voice calls out from the clearing behind me. I'd been expecting Swish to come looking for me when he realized I wasn't at the service. But that deep, loose, and jaunty voice is definitely *not* Swish.

When I turn around, a tall, young, dark-haired man I've never seen before is watching me with a wary look on his face. Like *I'm* the intruder. I'm not supposed to be here, but this *is* still my family's property.

I stand up slowly and face him. "Who the fuck are *you*?" I ask with as much aggression as I can manage.

"Remington Wilde." He says his name like it's a title. Like he expects it to mean something to me. And it does. Even though I've never laid eyes on him before. His last name was among some of the very first words I ever learned.

Remington Wilde is the oldest son of my family's biggest rival.

His family's heir in training.

Just like me.

I've been raised to think of him as my nemesis.

I don't know what I expected him to look like. Certainly not so… *normal*. He could be any other teenager at my high school. Like me, he's taller and broader than average. He's got a basketball tucked under one of his arms and is dressed like he's been playing.

"Who the fuck are *you*?" he says just as combatively.

"Hayes Rivers," I answer and straighten my spine. The same surprise I felt flickers in his eyes for just a fraction of a second before he schools his expression—but I don't miss it.

Then, he starts dribbling the ball. His hand meets it every time it springs off the ground, but his eyes never stray from me. I'd heard he was a major basketball talent. But he attended the public high school, Lamar, and I go to the private Strake Jesuit. Our teams have never played each other. But if his playing is anything like his skillful but absentminded dribble, he was clearly born to hold a basketball.

"You're not supposed to be here," he says and draws my eyes back to his.

"Neither are you," I shoot back.

We stare each other down. The longer I look at him, the more I'm sure I've seen him before.

He narrows his eyes at me, crosses his arms over his chest and curls his lip. "I came to get a ball that came over the wall. But you look like you've been making yourself comfortable back here." He nods at the sleeping bag that's stretched across the huge boulder in the center of the clearing. I've been coming here since the day my father died. It's been my escape from an endless stream of people who have been at our house to pay their respects.

"So?" I respond with a defensive shrug. I nod at his arm. "Looks like you got your ball. Why are you still here?" I ask.

His eyes narrow briefly, but his expression stays neutral.

"I thought your old man's funeral was today," he says casually, quietly. And yet, the reproach in his tone hits me like he yelled them inches away from my face. A flush of shame washes over me.

Of course, he knows. Everyone does. His mother, the widely-respected Tina Wilde, sent flowers. Eliza hurled the vase against the wall when she read the card, and they were not invited to the funeral. But I know their family must be watching ours closely to see how things change now that my father is gone. I wonder, too. He looks nothing like the mythical foe I'd imagined he would. But our families have shared nothing more than the wall that divides our properties for the last— nearly—fifteen years.

He glances at his watch, frowns at it, and then looks back at me. "It can't be over already? At nine o'clock in the morning?"

I imagine St. John's United Methodist Church packed to the rafters with people, pretending to care that my father is dead, mingling with the handful that really do. I've been handed so many business cards this week by people hoping that *the Riverses will continue to be customers.*

I've thrown them all away.

"Nah, it's probably just starting." I kick at the leaf-covered ground and avoid his disapproving gaze.

"So…why are you here and not there?" he asks.

"I already said goodbye," I say with a shrug of my heavy shoulders.

"What about your mom? Your brothers? Don't they need you there?" he asks. Kindness softens the disapproval in his tone.

I don't like it.

I don't want it.

But I do feel a flush of shame that I'm not there for my brothers. I push that down and say words that are much closer to the surface and less problematic for me.

"She's not my mom," I say.

"Oh, she's not?" He looks genuinely surprised.

"Nope. She married my dad when I was seven," I say.

"So, they're your step brothers?"

"They're my *brothers*," I clarify. I hate that word. We haven't made that distinction since the first year our parents got married.

"Go be with your family, kid." He nods in the direction of the house as if he expects me to start off in that direction.

I bristle and plant my feet. "I'm not a kid, and you're not old enough to be calling me one," I say crossing my arms over my chest for emphasis.

He folds his arms over his much broader chest and straightens so he's at his full height. "I'm eighteen. In college. And *my* dad's been dead since I was two, and my mother hates the sight of me. So, I've been old enough for a lot of things for a long time." he says.

"I'm sorry about your dad," I say even though I don't hear a hint of grief in his voice.

"I was too young to say goodbye when he died. You're not. If you can't do it for yourself, do it for them." He puts a hand on my shoulder, and it's oddly comforting—not at all awkward.

I don't want kindness or comfort. So, I shake it off and scowl. "I'm surprised you even care. Don't the Wildes hate the Riverses? Isn't that why we've never even *seen* each other before?" I ask.

"First of all, it's the Riverses who hate the Wildes." He bounces his ball once. "And I've seen you before. Didn't know who *you* were. You and that little cheerleader girlfriend of yours come into Eat! over on Wesleyan. I work behind the deli counter. You probably didn't notice since you didn't take your sunglasses off the whole time you were in the store," he says and dribbles his ball a few more times.

"You w*ork* there?" I ask.

"Who else is going to?" he says.

"Doesn't your family *own* it?" I ask.

"Yes, and we all work in the businesses until we're old enough and smart enough to run them. We aren't like the Riverses, who give it to whoever blood says is next in line." he says, his dark eyes cocky and daring me to challenge him. I can't.

It's true. But damn if I'm going to let him know it bothers me. So, I smirk. "I'll say hi next time I come in. Maybe you can make me a sandwich," I say.

He snorts and but a smile curls one corner of his mouth. "*Today*, I'll cut you some slack and let you get away with that. But don't try that on a day that's *not* your father's funeral," he says and bounces the ball one last time before he tucks it back under his arm.

"Or what? You'll leave the mayo off my sandwich?" I scoff.

He snorts out a laugh and throws the ball so hard and fast that I barely catch it before it hits me squarely in the chest. "Nah. I'll use my hands to show you why I can call you *kid* any time I want."

I throw the ball back with as much force as I can. He catches it without even looking. Then he turns and starts to walk back through the little clearing in the woods that leads to the door I've never dared to open. It's the emergency access to Rivers Wilde, the neighborhood the Wilde family established when they bought this land from my father, right around the time I was born.

He's almost disappeared into the brush when he stops and looks back at me.

"Go to your dad's funeral. Trust me, you'll never finish saying goodbye, and you'll be glad you saw him this one last time."

He leaves, and after a few minutes, so do I.

Part 1

16 YEARS LATER
CASTIGNIOCELLO, TUSCANY
ITALY

Chapter 1

HELLO

HAYES

"Can you hold the door, please?" a voice calls from down the hall. This is the third time the doors have attempted to close and someone has stopped us. I'm standing by the button panel and have no intention of pressing the "Door Open" button.

"Excuse me," a woman behind me says and then a feminine finger complete with a short, but perfectly manicured, light pink fingernail slips around my side and presses the button just as the door is about to close completely. I was reading emails when I stepped onto the lift, so I didn't see who was standing right behind me. But now I can feel her. Her breasts press into the back of my arm and her perfume, something with roses, wafts up my nose.

If there were a single inch of space in the elevator, I would turn to see who she is. But there's not. As soon as her finger disappears, I press the "Door Close" button and keep my finger on it.

"That was rude," the she says as the door shuts in the face of the woman who called out for us to wait.

"Oh, well," I say in return. I look up at the top of the mirrored elevator ceiling. I can only see the tops of our heads. Hers is crowned by a mass of blond waves that appear to tumble down her back. It's pushed off her tanned, delicate shoulders. Each one is bisected by two skimpy black strips of fabric holding up what must be a very lightweight shirt.

As the elevator stops on consecutive floors and people step off, it becomes less and less crowded. But she stays pressed to my back, and her hand moves, like she's fidgeting with something between us.

I wonder briefly if she's a pickpocket, and just as I start to turn around to ask her what the hell she's doing, she speaks.

"Please don't move. My necklace is snagged on your shirt," she says with enough alarm in her voice to halt my movements.

The elevator reaches the next floor and a couple gets off. She and I are the only ones left.

"Shit, I can't get it loose," she mutters. I start to turn again. "If you move, it'll break the chain," she says again in her voice which calls to mind smoke. And rain. And sex.

"Yes, got it," she says right as the door to my floor opens. She steps back and the rush of cool air between us isn't refreshing. It's just a very sharp contrast to the warm, soft heat that had just been there. I step off the lift and turn around. I stop in my tracks. Her eyes are wide set and almond-shaped. Their color is a medley of the same blues and greens of the sea that surrounds this villa. Not clear, but compelling and inviting. They make her face, which is a very nice face, completely extraordinary.

Her gaze is direct and questioning while our eyes are locked. Then, it travels down my chest, lingers at the waist of my low-slung shorts before they skim my bare legs and my sneakered feet.

I cough, and she looks back at my face. The muscles in my chest tighten at the naked admiration in her eyes.

"Hello," I say and extend my hand. She flushes the prettiest shade of pink and tucks her hair behind her ear.

Damn.

She's got the doe-eyed, sex kitten look down to a science. Her eyes are wide with surprise. Her lips are parted...*fuck*, her lips are perfect.

She looks like a fucking snack—the perfect portion of everything I like. But it's the one thing I know about her that corrals the compulsion I have to find out if that sweet pink mouth is as soft as it looks.

"Hello," she says slowly, a tentative smile spreading across those lips. Her voice is even sexier when paired with the vision standing in front of me.

She holds out her hand and shakes mine. When our palms touch, my pulse jumps and every one of the thousands of nerve endings that run along the surface of my skin wake up. She flushes even darker as our fingers wrap around our hands. We hold hands for a beat longer than necessary before she gasps softly and pulls her hand away.

"My necklace," she says as if she's explaining. She holds her open palm out to me. A delicate gold chain with a pendant in the shape of a raindrop hanging from it sits in the center of her hand.

"Is it broken?" I ask and cup her hand in mine and lift it up so I can see better. It's not necessary, but I like touching her. She steps closer to me.

"No, but I had to unfasten it to get it unhooked from your shirt." She pulls her hand out of my grasp and drops the chain into my still up-turned palm. "Would you mind?" The heat in her voice turns that question into a not-so-subtle "come hither." The unmasked attraction in her eyes hits me like a fist to my chest, and I have to clear my throat before I can respond.

"Of course," I say. She turns her back to me and bows her head. Those tumbling curls spill down to the middle of her back. Her black camisole skims her waist and exposes a bare slice of smooth, tanned skin.

She's short, a whole foot shorter than my six foot three—and petite. Well, except for that ass.

Shit.

I'm an ass man and that is one of the finest I've ever seen. Clearly genetics and exercise have been making magic back there because it's fucking perfect. Her hips flare and then bam! There it is!

She cups the curtain of hair and sweeps it off her neck and lays it over one shoulder. I step forward and take in the creamy soft expanse of skin that covers her back and neck. She glances over her shoulder at me. Her lower lip is captured between her teeth and her eyes are hooded as she looks up at me through her lashes. "You okay?" she asks when I don't move or say anything.

Get your shit together, Hayes.

"Sorry." I shoot her an apologetic smile. "Turn around," I say, and she nods before she does. I reach over her and drape the chain across her neck. I look over her shoulder. The teardrop is resting in the middle of her chest. I drag it slowly up and into place. I watch, transfixed, as it glides over her skin like I imagine my own fingers would. When it slides into the small hollow between her collarbones, I draw the clasp together at the nape of her neck.

I fumble with the tiny closure a few times. "My hands are big." I apologize as my fingers brush the soft skin of her neck. She exhales sharply, and gooseflesh ripples over her skin. There's no air-conditioning in the hallway. I smile to myself. Maybe this weekend won't be as mundane as I'd feared. I manage to close it, and she turns around and rewards me with the prettiest fucking smile I've seen all year.

The loud trill of my phone fills the air like a siren, and she jumps back. I glance at the phone in my hand and grimace. "Excuse me, I have to take this," I say, and send her an apologetic smile.

Her answering smile is the epitome of grace. "Of course. I'm on this floor…maybe I'll see you later."

"Absolutely," I respond before I turn toward my room and answer my phone.

"Hayes, honey, you there?" my aunt Gigi asks as I walk into my room.

"I'm here. How's my favorite girl?" I ask.

I flip the switch on the air conditioner, pull my shirt over my head, and go stand beneath the wall unit that's perched above the south facing window.

"You sure know how to make your Gigi feel special, Hayes. How was your flight?"

"It was good. I worked," I tell her.

"Of course, you did. Now, before I get down to business, I want you to make me a promise," she says.

"That's not fair. I can't agree to promise if I don't know what you're going to ask," I cajole her. Even though I know exactly what she's going to ask.

"Don't be smart, Hayes," she chides me in the way only she can.

"Pardon me," I apologize sincerely.

"I want you to promise me you're going to try and have a good time. Don't scowl so much. That face of yours is so handsome when you smile, honey," she coos.

"Okay, sure thing. I promise," I say.

"You're lying, but I love you for humoring me," she says airily.

"It's what I live for," I return dryly.

"Don't be smart. I'm helping the movers sort boxes and they can't find the box with your crockery." She sounds distressed.

"What's crockery?" I ask and lean against the door of my room and gaze out the window at the copse of pine trees that provide a natural border for the property and perfume the air all year round.

"Your plates, glasses, bowls," she explains.

"Oh, that's because there are none. I never eat at home. I didn't see the need for them," I answer honestly.

"Oh, Lord, Hayes. People will think you were raised in a barn," she cries.

"No one will think I was raised in a barn," I say dryly.

"I'm going to the Crate Barrel in Highland Village to place an order. I don't know if they deliver, so you'll need to pick it up when you get back. I'm just going to go over the list of things I'm getting," she says.

"Thanks for doing this for me, Gigi," I say.

"Well, it's the least I can do since I won't be here when you actually move in. And I should be thanking *you* for going to the wedding for me, honey. I know he's a pretentious little shit, but his mother was my dearest friend in Positano. I would have hated to not have anyone there. And *maybe*," she drawls conspiratorially, "you'll meet the girl of your dreams," she ends hopefully.

"Have you seen Thomas?" I ask, changing the subject.

"No." She sniffs like she smells something bad. "He and I haven't been in touch at all. I just shudder to think what the foundation would look like if he had even one more year with it. I'm so glad you're moving back here," she says.

"Nice to know you'll miss me," I say dryly.

"Of course, I will, baby. But I'm glad you're getting on with your life," she says. But I can tell there's something on the tip of her tongue by the way she catches her breath at the end of that last sentence.

"What's going on?" I ask and brace myself. My aunt is the most direct human being on the planet. The only thing she's ever been hesitant to talk about is Renee. "What did she do this time?"

"She accepted your offer," she says.

"How do you know that?" I ask. I put her on speaker and open my email application.

"Well, I was at that lovely restaurant in your new neighborhood… oh, Hayes, I *love* it here," she says dreamily.

"You were about to tell me how you know about Renee," I say impatiently.

"Oh, sorry, I just get so carried away talking about this place. The Wildes have done such a good job—"

"Gigi…"

"Okay, sorry," she says like she's being put upon.

"Just tell me about Renee," I say with feigned patience. She doesn't like to be rushed. And slows down purposely sometimes when she is.

She clears her throat, and I can just see her, tucking her feet underneath her and sweeping her dark, salt-and-pepper hair off her shoulders before she speaks. "Well, like I said, I was at a restaurant. Her lawyer was sitting at the table right behind me!" she says triumphantly.

"How did you know he was her lawyer? I don't think I'd know him on sight, and I've sat across the table from him at least a dozen times in the last two months," I say.

"Hayes, you know I never forget a face. Also, I heard him say her name. It's why my interest was piqued in the first place and then I realized who he was and what he was talking about," she explains. "Stop interrupting and listen," she says impatiently.

"Excuse me, go on," I say sarcastically.

"Of course, he had no clue who I was. He was celebrating. His thirty percent is more than you should have given that disloyal little bitch all together," my aunt says in her most severe voice.

"I'm just glad it's done." My voice is toneless. Renee, my ex-wife and my biggest regret, sued me two weeks ago. Gigi introduced us. We were all in Carmel for an annual party one of her friends throws every Fourth of July. I had just finished my MBA at Wharton and was working for a KPMG in Rome. I'd come out for the party because I was turning twenty-five and had somehow managed to let Gigi convince me that I needed to find a wife. This party, she said, would be crawling with women who would be suitable. Suitable meant she'd be from a wealthy family and a well-trained socialite who never put a foot out of place publicly.

Renee—on paper—was perfect. That she was sexy was icing on the cake.

I learned early on one of the hazards of having a lot of money. Your worst impulses have all the fuel they need to turn into your biggest regret. We were married within weeks of meeting each other. Our alcohol and sex-fueled dash down the altar had lasted a grand total of twenty-two days. Once the booze wore off, the sex got boring. Once that was gone, we realized we didn't even like each other very much.

When we divorced, everything I'd earned during our marriage was half hers. That was barely anything, considering we were officially separated less than thirty days after we found each other.

Our divorce finalized on my twenty-fifth birthday. The same day my inheritance from the Rivers Trust, and what Swish had been setting aside for me for the last ten years, all vested. She'd never known the details of it. There was never any need for her to.

I gave her enough money to get settled in a new place by herself and to give her breathing room until she could find a job.

She found a new husband before she found employment, and I was off the hook for alimony.

Then, a year before my thirtieth birthday, coincidence created a set of circumstances that set us on a course for a much-less-than-amicable reunion. A job took her and her new husband to Houston. Less than six months later, he'd left her for another woman, and her divorce was being formalized.

The Houston press was in a tizzy about my impending return. Would I be able to navigate the treacherous swamp of Houston's upper-class society when I spent my formative years in Europe? Did I even still speak English? How had becoming one of the wealthiest men in the country—practically overnight—changed me?

It was that last question that got Renee's attention. Though she'd never married without a prenup again, none of her husbands were green enough to let her walk away with more than enough to satisfy that "the lifestyle to which she was accustomed" clause in their prenups.

When she heard that I'd gone from successful accountant to the new "Rivers King," as they called me in the press, she pounced and sued me for a share of my inheritance.

She argued that it should have been counted as community property because I concealed its existence from her and because it matured while we were still legally married.

I pushed back. She was asking for thirty percent of my estate. I wasn't willing to give her thirty *cents*. The day after our first court hearing, she showed up at my house with a bottle of wine and an offer for settling. I slammed the door in her face.

The next morning, she sat down on a local talk show wearing sunglasses and implied that I'd removed her—physically—from my house. The police paid me a visit and set the rumor mill spilling.

My lawyers advised me to settle. Gigi wanted me to fight back. But I didn't want a court battle. She just wanted my money. And that is the one thing I have plenty of. It kept the foundation's and family money out of her reach.

"Don't let it get you down," Gigi says. She mistakes my silence for sadness.

"I'm not down. I'm glad she's gone," I say honestly. It's true. I hope our paths never cross again.

"Most people aren't so calculating," she says. "You had one bad experience. You can't stay single forever because of it."

"Why not?" I say it like I'm joking, but I've actually considered it.

"Don't say things like that! People will start thinking you're like that George Clooney - waiting until you're gray before you finally settle down," she says.

"He looks like he's doing all right," I say frankly.

"Hayes McGregor Rivers," she says sharply, and I laugh at how riled up this topic always gets her. "I know I got Renee wrong. But, in my defense, I didn't think you'd marry her a week after you met. If you let me leave this earth without grandnieces and nephews, I'll haunt you forever," she says.

"Well, that doesn't sound so bad. I like having you around," I retort. She lets out a pained, long-suffering sigh.

"You're thirty. You need to start thinking about it again. Especially if you're going to make a successful transition back into Houston's society."

I can't suppress my groan. We've been having this argument for the last year.

"Gigi, let me do one thing at a time. The foundation needs my attention right now. The wife hunt can wait."

"Well, there are lots of eligible girls from very nice families in Houston," she says.

"Gigi—"

"Oooh, if I'm here more often, I could be your matchmaker," she says hopefully. I start to quip that she's done enough by introducing and encouraging my liaison with Renee. But it goes beyond whatever her hopes are. I have watched one marriage of convenience after another fail and fall apart. It's the last thing I want. So, I level with her.

"I'm not interested in being with anyone who would use a matchmaker. Especially not if it's any one of the women you're talking about. They wouldn't care if I was eighty, sterile, and impotent. They want my money and they want to secure themselves a lifetime of monthly checks in the form of child support when they birth little Rivers heirs, and they would sleep with our gardener to make sure they got it even if I couldn't give it to them," I say.

She's completely quiet.

"Gigi?" I call her name.

"You need to think about who you'll move on with," she says finally. Her voice is completely normal. I put her silence down to a bad connection.

I've already moved on. To a place where choosing a wife will never be an impulsive, uninformed act again. I'll never put Kingdom at risk like that again. "I will. If *you* will drop this conversation," I say.

"Deal. I had lunch with Henny yesterday," she says perkily, and I relax a little. Rivers Wilde gossip, I can deal with.

"How was that?" I ask.

"She looks *wonderful*. Retirement agrees with her. We ate lunch in her pool and drank an entire bottle of wine. Her friend Sally made lunch. It was grand." She giggles to herself. "I was sick to my stomach when I got home, but it just made me think about how much I miss living here," she says dreamily.

"Perfect, I'll buy you a house and you can move with me," I say.

"I-I couldn't leave Positano, but I'm thinking with you gone, it won't feel like home. I spent the first twenty-five years of my life in Houston. Being back here, especially in Rivers Wilde… I'm tempted to start spending part of the year here. It's charming," she says happily.

"Charming isn't how I would describe it, but I think you being there would make it feel less like hostile territory," I say.

"I wish your brothers would come home. You need them. Though, with that dreadful mother of theirs, I can understand why they scattered the way they have," she says ruefully.

"They will," I say with more confidence than I feel. I certainly *hope* they will. So far, their responses to my request have been less than promising. But Gigi's right, I need them. They're all the real family I have left.

Houston doesn't feel like home anymore, and I have to find a way to make it so. Having them around might make that easier.

"Oh, dear." My aunt sounds dismayed. "I shouldn't have mentioned Renee. She always spoils the mood."

"She's good for that," I say.

"Just goes to show how money can't buy you anything that matters."

"Right," I say shortly. Talking about Renee and money are two things I'd always rather not do. But when I think about all the money I spent to book this particular suite in the hopes of finding quiet, and how that, too, has managed to elude me, it makes me downright antsy.

"All right, baby, you go on. Just promise you'll try to have a nice time," she says.

The image of the bombshell I met on the elevator flashes in my minds eye. "Don't you worry. I plan to do just that."

Chapter 2

GOLD DIGGER

HAYES

"This is paradise." A female voice drifts into my ear as if carried by the light sea breeze and interrupts my afternoon nap. Normally, I'd ignore them and get back to sleep.

But the American accent reminds me that the woman in the elevator is on this floor too, and that my room is one of only two on this level.

I open my eyes. I squint against the afternoon sun's glare and sweep my gaze over the huge veranda. I'm as alone as I'd been when I first came out here to lie down.

Did I dream it? Maybe Gigi had been right and I needed this break.

I abandon my lounge chair and walk over to the ornately-carved stone wall that also serves as the veranda's railing. I rest my forearms on the smooth, sun-warmed cement rail and take in the view. It doesn't have the glittering yachts and glamour of The Amalfi Coast where that I called for the last fifteen years. But this little stretch of shoreline in Tuscany has its own undeniable charm.

The sweeping greens and blues of the sea, sky see to go on forever and is dotted with lush landscapes topped with sprawling villas. The light breeze isn't stiff enough to do more than ruffle the very fine hairs on my arms. But it carries with it the smell of lemon and pine. The salt of the sea spray gives the air a bite that's softened by the sound of the sea's lazy current.

The sea stretches and disappears into the curve of the horizon. I gaze at it and understand why people thought the world was flat. From here, I can imagine falling off the illusion created the sea's glancing kiss with the sky.

The mossy cliff that runs along this stretch of beach surrounds the villa, making it feel secluded even though there are neighboring villas on either side.

Raucous laughter and unintelligible shouts spill and splatter all my silent reverie. So she's on a girl's trip. At least I know I'm not hearing things.

I hoped that if I had neighbors, they would be people who wanted to be as far away from the festivities' noises as possible.

My relaxation disturbed, I pull out my phone and scan the emails I've been ignoring since I arrived in Pisa.

I scroll through email after email of bad news. Kingdom is being hit with lawsuits left and right. For everything from breach of contract to improper dismissals.

My uncle's failure to manage Kingdom and all of its holdings properly is nothing compared to his lack of transparency and attempts to hide the company's building problems.

Since Swish died, he's stacked the board with his minions instead of competent people. We are in violation of hundreds of regulatory guidelines in nearly every facet of our business, and everyone is looking to me for answers I don't have.

It's been a few months since I stepped into the role of Chairman of the Board. The first email I received in my official capacity was from my newly-appointed executive assistant. In it, she asked me to send her a guest list for my swearing-in ceremony and banquet. My reply informed her that, until we had something *real* to celebrate, the banquet was postponed. The days of keeping up appearances are over. I've been working flat out, eighteen hour days, seven days a week since day one.

When Gigi asked me to attend this wedding on her behalf, I said no. The ship is *finally* turning in the right direction. I couldn't afford the time off.

She told me I couldn't afford not to take it off. When I tried to contradict her, she told me not to talk back, and booked my flight. So, here I am.

"God, Cass. *Why* did you bring her?" one voice drones as if she's in pain.

"Actually, I brought *you*. She's my plus one. And she's having a hard time, so you guys better not be dicks," Cass responds.

"Well, from what I heard, it's her own fault," another voice chimes in.

"And why is she dressed like that? I mean, if I had thighs like that, I'd never wear shorts."

"I think her thighs look great," Cass says defensively.

"I mean, she's pretty, but…like…how can she even afford this trip? This room? I heard no one will hire her," a chorus girl says.

"That's none of your business, you guys." Cass's voice is rising in anger.

"Well, if her gold-digging ways are going to reflect on us—"

"You're only here because Liv was nice enough to let you use her room block despite the fact that you're not wedding guests. And if this is how you feel about her, then just keep your distance this weekend."

I like this Cass.

There's a beat of silence before one of the voices responds in a whiny bray. "She has a lot of nerve showing her face—"

The sound of the door's squeaky hinges brings the conversation to screeching halt. "I'm baaaack!" A voice gushes and I recognize it as my mystery lady from the elevator.

"Oh, hey. Couldn't sleep?" Cass says in a much thinner, more hesitant voice than the one she's been using since they came outside.

"No. I was just so excited thinking about all the rich guys who'll be here this weekend," she says in a singsong voice.

I freeze. Suddenly, I wish I'd gone inside. This is the very last thing I need or want to hear.

"I mean, it's an Italian villa. It's bound to be crawling with them," Cass says and her discomfort is loud and clear even from where I'm sitting.

"Exactly, ladies," elevator girl crows. "If you want me to teach you, all you have to do is ask. It's not that hard. Men with money are the *best* boyfriends. They're usually so busy making it they don't have time for you. You might only have to fuck him once a month," she says. A chorus of uncomfortable giggles ripples through the crackling air around me.

I know firsthand about women like her.

I've just finished freeing myself from the clutches of one.

My amusement, interest, and good mood fizzle all at once. I start to head back inside. At least I'll know who to avoid tonight.

I'm almost to my door when my phone starts to ring.

The loud trill fills the air like a siren, and the conversation from the next balcony comes to an abrupt stop.

"Oh my God, is someone there?" I hear one of the chorus girls say right as I shut the door behind me and answer the phone.

Chapter 3

DOLCE VITA

CONFIDENCE

"*Who* is *that?*" I lean over to Cass and whisper without taking my eyes off the tall, well-built man striding into the tent. He looks like he's the sovereign of something—a country, a business, a thousand women in a harem somewhere and is about to declare himself our ruler, and demand we pledge our loyalty or die.

He's even more beautiful in that suit than he was in that hallway this afternoon. I can still feel the soft brush of his fingers on my neck. The way my breath caught in my throat when he'd dragged the pendant up my chest until it nestled into the small hollow at the base of my throat.

His dark, wavy hair is just long enough to curl right at the edge of his crisp white tuxedo shirt. It's unruly and perfectly artless in a way that no human hand, and no amount of pomade, could create. Those silky dark-chocolate waves are the work of God himself.

His profile is strong and bold; his nose prominent and straight. His lips are set in a straight line but I can see their fullness, even in his profile. And Lord Almighty, his jaw. It's chiseled and wide and covered in a beard low enough to be a five o'clock shadow, meticulously groomed, so you can tell it's not.

His tall frame is poured into a black tuxedo that fits him perfectly. Heads turn as he crosses the room. And I can't blame them—not even a little bit. He oozes sex and power. His long strides eat up the floor, and he reaches the lone empty table at the back of the tent quickly. When he's adorned the chair with his glorious body, he turns to face the front of the room where the bridal party is sitting and giving their speeches.

"Who's who?" she asks, and pokes her head around the room. I tug her arm and nod at him.

"Him. Also known as the man of all of my dirty dreams," I purr excitedly, my eyes trained on the finest specimen of man I've ever seen this close up.

"Ohhh," she drawls, eyes widening with interest and props her chin on her hand and ogles him.

"That's Hayes Rivers," the woman on my right says. Cass and I both turn to face her, surprised by her interjection.

"Heir to Kingdom," she says when neither of us respond.

"I knew it. He looks like a king. Which kingdom?" I ask. I'm already imagining myself in a ball gown, crown on my head, walking down some long, red-carpeted aisle where he's waiting at the end.

"No, not *a kingdom*." And just like that, she kills my dream. "*Kingdom* is the name of his family's business. He inherited all the money when he turned twenty-five. And now he's the new Rivers king," she says.

"How old is he now?" I ask, my curiosity overtaking my normal abhorrence for gossip.

"He must be thirty…he's one of the richest men in the freaking world," she exclaims.

"Really? Why's he here?"

"His grandmother is friends with the groom," our little canary says. "I can't believe you've never heard of him. His return to Houston is all anyone's talking about," she says and looks at both of us like we're crazy.

"I don't live in Houston," I say.

"Well, *I* heard…" Her eyes dart around as if checking for spies and then she leans into us. "Apparently, he had a fight with his ex. And it got *physical*," she grimaces. But her eyes are twinkling. "I'm not one to gossip…" she says and Cass and I exchange a *yeah, right* look.

"But she was all over the place wearing sunglasses. No one saw her, mind you, and she never said, but it was obvious he roughed her up," she says.

My lawyer hat comes on and my eyes slide away from the delicious man to her. I make sure there's no warmth in them and her silly, careless smile falters.

"That's actually the exact opposite of obvious," I say dismissively.

"Only if you're blind. I mean, yeah, he's nice to look at, but he looks so angry, don't you think?"

I glance at him, and just then, like he knows what she said, his jaw clenches.

"Well, if people were talking about me like this, I might be angry, too," I say and Cass pinches me.

"Well, if you think you know better, you can ignore me. But don't say you weren't warned," she says and turns back to the victim on her other side.

As if I need any warning. I can smell a violent man the minute he enters the room. I grew up with them under the same roof. I watched them do more damage than any of the natural disasters that were a way of life for us in the Mississippi Delta.

I lean toward Cass. "He's staying on our floor," I whisper. I can't take my eyes off him. My whole body is tingling just from looking at him. "Thank you, God," I say, pressing my hands together in gratitude.

Cass laughs. "I mean, he does clean up nicely, but he looks like he'd be more comfortable in a boxing ring than on a dance floor," she says.

"Yes, exactly," I practically purr before I take another sip of my gin and tonic. My thighs clench when I think about how rough things could get.

"His nose doesn't look like it's been broken, though," she muses.

"No one's perfect," I joke, and take a final swig of my drink.

"Enjoy. My fantasy Italian fling is more in the style of Jude Law in the *Talented Mr. Ripley. He* looks like he could eat Jude Law in a single bite."

"Or me," I drawl with a wink and stand up. I run my hands down my dress.

Cass grabs my arm and yanks me back down in my seat. "Where in the world are you going? You are *not* going to approach him," she says as if scandalized.

I glance over at her and grin, because I am *so* going to approach him.

"You never approach anyone. You're still getting over Nigel. Who *are* you?" she asks, green eyes wide with surprise.

"I'm Confidence Ryan, and I'm about to go climb my very own Mt. Olympus," I say with a suggestive waggle of my eyebrows.

"Are you drunk?" she asks when I start to stand up again.

"Yes, but so what?" I say.

"You'll regret it in the morning," she frets.

"Maybe…" I shrug.

"This isn't you." She peers up at me.

"Again, so what?" I shrug off her questions. "I'm in Italy. I'm single. And I think that if I'm ready to walk over and put my ass on a table for another man to make a meal of me, then I might be over Nigel," I say.

"True facts," she says with an enthusiastic nod.

"And if I have regrets…then, at least it will be for something worth regretting. I want to know what that kind of regret feels like," I say in a moment of rare vulnerability.

"Okay," she says, relenting in her attempts to stop me. Even if she doesn't sound convinced.

"Just be safe. Get your own drinks and drop your glass so it shatters if you need a rescue," she says and takes a sip of her drink.

"I won't be breaking any glasses. If I need a rescue, I'll do it myself." A sudden bolt of doubt flashes through my mind.

This *is* very unlike me.

I self-consciously glance down at myself.

"Do I look okay?" I cast a sheepish glance at Cass. My bravado has failed me now that I'm about to walk the walk.

"You look better than okay. You look wonderful," she says with all of the sincerity of a dutiful and loving friend who would never say anything other than how wonderful I look.

I lose my nerve and lower myself back into my seat. I grab my wine and take a moody, resentful sip.

Cass puts her drink down and grabs my forearm.

"What happened?" Her dark brows are furrowed in concern. "I thought you were off to get laid."

I sink down in my seat and pout.

"Why in the world would he be interested in me? She said he's filthy rich or something. He's young and hot, too. Do you know how rare that is? I bet he's engaged to marry one of those princesses—Eugenie or whatever." I fling my hand in his direction, but my eyes are fixed on the drink I'm lifting back to my lips.

"If he is, then I feel sorry for *her* because he's going to be leaving here with the hottest woman in the room," she says with a little too much enthusiasm. And I roll my eyes.

"Confidence, you're a *catch*," she exclaims.

I give her a disbelieving look. "Oh yeah, I know thousands of eligible, sexy men who are beating a path to be with a broke, failed lawyer whose family is a poster for dysfunction," I say grumpily.

"That's not all you are," she whispers fiercely, squeezing my arm. I chuckle—it's humorless, short ,and dry.

"Well, I'm glad you agree that it's *some* of what I am," I quip and take another swig of my wine.

"For God's sake, one lost job doesn't mean you failed," she cajoles.

I throw her a glance. "I was almost disbarred."

"That was all that fucking Nigel's fault," she reminds me.

"True. But it's certainly *not* his fault that I've spent sixty percent of my life savings in the last three months. A good chunk of it on this last minute, incredibly glamorous vacation. Who doesn't find a financially irresponsible spendthrift *irresistible*?"

"You think anyone worthy of you will care about any of that?" Cass asks me softly.

"One of us will have to care. Even a lifetime of sex with that beautiful man won't make up for my flagrant disregard for budgets."

She chuckles. "Now you're just being dramatic. At least you have your life savings. If I lost my job, I would have to move back home with my parents after one month," she says and nudges me with her shoulder.

I sigh and look back at my man… God, I'm ridiculous. He's not my *anything*.

"I've never broken a rule my whole life, Cass," I say to her. "I didn't even shave above the knee until I was twenty-one. I did whatever I thought I had to, to get out of Arkansas. I had a good run, and in one fell swoop, I've managed to ruin my life." I drain my glass and drop it on the table. "So, If I'm hanging out in rock bottom city, then I'm at least doing it in style." I wave an arm around the opulently decorated room to make my point.

"Well, you can thank Jules for being smart enough to land an Italian count with enough money to pull off a party like this."

"To Jules," I say.

"To Jules," she repeats as we clink our empty glasses.

"You know what?" I ask and stare at the bubbles clinging to the lip of my glass. They remind me of myself. I'm holding on. Long after life should have swallowed me whole.

"What?" Cass asks when I don't continue.

"I've found that rock bottom might be the best thing to ever happen to me. I've spent the last three months shopping, traveling, eating, and sleeping to my heart's content. Sure, after this, I have to move home. But, have you seen how round my ass has gotten?" I lift and point to my silver sequined covered backside and wink. "It's amazing, right?" I grin at her.

"It's got that Beyoncé circa 2014 magic," she says with authority and we clink our glasses together.

"And you have not hit rock bottom, TB," she says reproachfully.

"No, I have. Really," I assure her with a falsely proud smile. "But, I have a plan. And being back home will light a fire under me. Not to mention taking this trip has brought me perilously close to poverty. It's time to give up my apartment, go home, and regroup."

She pats my arm consolingly. "Well, if all of that fails, you could turn your new hobby into a business," she says.

"Yes!" I clap my hands and hoot with laughter. "Like I could be some sort of plus one for hire."

"You've had enough practice in the last few months," she ribs me.

"I know," I crow with delight. "Weddings are such a *score*. I mean, I have classy-as-fuck friends, so the venues are always marvelous, and I get it at the block rate." I laugh out loud and stop when I see Cass isn't laughing with me.

"What?" I ask and blush.

"I'm glad you're letting that crazy dark hair go. Your hair is the prettiest natural blond I've ever seen. I've missed the fits of jealousy I used to have every time you wore it down."

"I *do* look good, don't I? A life of leisure is apparently the real fountain of youth." I wink. "But tell me why you're looking at me like my mom did the first time I managed to bait a hook myself," I tease, but I'm blushing at the unfiltered pride in her eyes.

"It's just that I'm glad that you're doing what makes you happy. It *is* slightly reckless to blow through your savings this way. But, I also know that you're a brilliant, passionate attorney, and the minute you're ready, you'll have a score of job offers. I'm thrilled you're being a sexy, lazy, beach bum for once in your life. You've earned it," Cass says with the most sincerely delighted smile on her face. I smile back at her with equal delight.

This is why she's my best friend. She loves me as much as I love her. And when I'm happy, she is too. My heart swells with gratitude that I have her in my life.

I look back at my *dream man*. He's sitting with his arms crossed watching the dancing people like he'd rather be anywhere else. His heavy, square chin has a cleft.

I want to stick my tongue in it. I regain my resolve.

"I'm about to add slutty to that sexy and lazy," I say and give her a bawdy wink. Then, I stand up again before I lose my nerve. I'm about to turn and walk his way when I remember something and lean down to talk to Cass.

"The guy behind the bar—his name tag said Luca—he's a dead ringer for Jude Law, and I saw him checking out your ass when we walked through earlier," I say.

She leaps out of her seat. "I can't believe you saw *him* and didn't tell me." She scowls and starts to gather her phone and the lipstick and gum that spilled out of her tiny gold clutch.

"How was I to know what you were in the mood for? And if I told you every time a guy checked you out, we'd be here all night."

"You sweet talker." She swats my arm and presses a quick kiss to my cheek. "Be safe, have fun. And remind me to stick an extra-long pin in my Nigel voodoo doll when we get home."

"I love you," I say through a giggle.

She really has a Nigel voodoo doll at home. It's a pathetic little stick figure made of popsicle sticks. All of its limbs are broken.

"How could you not?" She wiggles her fingers goodbye and disappears into the crowd. I run my fingers through my heavy hair. Thank you for low humidity and great hair products. There's not a hint of frizz in sight, and there hasn't been since I got here. I take all of this as an omen. Beautiful setting, great company, best hair day of my life—the stars have aligned. Of course, the man of my sexual dreams would be here, too.

With that thought, I take a deep breath and turn to face my future conquest.

I hope that tonight, though, I'll be the one who's conquered. I'm five foot three. Tall, well-built men are my weakness.

The strapping, dark-haired Duke of Midnight across the room looks like he might be up for the job. I say a quick prayer that I didn't misread things in the elevator this morning and that I'm not about to make a fool of myself and start toward him. As I weave my way across the moderately populated dance floor, I lose sight of him once or twice. But when I step off the other side of the dance floor, my view of him is completely unobstructed. When his eyes swing in my direction, they land on me right away. His eyes sweep up my body, his head's angle marking their current position. My feet, my legs, my hips, stomach, my breasts, and on my face.

I feel a shot of confidence that propels me forward. I've never done anything like this before. But when I saw him this afternoon, I thought, *mine*.

Despite my little blip of doubt, I'm excited about the possibility of having a night with him. That's all I really want.

Since we've been in Castiglioncello, I've felt different—freer, happier. It's the most beautiful place my admittedly limited travels have ever taken me. The sea's perpetual whispers and roars lend an air of magic to the cove of neighboring villas we're staying at this weekend. As soon as we stepped off the dreary shuttle that brought us the forty miles from the airport in Pisa, I knew this would be a trip I'd never forget. Until now, I thought it would be because of the spectacular views, the clean, fragrant air, and being with Cass. Yet, as I approach Mr. Tall Dark and Glorious, I know that this is going to be the experience that defines this trip. Lord knows, I was in desperate need of something glorious and unforgettable right now.

When I'm two tables away, his eyes come into focus. Like my mama would say, *Lawd ha'mercy*. While I'd been gawking at his body, the shadows in the hallway had been hiding the real treasure. They're a heart stopping disc of pure hazel ringed in what could be a mossy green or nutty brown…the light doesn't allow me to see clearly. They're fringed by a thick tangle of lashes and burning with intelligence and…wariness.

He stands up just before I reach him.

His tall, broad frame is a little leaner up close. "Hello," he says and takes my hand. He presses a kiss to it and offers me a seat by pulling the one next to him out.

Holy Father. If this is how they make men in Europe, then I was born in the wrong place. Because this man is straight out of one of those fairy tales that I never believed in because I never saw a girl like me in one of them.

"Thank you," I say demurely, the flutter in my stomach turning to a vibration as I plant myself in the offered chair.

"You're welcome," he says noncommittally and then just watches me. That trace of wariness grows as he observes me.

"Why aren't you dancing?" I ask.

"I don't dance," he says shortly.

"Oh. Okay," I say with a grimace of shame when he doesn't speak. I feel a surge of mortification when I realize that I have, in fact, been too presumptuous.

"I don't know what I was thinking," I say. I wish I could snap my fingers and make myself disappear. "I thought…maybe when we saw each other earlier on the elevator…that you seemed interested. I'm sorry. I'll just…" I start to stand up and pray I can run in these stupid shoes that I spent too much money on. I want to cry. I scrape my chair back and he grabs my wrist.

"No, don't go. I'm glad you came." His voice is deep and smooth like the molasses in my grandmother's gingerbread cookies. And he's American, too.

Thank you, God, I mouth down to my lap before I look up and smile.

"My mouth is good for a lot of things…small talk just isn't one of them," he says, gaze smoldering and yet so relaxed. I'm so startled by the innuendo that a bubble of laughter escapes me. I cover my mouth with my hand. He reaches over to stroke the back of my hand and then circles my wrist. He tugs my hand away from my mouth. "Your smile is beautiful."

"Oh, my…" I sigh and my stomach does a somersault. I can't believe this is happening. He's actually into me.

He gives me a small, quick smile that I feel a surge of pride at having pulled it out of him.

"So, you're in business?"

"That's cute," he says quietly and takes a sip of his drink.

"Huh?" I quirk an eyebrow at the sarcasm in his voice and the sardonic smile that's ice cold.

"Not here on business. I'm just an ordinary man." His glass hovers in front of his lips and he watches me out of hooded eyes.

"There's nothing *ordinary* about you," I say and stick my hand out. "I should introduce myself. I'm Confidence Ryan, and I don't really know the bride or the groom, but I'm my friend Cass's plus one," I say.

"Your name is Confidence?" he asks, perplexed.

"I know, it's kind of weird at first. But I promise once you get used to it, you'll see it's actually a really great name," I assure him.

"No, not weird at all. Hayes Rivers," he says without any other detail. Not that I need any more for what I'm hoping is going to happen. But his smile doesn't quite meet his eyes.

"I love that name. Is it a family name?" I ask.

His smile dims slightly. "No," he says shortly.

"Well, my parents named my siblings and me after things they hoped we'd grow up to possess. I definitely lucked out. My siblings are named Happiness and Fortune," I tell him and then wish a hole would open up and put me out of my misery.

Why am I not better at flirting?

It's his turn to laugh, and he says, "Now, that is a great line." He shakes his head. "Can you imagine if people actually gave their children names like that?" he asks and I cringe. Hard.

He stops laughing. "Oh…"

"Yeah," I say slowly.

"I'm sorry," he says quietly, real contrition in his eyes

"No, it's okay. I'm used to it and they grow on you," I say and change the subject. "So, you friends of the groom?"

"No, my aunt is. She couldn't go, so I came in her stead."

"Well, you're a lot nicer than an RSVP and a gift card that most people send when they can't come to a wedding. It's nice of you to come. Even though, I bet it wasn't that hard of a sell. It's beautiful here," I say.

"I'm not nice. My aunt raised me. So, when she asks something of me, I do it." He shrugs and takes a sip of water, and I glance back at our table for a second to see if Cass is back. She's not.

"May I?" he asks, and I turn back to face him. He's watching me expectantly.

"May you what?" He nods to the table. His hand is hovering right above my wrist.

"Oh, you want to…" I ask in surprise, but smile and nod. "Feel free to put those big hands wherever you'd like," I say and groan internally at how thirsty I sound.

He smirks a little before his thumb swipes once on the tender skin on the inside of my wrist. I shiver and bite back a moan at the tremor that runs down the center of my body. I'm shouting *YES* in my head.

He lifts my hand to his face. His breath tickles me before he draws in a deep breath, his eyes closed as he rubs his nose back and forth across my wrist. My insides liquify.

"You smell like roses," he whispers so softly, his breath floats over the inside of my forearm and a tingle dances all the way up my arm.

If I'm dreaming, please don't ever wake me.

I lean into him and put on my sauciest smile. "It's this body lotion I bought in duty free—"

"It smells cheap." His voice is no longer soft and seductive. Heat rises up my neck and spreads on my cheeks as his words sink in.

I yank my hand out of his grasp and lean away. "Excuse me?" I ask in an affront.

"Didn't anyone tell you before you came over that I only entertain women who already have money?"

"'Entertain?'" I put the words in air quotes while I gawk at the man who just turned from a prince to a toad in less than three minutes.

"I'm not interested in being your next payday," he announces.

My jaw drops.

"Don't feel bad," he says without looking at me. "Go try it on one of the drunker, more persuadable men here. I'm sure you'll leave with enough money to at least cover your expenses," he says and my head snaps back so hard, I'm surprised it's still attached to my body.

His gaze flits over me. "No question. You're a knockout. But, if you're looking for something more than a weekend, I'd suggest you invest in your look. Off-the-rack dresses aren't going to cut it with this crowd. Dress for the job you want, and all that," he says and falls back in his chair.

Each insult and insinuation is barbed with contempt. They flay old wounds wide open.

"You jerk," I spit and lean forward so I can look him in the eye when I tell him to fuck off.

They're cold, dark, and shuttered. He looks like a completely different person than the one I met on the elevator. I wonder who put that look in his eye. I know it's not me. The disillusionment I see is deep-seated. Despite the warm May sea breeze passing through the tent, goose bumps replace my tingles.

"Do better research on your next target. Approaching me at an event like this was a dead giveaway about your motives. You should have bumped into me at the airport or something less obvious." His voice is devoid of any emotion, his gaze moves to the dance floor. His gaze is observant but detached. "Hmm…it's a shame, I think we would've had a great time together," he says while he looks at me like I'm a car he's thinking about buying.

I wonder for a minute if I'm being punked. I glance around the room. The music, the tinkle of silverware scraping plates, people shouting to be heard over the noise are still there. No camera crew is rolling in to surprise me.

Nothing changed. No one's watching us. I look back at him.

"Are you serious?" I ask him. I look closely at him for a sign that maybe he's kidding.

Nope, that disdain is real. He frowns and adjusts the cuffs of his jacket before he leans forward. "Let me spell it out." His eyes skim over me again. "Based on your lack of…polish," his eyes roam my body, from head to toe and a flush burns over my skin in their wake, "I'm assuming you're new to this scene. All the regulars know better than to try a trick like this. This place is littered with rich men. I'm sure you'll find one. You can thank me by calling out my name when you pretend he made you come," he says without a hint of humor and adjusts his cufflinks.

I clasp my purse to my chest in shock.

He looks back at me with complete disinterest.

"You're the one who claimed to be the expert at landing rich men. I'm just trying to make sure you don't look like a fool in front of your *friends*." He leans his head in close like he's sharing a secret. "Just a heads-up, they don't seem to really like you very much," he says.

My heart plummets to my toes.

"Were you listening to us?" I gasp in horror. We thought we heard a phone ring, but one of Cass's debutante friends said it came from the terrace.

"It was hard not to when you were speaking at the top of your lungs," he says.

I stare unseeingly at the room full of revelers who have no clue that this man is taking a pickaxe to my pride. I shake my head. He's taken my words, spoken in a moment of pure self-preservation, out of context. But I'll be damned if I'm going to explain myself to him.

"Don't look so down in the mouth. You've been spared a night of pretending that you're turned on by anything more than the diamonds in my watch."

And just like that, he turns away and faces the front of the room again.

I don't know whether to be angry, offended, sad, or ashamed. I settle on all of the above and they move through me like lava pushes its way past the earth's crust. I stand up, step right in front of his face, and let them spill.

"Oh, no you don't," I snarl.

He has the nerve to look surprised that I'm still there.

"What?" I widen my eyes in an exaggeration of his own expression. "Did you think I was just going to slink away in shame?" I glare down at him. "I'm not the one who should feel ashamed. You are a *pig*." I spit the word at him. He looks back at the dance floor.

"You don't get to accuse me of being some sort of gold digger and then turn back to your entertainment like it's not a completely unwarranted insult," I say and nudge his shoulder with one of my fingers when he doesn't look up. He glances up at me and sighs as if I'm tedious.

"Actually, I do get to do that. I just did. And, seriously," his eyes flit over me from head to toe again, "think about investing in your look. At least if you want to be someone to take out in public," he says and turns his stony expression back to the dance floor. Those words, spoken so casually, hit their target with the precision of fast flying bullets.

I imagine what it would feel like to slap that smug look off his face. But imagining is as close to satisfaction as I'll ever get. I have enough problems without adding an arrest in Italy to it.

"And you should invest in fixing your terrible personality," I snap, completely enraged by him.

"Sure. I'll take your advice if you'll take mine," he says.

I bend down so I can put my face in his. I see a flare of heat in his eyes, but I can't tell if it's ire or desire. Because even as I face off with him and burn with real dislike, I can feel a tug between us. His mouth is inches from mine and I can't keep my eyes off it. Before he shutters his expression again, he looks at my mouth the same way.

That bored, blank expression is back, and I pull back from him. "I don't know what kind of upbringing you had that you feel like you can talk to someone the way you just talked to me. Your money doesn't make you better than me or anyone," I say.

"Hmm," he says and stands up and takes a step toward me. The heated expression in his eyes makes me take a reflexive step backward.

"Hmm, what?" I ask.

His hand darts out and he grips my hip before I can take a second step.

He trails a finger down my arm and wraps his fingers around my wrist. He presses the pads of his fingers to my pulse point.

"It's a shame…you're fucking beautiful," he whispers, and I can hear real regret in his voice. It offends me at the same time as it thrills me.

Damn him for being an asshole while looking the way he does.

"Let go of me," I say, but I make no effort to free myself.

"I don't want to," he says quietly. "You don't want me to, either." His thumb strokes my pulse point and I shudder. I tug my arm free. No way will l give him the satisfaction of knowing that his touch is the most exciting thing I've felt in a long time.

"*Tesoro dolce,*" he murmurs.

"I don't know what that means, but you better cut it out," I warn him.

Because when he does, I want to stop and listen, even though I have no idea what he's saying.

"Why? Don't you like it?" he asks silkily.

"No, that's probably the word for streetwalker or cum dumpster or something," I grumble.

His hand skims my hip and the rest of my body quivers, throbs, tingles, and yearns for the same treatment.

"I can teach you. While I fuck you. I think you'd still let me," he says and that wakes me up. I pull out of his grasp.

I cross my arms over my chest and glower up at him. "Right, you called me cheap, and now, you're calling me *easy?* " I say in my best offended Southern woman voice.

"I wasn't calling you easy, but if you *are…*" He raises his eyebrows suggestively. "I'll overlook the cheap and even take you back to my room," he drawls with an amused smirk on his face.

I have never itched to slap someone more than I do right now.

"Fuck you!" I spit.

"See? We want the same thing," he quips with a grin that's cold as ice.

"You must be in a world of pain to act like that. You're a total asshole and you should be ashamed that you take joy in trying to make people feel small. You failed, by the way. Good night." I spin on my stupid heels and walk with as much ass shaking as I can back to my table.

"Ugh, who cares?" I mumble as I arrive back at my table full of strangers and no Cass.

"No luck?" my doggedly gossipy neighbor asks when I sit down. "Don't worry, he looks like he would break you in half," she says with a conspiratorial wink.

That's exactly what I'd been hoping.

I drop down in my seat and grab one of the sesame rolls from the breadbasket and slather it with the fancy butter that's served with every meal here. I'm about to take another huge bite when I remember the little joint I dropped in my purse, and I decide that I'll just do another one of the things on the Confidence Gone Wild list.

I grab my purse and head toward the back of the tent. When I get to his table near the rear exit, I give him as wide a berth as I can when I walk past him and push the flap of the tent open.

"Where are you going?" His hand is around my wrist and it brings me to a jerking halt that nearly sends me tumbling into his lap. I brace myself with a hand on his shoulder.

"None of your business, you rude man. And if you're thinking about apologizing, you can save it. I'll *never* forgive you." I yank hard.

He doesn't let go.

"It's not safe out there. The path is uneven and the steps are slick," he says.

"Thanks for the tip. I'll make sure to break my neck," I say with as much asperity as I can muster, and he has the grace to wince. "What? I thought you'd like the thought of that," I grit out and pull my arm again—in vain. "Let *go*. You can't manhandle me like this," I say when his grip only gets tighter.

"I'm not manhandling you," he says, but his grip on my arm loosens, "and I'm not letting you go until you turn around and head back into the party. Think of all the potential benefactors you'll miss out on if you plunge to your death," he says sarcastically.

"Are you actually making fun of me?" My anger is reaching a boiling point. I need to get out of here. I narrow my eyes at him. "If you don't let me go, I'm going to scream," I threaten.

He lets go immediately, and I see a flash of worry in his eyes. I recall my gossipy table-mate's comments about him and his wife and immediately feel guilty.

"I wasn't really going to scream. I just wanted you to let go," I say quickly. Then I square my shoulders and look down my nose at him. "Enjoy being miserable. Sorry I ever met you. Goodbye," I say and turn to leave.

"If you insist on going, I'll go with you," he says and starts to stand up.

"No, you will not," I say and rush out of the tent before he's fully on his feet.

I slip my nude sling backs off my feet and fumble until I have a good grip on the railing of the staircase. It's dark, and the moon is the only source of light, but the path is completely canopied in trees so in the places where the leaves are dense, it's pitch-black. The sound of the sea is very close; the breeze whips up the skirt of my salmon-colored dress. I love this dress. I can't believe he insulted the way I'm *dressed*.

"For God's sake, wait. This is *actually* completely crazy," he calls after me.

"Then why don't you go back to where you were *actually* being a jerk?" I call back over my shoulder.

I pull my phone out of my purse and fumble to find the flashlight button. The light is comforting, and I take one more step before I look back.

"Confidence, come back before you get yourself killed," he shouts, and he actually sounds concerned.

He's good.

"Just one less evil gold digger in the world, right? Leave me alone." I grip the rail and take another step. My heart and foot plunge simultaneously. There's nothing but air under my foot.

"Woaah!" I find my balance quickly. I glance down to see the gently lapping waves of a small inlet. I sigh in relief and sag against the rail.

"No, Confidence!" is the last thing I hear before the awful crack that seems to split the night in half. The entire rail collapses underneath my weight, and I fall backward off the side of the cliff. My scream is swept up by the wind and carried off in a soundless current.

I close my eyes and imagine the sea rushing up to meet me. The last thought before my world goes black is that I wish he'd at least kissed me before he opened his mouth and ruined it.

Chapter 4

THE LEDGE

HAYES

I break into a sprint when I hear the crack of the wooden railing. My stomach sinks like a twenty-pound stone in water. I slow down just in time to stop myself from following her over the ledge. I stand in the spot where I'd seen the flutter of pink fabric before she disappeared. One shoe and her small gold handbag are scattered on the ground close to where she had been standing. I close my eyes, count to three, and prepare myself for whatever I might find.

It happened so fast. I know that it's a long drop from there to the shallow pool of water that's been formed by erosion.

Trepidation and horror make my heartbeat slow down even while it thuds hard against the cavity of my chest. I hold my breath and look down.

Relief floods me, fast and wild, and it makes me dizzy. Her fall was broken by a ledge jutting out of the side of the stone face of the cliff. This cliff has dozens of them. It's an elite rock climber haven, and every autumn, just when the weather starts to clear and cool, they descend to risk their lives climbing cliffs like this all over Tuscany.

The sound of the sea roaring is gone, and I realize that it hadn't been the sea I'd been hearing. It was the rush of my own blood as I imagined the worst. It's actually very quiet here. The water laps gently on the rocky shore, the waves break in the distance. Behind me, the strains of music from the tent create a strange dichotomy. They have no idea what's happening out here. And, I'd like to keep it that way as long as I can.

I pull my phone out of my breast pocket before lying on my stomach. I slide forward until my head dangles off the ledge, and I can see her clearly. She's a little less than ten feet down. Not too far, but not close enough that I could reach her by extending my arms.

She's moved since I first spotted her. She'd been lying on her back, legs splayed. Now, she's curled up in a fetal position. That she's been able to move herself is a very good sign.

"Confidence," I call down. She doesn't speak, but whimpers loudly and nods.

I assess the ledge. The thick coating of moss covering it is a blessing and a curse. It saved her from landing on hard concrete, but it's also slick and will make moving around on it treacherous. The piece of rock she landed on looks to be about ten feet long and eight feet wide. It's not small, but there are only about five feet between her and its ledge.

If she rolls over a full body turn, she'll fall off. I glance up at the sky. It's dark, but the moon is very bright. The cloudless sky is good news. But even that comes with the caveat of the unexpected showers that are very commonplace in Tuscany during the summer.

I need to get help in a hurry.

I dial the pre-programmed number for the villa's security and explain to Marco, as succinctly as I can, what happened. Just as I hang up, she moves her foot, and a loud, gut-wrenching moan floats up to me on the wind. I drop my phone next to me and clear my throat before I speak.

"Confidence, can you hear me?" I shout down.

She nods and puts a hand on her head and starts to roll her shoulders.

"Don't move, please!" I shout. She freezes immediately.

"The ledge is five feet from your left. Don't go in that direction. Can you roll backward until you touch the cliff wall?" I ask. "In fact, if you could just not move at all, it would be best. Does anything hurt?" I ask her.

"Oh my God!" she shouts tearfully. "Everything hurts. So much."

She cries, but she does what I ask. When she reaches the cliff wall, she scrambles up to sitting and looks up and over her shoulder at me.

I can only see the shadow of her profile in the inky moonlit dark. "I'm really scared," she says softly, and the vulnerability in her voice twists my gut.

"I know." I breathe and then realize I whispered it. "Help will be here soon, okay?" I say in a louder voice.

"You're rich, right?" she calls up to me.

"What?" I call back in surprise.

"You said so," she presses impatiently. "It had better be true. Sending a dead body overseas is expensive. My mother doesn't have the money." She's talking quickly, but her voice is thick with emotion and pain. "Since it's your fault this happened, you have to promise to pay to send me home, so I can be buried next to my grandparents and as far away from my father as possible," she says.

"You're not going to die. It's lucky I'm here," I call down.

"Yeah, in the same way it's lucky to be mauled by a bear," she yells. The bark of laughter that springs straight from my gut surprises me. And she has a sense of humor.

"I don't know how that's lucky, but we've already learned that you and I don't share a lot of common perspectives," I joke back.

"I can't believe you're making jokes when I'm about to die!" she screams, and the pitch of terror in her voice is enough to squelch my little burst of levity.

"You're not going to die," I tell her.

"I will *never* forgive you. Not for what you said and not for killing me. I will haunt you from the grave," she shouts. I remember about Gigi's threat earlier and almost laugh. Almost, but I don't dare. Not yet.

"I haven't asked forgiveness. I gave you an honest assessment. And for the final time, you're not going to die," I tell her.

"What do you mean for the final time?" she cries up to me. "You mean you'll stop reassuring me? You'd just let me sit here and panic about dying and not try to make me feel better?" She's nearly screaming and her words are punctuated by sobs.

"You're making yourself hysterical," I call down in a voice that I hope doesn't betray my unease.

"You'd be hysterical if you were the one down here facing impending death," she cries angrily.

"I promise you're not going to die," I repeat.

"Don't say that. You can't promise that. Everyone dies. I had a feeling something significant would happen while I was here," she says mournfully. "Twenty minutes ago, I thought it was that I would get to have a fun little fling with a sexy stranger. Hahaha, what a joke," she cries.

She turns her head more so that nearly her full face is visible. A beam of moonlight breaks the dark shadowing them. I can see those eyes that tempted me so much tonight. Her face, even while twisted with pain and fear is like a painting—with features that separately you'd never think to pair together. Big eyes, a tiny nose. That lush, but small mouth… Yet they come together and create an expressive, very interesting, and beautiful masterpiece.

My phone rings, and I answer it with my head still over the side so I can keep an eye on her. "One sec, it's about the rescue," I tell her before I put it to my ear. Marco starts speaking right away and my heart sinks when he gives me the status.

"What's wrong?" she asks as soon as I hang up.

"Nothing's wrong—"

"Your face says otherwise," she snaps. "Just tell me because I'm freaking out down here," she says.

"It's not a big deal," I reassure her. "The station's rappel team is one man short tonight. One of the guy's wife went into labor about an hour ago," I tell her. Her eyes widen in horror. She pushes up to sitting and scoots closer to the cliff wall. I listen for signs of cracking or shifting in the rock. I hear nothing and exhale in relief. "There's a team thirty minutes away, and he's already on his way to them."

"This is what I get for being so goddamn selfish. I'm going to die on a cliff in Italy and all because I wanted to live a little," she cries.

"You're not going to die," I repeat what has become my refrain.

"Oh, the irony," she shouts and throws an arm over her eyes.

"Well, it will certainly be a loss for the theatre, if you decide to throw yourself to your death," I say dryly.

"It's not funny. You come down here and see if making jokes seems like a nice thing to do," she says, her eyes still covered by her arm.

My anxiety and guilt are tangling with each other. I don't know what to do and everything I say seems to only make her more upset.

"Do you want me to go get your friend?" I ask, feeling like a failure.

"No. Please don't leave me." Her hand stretches out to me. And she looks up over her shoulder again. Her eyes are full of sorrow. "She's having the time of her life. I've already ruined her trip by coming in the first place. I don't know why I did," she says.

"I'm sure she's glad you came and maybe—"

"I need to confess something," she calls, lips having been pursed in pain and now they twitch. I feel a prick of unease.

"No, you don't need to confess anything. And it wouldn't even count, I'm not a priest," I call down. "Save your energy and try to think about something—"

"You will *listen*, you owe me," she yells in a high-pitched, primal voice that is rich with anxiety and fear.

I give a sigh of resignation. I need to do whatever it takes to keep her calm and still while we wait.

"I'm listening. But not because I think you're going to die," I say.

"I got fired from my job three months ago. It was my dream job. And I was supporting my entire family with it. And I haven't told my mother what really happened. I've lied to everyone," she says in a rush.

"You don't have to—" I try to stop her, but she just keeps pushing forward.

"I wish I hadn't because I'm going to die, and those cunts who were making fun of me are going to think I'm really someone who uses men for money," she says angrily.

"Aren't you?" I ask her.

She glares daggers up at me. "Really? I mean, if I were, I'm clearly terrible at it. You practically threw me off a cliff to get rid of me," she says.

I laugh despite the real anxiety I'm feeling waiting to hear back from Marco.

"I thought you were about to confess lies. You're just telling more of them," I quip.

"Just because you didn't put your hand between my shoulders and shove me, doesn't mean you're not the reason I'm out here," she snaps.

"Sorry." I feel instantly contrite.

"I heard them talking about me. Out there on the balcony," she says quietly. "I was leaving and came back for something and overheard them. I just wanted to make them think that I didn't care. But, of course, I care. But all anyone knows are the rumors. And they would rather believe the most ridiculous theories, with no basis in fact, than hear the boring truth," she says. I know exactly how that feels. Renee dragged my name through the mud, and I know most people believed her.

There's an instant kinship, an invisible knitting of recognition and connection that I feel for her. I've been struggling with this very thing since I moved back to Houston. And I've had to endure gossip, not respond to innuendo and have everyone think *Oh, look at the size of him. Of course, he choked her out* or whatever. The gossip campaign that Renee started has died down in fervor, but I know that these people think they know things about me. And they know absolutely nothing.

"Tell me what really happened," I hear myself asking before I can think about it. It would be bad form not to ask, I tell myself. But I can't deny that I'm eager to know more about this woman who has me lying on my stomach with my head dangling off the edge of a cliff in the dirt, playing the role of confessor.

"I was living in Nashville. I had a great job at the Southern Poverty Law Center right out of law school. But the money was shit, and I wanted to be able to do more for myself and my mama. So, I started applying for jobs at law firms. Big ones where I swore I'd never work. I went to a shitty law school, but I was first in my class and I wrote an article that the Harvard Law Review published. So, I had no problem finding a job. I moved to Washington, DC. It was great. The cost of living was crazy. But I was renting and took the train in. Everything was great until I started seeing someone at work," she says.

"Well, I don't know how you could have foreseen that wouldn't go pear-shaped," I say sarcastically.

"Oh, it gets even worse. He was my boss," she drones.

"Oh." *Damn.*

"That's not the best part."

"What? Was he married?" I joke.

"Engaged," she says quietly.

That was the last thing I was expecting to hear.

"Shit, I keep putting my foot in my mouth with you, don't I?"

"You did say you were terrible at small talk." She laughs with real humor and shakes her head in what I have to guess—because I can't see her face—is chagrin.

"I lived in Rockville. That's a suburb of DC. It was affordable and not crowded, you know. I didn't really spend much time in DC beyond work. I didn't have any friends there, so my time in the actual district itself was limited to my office in Chinatown. But earlier this year, I ended up having an unexpected free afternoon after a deal closed early. You have no idea how rare that is. It's fucking brutal, that life. I worked like a mule at harvest time. On the days we were prepping for a deal to close, I would go forty-eight hours with no sleep. I never complained. I was proving to be something of a wunderkind in the practice that dealt with large insurance settlements. We were charting courses no one had ever even thought of. I was making an impact, and I was making money. I never complained about the shitty treatment, the shitty hours, and the constant sexual harassment."

"That intense," I say.

"It was. But like I said, it had its upsides," she says, and she sighs up at the sky in nostalgia. "On the first free day I'd had in a year, I woke up feeling like doing something special. I decided to go to Dupont Circle and walk up Connecticut Ave to Nigel's favorite store—so I could buy him a fucking *tie*. He was in California for the week and I thought I'd be wearing it, and nothing else when he got back in a couple days…" The image she paints turns me on until I remember that she did that for another man. The surge of jealousy I feel is dismissed for the ridiculousness that it is. She's not mine. Nor do I want her to be. But I have to admit that seeing her naked with only one of my ties around her neck would have been fucking nice.

"Well, turns out his 'I'm going to be in California for work all week' was a lie," she says.

"He was at the store?" I ask.

"Yup, with his fiancée. I saw him, and at first, I was excited. I called his name. They both turned around. You should have seen his face." She snickers, and it makes me smile, too. "It was the classic, *I think I'm going to shit myself, so I'm clenching my ass as hard as I can* face." She laughs to herself and I find it miraculous that she can laugh at the memory even while she's lying there in pain.

I feel my first pang of doubt about the conclusions I drew about her.

"Can you believe that at first he tried to act like he had no clue who I was?" she says, and I guffaw incredulously.

"No fucking way."

"Oh, *way*," she says.

"I mean, *hello*, motherfucker. Your tongue was buried between my thighs two days ago, remember that?" She laughs and I do, too. But my laugh isn't a loose, easy one. It's knotted around the discomfort I feel every time she refers to her sexual relationship with that man.

I don't like it. Not one fucking bit, and I have no idea why or where that feeling came from. Because honestly, half an hour ago, I didn't give two shits whether I saw her again or not.

"'Come on, Rebecca, *look at her*, would I date a girl who shops at *The Gap*?'" She says this in a deep voice that I'm assuming is meant to be the boyfriend. "I mean, who says things like that?"

"Well, apparently, your boyfriend. So, what'd you do? I hope it was worse than throwing yourself off a cliff because what he did was way worse than what I did…and look how you've punished *me*," I quip.

And when she laughs, I feel a swell of pride. And then immediately wonder who the fuck I am. Maybe I've had too much to drink.

"I didn't throw myself off a cliff, and I wasn't trying to punish you. You're so vain. Not everything is about you," she says angrily but with no malice.

"Anyway, I wish I'd done something to punish him then. It would've been much more satisfying getting arrested if I'd actually done something to earn it," she says irritably.

"You're like one of those Russian dolls. So many layers," I say in wonder.

"Huh?" she replies.

"Nothing, keep going," I prompt, eager to hear what came next.

"He had the nerve to call security. In seconds, they swooped in and escorted me out. I was truly speechless. Shocked beyond belief."

I can be ruthless with people I'm not happy with. But, I can't imagine pretending not to know someone you've been intimate with.

"What next?" I ask, intrigued beyond belief.

"I get back to work and find out the girl he was with is the daughter of our firm's managing partner. Overnight, my job became a different kind of hell. It wasn't just long hours and hard work. It was *impossibly* long hours, being assigned to cases in practice areas like white-collar crime—places where I had no expertise and no interest. They gave me all these extremely technical questions to answer for super valuable clients. Then they'd tell me they needed the answer back in a matter of hours. These questions required a full day's worth of work in less time than I was given to complete the job. So, of course, I made mistakes. I fucked up assignments. I took too long to return phone calls. Whatever you can think of, I did it. I was constantly being called to task," she rants. "They started saying things like, maybe I couldn't do the work because I didn't go to Harvard or Cornell like everyone else. For nearly an entire month after the incident at the store, they did everything they could to get me to quit.

"I knew what they were doing. I tried to stay strong. I was finally taking care of my mother the way she deserved. So, I hung on because I liked the money too much, and I thought I could outlast them. I'd never lost a fight in my life. And I have fought some really big demons," she says, and her voice is clogged with heavy emotions.

"Wow," is all I say, despite the dozens of questions I want to ask. Her honesty is so refreshing. I want more of it.

"But one day, the fuckup was *too* big. And a partner threw an entire three-ringed binder at me from across a conference room," she says.

I was stunned at that.

"I *know*," she says as if she can hear the shock in my silence. "No one did anything. In fact, they asked me to clean up the papers that had fallen out when it slammed into the wall next to my head. I started to think about quitting. I decided that there was no amount of money worth all of this. And if, at the age of twenty-eight, I was making nearly two hundred K a year, it meant I could find something like that again, right?" she posits.

"Right," I agree.

"Wrong," she deadpans. "When I leave here, I'm moving back home to Arkansas because I can't afford my rent in DC anymore. This trip was my last hurrah. But now, I'm going to die." Her chest rises and falls rapidly as she tries to catch her breath after that diatribe.

I ask her the question that's been on the tip of my tongue.

"How could you not know that your boyfriend had someone else in his life?" I hear a voice in my head say, *Not now, she's in the middle of what she believes could be her deathbed confession.* But the woman I'm looking down at, that I'm listening to—that woman is smart and damn perceptive.

So, I double down when she doesn't respond right away. "*Really*. How could you not have known?"

"I ask myself that every day," she responds miserably.

"You seem like an astute person," I muse.

"Then *you're* clearly not," she says with disdain.

"Thanks, that's nice," I say dryly.

"Haven't you been *listening* to my story? Don't you see the parallels?"

"Parallels?"

"Yes. *He* fucked me on the down low, but basically said I was too low class for him to be seen with in public. *You* wouldn't even fuck me. And you made it very clear that even if you *could* lower yourself to being with me, I was too cheap to do more with than that," she says without any recrimination at all in her voice. "I must be the world's biggest kind of fool. I keep meeting and liking the same kind of guy," she says.

"Hey, I am not the same kind of guy as *that* asshole," I say.

"What says you're not? Certainly not the way you spoke to me. I mean, you being out here on this ledge is nice. But considering how it's your fault and all, you leaving me alone out here would make you a pretty evil son of a bitch, so… I'm not sure that I can see any real difference between you and my boyfriend of five years except he kept his sense of superiority hidden for much longer than you did." She lays this indictment on me with the force of a sledgehammer.

Swish would be so disappointed in me right now, and there's nothing worse than feeling that certainty settle down on my shoulders.

"Anyway, all I'm saying is, clearly, I have a type. With Nigel, all I lost was my job. You're about to cost me my fucking life," she says.

"Don't say they actually fired you. Didn't you have a contract or something?" I ask, ignoring her melodrama.

"I know you only date heiresses, so you wouldn't know much about jobs and employment like the rest of us working stiffs," she snarks. She's making a joke, but a lash of shame strikes me right in the center of my chest when I remember the way I spoke to her.

"Most of us who have jobs are what's called *at will*. I can quit whenever I want, and they can fire me for any reason. They found their reason and fired me," she says simply.

"What did you do?"

"Nothing. I left. They offered me money to sign a nondisclosure, something saying I wouldn't sue them for wrongful termination. I was tempted. That money would *not* have gone begging."

"So, you signed it?" I ask.

"Hell *no*," she says like it's the stupidest question she's ever been asked. "Of course not. I would dance naked on a pole in Little Rock before I took their hush money. I've worked too hard to let them drag my name in the mud. That is *my* story. And I'll tell it if I want to," she declares.

"So, have you?" I ask.

She sighs loudly. "No. Because it would destroy what's left of my career. No one would ever hire me again. But I hope they spend the entire three-year statutory period looking over their shoulders for that lawsuit. They're playing games. I'm playing for my *life*. I have one shot to escape the future that I was born to, and I'll be damned if they take it from me," the lioness on the ledge roars.

God*damn*.

She's sexy as fuck when she's angry. Her voice is strong. There's no fear. No apology.

"Nigel made sure to stop by my office on my last day and tell me how sorry he was that things didn't work out. He told me that I should lower my ambitions. I had a great body, a decent face, and amazing hair. But my pedigree was all wrong. 'Stop punching above your weight, find your kind,' he said."

"Shit. He's a proper asshole," I say.

"He's worse than an asshole. He's a hemorrhoid. Useless, painful, and rotten on the inside," she says with real scorn. "My *kind* are hunters and trackers. We're keepers of tradition. We're salt of the earth. I refuse to feel ashamed of that."

My dick gets hard. Like her words are her mouth and they're wrapping themselves around it, sucking the way I like it - hard.

Fuck. Me.

I'm about two minutes from jumping down on that ledge with her and finding my way under that little dress and making both of our dreams come true.

"Oh, about two weeks after I left, Nigel had what he called a 'crisis of his conscience.' But really, what he meant was that he wanted to fuck me again."

My dick deflates. "Please spare me the details."

"Oh, stop being a prude," she says, misunderstanding my request. "Nothing even happened. I got home from another awful interview and found him sitting in his car outside my building. I lost it. I took my briefcase and started pounding his car. I broke his headlights and put a good dent in the hood before he drove off."

"Did he leave you alone after that?"

"Yeah. He sent the police to me instead."

"*Shit.*"

"Yup. Then, I got a call from my old partner," she says.

"About *him*?" I ask.

"No. When I was fired, we were waiting for a ruling on a pro bono case I took on for the firm. Flood victims suing the insurance company for failing to pay legitimate claims. The ruling came back and we won. Big time. There was an appeal filed by the insurance company, and they wanted me to help with it," she states. "Said they could get the DA to drop the charges if I did. So, I did. I could have been disbarred if I'd actually been prosecuted," she says.

I whistle, impressed at their nerve. "Why didn't they just assign another attorney?"

"I'm regarded as the foremost expert in the area of disaster relief financing for municipalities and regulated businesses like property and casualty insurance companies," she says.

"That sounds impressive as hell, but it's all Greek to me. Tell me, in plain English, what that means," I ask her.

"Well," she sighs, "when I was in law school, I wrote this article for a prestigious law review about the economics of hurricane disaster relief and how wrong we get it. That we focus on the bulk of the money of the issues that are sexy and headline worthy. Like helicopter rescues and helping resettle displaced people in new cities and states. But what about the people who stay? Whose homes aren't washed away, but simply flooded. The news cameras ignore them. It's not sexy to sit in your house and suffer quietly. No one wants to tell stories that would force us to really think about how we treat poor people in this country. So instead, we see the people lifted out of their homes by helicopters, moved to entirely new cities, given new clothes, new lives, and that makes us look benevolent. And I've been advocating for the litigation of cases that will force the federal circuits to take a position. Or maybe even make it to the Supreme Court." She shakes her head. "Gah, sorry, I could talk about this all night," she says.

"I could listen to you talk about this all night," I confess.

"Because of you, I'll never get my Nobel Peace Prize. I had so much potential," she cries and shakes her fist up at me.

"Stop speaking of yourself in the past tense," I chide her gently.

"You've ruined my life," she yells up at me. "And you know what's worse?"

"What?"

"Forget it," she says.

"Forget what?"

"Nothing," she responds sullenly.

"Okay," I acquiesce.

"I guess it doesn't matter if I tell you now," she grumbles after a few seconds pass. I smile but hide it in my voice when I speak.

"Shit or get off the pot, Confidence. Tell me or stop talking about it," I say.

"See? You're rude. But because I'm stupid when it comes to men, I like you." She says it like it's a fate worse than death.

"You do?" I ask, completely surprised and pleased.

"Of course, I do. I saw you and thought, *yes, he's mine.*" She leans her head against the wall and gazes up at the stars.

"Did you, really?" I ask. I like the way that sounds.

"Yes. Something is *very* wrong with me," she says miserably, and I snort out a laugh. "It's not funny. Every time I look up at you, I think about how much I want to kiss you."

Heat coils in my chest. "I want to kiss you, too," I admit.

"Of course, you do, now that I'm lying down here about to die," she says angrily. I laugh. *Again.* God, she's funny. "I should be inside eating cake, getting drunk, and taking some beautiful stranger to bed. What kind of karma is this?" She wails to the sky and slams her open palm on the ground.

I watch helplessly from this stupid ledge. I feel like total shit.

"I'm sorry about what I said," I start.

She doesn't respond.

I haven't apologized for anything in a long time. I don't even know if I'm doing it right, but her increased volume makes me think not.

These are my "What would Swisher Do" moments. As soon as I ask myself that question, the answer comes.

"It was shitty, and I was an asshole for no reason," I call down.

"Yes, it was." She sniffles and looks up at me over her shoulders, which are pressed flat against the rock. "No one's an asshole for no reason. But, I really hope yours is good, because I want to forgive you," she says begrudgingly.

I laugh. "You sure about that?" I ask.

"Only because if I get off this ledge, I'll be able to have the night I wanted." She scowls up at me.

I like that scowl.

I like *her.*

Very much.

The fearlessness of her conviction is so fucking attractive.

It's a very rare trait. It's the lack of that trait that makes the saying, *and there are no atheists in foxhole*s very true.

But here she is. In her proverbial foxhole, and she's not finding her faith. Or compromising. I've only known four other living people who are like this, and three of them are my brothers. So, I give her a sign of respect that I give very few.

The truth.

"I can count my family on one hand. My aunt, my brothers. To everyone else, I'm a means to an end. And that end usually has some-thing to do with my money. I've stopped minding. I just wish I would meet someone who would be honest about it." I say the words out loud that I've only ever let fester in my chest, and they sound as awful as they feel.

Her voice softens. "Oh, Hayes—"

The blare of sirens and the glowing from their flashing lights cuts her off.

The spell is broken, and I switch to action mode. I speak quickly and urgently down to her.

"I told them not to alert anyone inside. But it's going to be impossible for them to get out here without that now. And people are going to come out and see what's happening."

"Of course, they will," she says dejectedly. "For once, I'd love to not make a dramatic exit." And I feel her pain. More than I can say.

"I'm going to go and make sure they don't come too far, and I'll do my best to make sure your dignity is in one piece when the night is over," I tell her and start to get up.

"No, you can't leave me alone with them!" she cries out, and her eyes widen with fear. "What if they drop me? What if I fall?" she cries. Her chest heaves and arches her back off that wall.

"No, don't worry, and don't move. I won't leave until they get here, but I want to go and stand by the entrance to make sure that no one else comes out here. The last thing we need is for you to have to push through a crowd of people."

"I'm so scared. Please promise you'll stay close by. I just want to hear your voice, please?" She pleads with me with such earnest vulnerability that it makes me wish I could be the one to bring her up to safety.

"I'll make sure you're safe. And I'll be just behind the rescuers, okay?" I search her eyes until she nods.

She looks over to her left and whimpers.

"Don't look. Keep your eyes turned up here."

"It's so dark. I'm scared, Hayes." She hiccups my name, and my heart squeezes in my chest. A sudden gust of wind picks up her thick mane of hair and blows it wildly around her head.

She screams, "Oh my God, are there birds?" Her hands wave frantically around her body.

"No, it's just your hair, Confidence," I call. I look over my shoulder when I hear shouts and chairs scraping the ground.

"What if they can't find a way to get me up?" she asks tearfully.

"It's really not that far. It'll be a breeze, and I'll be right here. I'll make sure you're safe. I promise."

I've barely managed to keep myself safe. But I'll be damned if I don't excel at it for her. I hear the commotion before the back flap of the tent explodes open.

"Down here," I call out and start to lift off the ground.

"Haaaaaaaayes, I can't see you anymore!" she screams.

"I know, but I'm here. I need to make room for the rescuers. One second!" I yell, and then rush a few feet to meet them.

A woman in a short, multicolored sundress comes dashing out. Her eyes are wild with fear. She runs at me. "When I heard a woman had fallen, I was afraid it was TB, and then I saw *you*." She reaches me and shoves me in the chest. "And I *knew* it was her. What did you do to her?" she snarls in my face.

Then she crumples against my chest and covers her face with her hands. "I should have stopped her!" she wails.

I put my hand on her shoulder and pull her back. Her green eyes are clear of anger, and I can see her distress is real.

"Come on," I say, and start walking again. "I told her I'd be close enough to hear her, and right now, I'm not."

When I reach the rescue party, Confidence is shouting, "He left me!" over and over.

"No. I didn't," I shout over her.

"You did." She sounds unhinged. "You promised me, Hayes," she wails.

"I didn't leave. Your friend came down, I was just—"

"Oh my God! Cass!" she shrieks.

"TB, I'm so sorry, I'm right here, don't worry," her friend yells over her shoulder.

"So, what's the plan?" I ask one of the men who's talking on his walkie-talkie.

"We're just getting anchored, Signore Rivers," he says. "Then we'll send Danelo down to secure her harness, connect her to the rappel, and we'll pull her up. Once we're anchored, it will only be a matter of minutes," he says.

I exhale a sigh of relief I didn't even realize I was holding on to.

"Why don't you go sit there?" He nods at the stone steps where the rest of the guests are gawking. "You look very pale."

"No, I want to be close enough for her to hear me," I tell him. "I'll wait right here."

Chapter 5

TURD BLOSSOM

CONFIDENCE

"Thank goodness," Cass cries when my feet touch the ground after the rappel team hauls me to safety.

I wince at a shooting pain in my ankle and immediately bend my knee to take the pressure off it.

The harness is heavy, and when I try to stand on one leg, it's impossible. I sway a little until a pair of strong hands grab me by the shoulders and steady me.

"Let me hold you up." Hayes's deep voice makes my heartbeat quicken. I look up from the three pairs of hands that are working to loosen the various latches and clasps on the contraption that saved my life. When our eyes meet, his are full of worry and warmth that I hadn't seen up close. I'd been staring up at those eyes while I was sitting on that ledge. They had been my lifeline. I know he never felt fully afraid, but I did. When I landed on that ledge, it took me a full thirty seconds to convince myself that I wasn't dead.

"Thank you for staying with me." I reach over the men kneeled around me and grab his outstretched forearm.

"I'm sorry you were out here in the first place," he says. His eyes are close and hypnotically focused on my mouth. I look at his mouth, too. One of his hands leaves my shoulder and cups my face.

"You scared me, Confidence," he murmurs.

"You pissed me off, Hayes," I say softly.

"I'm sorry, if you are," he says.

"I hold grudges, so I'm not ready to accept your apology," I say honestly.

He smiles.

"I wouldn't expect anything less. But I'll work for it if I have to," he says. His hazel eyes burn into mine. I swallow hard at the heat in them. He's looking at me like he wishes we were alone. I do, too.

Something happened between us while I was on that ledge. I didn't feel it fully because no matter how much he did to distract me, I couldn't forget that I was a few feet away from falling off. But now that I'm safe and in his arms, I'm catching up. And my body is buzzing for an entirely different reason. I smile up at him, bright and wide with my perfectly straight teeth that my mom always called God's apology for fucking up everything else in my life.

"I'm so glad you followed me out, even though it was your fault. You kept me from going crazy," I say softly. We've run the full gamut of emotions, and we've ended up intrigued and much more than interested.

He leans in slightly—his eyes are open and on mine. My heart is thudding like I've just sprinted for a mile. My face is tingling. His fingers move in slow, small circles at the base of my neck; his thumbs massage the muscles that are clenched in my jaw. My head falls back and his fingers slip into my hair and cup the base of my skull. He cradles my head like it's the most delicate thing he's ever held. I'm liquifying. The adrenaline is mingling with lust, and I'm turned on in a way that I've never been before. What they say about near-death experiences making you horny is true. His fingers caress my scalp and send chills through me that curl into heat-seeking missiles that turn my entire body into an erogenous zone.

"I'm going to kiss you now," he murmurs and leans forward to brush a kiss on my mouth. But my lips want more and they cling to his greedily. Kissing him is like being hit with a thousand lightning bolts of full-blown pleasure. He feels like the most worthwhile regret I'll ever have. I want to make this count.

I sink my teeth into his lower lip and tug. He hisses, but he takes control of the kiss and covers my mouth with his. And then he kisses the shit out of me. It's so perfect that it feels like I fell off the edge of the cliff just so this could happen.

His lips are soft and demanding. I could get addicted to this man—really fast. My body is *singing* like it's just had that first, singular hit of its new favorite drug. He pulls back after one of the men working on my harness coughs loudly. I hold on to his lips until simple biology makes it impossible for me to hold on anymore. We smile like lunatics at each other. He looks like a kid on Christmas morning, and that's exactly how I *feel*. When they pull the harness off me, I know two things for sure. One, this was just the first of many kisses I'm going to share with him. And two, that I'll never forget him or this trip as long as I live.

"I still don't forgive you," I remind him.

"I want to make it up to you."

"Okay," I whisper when he leans away.

The harness loosens and the men crouched in front of me working it loose all stand. Hayes lets go of me, and I drop my leg back down for balance. I immediately regret my decision because pain—almost blindingly sharp—shoots up my leg from my ankle.

We're in my bed. The EMTs decided my ankle was only sprained. They put me in a soft knee length boot to immobilize it. Considering that I fell down that ledge, I'm amazed I walked away with that being the only thing wrong. I also walked away with the most unexpected, beautiful surprise. Hayes Rivers. He's still mostly pretty rude, but he's been attentive and tender. And I can't keep my hands off him.

"So, tell me, what's TB mean?" he asks. His breath is warm and tickles the fine hairs near my temples.

"Turd Blossom," I say, and his chest tightens against my cheek.

"What in the world is that?"

I laugh hoarsely and pat his chest softly. "And you call yourself a Texan," I say.

"Is knowing what a turd blossom is a prerequisite for being a real Texan?" he asks.

"No, it's not a prerequisite, it's a *requirement*. To call yourself a real Texan, you've got to have had some shit dumped on you and come up smelling like roses," I tell him.

"And how do you know so much about being a Texan?"

"I went to college in Texas," I tell him.

"UT?"

"Not UT, I couldn't afford that. I went to Texas State in San Marcos. It was like Paris, France compared to Amorel," I say and laugh as I remember how googly-eyed I'd been for the first couple of weeks.

"Where's Amorel?" he asks.

"It's where I'm from. Right in the armpit of Arkansas, just across the Tennessee border, and along the banks of the great Mississippi River."

"Is it a small town?" he asks.

I laugh. "That would be a generous description. We have one road running through town and really, it's just there because the railroad tracks need a place to cross." I laugh.

I wiggle the toes of my healthy foot along his shins. "It's why my feet are extra wide."

He laughs. "This because of your childhood? Or is this a random Confidence fact?" he asks.

"My childhood," I clarify. "I was barefoot all the time. Walking on hard ground with no shoes makes your feet spread and hardens them." I miss the springy, fertile, cool soil of Amorel beneath my feet suddenly.

"I played barefoot all the time," he says

"I didn't play barefoot. I *lived* barefoot. I even went to school without shoes. And so did a lot of the other kids."

"Barefoot? Were you…" He trails off like he doesn't want to say it.

"Was I poor?" I ask and laugh. "It's not a dirty word. I'm not ashamed of where I come from. Because look where it got me," I tell him.

"Well." He hums low in his throat like he's thinking deeply. "I think you defied the odds, getting out of there to where you are now." He leans back and looks down at me. "I have a feeling you left a string of broken hearts in town when you left, and I'm sure half of them never managed to make it out and come after you," he quips.

"Yeah, no." I laugh out loud at the idea. "There was nothing romantic about my existence. It was a hard life, but my town did everything they could to make sure I got out. And there was no string of broken hearts." I nudge the center of his chest with my nose. "I was too busy doing chores, hunting, cleaning, going to school, and reading everything I could get my hands on."

"See? You did what it takes to get out of there and your family helped you," he says.

"Not by myself. And not because of my family. At least, not my blood family. It was the sheriff, my school librarian, the woman who ran the food market. Family, for me, isn't because of blood. It's because we decided to be each other's support system."

A strange expression crosses his face. "What? Does being a trust fund baby negate the need for family?" I ask.

"Of course not. And I don't like that phrase. I've never been comfortable with the idea of being idle. I've worked since I left university. My brothers are the same way. We all have professions," he says.

I pull back. "Profession? That sounds fancy. What did you do?"

"Nothing as *fancy* as a big firm lawyer," he drawls. "I'm an accountant. Or I was," he says and for some reason it tickles me to death. I laugh.

"You're an accountant? You look like James Bond, the superhero version. I would never have guessed," I tease. Kinda.

"Yeah, and I worked for my family's company for a while. I'm the first Rivers in two generations to do so," he says with pride.

"But I think that if I didn't have the benefit of all that money, it would have been a lot harder."

I shrug, unimpressed.

"Sure, having to work a second job while going to school full-time meant college wasn't a barrel of laughs. But, you know what?" I ask him.

"What?" he responds with an indulgent smile.

"I don't even remember the hard work. I just know it's paid off. So, yeah, I come from one of the poorest places in the country. But I can also tell you that the more successful I become, the more terrible the people I meet are," I say.

"Oh, come on."

"It's true. There are five hundred people in my town. They're all like my family. They say good morning and they mean it," I say.

"Hmm, sounds nice."

"It was. That entire town raised me. When I left for school, over a hundred of them drove down to Memphis to hug me at the airport. They couldn't give me money, but they gave me the work ethic to fuel my ambition just because they love me. Now everyone around me wants something in return."

"Maybe. But I still think you defied the odds," he says.

"So did you," I throw back. "If you have disposable income, good health insurance, and job security, then you've defied the odds. Do you know how unattainable that is for so many people? The odds are stacked against most of us," I tell him.

"Honestly, I have no idea. I've never had to think about any of those things," he muses like he's never considered the mundane aspects of life.

Lucky him.

"Do you volunteer?" I cock my head at him.

"Like, you mean…my time?" he asks like it's the most far-fetched thing he's ever had.

"Yes, your *time*. You know, in your community? Worked in a soup kitchen, repaired a roof, cut grass, read to someone who couldn't read to themselves?" I ask.

"No… I support those things financially," he says.

I shrug. "Yeah, that's great. And we should all do that if we're able. But if you don't interact with the people you're writing those checks to support, you'll never see them as anything but poor. Which, contrary to popular belief, is *not* a character flaw."

He doesn't respond, and after a full minute of tense silence, I can't stand it anymore.

"I'm sorry. I'm just passionate about…well, about everything," I admit.

"Everything?" He laughs, and it rumbles around his chest and rolls over me like thunder. I snuggle closer to him.

"Well, yeah—everything I do, anyway. I don't see the point in doing something if I'm not all in. It'll take the same amount of time to do it whether I'm enthusiastic or not. And I've found my greatest passions that way. What you give is what you get… I acquired lot from my experiences, so I know that means I've got to give them my all, too."

He doesn't say anything and I start to feel uneasy. Me and my oversharing big mouth. "Did I just scare you off?" I press my forehead to his chest and close my eyes. "I'm a little neurotic," I say.

"Where did you come from?" He drops his chin onto the top of my head and pulls me close to him. He smells so good.

"Did you fall asleep when I was talking? I just told you. I'm from Arkansas—"

"That's not what I mean. I mean, I didn't know people like you existed…" He pulls back so he can see my face. I flush at the awe in his eyes.

"Oh, come on. I'm a clumsy, country redneck with a law degree and a nice ass," I quip to hide my embarrassment.

"Yeah, I can only agree with the nice ass part and I guess I believe you're a lawyer, but I need to see a diploma." He slides his hands down and cups the cheeks of said ass in his strong hands. "I'm sorry for what

I said to you. You're incredible. I have never met anyone like you, and I've never wanted a do-over so badly in my life." He rushes the words out in a clumsy, halting sentence. I school my smile before I tilt my head up at him. His eyes are so beautiful and they're fixed on mine in an open, honest, slightly vulnerable way.

"My mother told me that we speak from our brains, but we hear from our hearts," I say.

"Meaning you know bullshit when you hear it?" he asks with an amused smirk.

"I know bullshit when I hear it," I confirm. "And *that's* the only reason I'm forgiving you. I can tell you're really sorry. Also, it sucks that you have such shitty people in your life that you're walking around expecting to be used," I say honestly. He tenses again.

"I don't know that they're *all* shitty people. My brothers aren't. My aunt isn't. But otherwise, in my circle, money is more than just what you use to live. It's your armor, it's your power, your weapon—"

"You make life sound like a war," I say.

"Isn't it?" he asks.

"I mean, *I* don't think so and I've had some battles, but no. In general, I'm just trying to do better than the people before me so that the people after me have something worth taking care of, too," I say.

"That's all I want, too," he says and runs an absent hand up and down the small of my back. His hand is heavy and warm, and I start to feel the first call of sleep.

"The lady at the table told us your family is a big deal in Houston. What for?"

He takes a minute, his hands tightening their grip on my body. He hums contemplatively and sighs deeply before he speaks.

"I'm very wealthy. I have been since I was twenty-five. That alone makes me someone whose name people know. My father died when I was fourteen, and I went to live with my aunt." His lips twitch slightly like he's in pain.

"Was this in Texas?" I ask him gently.

"No, it was in Positano." He runs a hand through his thick, curly hair.

"Where's that?" I ask.

"Italy," he says.

My fingers drift down his face when I see the flash of pain in his eyes that the memory of it brings.

"That's a long way from home," I say.

"It was. And when I got here, I was so angry. At everyone. I didn't really know my aunt, and I resented having to come and live with her. I behaved like such a jerk. She sent me to a boarding school after I broke a window in her neighbor's house and refused to apologize," he laughs.

"She kicked you out?" I ask

"Yeah." He scratches his chin; the scrape of stubble under his nails vibrates against my ear, and I snuggle closer to him. His body is so hard, but it yields where I need it to, and I've never been more comfortable in my whole life. "We were at real odds with each other. She didn't know what to do with me, and I didn't know what to do with all of my anger," he says.

"How was boarding school?" I ask.

"Hell. I didn't speak Italian well; I was a loner, and the upperclassmen smelled blood in the water. And almost right away, they tried to make me their grunt. And that wasn't happening," he says coldly. I like that rough edge in his voice. I shiver and move closer to him.

"So, what'd you do?" I ask.

"The first one who got close enough to me got a bloody nose for his trouble," he says with grudging pride.

I nudge him and tighten the hands that I have wrapped around his waist. He's talking about it like it was no big deal. I can tell that now, it's not. But I can't imagine what he must have been feeling then. My heart aches for him. How can someone have so much and yet…

"So, you fought your way through school?" I ask him.

"Didn't get the chance. I was expelled when I broke the French ambassador's son's cheekbone," he says grimly.

"Holy shit." I grimace.

He starts to pull his hand back.

I hold his arms in place to stop him. "Please don't stop touching me; I like it. A lot," I say quietly.

His arms tighten around me, and I relax again.

"Did you hear about my ex? I'm assuming that gossip has made its way here," he says.

I nod.

"What did you hear?"

"It doesn't matter. I don't believe it," I tell him.

"Why not? Because I was nice to you tonight?" he asks in a voice that reeks with skepticism.

"Don't be a jerk," I say.

"I'm not being a jerk," he pushes back. "I just know what people say. 'Guy his size…'"'

"Well, my father was five foot, five inches tall, a hundred and forty pounds, and he's the most vicious human being I've ever met. He beat my mother until the day he died. His size had nothing to do with it. And it doesn't have anything to do with my brother who's the same size and just as brutal. I was bred by a violent man. I lived with violent men. I can smell it. My skin tingles." I look down at my arms. "The only tingles *you* give me are the kind that feel really good."

He nuzzles my hair with his chin.

"But…how did you end up in such a bad place with your ex?" I ask.

He stiffens and then clears his throat.

"I was living in New York after college, away from my family and with my brothers. All four of us in one city. It was…amazing."

His sigh is full of nostalgia, and I can hear the smile the memory has brought to his face. "I feel a but coming on," I say when he pauses a beat too long.

"But, I was also in a really dark place. I was almost twenty-five. My inheritance was vesting, and yet I still couldn't go home. I'd have the money, but none of the responsibility that made it mine. And I was obsessed with being ready to take the helm. My aunt always takes blame for introducing me to her. But if I'm honest, I thought finding a wife was the most important thing. Combine that with alcohol, youth, and more money than sense…and you've got a perfect storm.

"I married the wrong woman. We divorced. She moved on. I moved back to Europe. Five years later, her luck ran out and she was trying to get more money out of me. She came to my house one evening and I refused to let her in. She banged on the door for an hour. She only left when I told her I was calling the police."

"Why didn't you call them the minute she showed up? This sounds insane," I ask.

"Because I was, as always, thinking about what that would look like for the family. It ended up being a disaster anyway," he says.

"So, you've been in the position for how long?"

"Since I turned thirty, two months ago. It's been a total disaster. My uncle and stepmother have spent the last sixteen years making a mess of it. So, first order of business is trying to climb through all the shit they've piled on top of us."

"Ha, just like a turd blossom!" I wiggle my fingers against his ribs.

"I'm not ticklish," he says dryly.

"How boring."

"Listen, I like the idea of that nickname, but I can't see myself calling you anything that has anything to do with shit."

"Well, I don't need a nickname. I'm good with you calling me by my name."

He watches me with pursed lips. His eyes narrow and then he holds his wrist up so the face of it is in my line of sight.

"See those stones? Can you tell if they're real?"

I drag my finger over the halo of diamonds on his watch's face.

"I can't tell. I don't think I've ever seen real diamonds in my life," I admit and peer at them.

"What's your first impression?" he asks.

I examine them again. "They're pretty, but they kinda look just like the stones in a ring I bought myself for Christmas at Macy's," I muse.

"I think unless you're an expert, you probably can't tell them apart from other clear stones."

"So why do people pay so much for them?" I ask.

"They're rarer than most stones, stronger than most, too. So, yeah, there are lots of things that might look like them, but when you test their strength, they'll show you why they're worthy of the price tag."

His voice is roughened by exhaustion, but it's soothing. Everything about him is; his voice, his hands, his body, the way he touches me—it all feels right.

It's almost six o'clock in the morning, and we've been talking all night. The buttery morning sun peeks through the dark green wooden shutters that are ubiquitous to all of the villas along this stretch of coast. I watch the dust motes dance in the rays that fall on the tangle of white sheets that we've cocooned ourselves in. It's also a reminder that a new day is here and that in a couple of days I'll be on a plane back to reality.

"That's how I'd describe you," he says, and my eyes snap back to him. He's staring at the face of his watch still.

"How?" I ask.

"A diamond. Well, durable, rare, stronger than you look—a treasure." And when he says those words, I think how right they feel.

"I agree," I say, and then flush with embarrassment. "I'm not vain," I say defensively.

He disentangles himself from me, and I land with a small bounce on the soft mattress we're lying on.

I find myself looking up at him. He's propped his head on his fist, and he's watching me.

"There's nothing wrong with vanity, Confidence. I've never met a woman more entitled to her vanity than you. I'll call you…just that, *Tesoro.*" His fingers trail up my arm.

"That's what you called me tonight when you were being rude," I remind him.

"I didn't mean it then. But it turns out that it was portent." His fingers skim my shoulder and trip up my neck before they delve into my hair.

"I like that, even though you're just trying to make up for being such a dick tonight," I tell him dismissively. But inside I flail, flutter, and swell with pleasure.

"Yeah, I am," he says slowly.

I laugh at the surprise on his face.

"Is that rare?"

"Yeah, I'm not usually worried about making up for being anything. Most of the time, out of either necessity, obligation, or a combination of both, I'm forced to make hard decisions, to speak harshly to people I respect, to say no to people I love. But, right now, I feel like I can just be myself. And *remorse* is something I'm glad I can still feel. It reminds me I'm human," he says a little absently, like he's thinking out loud. His fingers skim—with no real agenda—up and down my side. "So, *this* is just because it feels right to say that I'm sorry." He focuses on me again, and when our eyes connect, we click into place like well-oiled gears and just look at each other. He's got a mole—tiny and the same color as his skin—on the left side of his mouth. His five o'clock shadow is heavy and rides up his cheeks. The light from the lamp overhead cuts between and lights his face so his lashes make shadows on his cheeks. I trail my fingers along the shadows and say, "Thanks for apologizing."

He sighs.

"I wish I could go to the beginning. When I saw you in the hallway outside my room, I should have dragged you into my room and kissed you," he says slowly.

"But I wouldn't change a thing. I mean, that kiss would have been awesome. But everything that's happened since was like a prelude to all of this. I've gotten the chance to know the man behind those lips," I say suggestively.

I lean up and kiss the tiny frown that's marring his lips away.

"And?"

"And now, this kiss is going to be something much better than awesome…it'll be honest," I say. I brush my mouth against his and I feel it in my core. Sexual tension inside of me. I'm *dying* to be with him.

"I like that," he says, then leans down and kisses me back. His lips are soft and insistent on my mouth, and I open for him. The pads of his long fingers scrape my scalp and his thumbs cup my jaw while we kiss. It is achingly tender, and with each press of our lips, my desire for him blooms even bigger and brighter. Our tongues do an erotic slide and rub that makes my toes curl. I've kissed my fair share of men, but this is different. It doesn't have an agenda. It's not foreplay. It's just a kiss for the sake of it. He groans into my mouth and bites my lower lip before he sucks on it. Heat floods my body. My heart rate rises. This kiss is everything. He's my river. I am drowning in him. And I don't want to be rescued.

"Your mouth…it's so fucking sweet," he whispers before we're kissing again. His hand slides from my hair down my back, grips my ass, and works its way back up to grasp the back of my neck and hold me in place while we share a kiss that's far beyond anything I imagined a kiss could be. Heat is licking at my skin; I feel like I'm on fire. I sink my fingers into his hair and nibble on his lips before I break our lip-lock. I drop kisses on his chin and underneath.

A yawn cracks my jaw and surprises me so much I almost choke on the air I inhale.

"Well, glad to know my kiss bored you to sleep," he says dryly.

"More like it wore my jaw out," I say and yawn again.

He yawns, too, then groans and pulls me into a bear hug. "Let's sleep. I have a call at nine a.m. and then I'll be working for the rest of the day."

He nestles his head on top of mine, tucks his hands underneath me, and pulls me flush against him.

I laugh at the way he's cocooned me.

"I would never have guessed you grew up sleeping with a binkie. You're a pro at the full body wraparound snuggle," I say.

"Binkie?" he asks sleepily.

"Binkie. That's what we call security blankets, stuffed animal, your mama's T-shirt. You know, something that you hold because it helps you sleep."

"Well, clearly, I'm a natural at the full body wraparound, because I can confirm, you're my very first one." He drops a kiss on the top of my head and sighs, deep and content, before his breathing evens out.

And I lie there and let myself enjoy what I know will go down as one of the best nights of my life.

Chapter 6

LOVERS

HAYES

"Woah… Hayes, this is a full one-eighty from where you were last night. Last night you said, and I quote, 'I would have fucked her, but I could never have brought her home.'" My brother Dare peers into the Face-Time screen on my phone.

I bristle. "I didn't say that."

"Actually, you texted it, but either way, that's how you described her. And now…"

"Things have changed, I like her. A lot. So, I need to know who she is."

His one-eyed squint full of skeptical amusement, he asks, "Who are you and what did you do with my older brother? Mr. I'll Never Date Seriously Again?" Dare frowns.

"Listen, I need to get in there. I just wanted to see if you could get me the background check without me having to use official channels. If you're just going to talk shit, I'll talk to you later," I snap at him and run my fingers through my hair.

"Wait, at least let me give you some advice. Because if nothing else, you know you're moving too fast, or else you wouldn't have called me," he drawls.

"It *is* too fast. But I need to make sure this isn't another Renee situation. Can you get it? Or not?" I fix him with a stony glare. He rolls his eyes in defeat but pushes back one more time.

"Why don't you just get to know her yourself? Don't freak out because you actually like her. I mean, it sucks that she's 'unpolished and unbred'—"

"Hey, I didn't say that," I protest.

"That's what you said it boils down to. And if you're really worried about *her pedigree*, maybe you're not ready to be with anyone right now."

"I don't give a shit about her pedigree. And don't be dramatic, Dare." I dismiss his rebuke.

"Hayes, a *background check* is fucking dramatic. And it's dishonest. What'll you do if she finds out?"

"How would she find out?"

"Well, hopefully, when you realize what a dick move it was and tell her," he says.

"I'm glad you've finally found a moral compass, Dare. How about you practice using it before you start lecturing me about honesty," I say sarcastically.

He laughs. "I've always had a good moral compass. Just not when it comes to my own life."

I frown at him.

He sighs and shakes his head. "Why don't you just trust what you feel, He-man?" He uses the nickname he gave me when our parents first got married. I lean against the wall and scowl at him.

"Because, I don't trust *myself*. Not anymore. I just inherited the keys to a kingdom, Dare, and whoever I'm with will have access to them. I need to be *sure*. If you can't do it, I have two other guys I can call," I tell him flatly.

He sits up and takes a deep breath with his vape pen in between his lips. "I got you, bro." He says it with barely tepid enthusiasm.

"Somehow, that doesn't inspire confidence, Dare," I mutter.

"Yeah. Well, I said I'd do it. I didn't say I'd pretend to enjoy it. I hope once it comes back, you'll find a way to tell her and apologize."

"Sure, any other advice?" I ask sarcastically.

"When you fuck her, only kiss her once and make sure when you come you aren't looking her in the eyes."

"I do not need any advice about how to fuck, Dare," I tell him and grimace in annoyance.

"I only meant until you get the background check results and can confirm that falling in love with her is safe."

"Dare…" I growl impatiently.

He winks. "I'll never lie to you. I know your bark is worse than your bite. And I'm your brother. We're BFFs forever," he chirps in a high-pitched voice.

"Shut up and get me the info," I snap, and I hear his laughter when I press the end call button.

I got a call from the office in the middle of the wedding ceremony. I stepped out of the tiny seaside chapel to take it and I've been gone for more than an hour. I had been more than ready to go find Confidence, but I needed to call Dare first.

I walk back to the terrace where the tent has been set up for two days. During the day, the flaps are raised, and you can see clear to the horizon.

Tonight, it's pouring rain outside. And the curtains are tightly closed against it. The ceiling is pitch-black and blanketed with thousands of rows of twinkling lights in the shape of stars. Huge, lush trees with golden, round imitation fruit hanging off them line the walls and act as cover for the seating alcoves tucked into the corners of the space. There are flowers everywhere that complete the look. It sets a beautiful scene. Yet, it all fades into the background when I finally see her.

Nothing in this room is nearly as beautiful, original, or fresh as Confidence. I've thought of nearly nothing else since I laid eyes on her in the hallway.

Her golden spun hair is swept off her neck and face and piled in a mass of curls on the top of her head like a crown. She's got some sort of jewelry interspersed in it and the stones fire like diamonds when they catch the lights from overhead. The thin white straps of her dress cling to her shoulders, but they look like they'd slip off at the slightest provocation.

A gust of wind.

The gentle nudge of my nose.

In the hungry grip of my teeth.

The lights overhead reflect on her bare back like a cloak of diamonds. How fucking appropriate.

I keep my eyes on her as I approach and watch the movements of her back and the elegant sway of her neck as she laughs at something. I can't wait to press my lips to that sweet, fragrant skin.

Her hand slides up to caress the very spot I was just fantasizing about. Her fingers linger there and her head lolls slightly. And like she can sense me, she turns her graceful neck until she's facing me.

The smile on her face when she sees me feels too good to be true. We hold eyes as I walk up to the table.

Am I being a fool?

Does it matter if it's just going to be a few days of fun?

Will a few days of fun be enough? I push aside the unease that pings in my chest at that thought.

Conversation stops when I get to the table. I smile at them, greet a few by name. Their response is universal and reminds me why I sit by myself. They all congratulate me on my chairmanship and a few ask for a meeting.

When I've finally done my social duty, I smile down at Confidence. "Good evening." A small dimple indents the middle of her right cheek. I run the tip of my finger over it and trace the underside of her lip. Her skin feels like the softest velvet. She blushes and tucks a thick strand of curls behind her ear and smiles wide.

"Did you rest this afternoon?" I tip her chin up with my finger, and her delicate throat bobs.

Oh, yes. There's *something* about her.

"Yeah, I did. How was work?" she asks. Her blue eyes catch the light and glimmer with desire. I stroke her shoulder and fiddle with the thin strap of her dress.

"I wanted to come and see you, but—"

"Excuse me, Mr. Rivers." A hand taps my sleeve, and I look down at the man sitting next to her. "Yes?" I glance down at him in irritation.

He gives me a wan smile and sits up straighter. "I just wanted to introduce myself. I'm Giovanni Caselli." He nods at Confidence. "I'm this young lady's escort tonight. I met her in the bar—" I immediately tune him out.

"Would you like a drink?" I ask Confidence. She shoots a worried glance at her companion and then back at me. "Maybe a limoncello, but it can wait. You just got here," she says.

"Mr. Caselli, if you would." I look down at the third wheel and scowl. "I'll have a whisky soda."

He only hesitates for the blink of an eye before he stands up. "Oh, it would be my honor to fetch you a drink, Mr. Rivers," he says. His thickly accented English is perfect and he bobs up and down. "Please feel free to use my seat while I'm gone."

Fucking coward.

I lean in and whisper in his ear, "*Invia un server con i nostri drink in modo da poterti concentrare sulla ricerca di un altro posto.*" Send a waiter with our drinks and find yourself another seat.

His eyes widen at my directive, but he nods, bows to the rest of the table, and with a furtive, "*Ciao*" in Confidence's direction, he darts off.

"What did you say to him?" she asks with a disapproving laugh. I drop down in the seat next to her and grab the leg of hers and drag it over.

"I thanked him for keeping my seat warm," I say with a shrug. My eyes sweep the rest of the table, and a few of the eyes trained on us zip away. But a couple actually gawk for another second before they bend their heads together to gossip.

"Why is everyone staring?" she whispers, her eyes wide as she looks around the table.

"They're shocked that I'm sitting here. I haven't had a plus one in five years. For me, these events are about business. It's a chance to catch people with their guard down, make a deal that would be impossible to hatch in a boardroom."

"So, you don't have business this time?" she asks.

"Yeah… You," I say.

She laughs. "You're so smooth when you want to be," she teases.

I pick up her hand and place it in my palm. She stops laughing and wraps her delicate fingers around mine. Her nails are painted a light pink. They're short, simple, but so fucking pretty. Just like her.

"But I can't seem to stop touching you," I say quietly and look back at her face.

Her eyes sink their hooks into me and reel me in. I go willingly. I want to backstroke in those baby blues. Her full, red lips are parted and soft.

She's practically drooling.

"Does it turn you on?" I ask, half teasing, half pleased as fuck.

She's good company. I feel completely comfortable with her. Like I do with my brothers and a very small handful of friends. She's smart and funny. And she looks at me and just sees a man she's attracted to. Not what I can do for her.

It's bad timing. I have so much on my plate. I have no idea what will happen when the wedding is over. But I know that I'd like to see her again. Is she even thinking about it, or is this really just the weekend fling she talked about last night?

"What are you thinking?" she asks.

"This and that," I say vaguely, but I add a smile so she doesn't pick up on the prickle of unease in my gut

I trace her finger absently and think about what I said to Dare. It's true—it would be seen as a misalliance. But it wouldn't be. There's nothing I've seen that says she's not amazing. I want to explore what we've ignited this weekend.

"What are *you* thinking?" I ask.

She raises her eyebrows in amusement. "Just that I'm sure everyone would be shocked to find that underneath your Duke of Midnight persona, you're really an introvert who creates distance to prevent being disappointed."

"I have no idea what the Duke of Midnight reference alludes to, but the rest is essentially correct," I admit with a shrug. I am very well aware of all of my shortcomings and of my character. The way my past experiences have shaped the way I build relationships. I see them as just part and parcel of who I am.

"*Duke of Midnight*… It's the title of a book I read a few years ago. A historical romance where, by day, the duke is an autocratic and powerful member of parliament. By night, though, he was a sort of protector of the poor—Victorian England's version of Batman. Anyway, no one would have guessed that his motivations were all about avenging his parents' murders and not about being the most powerful duke in the world. It's such a great book. And after yesterday, I think you'd be just like that if circumstances called for it." She smiles.

I hear Dare's voice in my head when she does exactly what he suggested I try—trusting how she feels and what I've shown her to decide if I'm worth knowing. I feel my first niggle of guilt about ordering that background check.

I swivel the small stack of delicate gold rings that adorn her middle finger.

She's told me about losing her job. If there's nothing more scandalous in her past than that, then it would be a good indicator that there won't be anything scandalous in her future. After Renee, I won't take any more chances with the women in my life. My responsibility is to make sure I pass on a legacy worth fighting for to the next generation. My personal desires come second to that.

My brothers have talked themselves blue in the face trying to convince me that I should date again. I've ignored them. They have the luxury of doing whatever they want. As long as I'm alive, it's my responsibility to continue the family name. Have children, grow what we have—to continue funding medical research, continue investing in the city that made us who we are. And to steer us in the direction of being what we've always been. Leaders, contributors, powerful, and respected.

The tickle of her fingers tracing my knuckles draws me back to the moment. I glance up at her face to find her watching our joined hands, lost in an internal conversation of her own. I watch her unobserved and lose the ability to breathe.

She's more beautiful than anyone has the right to be. And the longer I look at her, the more I'm sure she's the most beautiful woman I've ever seen. Her lush lips are coated in an obscenely sexy, slick, red lipstick. Her cheeks shimmer with what looks like gold dust. How fitting, since she looks like a very sexy fairy. Her dress is white lace confection that's stark in contrast to the smooth tanned skin of her chest and arms. Her hair sits in a blond knot that kisses the nape of her neck and I'm jealous of it. I imagine closing my lips over that spot and whirling my tongue over it before I sucked her hard enough to leave a mark.

She's still staring at our hands and her lips lift in a quirk.

She traces the network of veins that cross the back of my hand.

"You've got such big hands," she says absently.

"Yours are so small," I respond.

I feel eyes on us, and when I look back at the table, their eyes all dart away like roaches when the lights come on. I should give them something to make their gossip worth it.

"Let's dance," I say.

"I thought you didn't dance," she says.

I answer by standing up and holding my hand out to her.

"May I?" I ask with a formal bow.

She giggles, but pouts and points down at her booted foot with a frown. The large plastic boot that's holding her sprained ankle in place sticks out of the bottom of her long, flowing, white lace skirt.

"I can't dance on it; walking is about as good as it gets."

"You can if you're standing on my feet," I tell her.

Her eyes widen with surprise, and her mouth drops open in a happy smile. She stands up, grabs my hands, and beams up at me.

"That's the nicest thing, but I'm not exactly small and this boot—"

"You're tiny," I retort.

"I'm short, but I'm certainly more than a small handful." She starts to sit back down, but I put a hand at her waist and pull her gently into my chest.

"Well, it's a good thing I have these big hands, isn't it?" I murmur in her ear. I lead her slowly onto the dance floor and point down at my feet.

"Climb on." I hold out my upturned hands to her.

She gives me a slightly skeptical smile before she says, "Okay. But you better not let me fall," she warns, and then she puts one foot on top of mine.

"Never," I say and tighten my grip on her waist.

The song starts to fade and the next one starts.

"Oh, my goodness, is this Elvis?" she asks as she places the ball of her silver ballet-slippered foot onto my other.

"He's very popular in Europe," I say and smile as the strains of the song "Can't Help Falling in Love" start to play. I look up to the ceiling of the tent and thank my dad for the sign.

I slip both of my arms around her waist and draw her into me. The bodice of her dress has a V down the front that stops a few inches above her belly button. The one in the back is just as deep and twice as wide. She looks like an entire meal tonight.

I slide one hand up the expanse of velvet skin of her back and wrap the other around her waist.

"Slip your arms around my neck," I murmur. She does it slowly, her eyes on my mouth as her fingers link behind my neck.

Now, we're chest to chest, hip to hip, thigh to thigh, and cheek to cheek. Elvis is crooning about wise men and fools. This unexpectedly wonderful woman amazes me. And I can't help but nod in agreement when he sings, "some things are meant to be."

I lean in, brush a kiss across her soft, pliant lips. The touch pulses. The air is vibrating with attraction, and the pull between us is a living thing.

"Do you feel that?" she asks, her voice full of innocent wonder.

My short beard brushes the soft, sweetly fragrant skin of her cheek. "Yeah, I do."

"I think it's the air and the water. It's so beautiful here," she says softly. She drops her head on my shoulder. I glare down and her eyes are closed. A small smile pulls at her lips.

"I think it's us," I whisper in her ear and drag my lips to that dimple and drop a kiss on it. "You're beautiful."

"So are you," she replies with a drowsy smile, and I laugh dismissively. I step back and forth, my hand at her waist tightening to hold her flush against me.

"Not one single person has ever called me that before." I laugh.

Her eyes pop open and cast a haze of desire that traps me in its azure net. My heart jerks in my chest, and the laughter dies in my throat.

"Then, they must not have been looking at you at all," she whispers. Then, she takes my big hand into her much smaller, much prettier one, puts it to her delicious lips, and drags a kiss across my knuckles.

I'm moving in a small circle of slow two-steps. The music blends in with the rest of the background noise, and all I hear is the beating of my heart and the thud of my racing pulse in my ears.

There's a storm brewing between us. It's loud and it builds in a slow stream of tension that's permeating the air.

I feel it in my racing pulse.

I feel it in the tingle at the base of my spine.

And when she sways into me, *she* feels it in the ardent pressure of my rock-hard dick between us.

"Oh my God." She twines her fingers into the hair at the base of my neck.

Without a single thought for propriety or gossip, I bend and slip my arm under her knees and lift her in my arms.

A loud cheer goes up in the crowd as I shoulder my way through the dance floor and out of the tent.

"Oh my Lord, what are you doing?" she asks in a whoop of laughter as she tightens her arms around my neck.

"I'm taking you to the closest room with a door. When we get there, I'm going to throw up that skirt and take off whatever's underneath it and fuck you," I growl before I kiss her hard and fast.

We step into the carpeted lobby of the villa and scan the room until I see a swinging door with the light off inside. I head straight for it.

"This is crazy," she gasps into my neck. "I feel like I'm on fire, Hayes. I've never… I don't know what it is." She starts to squirm.

"I do. It's whatever fucking pheromone you're secreting. It makes me want to beat my fucking chest and rut with you while everyone watches," I say and kick the door open. I set her down before I feel around for a light switch. The bright fluorescent bulb flickers a few times before it floods the room with light. It's a utility closet with a waist-high counter running down the middle.

"Perfect," I whisper.

I wrap my arms around her waist and hoist her up, the voluminous layers of her skirt crushed in my hold. I stare at her face for just a second and I'll never forget the way her eyes burned with need right before I took her mouth in a kiss I'd been thinking about for almost twenty-four hours.

She opens like the beautiful flower she is, and my tongue slips into her sweet, warm mouth.

She's like nothing I've ever felt.

She feels like mine.

So much like mine.

For tonight, at least, she will be.

I drop her onto the work bench and break our kiss. I shove her lace skirt up to her waist, and her hand falls to my belt. I slide my hand up her thigh. "Your skin is so… soft. May I?" I ask.

She growls. "Please. Just touch me."

I kiss her again and press my palm to the damp, heated slip of silk between her legs. I pull it so it slides between her lips. She moans into my mouth and unzips my pants.

"Please hurry. I want you inside me so badly, it hurts." She moans.

I slip my hands back in between her splayed thighs, and I play with her pussy. I slip a finger inside her, rub her wetness up her slit, and rub her clit. She lets loose a broken sob when I pinch it at the same time that I nip the tender skin on her throat.

"What are you doing to me?" She pants and throws her head back. It hits the wall behind her.

"I'm about to fuck you until you come so hard and loud that they'll hear you in the other room."

"Yes. God." She groans and leans forward to wrap a hand around me. She strokes up, and I thrust up into her hand.

"I want you so badly," I growl and grab a handful of her ass and squeeze it until I'm sure my fingers will leave an imprint.

She moans, and her legs spread even farther apart.

"Then fucking take me," she says impatiently.

I pull her off the bench and turn her around.

I lift her skirt and expose her round, luscious ass. I slap it, and she jumps. But then her hips loosen.

"Let me fuck you how I know you need." I slip my fingers around the soaked piece of fabric that's drawn between her lips.

"Yes, please…"

"Why did you even bother wearing these?" I slip two fingers inside her and press up.

"Because I imagined that you might want to rip them off," she says and shoots a satisfied grin over her shoulder. I give the silk scrap of fabric a sharp tug, and they give up their hold on her body and fall into my hand. I stuff them into the pocket of my shirt. I push her legs even farther apart and thrust three fingers inside her. Her back arches and she groans into the table top.

"Your pussy is fucking unreal." I swivel my hand, and she pulses around my fingers and rotates her hips.

I pull out of her and fish a condom out of my pocket. I roll it on and spread her wetness from my fingers all over it.

"I want you so much." She moans.

"Then, get your pussy on my dick, *Tesoro*," I say and pull her back onto me. She thrusts back and starts fucking herself. I watch my dick glide in and out of her and wonder if I could build a shrine to her cunt. I grab her hips and slam up on her next downward slide. She screams, loud enough that it carries out into the hallway and mingles with the sounds of conversation on the other side of the door.

"Do you like that I'm fucking you where everyone can hear?" I whisper in her ear.

I slide the strap of her dress down, and I pull down the bodice. Her round, full-as-fuck, pink-tipped breast spills out.

"Yes," she pants in my ear.

"Why?" I rain kisses down her throat and bite her shoulder, nudging her entrance with the head of my cock.

"I want them to know I fucked my dream man tonight," she croons, and I laugh.

"Dream man?"

She turns her head over her shoulder and holds me in the sweet snare of her azure gaze. "Yes. My dream man. Who looks like a king and fucks me like I'm his queen. Who is so fierce and so raw on the inside that he bleeds everything he's feeling straight into his eyes." She pants.

My heart stutters to a stop at how sure she sounds and how good it feels to be *seen*.

I lean down, press a kiss to her mouth, and start fucking her again. She breaks the kiss and presses her face into the table with a deep, satisfied moan.

I sweep her few errant curls off her shoulders and press my mouth into the slope where her shoulder meets her neck and press forward with hard, shallow thrusts.

"Fuck, fuck, fuck, fuck." The feeling of being balls deep inside her is indescribable.

I *feel* like a fucking king.

I surge forward and drive her into the table. Her booted foot makes contact with my shin, and I ask, "Are you okay?" without slowing my rhythm. She nods. I fist my hand in her hair and pull a fist full of her hair back. I press our cheeks together.

"Jesus, you feel like a goddamn dream. I want to watch you come." I pull out of her and turn her on her back. I thrust back into her in one long, hard push of my hips.

"Ahhhhh," she wails, and I get to watch the achingly beautiful expression on her face when my name pushes up her throat and out of her mouth in the sexiest whimper I've ever heard.

I push even deeper.

"Yes, sing for me, *Tesoro*," I coax her. Her facial expression ebbs between ecstasy and pain, and then to bliss while I fuck her. My hand is grasping her thigh and her arms are flung wide on the table.

I pull the straps of her sleeves down so that both of her breasts are exposed to me. I bite down on one of her hard, pink-as-the-inside-of-a-seashell nipples, and she starts to cry my name over and over. I focus on the satin fist her pussy is making around my cock. I lose myself in her cries and race toward the relief I need like I need air.

I already want her again.

I bury my face in her neck, hold her succulent ass with one hand, and hold the other flat against the wall beside her head.

She presses her warm, soft lips to my ear and flicks her tongue along the shell of it. "There's a hurricane swirling inside of me," she whispers.

"That's *me*," I tell her between small nips at her throat.

"I'm coming apart." She moans.

My breath hitches. I pull back and look into her limpid, breath-takingly bright eyes. She touches her open mouth to mine and kisses me softly.

"It feels so good, I don't know what to do." Her breath comes in short puffs. "Like I've never..." She trails off.

"I know; it feels too good to be true, right?" I stare into her eyes and the naked desire in them, the honesty in her gaze, moves something inside of me.

Yes, I *like* her.

"Like...I'll never, ever get enough," she says in a low, but strong voice.

Her eyes light with a fierceness before her mouth is back on mine. She grips my neck, twines her fingers into my hair and pulls herself up my body.

Her legs tighten around my waist. I let go of her ass and press my other hand to the wall. "I want to make you come." She groans just as she lifts up and slams back down on my cock.

She squeezes me in rhythmic pulses that shoot pleasure straight to my balls. Like a slave following his master's command, I start to come in a rush that blindsides me.

My knees buckle and I close my eyes against the suddenly unbearably bright light in the room. She rides me through my orgasm and slips a hand in between her legs. "I can't come without my clit." She pants before she starts rubbing between her legs.

"Let me." I breathe and stand up. I take the condom off and toss it in the trash can next to the door. I spread her thighs and admire the sweet, wet, swollen pussy I just finished fucking. I bend and squat until my face is right where it wants to be. I lick her from the tender spot above her pucker all the way to her clit, and I pull it into my mouth. I suck hard, soft, flick my tongue, nip with my teeth until I know what she needs. And then, I eat her until she comes. Her hands fist in my hair even while she squirms away from my mouth. I press my palm to the center of her stomach and hold her in place and suck her clit until she screams my name. I want to beat my chest and throw her over my shoulder.

I stand up and stare down at her.

She's slumped against the wall like a rag doll. Her hair is spilling free of the pins she used to put it up, and now curling strands lay tousled all around her shoulders.

"That was…" She sighs and eyes me lazily out of half-open eyes.

"Yeah, it was…crazy," I say and tuck my shirt back into my trousers and fasten them.

She pouts.

I tug her dress straps up over her shoulders and cover her breasts.

"You're killing my dreams," she complains, a frown puckering a swollen, sultry mouth.

"What dreams are those?"

"Ones where you're not getting dressed and pulling my dress back in place," she says in a sexy tone.

"It's bad enough that I carried you off the dance floor and fucked you in a utility closet with a door that doesn't close properly," I remind her.

Her face flashes a hot red, and she sits up and crosses her arms over her chest and looks over my shoulder at the door.

"Oh my God, it's a swinging door, Hayes. What if someone saw us?" she asks.

"Then, they got a fucking great show," I say and run the tip of my finger over the gentle slope of her lips. "I'm only getting dressed so I can carry you up to my room. I think walking through the lobby would turn our tryst into *flagantre delicto.*"

"In what?" she asks

"It's Latin. Translated literally, it means a blazing offense," I tell her with a smile. "These days it's sort of synonymous for walking around in a state of undress." I start to lift her and she stiffens and puts her hands on my bicep to stop me.

"I can walk. You can't be carrying me everywhere," she says. Her brows are drawn, and she looks ready to argue. I kiss her, and she melts against me. I scoop her up and hold her to my chest, and her arms go around my neck. I take one last sip of her and then break our kiss. A satisfied smile stretches across her sexy lips and the protest she put up a second ago is gone. I kick the door open and step out into the hallway and start toward the rear of the villa.

"The elevator is that way." She points a graceful finger in the opposite direction.

"We're not taking the elevator," I inform her.

"Why not?"

"It'll take too long." I wink and start up the narrow stairs to my room. "I'm in a hurry."

Chapter 7

ANDIAMO

CONFIDENCE

"That was so beautiful, Hayes." I watch in awe as his fingers skip across the ivory keys of the piano and then stop.

"Thank you. My aunt Gigi taught me, and even though my hands are big, it came naturally."

We're seated at the piano, and Hayes is peeling back even more layers. He plays the piano beautifully. "So, this is like your last hurrah, too?" I ask with a waggle of my eyebrows.

"I wouldn't have thought of it that way, actually, but you've definitely put the hurrah into this trip." He waggles his thick brows back to me and gives my hand a squeeze.

"Well, I'm glad I could be of service." I snuggle into him. We're waiting for our airport shuttle in the lobby. Our flights are a couple hours apart, but we're heading to the airport early to avoid the larger crowds leaving later this afternoon.

Cass is asleep on the little divan in the corner. Her black fedora is pulled down over her eyes and she's got her sunglasses on.

"She had a good weekend." Hayes nods in her direction.

"So did I," I say. "Who would have known that you are such a

Renaissance Man, Hayes."

He presses a finger to my lips and looks around the room. "Shh… I like them being a little afraid of me." He laughs and I admire the way his shirt bunches around broad shoulders when they shake with laughter. I want to soak up *every* detail.

"I can't believe we're leaving today. It's been amazing." I drop my head to his shoulder and link my arms through his.

"I want to see you again," he says suddenly and my happy heart leaps in my chest. Warmth suffuses my body, and I'm surprised at how elated I feel. But I don't question it. None of it. This weekend has been magical and full of surprises. Hayes is the most magical one of all. I've never had such an instant and tenacious connection before.

"I would love that," I agree softly.

He reaches up and pulls his phone and a pair of black-framed glasses out of his breast pocket.

"Let's look at our calendars," he says and slips the glasses on his nose.

"Your glasses are hot," I say, admiring the profile.

"Right." He rolls his eyes dismissively. "First, what's your number?"

I rattle it off and he puts his in my phone. "What's the rest of your summer like?" he says.

"Mine is pretty open," I say cheerily. Inside, my stomach knots when I think about the absence of job interviews, or anything else, on my calendar.

"I'll be in Houston next week, I could fly you in," he says.

"Fly me in?" I question, and I feel the first prickle of discomfort.

"Yeah, you said Arkansas? I can send a plane," he says nonchalantly, his eyes still glued to his phone, his fingers flying across his keyboard.

"I can fly myself to see you." My pride is bruised a little.

"Why would you do that? You're not working, right?" he asks quizzically.

"Why did you get a job instead of living on your family's millions?" I ask him.

He pauses his typing and slides his gaze sideways in my direction.

"What?" I ask when he doesn't say anything.

"That's hardly the same. It's just a quick flight," he says slowly.

"To *you*, it's just a flight. But this is my first time out of the country and only the fifth time I've ever been on a plane. It took me four months of dedicated saving to afford the flight from Memphis to Austin when I left for college," I tell him. "I'll never see a flight as *nothing*. And given the way things between us got started, I couldn't even imagine you buying me a plane ticket—or anything else."

He stares at me for a long moment. His gaze is assessing, and I can practically hear the wheels spinning in his head.

"Fine," he says. "Then I'll come visit you."

"Okay…" I clear my throat. "I'm telling you it's probably not anything like what you're used to."

"I'm good at getting used to new situations," he says pensively. His fingers drum the piano keys lightly and make a tinkling melody that is so contrary to the heaviness in his voice.

"I just moved back to Houston, started a new job; it's been fine." He sounds like he's trying to convince himself.

I nudge his arm lightly with my shoulder. "You sound thrilled about it." He smiles absently but doesn't look away from the keyboard. "I don't know what I am," he says and shakes his head slightly. His lips quirk, and when he turns his head to look at me, conflict has muddled his normally clear gaze.

"What do you mean?" I rub up and down his arm.

"It's strange to step into the role as the head of a family that I don't really know. I was born to it, but that doesn't feel like enough of a reason. Does that make sense?" he asks.

I turn fully now and wait until he does the same and we're face-to-face.

I trace the uneven bridge of his nose and gaze into his keen, green hazel eyes while I try to find the words to answer him.

We only met two days ago. We bonded during a highly stressful moment. I was terrified on that ledge. I know how lucky I was. If I'd fallen on another part of that path, I wouldn't be sitting here. That *he* was there feels like a very significant detail. One that, despite being mainly a coincidence, I think it will change the course of my life. I overshared a lot on Friday night. I don't regret it. Yet without the rush of adrenaline from that evening and with our separation looming, my feelings aren't as sanguine as they were yesterday.

I'm grateful for the serendipity that brought us together. But lightning doesn't strike in the same place more than once.

I'm glad we didn't walk out of here and leave our reunion to fate. A tangible chemistry courses between us. It carries with it an effortless ease, an immediate comfort and mountain of physical attraction. He's powerful, brilliant, passionate, decisive, honest, funny, *and* he's kind. He's shown me all of that and it's only been one weekend. What would it be like to spend a whole week, month, year with him? I can't wait to find out. I have a feeling. *Just* a feeling… That *this* man could be *my* man. So, I decide I'm going to fake it until I make it happen.

I stand and extend my hand. "Let's go out onto the terrace. It's quiet and private." He nods and smiles up at me for a beat before he takes my hand into his and stands up.

We step out onto the red brick paved balcony. It's another beautiful, if unpredictable, day. Puffy light gray and white clouds dot the powdery blue sky, birds are chirping, the sea rolls and crashes, and the breeze blows lightly around us. From here, the menace of the rocks that I fell from is obscured by a blanket of pine trees. The beach below is beautifully kept, and the water is crystal clear.

He stands behind me, wraps his arms around my waist, and drops his chin on my shoulder. I cover his hands with mine and try to memorize the way it feels to have him surrounding me. He sighs—it's not a heavy sigh, but it's *not* one that says, "I'm content."

"I'm listening, Hayes," I say into the silence.

"Yeah, I can tell." His voice vibrates from his chest and resonates against my back. I feel the gratitude in his words, even though he didn't express it explicitly.

We speak with our brains. People hear with their hearts.

"I've been preparing half my life for a job that I don't feel even close to being ready to assume. My father, and then my aunt, told me repeatedly that I have something important to do with my life. And now, it's one of my strongest desires," he says.

"I think that's what everyone wants," I say.

"No." He shakes his head and his chin brushes my hair. I nestle tighter against him and his hands come off the rail and wrap around me. It's the most possessive yet tender embrace. "Some people just want to *be* important. There's a difference. I'm learning it now. I'm seeing it in you. Everyone I know is pursuing glory for themselves. Money for *themselves*. Prosperity for *themselves*." His arms tighten around me. "You're talking about preserving things that benefit your entire community. That's how I want to think about my family. If I only have this finite time to make my mark, then I want to do it in a way that matters. Like you said, make it count for more than just time spent," he says.

"Yeah." I nod, but inside of me, something is blooming. He listened to me. He thought about what I said and found value in it. I think this man might be a unicorn.

He tilts his chin in the direction of the horizon and says, "Those men who sailed out past what looked like flat earth and kept going even though they weren't sure they wouldn't fall off—they're the people I admire. They conquered the earth and then laid claim to it," he says.

"There's no conquering the earth." I scoff.

"Tell that to *them*." He nods at the horizon again.

I turn to face him. His eyes are bright and beautiful, and just looking into them steals my breath. But I force my mind back to the point I want to make. "Maybe it's because I grew up on the river. No levee we'll ever build is strong enough to hold back more rain than the human mind can imagine. Mother nature is merciless. It made me realize how really insignificant we all are," I say.

"You're only insignificant if you leave nothing worthwhile and lasting behind," he pushes back.

"How do we measure what's worthwhile? Who decides that?"

"What does history record?" he asks.

"Are you saying that if we don't write down what happened here this weekend you'll forget it and it won't mark a moment in your life that will influence how you make decisions in the future?" I ask.

"No, I'm not saying that. And that's a very nicely-made point," he says with respect in his voice. I shrug and turn back around to look out at the horizon.

"Until you've been overwhelmed by life—found a wave you can't surf, a mountain you can't scale, a river you can't cross—it's really hard to understand how small you are," I say.

"I guess..." he says.

"If I hadn't seen how Mother Nature gives not one whit about even the best-laid plans of men, I may not be sure either. To watch that happen is humbling, heartbreaking, and transformative. We don't *conquer* anything. We just have use of it for a short while, but those trees, they grow back.

"Those monuments? They need men to write their existence into history. On the other hand, the acts of bravery and kindness those horrible events inspire may not make it into history books. But they will pass from generation to generation by word of mouth. And when people hear about them, they'll get goose bumps," I say.

"So, instead of conquering, I should be thinking about contributing something lasting," he muses.

"That's for you to decide. But it's what *I* hope for. That I'll do well enough with my life that when my story is told or *read*..." I drawl and he laughs. "That people will *feel* something." I sigh and his arms tighten around me. "If you really want to make a difference, you don't have to chase horizons; just look around you and do something that calls you," I tell him. "This necklace?" I touch the small pendant at my throat.

"Yeah. I like to think of it as your fishing hook," he teases, and I smile.

"It was the very first thing I bought for myself when I won that case. It's a reminder that I may just be a drop in the bucket, but it only takes one drop to overflow it. Little old me… I did something. We *all* can," I say.

We stand there quietly for a few minutes. "I'll get off my soapbox now," I say sheepishly.

"I like the way you look up there," he says quickly and presses a kiss to my cheek.

"That's because you've only had one weekend of it," I joke.

"I think if I'd had any more, I'd be trying to find a way to keep you right where you are for as long as I could," he murmurs in my ear. And my heart that's been tripping all weekend finally gives up the ghost and falls.

Chapter 8

SURE THING

CONFIDENCE
One Month Later

"You miss me?" I murmur softly as soon as the call connects.

"Too much." The words, enveloped in Hayes's fatigue-roughened voice, deliver a delicious jolt to my heart.

"I miss you, too," I say and hug my pillow tightly to my chest and inhale the lingering scent of him on it.

"I'll be back next week, and I think I can come up on Thursday, so we'll have an extra day."

I feel a pang of guilt that he's the one doing all the traveling.

"I can't wait until I can come and see you…" I start and then trail off because I know what he's going to say. This is our constant argument.

"I can't wait for that either. Say the word. I'll make it happen," he says and a yawn escapes.

"Do you want me to get us a hotel in Memphis next time?" I ask him and do the math in my head really quickly. I should be able to swing it even after I pay Mama's rent for the month.

"No, I like staying at your place," he says. He sounds sincere. But I've seen pictures of the house Hayes grew up in, in Houston and the villa he lived in with his aunt in Italy. Our double-wide is clean and cozy, but it's a huge step down in terms of the luxury he must be used to.

"My bed is so small. Don't you want a weekend without your feet hanging off the edge?" I ask.

"Nope. That small bed means you can't roll away in the middle of the night. In fact, when we get a bed, I think we should make sure it's not too big," he jokes.

"We're getting a bed?"

"Yeah. We are. One day. And in the meantime, I've never slept better than I do in yours. With you beside me." My heart is… it's going wild. Every word he says is kryptonite. I'm falling so hard for him. He talks about the future like it's a given.

"You sound so sure."

"I am. I'd lay good odds on us," he says easily.

"I would, too." I sigh. I'm so happy, it's surreal. We're such an unlikely pair. Our paths should never have crossed. But here we are. There's something really right about us together. His visits have been so easy. Not a moment of awkwardness. My mother loves him. The people he's met in town think he's some sort of rock star and he's nothing but gracious and patient with their questions about what he does. He brought Tripp, my neighbor's nine-year-old, a new fishing rod this weekend because he overheard him talking about his being broken last time we were down at Harps for groceries. He's brought my mama every book on Abraham Lincoln he can get his hands on, and they sit and talk outside together every night after dinner.

"Your mother home?" he asks.

"Yeah, she has a night off," I say, and then nearly crack my jaw on the yawn that follows my words.

"Get sleep, my little treasure. I'll call you in the morning. Tell her hi for me," he says.

"Okay. I will." I never know what to say in return because Hayes's family isn't around. I know he's close to his brothers, but he talks to them less often than we see each other. "Sleep well," I tell him

"Sweet dreams."

And then he disconnects.

When I drift off a few minutes later, it's with my pillow cradled in my arms, a smile on my face, and a song in my heart.

Chapter 9

WILD RIVER

HAYES
One Month Later

"All of these rivers—St. Francis, the White, and the Arkansas—come together and empty into the Mississippi from this delta," Confidence points out to me.

"So, it must have been booming once," I say and look around at the dead downtown of Amorel. There's the one church building that looks like an ice sculpture that's melting, and the two long park benches chained to the ground in front of the town's police station.

"It still is," she tells me. She's been idly running her fingers through her hair and she slips the end of her ponytail in between her smiling lips.

"Yeah, all of these abandoned buildings scream a booming town." I laugh and she bumps me with her hip in reproach.

"No, but the blues festival that still happens every single summer does." Her voice is tinged with defensive love and brims with pride.

"You love it here, don't you?" I ask her.

"I'm proud of its persistence," she answers after thinking for a minute. "It's seen every boom and survived every bust since it was settled in the 1800s. But…the river has given it a constancy. It's made the soil here some of the most fertile in the world. Most of the forests have been cut down, but look at how ardently what remains still grows. There's only a small fraction of people who live here when you compare it to before."

"Where'd they go?" I ask.

"To the city for jobs. Like me." She shrugs and leans back into me.

We're driving back to her mother's house after a day spent sight-seeing or maybe just seeing. This is my fifth trip here in eight weeks. It's the first time we've ventured beyond her small town. She drove us out in her mother's beat-up, old Oldsmobile Delta 88. I'm driving us back. The front bench seat that lets her sit right next to me is the only thing that has made driving around in a car with foam and wires poking out of the seats, no air-conditioning and a barely-functioning radio through the swampy Mississippi Delta bearable.

We roll over the railroad tracks that seem to run through every town in this part of Arkansas and turn onto her mother's street.

"The place still calls me sometimes, my love for it… This is where blues was born," she reminds me for the hundredth time. I just smile and nod, grateful that the sun is setting and taking the punishing heat with it. I glance at her. I've noticed that when she's happy, she tucks a lock of hair between her lips. Today, she's done it so much I've lost count. She gazes out of the window as we drive into the wooded area where her mother's house is.

"The delta is the soul of the South. And while the rest of the South is looking to become the 'New South,' we still own our past. Can't forget that at the same time that we gave the nation the blues, we also harbored the KKK. And then, in the sixties, it was a steaming cauldron of social change. So, yes, we're flawed, but we persist."

We fall silent for the rest of the drive. It's nearly a mile down this dusty road, lined with white clapboard houses that sit on at least half an acre of land each.

"Do you think you'll want to come back here and settle?" I ask her, and my throat closes around the question because I'm desperate for the answer to be a very firm *no*.

"It's home. But, it's also got so many bad memories. Between my father and the river, living here was like having a devil at my front and hell at my back. As much as I love our way of life, I've never felt like this is where my life was supposed to take root," she says. "The first flood I was old enough to remember was when I was twelve. I saw how we were left holding nothing, and it made me want to do what I could to make sure that next time we'd do better than just barely survive. I think I can do that more effectively outside of here," she says without hesitation.

The knot in my throat unclenches, and I smile down at her as we roll into the parking spot under her mother's covered carport.

"I understand that," I say simply. Because I do. It's how I used to feel about returning to Houston permanently. But now, I can see how much potential the city has.

I push the gear shift into park, unbuckle my seat belt, and give her a kiss. She cups my neck with both of her small, strong hands and kisses me back. Her mouth tastes like sunshine and water and trees and smoke. I pull her onto my lap until she's straddling me. "You're so sexy when you're up on that soapbox," I murmur against her lips.

"Yeah, well, my convictions give me the feels…" she jokes.

I don't laugh. "I know, and *that* gives me feelings, too," I say, refusing to use that ridiculous slang.

She hums and rolls her hips in my lap. "Hayes…" she drawls lazily.

The storm door at the back of the house slams against the wooden frame and startles us both.

"You two better get out of there like that before Sheriff Tommy sees you." Her mother's distinctive raspy drawl reaches us through the open window.

Confidence jumps so high she hits her head on the sagging ceiling of the car. "Ow," she complains and rubs it while she climbs off me.

"Go on." The door wrenches open, and I look up at her mother's ever present, good-natured smile.

"Hey there, Ms. Dorothea, you look nice tonight." I smile back.

"Don't try to charm me, you handsome devil," she chides.

"I'm not," I insist and take her hand in mine while I climb out.

"Well, why the hell not?" she asks and then cracks herself up laughing. I walk over to the other side of the car and pull the heavy door open for my girl.

"Hey, Mama," Confidence calls as she slides out. She mouths a silent *thank you* before she leans over the top of the car to face her mother.

"Hey yourself, baby. I've got Bingo, and I'm gonna be late, so I'll see you later." She smiles at her daughter without moving to get into the car.

They are mirror images of each other. Except for the deep lines that bracket and shape Dorothea's tanned face, they could be twins. Thick blond hair, vibrant blue eyes, small but generous mouths. They're even the same height. But where Confidence is shaped like a classic coke bottle—all curves, tits and ass—her mother is as spare as a reed.

"Hayes is leaving tomorrow," she reminds her.

"I know he is. I'll see y'all for breakfast." She winks at both of us before she gets in her car.

"I'll be back at the crack of dawn, so y'all should get to bed early so that when I wake you up, you don't feel like you've been hit by a two-by-four," she calls out of the open window before she turns the key and the powerful engine roars to life.

"Last one in the hot tub brings the beers," Confidence calls out to me as she runs toward the house. In a blur of tanned limbs and blond hair with a huge smile on her face, she disappears inside.

"It's about time," Confidence shouts when I step out onto the deck.

"Says the girl who wore her bathing suit all day. Some of us had to change." I scowl at her, hand her a beer, and step into the huge hot tub on her mother's deck.

She takes a swig of the beer, and some of the cold foam dribbles down her chin and lands on her bare chest. "Ooooh, that's cold," she purrs and casts her head back slightly, her eyes gazing downward at me suggestively. As if I need any suggestions. I lean down and lick it off and then drag the tip of my tongue up the damp, salty skin on her neck.

"Mmm, you smell like everything I love about this place," I tell her and drag her onto my lap.

The bottom of her bikini is crammed between the two firm, with-just-the-right-amount-of-cushioning ass cheeks that fill my hands.

"And what's that?" She straddles me, presses her chest against mine, and wraps her arms around my neck. Her breasts spill out of the sides of her skimpy bikini top, and the slide of her skin against mine gets me hard right away.

"Smoke, water, trees, clean air," I murmur in her ears.

She sighs and throws her head back to gaze up at the sky that covers us like a black, diamond-encrusted blanket. I nibble on her neck and run my teeth along her throat. A tiny shiver ripples over her body, and she drops her head onto my shoulder.

"I hated having to move back home a couple months ago. I'm still dying to get out of here, but seeing it again through your eyes has made me appreciate it all so much more." She sighs and rolls those talented hips over me before she slips off my lap and into the water.

She reaches behind her, and a few seconds later her bikini top floats to the top of the water. She reaches into the water and pulls my already hard cock into her hands. I grip the sides and I lift my hips so I float right above the seat I'd been resting on. Her thumb swirls around the dark red, swollen head that pokes out of the water

"I'm all in favor of blow jobs, but it's not worth your life, " I tease and thrust up into her hand.

She smiles a secretive, pleased smile before she releases me. She pushes her juicy, firm breasts together and then slides forward and captures my cock in the tight channel she's made between them.

"I'll do you one better," she says, her accent stronger with her drawled promise. She presses her lips to my swollen head and slides up, at the same time that she opens her mouth and takes me into her mouth while she uses the water and her breasts to create a sensation I've never even imagined before. I groan and grab the sides of the hot tub to keep from sliding under. "Holy shit!" She keeps her eyes on mine while she moves up and down in the water.

"Hold them." She gasps and nods to the sides of her breasts. I put my hands there and she moves hers to cup my balls. She rolls them lightly in her hands, her up and down slide never faltering, her mouth sucking the head of my cock with her every downward stroke of her breasts.

"I'm going fucking crazy." I groan and stroke her nipples with my thumbs.

"That's the plan." She gasps and then she proceeds to make sure her plan succeeds.

"You're amazing," I breathe out.

"You make me feel like I can do anything," she says, and I start to come. Without any warning, spurts of cum shoot out of my cock and splatter on her chin and her cheeks before she closes her mouth over me and takes as much of me as she can into her mouth. My fingers dig into the abundant flesh of her tits, and I only realize how hard I'm pressing when she winces.

"Fuck, I'm bruising you," I say.

"Yes." She gasps. "I want your bruises." I buck up into her mouth. She sucks the head of my dick one more time before she slides up my body. When we're face-to-face, she says, "I want to look in the mirror on Monday and see your fingerprints on my skin and remember how it felt when you put them there." My pulse jumps in my throat. I cup her cheeks and caress them with my thumb. Her bright eyes, the ones I've seen in every dream I've had for the last two months, are fixed raptly on mine, and I decide to go for broke.

"I'm about to ask you something," I tell her.

She stills the up and down movement of her hips. "You're going to ask me something?" she says quietly.

"Yes, I am," I say softly. I drag my thumb across the lips I've been kissing all day.

"I want you to move to Houston," I tell her. "Come live with me."

Her breath hitches, and she drops her face into my neck.

"I haven't found a job yet, Hayes," she responds mournfully, and there's an instinctive tightening in my chest.

I knew this is what she'd say. I force myself to relax. But I can't do anything about the urgent beat of my heart. It wants this too much. *Needs* it too much.

"I can help you with your job search," I remind her.

"I shouldn't *need* help. I have an excellent résumé. I'm *the* fucking expert in a whole practice area," she says, and her voice is full of frustration that cuts at me. "There's not a single environmental law practice worth anything that'll hire me. I think I've been blackballed," she fumes.

"If you would let me make a call—"

"No, Hayes. I don't want that," she fusses at me.

"Is your pride more important than being with me?" I ask her quietly.

"That's not fair. And I shouldn't have to choose," she shoots back, pulling herself back from me.

"Life isn't fair. And I don't see why it's a choice. Why does your pride take a hit from letting the man who loves you help you? Wouldn't you help me if I needed it?"

"As if you'd ever need my—" Her eyes widen and her hands cover her mouth. "You lo-*love* me?" she stutters through the finger she pressed to her lips.

Her wide blue eyes are full of surprise. They glitter in the gloaming light and the ire that was in them from our argument is gone. Joy—unfiltered, unadulterated, replaces it. She's fucking beautiful right now, and I wish I had my phone so I could capture her like this.

"Of course I do. I'm sorry you're surprised by that," I say and lean in to kiss her soft, pliant mouth. She doesn't kiss me back, so I pull back.

"You don't need to say anything," I tell her quickly. And I mean it. I know Confidence loves me, too. Of *that,* I have zero doubt. So, I go back to the subject that I've prepared to stand my ground on. "Just tell me you'll think about moving," I add.

She smiles, but there's still hesitation there.

"I will think about it, but first I want to visit. Meet your family. Is that okay? Just feel like things are more certain. Do you understand?" she asks.

"Are you not sure…still?" I ask, unable to quell the irritation.

"About us, of course, I'm sure," she says, and her hands cover mine. She tries to reassure me with her smile, but I don't return it.

"You'll never understand, Hayes, how badly I need to get there on my own. I know you're not him. I know you'd never humiliate me like that, but I also need to be able to feel at peace when I lay my head down at night. That will come from knowing that I got a job because I deserved it and not because anyone helped me," she pleads with me to understand.

And, I do understand. I just don't like it.

"You lying next to me without me having to think about what time we're leaving for the airport the next day would go a long fucking way to doing that for me," I snap.

She snags her floating dark green bikini top and smiles up at me. "Come here," she says and steps out of the tub. "So, I'll visit?" she asks and I look up at her. Her eyes are pools of blue destiny, and I can see my future in them.

"Yes, but please let me send my plane," I say.

"How about you just buy an economy class ticket?" she asks, and I stop and place my hands on her shoulders and turn her to face me.

"You're going to have to be comfortable with the fact that I have money. I'm not ashamed of it. I'm going to spend it. And sometimes it will be in frivolous ways that are simply about making my life simpler. We grew up differently. My world is different. And there are parts of being in it that aren't always comfortable, but they're necessary."

"Necessary for what?" she asks.

"To preserve order. To preserve the legacy my ancestors built. To repair the damage that's been done by the vacuum of leadership my father's death created."

"What will *your* legacy be, Hayes?" she asks and crosses her arms over her chest.

"I don't know. It's larger than me. My family, what I do with my time as head of it will be here long after I'm gone. And my stewardship of it will determine its future. When I was a boy, my father used to recite a line from Shakespeare's *Antony and Cleopatra*. Have you read it?"

"No, only *Romeo and Juliet* in high school," she responds.

"*Antony and Cleopatra's* basically the same story but with adults and in a historical setting. Anyway, my father would recite this line from it and tell me that it was the way any great leader thought about their responsibility." I close my eyes and recite from memory.

" Give me my robe, put on my crown; I have Immortal longings in me."

She nudges me. "Translation?"

"She was talking about dying for what she believed in. Bu*t I* think of it more as believing in something that will outlive you and making sure it does your name justice. My uncle has forgotten that. He's been thinking about right now for so long, he's lost sight of the future. The next few months are going to be intensely focused on trying to correct its course. But I want to focus on you, too," I say.

"I'll visit. With the intent on scoping it for a move," she says.

"You'll like it," I say.

"I don't doubt it's a place I'll like very much," she says and smiles at me with a plea for understanding in her eyes.

"Fine," I say and let it go, because I don't want to fight about it anymore.

"Now, come on—I have plans for you." She pulls me to standing. "Don't let me forget to drain this in the morning. Mama uses it almost every night she's home, and I'd hate for her to be soaking in your cum tomorrow night," she says and then she saunters off, that round, sweet ass completely bare as her bikini nestles into the hot crevices of her body.

Speaking of places we like very much… I catch up with her in three strides, snag her around the hips, and hoist her over my shoulders.

She starts to pummel them right away. "Put me down," she shrieks through a giggle. "This is *my* seduction, Hayes Rivers." She wiggles and rolls.

"Oh, my *Tesoro*." I tighten my grip on her and smack her ass just hard enough that I know she'll be distracted by the sting and turned on by the promise in it. "This seduction is all me," I tell her and open her bedroom door. I toss her onto the pile of crumpled sheets on the bed.

I pull my cock out of my shorts and run my fist up the length. Her tongue darts out and she swipes it across her pink, plush lower lip.

"Take it off. All of it," I command.

"Yes, baby." She spreads her legs so she's on full display.

"For the rest of the world, you're strong. Everywhere else, you're untamable. But here, you'll let me have whatever I want, won't you?" I ask.

"Yes, anything," she says.

"God, I want to fuck you in public so everyone can see what I get to indulge in every night." I cup her ass in my hands, then without another word I slam into her and nearly pass out from how wet, hot, and hungry her pussy is. She closes around me and her back arches off the bed. "Yes," she moans low and deep in her throat.

"You love me, Queen?" I ask her and slam into her again. The entire length of her voluptuous, beautiful body slides up the bed.

"Yes, King," she groans, but the king is garbled by another groan. I pull out, throw her legs over my shoulder and close my lips around her clit and suck.

She tastes like chlorine, salt, sweat, and mine. And I eat her like she is. She holds my head in place, as if there's anywhere else in the world I'd be right now besides in her bed, between her legs—eating her fruit and drinking her ambrosia.

I flip her on her stomach, pull her by the hips until her ass is in the air. I grab the bottle of lube by her bedside and pour it over her sweet pucker. Then, I slide a finger inside just to my first knuckle and she bears down on me like she knows what the fuck she's doing.

"You like that?" I ask. She whimpers and nods, sending her thick curls adrift over her shoulders and down her back.

That's my girl.

I slide another finger inside her, stretching and coaxing her open. She moans low in her throat. "Please, I want you," she cries into the pillow.

I pour more lube over her, coat my dick and then replace my fingers with it. I press forward and probe her sweet, tight pathway to nirvana. I watch a bead of sweat wind its way down the center of her back. I lean over her and catch it on my tongue.

"Haaaaayes!" She calls my name like she's making a wish just when I slip past the first tight ring of her ass. She moans, and the sound catches in her throat on the beginning of a sob.

"Does it hurt, *Tesoro*?" I whisper in her ear.

"So good." She moans and nods, her fingers clutching the sheets convulsively. But she bears down and opens for me. I press a kiss to the center of her back and grip her hips.

"Good." I grunt and bury myself to the hilt. I snake around her thigh and find her clit. I swirl the tight bud under my thumb, and the slick evidence of her arousal coating my fingers nearly makes me blow my load.

"Take all of it." I roll my hips. "And you're going to love all of it, just like you love all of *me*."

"Yes. *So* much." She groans her agreement like she's pledging her life to me, and I fucking want her to.

"Show me how much." I wrap my hand around her throat, hold her hip with the other, and fuck her like she's mine to break.

And I *want* to break her. In a way that only I can put her back together again. When she comes, it's with curses and my name on the back of a scream that rips out of her throat. Her body trembles uncontrollably and she collapses on her stomach; I think *this* could be the answer to world peace.

I flip her onto her back and lick my way up past her hip bones, swirl my tongue into her belly button, and I put my hand in the center of her chest and feel that strong, bold heartbeat. I slide farther up and replace my hand with my lips and then rest my head against her breast bone, so that her heartbeat mingles with the rush of my own in my ear.

I can't believe how much I feel for her. How much I've felt since I met her and how tied my entire future feels to hers.

Chapter 10

THE RIVERS RECKONING

HAYES

"Welcome to Rivers House." Poppy, our head of household staff, smiles warmly at Confidence as we approach her in the foyer. She's standing there like an army general waiting for her troops to fall in line so she can give them their marching orders. She's holding her ever present black spiral notebook. A key chain hangs off the belt of her black service dress. She has one of those faces that never shows its age. She could be thirty or she could be fifty. The threads of silver in her dark hair are the only clue as to which end of that spectrum she falls on. Her warm, but restrained smile doesn't falter once as she watches us approach.

"Ms. Ryan, I'm Poppy Patterson. I'm the house manager and I will be at your disposal while you're our guest," she says smartly.

"Thank you. This is incredible. Please, call me Confidence," she says and extends her hand to shake Poppy's while her other one squeezes my hand tightly. "I'm really happy to be here," Confidence gushes. My stomach knots, and I wonder how long that will last.

"Excellent." Poppy's smile broadens for an instant before her more efficient one is back in place. "Your rooms are ready, and one of the boys is delivering your luggage now. Mrs. Rivers sends her apologies.

She's out for the afternoon but looks forward to meeting you at dinner tonight," Poppy explains to Confidence.

"Where's everyone else?" I ask, relieved that Eliza isn't here.

"Your uncle and aunt drove out to Brenham today. They won't be here all weekend," she says with a glance at her notebook. Thomas is such an asshole. He thinks his little decampment is a slap in my face because I asked everyone to be here for Confidence's visit. Gigi's back in Italy, but she will be back next month.

"Dare is in town, but we haven't seen him." Poppy continues down her list. "But we expect him to be here tonight. His mother has suspended his credit cards. That usually lures him in," she says with a short smile. I look at Confidence and know that behind that even smile on her face, she's got to be thinking that this is totally fucked up.

Fucking Dare.

"Okay, we're going up until dinner. Thanks for the updates," I say and start to move past her quickly.

"Dinner will be served promptly at seven. Call down to the kitchen if you'd like to take refreshments in your room between now and then, but the dining room won't be available for you until dinner. The staff is setting up for this evening," she finishes.

"If you'd like to have your dress steamed or pressed while you're waiting, just dial down to the laundry and someone will come to collect it," she says to Confidence.

"Hayes, your suit is already pressed and in your wardrobe for tomorrow. Mrs. Rivers asked me to remind you that you're dining with the Bains, the Barras, and the Hassans. I've emailed you some general background information so you can read it before dinner," she reads from her notebook.

"Thank you, sounds like everything is in order," I say.

"As always," she says brightly.

"As always," I agree readily.

"Please let me know how else I may be of assistance," she says before she turns to Confidence. "Enjoy your stay," she says with a slight bow before she turns and heads toward the service wing of the house.

"Wow, is it a special occasion? You didn't tell me dinner was an event," Confidence whispers and glances back over her shoulder as if she wants to be sure no one is following us up the stairs of my family's house.

"It's not. Friday dinner is always like this. We dine with business associates and friends every Friday. Eliza and my aunt Mae usually plan the guest list, but it's nothing special," I say casually despite the knot in my stomach.

"Sounds intense," she says with a grimace.

"Yeah, well…my family is intense. And this house doesn't help. It feels like a crypt. I spent half my life here. But I can't wait for my house to be ready because I hate living here."

"Ouch," Confidence squeaks, and her hand flexes in my grip. I realize we've stopped walking, and I stare blankly at her.

"You're going to break my hand, Hayes," she complains, but her eyes are full of concern as well as pain.

"Shit, baby, I'm sorry," I say. I drop her hand and sit down on the stairs just like I had as a boy when I hadn't known where in this house I would be safe.

"Are you okay?" she asks and sits down next to me.

The steps in the house are as long and wide as park benches, and I used to sit on them and read, write, listen to music—whatever. And yet, this whole house feels like a strange place.

"I don't know. I've been back for almost six months and it still feels like I'm a guest. This house…" I glance around at the ostentatious ceiling and walls full of art that have no meaning to me. "I don't think it can ever be home. At least, not with all of these people living here. To them, it's free accommodation and they're not the least bit interested in how or why we spend so much money and time to maintain it."

"If you're not going to live here, do you think you could sell it?" she asks. I rear back in surprise.

"Of course not. I couldn't sell it. It's my family's home," I say sharply.

She looks surprised, too. "I'm sorry, I just…" She puts a soothing hand on my shoulder.

"God, I'm sorry. Yeah, there's just so much going on, *Tesoro*." I stroke her cheek.

"I'm sorry," she says, her face full of worry, and I feel a flash of guilt for my outburst. This isn't how I hoped our visit would start. But I can't lie to her, so I tell her. "I've been stressed out thinking about you being here. My family is complicated. We all coexist in this space. But none of us really like each other. I'm worried about you seeing that," I confess.

"Why? You're not them. Why would I hold it against you?" she asks. The question pisses me off.

"Because you're only here for a fucking visit," I say through a clenched jaw. "I want you to stay. But you're not sure. And now my fucked-up family is going to scare you off. "

This is hard for me. I don't do this—opening up—but with her being here, seeing her in the context of this house, devoid of warmth and love, I realize that what I'm offering her may not be enough.

"Is that what you think? That your family could scare me off?" she asks, incredulous.

"Not that I would fucking let you go. But I don't know how to do this. I don't even know how to say all this romantic shit without sounding like an asshole, Confidence," I say, and she giggles.

"It's not funny," I snap.

She sighs and stands up.

"Take me to your room. I want to show you something," she says and holds her hand out to me. I take it and use it to pull myself up.

I open the door to my room and she starts to strip. My cock stirs at the sight of her smooth, tan skin and the swell of her tits.

"Good idea, I'll fuck you until you can't walk. Much less, run off," I say and start to take my clothes off, too.

"Hayes," she says from underneath the T-shirt that's covering her face. "Sex isn't always the answer," she reprimands.

"Why not? It sure as hell feels like an answer," I joke. Only partly.

"I want to show you something," she says again and then turns her back to me.

"You see?" She looks over her shoulder at me expectantly. I scan her back and then I see it. My eyes snap back to hers. She's grinning from ear to ear, those plump lips parted to reveal her white, bright smile. Her eyes are full of triumph.

I look back to her lower back, in between the Dimples of Venus is scrawled *ADORO IL FIUME*—I love the river—in the same font as my family crest.

I kneel down to get a closer look and run my fingers over it. Gooseflesh erupts on her skin. I press a kiss to her lower back and stand up, turning her to face me.

"What do you think?" she asks.

"You did that for *me*?" I ask at the same time.

"I love it," I respond.

"Just for you," she says, and we speak over each other again.

She cups my face in her hands and whispers, "*Ti amotu sei il re del mio cuore.*" You're the king of my heart.

I can only stare at her while my heart races happily toward the edge of the cliff called Confidence and takes a flying leap.

"You learned Italian?" I ask dumbly, too shocked to say anything that makes any semblance of sense.

She laughs. "Well, not entirely. But enough for my big reveal," she says.

"You tattooed my family's name on your body?" I ask, stupidly.

"Well, yeah," she says, and I don't hear any regret or doubt in her voice. "I've never really been in love before, Hayes. Not until you. Not until now, and I figured I should commemorate it. Because this love… it's everything. You're everything. These last two months, you've shown me so much. Taught me so much. Shared so much with me. And I don't want you to worry. I'm the surest thing in your life. I love you. I want to move. I'm ready to live my life. I'm ready to take a chance. You're my lover, my brother, my father, my friend, my person. I need you. It's not you I'm unsure about. It's life. Nothing your family does or says will change how I see you," she says, and when she kisses me, I almost believe her.

Chapter 11

FLOOD

CONFIDENCE

Cardi B's "Bodak Yellow" bursts into my brain and I wake up with a gasp. I grab my phone, silence the alarm and glance around the room.

When my gaze drifts to the west-facing bay window, my heart lurches into my throat. My phone, forgotten, falls silently onto the thick down comforter of the bed. I slide off the bed and walk over to the window for a closer look.

I knew a storm was brewing in the gulf, but I hadn't really paid attention because it was supposed to miss the part of the delta where my family was.

When I stepped off my flight this morning and saw the gates packed with stranded passengers because flights out were being canceled, I started to worry.

I hate storms. Houston, though usually spared the brunt of the wind damage, always got a lion's share of the rain when storms came into the part of the gulf where the city sat. Having a port had made it the powerhouse trade behemoth that it was. But being that close to the water also meant that its flat landscape, the bayou that ran right through the city—and its below-sea-level altitude—made it ripe ground for the kinds of floods that most other major cities had managed to design away.

The wind is having its way with the huge walnut trees that line the drive of Hayes's family home. They're waving violently back and forth, hurling their leaves into the air with terrifying speed. The rain is falling in sheets that look like liquid glass. The wind is blowing it sideways, too, and it's sheeting against the window.

It looks like the world is ending.

But even even if it wasn't raining, it's how I felt right before I took the Xanax that knocked me out.

I grab my phone from the floor and re-read the email from the recruiter. The job of my dreams, located in Houston, had been submitted to her agency just this morning. It's the best career news I've had in weeks. Until I saw the employer is Wilde Law.

Hayes hasn't said much about his rivalry with the Wilde's but I know that going to work for them wouldn't be welcome news.

My phone starts to ring again, Cass's name flashes on my screen.

"Oh my God, Confidence. Thank God you answered," she says as soon as I accept it.

"Hey, I meant to call sooner but I passed out as soon as I got —"

She cuts me off with a wail that dread fills me.

"Cass, what's wrong?"

"I don't know what to do. We're stuck." Her speech is muffled like she's covering her mouth.

"Where are you?" I ask, but I already know. Her parent's house is in a part of the city that floods even during normal storms.

"My parents'. I came last night because they didn't want to leave their house, and I didn't want them to be alone." She lets out a wail that scares me.

"Cass, what's happened?"

She clears her throat and speaks through a watery broken voice. "We woke up this morning, and there was maybe three inches of water in their house. This neighborhood always floods, but not their house. Never. But it did today. And we did our best to get all of their art and electronics up on top of the dressers, on top of appliances. And we thought if the rain slowed down we could get out."

"But you can't?" I ask, trying to keep my voice calm and my mind clear. They need solutions, not hysteria.

"We made to the neighbors'. TB…" She sniffles "We had to wade through waist high water full of only God knows what to get here. My mom almost drowned us because she was freaking out."

"I didn't realize it was that bad." I say, horrified.

"Are you not watching television? It's national news" she shouts into the phone.

"I'm sorry. I got in super early this morning, and I passed out. Cass, are you safe at your neighbors'?" I ask. "Aren't they a one-story house, too?"

"They have a loft," she says.

"Oh, good." I sigh in relief.

"But there are twenty-four people up here. It's small. And my mother doesn't have her insulin," she says, and her voice pitches in an awful spike as her panic rises.

"Okay, well, the rain will stop and the water will recede, right?"

"Yes, but not in time. There's one bathroom, no power, and all of these people." Her voice has dropped again and breaks on the last word

"What can I do?" I ask.

"I don't know…nothing," she says sadly.

"Cass…" I shove my hand through my hair and stare helplessly at the wall.

"It's okay. I just wanted you to know where I was. Someone's called the city, and they say they'll try to send a boat around before it gets dark. But once it gets dark, they're not going to keep the rescues up. I need to get her out of here," she says. Urgency coats her voice, and my stomach wrings in my gut while I fret about what to do.

"Listen. Save your phone battery. Let me go find Hayes. I'll see if he can do something to help," I say and pray I'm not over promising. But I know she needs the lifeline of hope I'm giving her, too, so I inject my voice with confidence I don't feel.

"Oh, TB, that would be great." She sounds giddy with relief. "I'm so worried about my mom. And my dad is sitting in a corner, sort of talking to himself. They've lived in that house for almost forty years, and in just a few hours, it's nearly gone." Her voice is barely a whisper when it breaks on that last word.

"Oh, babe, I'm sorry. Let me go and see what I can do," I say, and then hang up before she can respond. My fingers tremble and my stomach feels like it's hooked to a hot-air balloon.

I dial Hayes and hold my breath, praying he'll pick up.

"*Tesoro*, I'm in a meeting," he says in a hushed voice after the third ring.

"Cass just called. Her mother doesn't have her insulin, and the city is sending boats 'round for rescue, but they're going to stop when it gets dark," I say.

"Excuse me, I have to take this," Hayes says, and I hear the murmur of voices behind him before a door closes.

"Where are you?" I ask him and rummage through my suitcase for clothes. My muscles protest when I bend over and I can't believe that a few hours ago, I'd been folded in half, trapped between Hayes's incredible, huge muscled arms while he drilled me into the mattress and made me come so hard I know that the whole house must have heard me screaming his name.

"Oh." He sounds like he needs to stop and think about it. "I'm downstairs. I'm having an executive team meeting," he says. "Wait. *Sugar Land's* flooding?" he asks.

"No. She's at her parents' in Meyerland," I explain.

He lets out a long, low whistle and says, "Shit. We've had it on in the background nearly all afternoon. It's a fucking disaster. I don't understand how this city hasn't done something to stop this from happening every fucking year. And why those people keep rebuilding in the same spot," he says disgustedly.

"Her parents' house has never flooded before. Never. This isn't a regular storm, Hayes. And even if it had been, I don't think assigning blame to anyone right now is helpful," I snap at him.

"Give me an address; let me make some calls," he says.

"It's nine-zero-nine-nine Indigo, off Chimney Rock on the eastbound side," I tell him.

"How the hell do you know which side is the eastbound side?" he asks.

"I've heard her say that before, Hayes. Can you ask me these questions later? Please make that call." I'm practically yelling.

"Hey, it's going to be okay," he says softly, soothingly into the phone.

"Don't try to calm me down, Hayes. I'm not going to calm down. Cass sounded scared. I know you don't understand how urgent this is because you've never been forced to try and stay afloat in water you have no choice but to swim through. But every second counts. Please. Make that call," I say through gritted teeth and then hang up.

I start to throw my jeans on but realize there's no point in getting dressed. I don't know anyone in this house, and I have no clue where Hayes is in it.

I sit back down on my bed and stare at my hands. A minute later, my phone rings. "King" flashes on my screen, and I pick it up before it has a chance to ring again.

"*Tesoro*, I spoke to my contact at the mayor's office. They're going to add her to the emergency list, but they may only be able to take the people who absolutely need to leave," he says in a rush.

"Okay." My answer comes out in a stuttered sigh as I try to think about what I can do. I know Cass and her dad will go crazy if her mom is taken and they can't go with her.

"Listen to me. If they can't take your friend, I'll go get them myself when I'm done. My brother Beau's truck is parked at the house while he's away. It's one of those monster trucks and it's lifted more than six feet off the ground, and it'll get through that water. It only seats five; we'll only be able to take three other people."

"I can stay home to make room for one more," I say immediately. "If the rain doesn't stop and they're not rescued, they'll end up spending the night on their roof and I can't even imagine that for Cass," I say.

"Okay." He blows out a breath and says, "Let's hope it doesn't come to that. That truck is a nightmare to drive on a dry, clear day, but if the city doesn't come through, I will."

FOUR HOURS LATER

"Oh my God, TB, thank you so much," Cass cries and throws herself into my arms as soon as she and her parents trudge into the foyer. They're soaked, but safe. I look over her shoulder and take in the six other people Hayes brought with him. I only recognize Mr. and Mrs. Gold, Cass's parents. The other three are a small, pretty woman and two children, a boy and girl, who, judging by their appearance, are between the ages of ten and twelve. The girl is as long and skinny as a beanpole, and her big eyes scan the room in amazement. Her mother puts a hand on her shoulder and says, "Stop staring," and then smiles apologetically at me. I smile back and turn my attention back to Cass.

"Where's Hayes?" I ask her.

"Parking the truck. He dropped us off first. You should have seen him, TB," she says, wide-eyed. "The police put a blockade up on the street to stop any more rescue attempts. He drove straight through it. He backed up right to the front door and even though he only had enough seat belts for—"

"What is happening here?" A woman's voice, as cold and clear as a bell calls from behind us. I jump, and right before I turn around, I see the little girl's eyes nearly bug out of her head with fear before she ducks behind her mother's legs. The little boy's eyes narrow, and he steps in front of his mother and his sister.

"Uh, hi," I say and wave at the redheaded Jessica Rabbit look alike, down to the red dress wrapped around her impossibly exaggerated curves and bright red lipstick. She stares down at me with hostile eyes and frowns.

"Who are you?" she asks through her pinched lips.

"I'm Confidence Ryan," I say. and try not to sound like I want to piss in my pants.

"I don't care what your name is, girl. I want to know what you and this ragtag mob of interlopers is doing standing in my foyer?" she shouts and the little girl starts to cry.

I let go of Cass completely and walk toward her. "I don't know who you are, and I'm sorry that you're walking into an unexpected scene, but we are all guests of Hayes—" I start.

"Hayes?" she asks like she has no clue who that is.

"Yes, Hayes." I cross my arms over my chest and eye her suspiciously. "Who are *you*?" I snap at her.

"I am Mrs. Eliza Rivers and this, you little guttersnipe, is my house," she responds haughtily. Then, she pulls a small pearl-handled revolver out of her purse and points it squarely at my chest in a grip that tells me she knows how to hold a gun, but no idea how to aim it. I don't move, but my heart is sprinting like a hare running from a hunter. I stare at her, beyond shocked.

Behind me, pandemonium breaks out. I can't hear anyone clearly, but they're all shouting. The children are both screaming. Cass grabs my elbow and tugs me backward.

"TB, let's go," she says, her voice a desperate whine.

"No. We're not going anywhere." I shake her loose. I take a step closer to the woman pointing her gun at me and look her square in the face. "This is not *your* house, and it hasn't been for a long time. I am Hayes's guest. So are these people, including the children you're pointing a weapon at."

Her expression falters briefly, and then she tightens her grip on the butt of her gun. "How do I know what you're saying is true? Where *is* Hayes?" she asks, her voice slightly fretful. I want to turn around and assure the people behind me that everything will be okay. That she's about as harmless as a fly. But I don't dare take my eyes off her. Because she is actually very dangerous. Especially with her clear lack of practice.

"He's parking. He'll be right in. Please, put the gun down; you're scaring the children," I say in a voice that I hope is deferential and conciliatory.

"That's what they get for scaring *me*," she says and I gasp at her callousness.

"You can't mean that, " I gasp before I can think better of it.

"You bet your ass, I do, " she says jauntily.

"Eliza, what's going on?" Poppy's voice sounds from over my shoulder, and I still don't dare turn around but sigh in relief that some-one who can vouch for me has finally arrived.

"I've told you to address me properly in front of guests, Poppy," she snaps. "This *girl* says she's Hayes's guest along with all of those people. I know nothing of it, so I'm exercising my right to stand my ground," Eliza explains as if it makes perfect sense.

"Do you pull guns on every unexpected guest in your home, Mrs. Rivers?" This comes from Cass's father who hasn't said a word since they arrived.

"No. Only the ones who very clearly don't belong," she returns.

"El—Mrs. Rivers," Poppy interjects and rushes past me to stand in front of her on the stairs. "You knew Ms. Ryan was visiting. I informed you that Mr. Rivers was bringing back guests to stay for the night because of the flooding," she says. She stands right in front of the gun and puts a hand on it.

"Poppy, be careful," I call to her.

"It isn't loaded," she calls back to me without turning around.

"What? Are you kidding me?" I yell and start for the stairs, too.

"Why did you tell her that? You idiot!" Eliza shouts. Poppy's yelp of pain is a beat behind the crack of Eliza's palm against her cheek. The room's incredible acoustics meld the two sounds together in a sickening rhythm.

I skid to a stop right at the foot of the stairs and freeze in shock.

What the actual hell is going on here?

"We're leaving," Mr. Gold says and I finally turn around to look at the poor people who have escaped one nightmare only to find them-selves in the middle of another. And I'm sure they're thinking they'd rather take their chances with Mother Nature than deal with this insane woman.

He's standing guard in front of everyone else. I catch a glimpse of Cass's face and she looks green. "We'll get a room at the Ivy for the night. Confidence, you're welcome to come with us," he says gravely, his dark gray eyebrows drawn in extreme concern as he surveys the scene unfolding in front of him. "In fact, I would like to insist that you do," he says. I've only met him once before at our law school graduation, and I was struck by how gentle and quiet he had been. He's a small man—so much like my father, I'd thought. But without the sadistic spirit that inhabited him. What must he think of me right now?

"Where in the world is Hayes?" I groan when all other words fail me. I pat my pocket and curse my decision to leave my phone upstairs when I rushed downstairs.

"Confidence, we're leaving. I just ordered an Uber, and he's only two minutes away," Mr. Gold says again, and this time, his voice is firm and commanding. "Tell Mr. Rivers thank you for rescuing us. We owe him a huge debt, but we don't want to impose, and clearly, it's not a good time." He nods pointedly at the insane woman standing on the stairs watching the chaos she just created with a pleased, smug smile on her face. Poppy has disappeared in the five seconds since I looked away.

"An Uber?" I exclaim. "Bu-But, I have your rooms ready. I didn't even give you the towels," I say, completely dejected and helpless to stop the situation from spiraling. I point to a stack of towels and a thermos of coffee that Hayes's housekeeper, Matilda, gave me to bring down with me.

"What's going on?" Hayes asks, and I look over to see him standing in a doorway that I hadn't noticed beneath the stairs. The rain has had its way with him. But unlike the rest of the soaking wet people in the room, he looks more like a sea god than he does a drowned rat. His hair clings to his forehead in dark wet waves and water runs down from one of them, through his dark gray T-shirt, and it's plastered to his body like a second skin. His jeans, the same. His eyes sweep the room, moving from each one of us to the next when he doesn't see whatever he's looking for on our faces.

"Mr. Rivers, I was just saying that we're so grateful for your kindness. You were heroic today. But we've decided to head into Rivers Wilde for the night," Mr. Gold, clearly the group's designated speaker, says. "We have Carly's insulin, and little Micah has his inhaler. So all we need is a dry, warm place to lay our heads," he says.

"And I told you, you could do that here," Hayes says quietly and walks over to me. "What happened?" he asks.

No one says a word.

"Eliza, what happened?" He squares his gaze on her, and even though I'm not looking at her, I see the moment he gets to the gun. His face turns white and then blood suffuses his cheeks and looks like the top of his head might pop off.

"Did you point your fucking gun at my woman?" he asks, and his voice ricochets off the walls of the house's cavernous space in a terrifying echo. The little girl starts to cry again, and my stomach cramps into a knot. This is beyond disastrous. I can't imagine how Hayes lives with people like this.

Eliza's face never loses its smugness, but she starts backing up the stairs.

"I don't have to explain myself to you, Hayes Rivers. You're lucky I didn't shoot her," she says, and then like the rat she is, she turns and runs up the stairs.

"I'm so sorry. Perhaps it would be best for you to stay somewhere else tonight. I have a suite of rooms at the St. Regis. The road between here and there is clear, and I'll have our driver take you over," he says to the crowd, but he doesn't look at me. "I'll go make arrangements."

And then, without another word, he turns and leaves the room.

Chapter 12

NEED

HAYES

"I'm sorry about last night," I say as soon as I walk into my bedroom. Confidence is halfway out of bed and stills mid-motion. She wraps the sheet around her bare body and sits back down, her profile to me as she stares ahead for a beat, and then turns to face me.

Her eyes are flat and cold, and I could kick my own ass for the way I behaved.

"For what? For not warning me that your stepmother had no clue I was coming? Or for not warning me that she's a lunatic who's fucking packing heat?"

I groan silently, guilt gnawing at my gut. "*Tesoro*—"

"Or," she cuts in, her voice hard as nails, "is it because *after* she pulled a gun on me, my best friend, her family, and small *children*, you promptly disappeared and haven't been heard from since?" she asks.

"I'm sorry. I needed to clear my head. I went for a drive. Yesterday was intense, and I meant to come back, but I passed out in my car and just woke up," I tell her. I don't tell her that I drank half a bottle of Jack Daniels and then threw it all up before I passed out. She looks like she's ready to murder me.

"This is not what I expected when I came to visit, Hayes," she says, and my stomach sinks. That goddamn Eliza and her crazy ass antics yesterday.

"I know. The storm threw everything off. Going out to get your friends…" She drops her head into her hands and falls back onto the pillows. Her sheet falls, revealing her perfect, spilling-out-of-my-hands, marshmallow-soft, pink-nippled breasts. And like an addict whose poison is being served up to him on a silver platter, I start walking.

"Thank you for that," she groans. "Good Lord. What the hell? This trip…" She sighs just as I get to her side of the bed.

I stare down at the goddess in my bed. This nymph who has me under her control. She's like nothing else I've ever known. Brave, kind, honest, funny, sexy, and so fucking brilliant. She's the catch of the century, and she's mine.

For now.

I close my eyes at the stab of pain in my chest that accompanies that thought.

There's something that happens when I see things through Confidence's eyes. She reveals my blind spots, and while I'm glad to know the places where I was failing in the basic human decency department, what will that mirror reveal when she holds it up to my family. So far, it's revealed dysfunction and division. I'm afraid that when she leaves here in a couple of days, she'll think less of me, and I'll think less of me, too. I want to sanitize everything. To hide the ugly. But I'm going to be asking a lot of her.

She needs to see exactly what she's getting into. I just have to hope that when it's over, she'll still want me and all of the baggage I come with. And if she does, I hope it's not because she thinks my money or connections will make up for it.

I feel guilty for having that last thought. She's nothing like that, and I know if I end up sleeping under the 610 Freeway, she'd be sleeping with me. I love her. She loves me. I want to show her that I can take care of her more than just financially.

"King," she calls softly. Her hand comes up to grab mine, and I finally look at her face. She's the most radiant woman. She's got this peace about her that's there even when she loses her cool.

"Yes?" I ask and trace one of her pretty nipples with the pad of my thumb. She sighs and smiles. Her eyes fall to half-mast as her nipple stiffens under my touch.

"Yesterday was crazy. Everyone was on edge because of the weather.

But, I wish we could press the reset button on all of this." She sighs. I push aside the thought that the weather had nothing to do with Eliza's behavior.

"Come on, I need a shower; I need to eat you. I need to fuck you. Let's do all three right now," I say.

She smiles and lets me pull her up to sitting. Then she unbuckles my jeans, unzips them, and pulls them down at the same time as my boxers. My dick is hard and her mouth is hot when she wraps her lips around it and sucks the head at the same time her tongue flicks the slit. I pull my shirt over my head and fist my hands in her hair while she works her magic with her talented tongue. When I can't wait for her anymore, I let go of her head and slide out of her mouth.

"Get up here," I gesture for her to wrap her legs around my waist and she laughs her deep, throaty laugh before she does what I say. I put my hands on the curve of her waist where it flairs into her hips and lower her down onto my hard-as-a-rock dick. I walk us like that into the bathroom, and I step into the shower, press her against the wall and start to fuck her. Her hands fly up above her head and use the wall at her back and my dick to hold her up. I turn on the water and hiss when the cold spray hits my back and starts beating down on us. "Hayes." She moans my name, and I fuck her harder.

"I'm going to make you come," I say and throw my head back into the spray of water before I lift her off my dick and put her on her feet.

I drop down on my haunches, spread her cheeks and flick my tongue over her tight puckered asshole. I keep it there, push in a little and trap the now warm shower water on my tongue and then slide down to her pussy and put her clit in my mouth with the water around it and bite it.

Her knees buckle, but the shower muffles her scream. I find that I don't like that at all. I reach up, turn the water off, and press my hand into her back to bend her in half. She braces on the wall and I slip my cock between the warm, wet lips of her pussy and drag it back and forth.

I slide up and into her in one smooth, easy stroke. She gasps and slaps a hand on the wall. I grip her hips, slide one hand to her clit and rub.

I dive into her.

Pull out.

Thrust up.

Drill hard.

Fuck her fast.

Then, I slow down and make love to my woman until she comes.

She screams my name and creams all over my dick, bucking her hips and clenching her trembling thighs so that when I start to come, my hips are trapped in the cradle her body has made for mine.

"You're going to end me." I groan.

"No baby, this is where you begin." She pants, and when I pull out next, she hops down, whips around and falls on her knees.

She cups my balls with her hand and fists my pulsing dick with the other and puts me into her mouth and sucks me so hard her lips hollow.

I push her hair back off her face, and she looks up at me. Her eyes water when my dick hits the back of her throat, but she doesn't quit. *I love you,* I mouth down and she winks before she closes her eyes and hollows her cheeks.

When I come, she catches what she can on her tongue. I pull her up, turn the water on, and rinse her clean.

By the time we get out of the shower, we're right again. I'm hoping that tonight's dinner won't be a disaster. I mean, it's just food and a few friends. What could go wrong?

Chapter 13

LET THEM EAT CAKE

CONFIDENCE

"I'm so glad he didn't cancel." The woman next to me looks down the table to where Hayes is sitting. "These flood watches are so tedious," she says to me like she expects me to agree with her.

I force the sincerest smile I can muster. I'm sure it looks more like I'm suffering from a bout of constipation. And the churning of my stomach says that if I'd been able to put anything in it since this morning, I might actually be unable to evacuate it from my body.

Tedious is the very last word I would use to describe this dinner or this day. I can't believe that, on my first visit to Houston, the weather has taken such a huge turn for the worse. Hurricane Harvey has dumped historic levels of water on the city of Houston. The flooding has been catastrophic for a lot of the city. And yet, here we sit.

The dining room has a glass dome in the center and the clatter of the driving rain against it reminds me of the way it beats down on the corrugated metal roof of our mobile home.

I push the food around my plate as my appetite refuses to cooperate. I've never heard of, much less eaten, some of the things they've served today. I've always been an equal opportunity eater. But today, not even my mother's chicken fried steak could tempt me.

"Where did you say you were from?" The woman who hasn't bothered to introduce herself demands.

"I didn't," I say and smile. I refuse to accommodate this woman's snobbery. If she wants to know, she'll have to introduce herself like a normal person would.

"Oh. Well." She smiles coldly. "I'm Davina Bain. Our families have dined together for almost twenty years," she informs me and then glances around the table with distaste. "Though, I have to say that the quality of the attendees has been diluted since Hayes got back. He was raised in Italy. And in the countryside or something dreadful." She frowns disapprovingly. "I heard he's taken up with some nobody he met in Europe." She says it like it's a total scandal. "Anyway, you're such a pretty thing. Who are your people? A girl that looks like you is exactly what he needs to soften up his image," she says, and I look at her like she's an alien.

"Did you really say that?" I ask and she must mistake my anger for something else because she pats my hand.

"Don't mind all the talk about him hurting that girl," she says, her smile thin and empty. "He's richer than Croesus. It'll make a couple of black eyes a year worth it."

It takes Herculean strength to keep my hand in my lap when all I want to do is slap her. I'm reminded of something I learned from the sharp bite of my father's rage. There are devils walking around in skin that makes them look like normal human beings.

"Who are your people?" she asks, her eyes scanning the table while she sips her soup.

"I'm Confidence Ryan," I tell her. "I'm from Arkansas. I'm the nobody he met in Europe," I inform her with a smile. And I enjoy the momentary flash of panic in her eyes as she realizes who she's been talking to. It's gone as quickly as it came and in its place is a smug, disdainful frown.

Her eyes, once friendly and bright, dim. She sniffs as if something distasteful wafted into her nose.

"Well," her eyes flick over me as if she's trying to find what she missed in her initial assessment, "at least you look the part," she says before she turns away. Dismissing me in a way that feels eerily familiar. It's reminiscent of the way Hayes looked at me that night in Italy. Like I'm beneath her. That memory still makes me queasy. Being with Hayes's family and friends tonight has made me queasy. I look around the huge table. Almost everyone is engaged in a one-on-one conversation. Except Hayes, who's watching me with a scowl. His stepmother made the seating chart—who has a seating chart for regular dinner?—and when Hayes took his place at the head of the table, I was unceremoniously asked to vacate the seat next to him for Mr. Jones and shown to a seat all the way at the other end. Hayes didn't say a word. Between that and the rain, I feel stressed out on a level that has me wishing I could go for a run. And I hate running. With a passion.

"You understand, don't you? It's protocol," his stepmother said as she led me to my seat. I didn't answer because I knew she didn't really care if I understood. She'd made her feelings about me plain when I saw her right before dinner. She leaned in, pretending to hug me, and whispered in my ear, "Don't get too comfortable. I'll be damned if the next Mrs. Rivers is another nobody from nowhere." Then she'd pulled away and smiled brightly and said, "We're thrilled to have you, dear," loudly enough for everyone to hear.

I don't know if I'm going to tell Hayes any of this. What would be the point? He can't do anything about it, and I can see that he's trying hard to continue the traditions of his family. Even if they are dumb and useless ones.

We haven't had a moment alone since we came down for dinner. And now, I've been dismissed as lacking by a woman who spent the first forty-five minutes of dinner telling me all about the piping for her new window treatments.

"Most of them are fine," the woman next to me murmurs in my ear.

"Excuse me?" I turn to look at her. She's a pretty woman in her late sixties with skin the color of hazelnuts, eyes the color of coffee, and a warm smile.

"But some of them are a bunch of stuck-up assholes." Her whispered words are colored with humor. "We're only invited because the previous Mr. Rivers and my husband were friends. It's only since Hayes got back that we decided to come at all. Trust me, honey, you'll be glad they don't talk to you," she says with a wink.

"I like you." I stick my hand out. "I'm Confidence. Yes, that's my real name," I say before she can ask.

"I'm Mary Hassan, and what a fantastic name," she compliments sincerely.

"Thank you," I say in kind.

"Well, I know a little something about sitting at tables you weren't exactly invited to, so I can empathize," she says. "And, I have three grown daughters. You look about their age," she says. And I think how lucky those girls must be.

Those girls are lucky to have a mother whose eyes light up when she talks about them.

"Do they live in Houston?" My heart jumps in hope that maybe I'll make some new friends.

"No. My oldest and her husband are in DC. My middle and youngest both live in the UK," she says.

"Wow, that's amazing. I just took my first trip out of the country this summer. I can't imagine living overseas. What took them there?" I ask.

"My baby got a job; she's a lawyer—"

"Oh, me, too," I say excitedly.

"Are you? I should introduce you. They'll all be here for Christmas. Just three more months," she says happily.

"I'd love that. I'm moving here. My best friend lives here actually, but I would love to meet more people," I say gratefully.

"You'll love them. My middle is married to a real life Duke and lives in England," she tells me proudly.

"Really? What is that like?" I ask, looking around this room and thinking I can barely handle these entitled rich people. How would I deal with aristocrats?

"She had a hard time with some of the people in his circle. She's not what a countess looks like over there, but she's won them over now," she says.

"That sounds like a hard transition," I muse.

"It was. But for her husband's sake, she worked her way through it. And now, she's just like one of the locals. She even teaches a coding course at the local high school," she says. I smile at the pride in her voice and reach for my drink to avoid having to speak.

Hayes is no earl. But around here, he's like royalty. And given my less-than-warm reception, I'm worried about being his partner. I think that's where we're going. He wouldn't have asked me to move in with him if he didn't think so. I wouldn't be considering it if I didn't, too.

She touches my arm. "I saw you come down with Hayes. You make such a beautiful couple."

"Thank you so much." I glance down the table at him just as a man dressed in one of the dark blue valet uniforms rushes into the open doors of the dining room and bends to whisper in his ear.

Whatever the valet says can't be good. Hayes's jaw clenches and his brow furrows. Then, he tosses his napkin down on the table and stands up.

"Excuse me, everyone," he says. I watch him in hopes that he'll make eye contact with me. He doesn't.

I war with myself, watching the door, and unsure whether or not to follow him. Mary touches my arm again, and I glance at her.

"I'm so sorry," I say. "What were you saying?"

My eyes dart back to the door for a second, and when I look back to her, she's smiling sympathetically.

"That's one of the benefits of being someone's other half," she says. "You don't have to wait for them to say they need you. You just go because you know they always do."

She cocks her head to the door. "See you later," she says.

We share a smile, mine full of gratitude for this unexpectedly kind woman being here tonight. I start to stand up, and she touches my arm.

"We own Palmyra, it's a Middle Eastern Restaurant in Rivers Wilde," she says. "Come visit me, I'm there on weeknights." She squeezes my hand, and I squeeze hers back.

"Oh, that's my favorite. I'll come see you," I promise.

"I'm so glad he has someone like you. He's going to need you." She nods at the empty seat at the head of the table.

I want to ask her what she means, but at the moment, I'm more concerned about Hayes. I walk out of the dining room, and the weight of the stares on my retreating back is heavy. The whispers are loud, and I'm sure everyone is wondering who the hell I am. I want to turn around and yell, "I'm his," but that would just delay. And something tells me I need to get to him as fast as I can.

I step into the hall and look both ways down the long, dark passage. I have no idea where he went. I'm turning left when a loud crash of glass has me turning right. I run down the hall. Muffled, but loud voices spill into the dark around me.

"You can't keep doing this, Dare," Hayes says.

My hand freezes on the doorknob. This is his younger brother. The one Poppy mentioned earlier.

"I didn't realize I couldn't come to my own family's home," the other man slurs.

"I didn't say that. I just wish you would lay off the alcohol and only God knows what else you're putting into your body," Hayes says, his voice tight with restrained anger. "Confidence is here, and I'm trying like fuck to make sure she wants to come back." I know he's been on edge about my visit. But it's jarring to hear the anxiety so clearly in his voice.

"Well, from what you told me, it sounds like she lives in some shit hole mobile home in the middle of nowhere." I'm startled by how much he sounds like Hayes. The drunken slurring of his words is the only way I can tell the difference. That, and the ugly insult in his tone.

"Shut up," Hayes snaps.

"I'm sure she got one look at this place and realized she hit pay dirt. She isn't going anywhere. Trust me," he says.

The words and the ease with which he flings them feel like a lash across my heart. Is that what everyone thinks?

"Dare," Hayes says, the warning in his voice making the hairs on the back of my neck stand up. I'm caught between wanting to go in and needing to hear how Hayes will respond.

"Oops, I forgot. You fucked her and forget you begged me to run a background check on your little gold digger." Those words hit me like scalding water. I cover my mouth to muffle my gasp of pain.

"Dare, don't say another fucking word—"

"I'm shocked as shit she's here. I mean, she's cool if you're just looking for a good regular fuck, but to bring her home - " His words turn in a loud groan followed by the sickening crunch of bone meeting bone.

"You broke my nose, you asshole!" Dare shouts before more glass crashes to the ground.

The telltale sounds of a tussle—grunts, curses, furniture scraping the floor, glass shattering—fill the air. I open the door and see two men, both big and tall, on the ground in a hopelessly well-matched tussle.

I know I should call for help, or step in to stop the fracas. Yet, I do neither of those things. Instead, I just watch the two men fight. My eyes remain on Hayes, the man I love. He still looks exactly the same, but at the same time, so different.

I can't move.

I can't breathe.

He ordered a background check? He knows every ugly thing about me. And to think I've been feeling guilty for not telling him about the potential job at Wilde Law.

Anger, betrayal, and fear whirl furiously inside and the sound of my blood rushing in my ears mingles with the sounds of violence coming from the other room.

These are sounds of my childhood. Furniture breaking, grunts of pain, crunch of fists, crack of slaps. I'm twelve years old again, caught between the devil and hell—I don't know which direction in this house of horrors to turn.

I walk down the hall, opening doors until I find our room. I sit on my bed and try to figure out what the hell I'm going to do.

I've just started to drift off when our bedroom door opens. My eyes snap open and I stare unseeingly at the wall as I wait for him to say something. He slides into bed with me. I can smell sweat, blood, and liquor on him. His body is cool, the stubble on his face is slightly damp as he presses his cheek to mine and wraps his arms around me. A fraught and angry energy emanates from him. And like the fool I am, all I want is to soothe him. I lift his knuckles to my lips and kiss the sore, stiff, red joints.

He turns me around, and without saying a word, kisses me.

We make love for an hour, maybe more. We find a calm that always exists in the sanctity of our bodies' communion. When we are together like this, it's easy to forget that anything else matters.

We roll out of bed and shower at 2:00 a.m. I kiss his bruises without asking how he got them. He accepts my kisses without offering any explanations. We go back to bed and do it all over again. I fall asleep on him, sated but dreading the reckoning the sunrise will bring with it.

Chapter 14

PRIDE

CONFIDENCE

My phone beeps with a new email and I look over at my window and see the first hints of sunlight peeking through my curtain. Hayes stirs beside me, and I decide to ignore my phone. I snuggle into him. "Good morning," I whisper into the back of his warm, muscled shoulder.

"Morning," he mumbles sleepily, his arm snaking behind him to pull me closer. "I need to tell you about last night." His voice is partially muffled in his pillow, and he turns to face me. His eyes are clear, and I realize he's been awake longer than I realized.

My heart falls. I'm dreading what I know I must say. What I *must* do.

"I already know," I confess.

His muscles tense. "*What* do you know?"

I gaze at him.

I love him.

But I can't be with someone who thinks those things about me.

I push out of his grasp and sit up and pull the covers over my chest. I stare at my fingers, twirling the rings the way he does all the time.

"You know why I wrote that thesis?"

"Huh?" he frowns, his brow furrows at the abrupt turn in our conversation.

"I wrote it because I love the river. But I wanted to protect my people from the destruction it always causes." I choke on a sob.

"Hey…baby." He starts to sit up and put his arm around me. I shake my head and climb out of bed, taking the sheets with me. I sit on the large window seat, and a tear splashes on the blue-gray fabric I'm cocooned in. The tiny moist spot bleeds to form a quarter-sized stain. I wipe at my eyes with a brutal pass of my hands.

I take a shuddering breath and stare at my hands while I try to collect myself. Growing up, I watched year after year as the river banks swelled when the rain overwhelmed it. And its lazy, tranquil flow would transform into a beast. It laid waste to every single plan, hope, home, heart that was in its path. When it receded, it would leave everything covered in mud and dirt. Some things would never recover. Like me. Now, I look back at him. He's watching me with a perplexed expression on his face.

"I know rivers, but you made me forget the danger. I forgot to cage my love for you. And now, I'm drowning in it," I whisper.

"Confidence, you need to stop speaking code. Tell me what the fuck is going on?" He raises his voice in frustration. "Why are you crying? And why can't I touch you?" he asks, his voice even louder, and he sounds as angry as I feel. I glance at him and it pisses me off that he doesn't look panicked or worried.

"You've ruined everything!" I shout, suddenly overwhelmed with anger, sadness, disillusionment, despair.

"You need—"

"I don't *need* to do anything," I say in defiance.

"Yes, you fucking do," he snarls.

I cross my arms over my chest. "I'm not saying I thought this was going to be forever. But over the last couple of months, I'd let myself imagine the possibility…" I say while I throw my charger, laptop, phone, and books into my shoulder bag.

"Okay." He shrugs. "What's changed since you fell asleep on my cock six hours ago?"

Of course. It's always about sex with him. I shake my head and slip my feet into my shoes. I can't even look at him.

Queen.

I love you.

Respect you.

All lies.

"You ordered a background check on me?"

His face pales.

My stomach falls, and my anger crests. "Because I'm 'hot enough to fuck, but not good enough to bring home'?" My lip curls in a sneer.

"Who told you that?" he asks, and my heart sinks.

"Well, at least you're not denying it." Suddenly, I'm exhausted. It makes the sadness heavier. "I can't believe you talked about me like that," I say, my traitorous voice breaking.

He shakes his head and reaches for me. The warmth of his hand resting on my shoulder suddenly feels like a branding heat.

"I didn't mean—"

I step away. "Don't you touch me," I snarl.

"Confidence, what the *fuck*? Who have you been talking to?" he demands.

My stomach cramps, and I hug my arms around my middle.

My heart is sick.

I'm sick.

How in the *world* could I have fallen for this shit again?

I *tattooed* this motherfucker's name on my body.

I square my shoulders, drop my hands and straighten up so I can look him square in the eye. "I *heard* you last night. I followed you when you left because I thought maybe you needed me," I tell him and watch his face fall.

He groans and for the first time since I've known him, I see fear in his eyes. My own fear feeds on it. The ache in my stomach sharpens. Things are about to get worse and I'm scared by how viscerally I feel the loss already. I've fallen so thoroughly and irredeemably in love with him. Just in time for him to break my fucking heart.

"No," he says sternly. "You've got *all* of that wrong. I ordered it before we were together in Italy. Weeks later, when it showed up, I couldn't remember why I thought I needed it. I never opened it."

"You didn't?" I ask, and I feel a flicker of hope that maybe I misunderstood.

"No." He sighs. "I decided I could overlook everything that was wrong about us. Your lack of money, your lack of a name. I already knew about the scandal surrounding your career," he says.

I pale. But I set my jaw and narrow my eyes at him.

"You've *overlooked* them?" I ask, almost daring him to repeat himself.

"Yes. I decided it didn't matter," he says like he's being a benevolent ruler. Like he's looking down his nose at me.

My hackles shoot straight up. "I didn't ask you to overlook *anything*," I hiss.

He comes to stand in front of me and reaches for me. "No," I say quietly.

"Let me explain." His voice is thick and gruff. Angry.

Fuck him.

I don't want him to explain. I want him to have never said it. The scene from last night replays in my head, and my anger is only outmatched by the ton of pain in my heart. I turn to face him. "I may not have a name. Maybe I didn't know where Positano is or what some random Latin words mean…or whatever." I narrow my eyes at him and stab the air with my finger. "But I'll tell you what. My mother worked her way up to manager at a small plant in Tennessee at a time when it was really hard for women to do that. *While* she lived with a husband who treated her like a punching bag and a son she was afraid of. And she put up with that shit for *me*. She worked a second job to help pay tuition to put *me*," I say, pointing at my chest, "through college. And law school. Because she looked at me and saw what you and the rest of your stuck-up friends fail to see. *All of my potential.*"

I wave my hands in the air around my head, my fingers pointing down to my body. His expression is one of pure shock.

"I was raised to treat everyone with respect," I continue. "I was raised to be proud of my integrity, my loyalty, and my kindness. My name means something because I've *made* it mean something."

"Confidence," he growls.

"You don't have the right to say my name," I snap, and his eyes widen. "I'm not going to let you or anyone else look down on me because I don't have money and my last name isn't on a stadium or museums or a hospital somewhere."

"Fucking hell, Confidence," he grinds out, his eye burning into me. His jaw flexing from the effort he's making to not say more.

As if he could say anything to make this right.

I shake my head. "You've had everything handed to you. And yet, here we are." I fling my arms wide in a sweeping flourish that covers the whole room. "In the same place. At the very same time. Who's slumming?" I sneer. "And who leveled up?" I give him a hard, challenging look. "Who should be looking down on who?"

"I don't look down on—"

"The one who's here because she worked, scraped, and beat back the crabs trying to pull her back into the barrel?" I take a step closer to him. "*Or* the person who's here because he was lucky enough to be pushed out of a gold lined pussy?" I give him a disdainful head-to-toe assessment.

His eyes narrow, his jaw flexes, and he rears back. "What did you just say to me?" he hisses.

"Did you let the pretty dresses, law degree, and good table manners fool you?" I ask. "I grew up with a trucker hat turned to the back, jeans tucked into my muddy hiking boots, a hunting rifle slung across my back, and a bowie knife tucked into my waist. I've been thrown to the wolves, and I have killed every. Single. One. Of them." I am aflame with indignation.

"You need to calm down," he says and has the nerve to reach for me.

"No, I don't," I huff and grit my teeth. "You are *never* going to insult me again. You don't deserve me."

I can't believe I was fretting about taking a job that might offend him.

I shake my head to clear it and stand.

He moves fast and grabs me by the forearms. He presses his forehead to mine, our noses touch, our breath mingles between us, and his eyes burn into mine with possessiveness and determination.

"You're right. I don't." He pins me in place with his eyes "I *know* it. You know it. And yet, here we are. In the same place at the same *fucking* time," he says, throwing my words back at me.

"We're done, Hayes. Let me go."

He ignores me, holds me even tighter. "You take everything I give you. Even when it hurts because you know I'm going to make you come so hard you can't breathe. You sleep next to me with your fingers linked with mine because you love me. We are not even close to done," he grits out and I try to pull myself loose.

Right now, I'm caught between wanting to sob in his arms and wanting to kick him in the balls.

"Let go of me," I growl.

"Never. You will *not* walk away from me because of some bullshit like this."

"It's *not* bullshit. I've spent the entire weekend with your crazy-ass family and their friends," I shout back at him and shake myself loose. This time, he lets me go. "Are these *really* the people you want to surround yourself with? You talked about your family doing good. What *good* does it do to get dressed up for a six-course meal just because it's

Friday? I mean, it's like fucking Versailles. Your city is drowning and you're dressed up because it's *Friday*."

I pack my words with scorn and hurl them like bullets. When his face turns red with anger, I know I hit my target. He grabs my wrists and pulls me back.

"You overheard me and Dare , but you still let me fuck you last night. Were you planning to leave me when we woke up?" he asks angrily.

I flush because the way he says it makes it sound…treacherous. I glare up at him. "I didn't know what I was going to do, Hayes. I was confused!" I shout, frustrated and defensive in the face of the accusation in his eyes.

"Did you know you were going to leave this morning?" His voice is ice cold.

I swallow thickly, but I don't let him intimidate me, I look him straight in the eye. "Yes."

He drops my wrist and stares back at me.

The betrayed expression on his face makes my skin prickle with guilt. I shake it off. "Maybe if that craziness with Eliza had felt like a fluke, or the dinner guests hadn't made me feel like something a dog dragged in from outside. Or knowing that your brother thinks I'm already measuring for drapes and counting your money. But I don't want to live in chaos with people who hate each other—and who hate me. I mean, she slapped the housekeeper!" My arms fling out in front of me.

His hands take the opportunity and grab hold of me. I don't fight him. "I'm not them."

"But you are. You can't help it. They treated me the way you did the night we met," I say with a stony glare.

He flinches.

Good.

"You have to forgive me for that. And it can't be the reason you walk away," he says.

"I don't want to fight in the place where I'm supposed to be safe. I want a calm, quiet home. *That* is my reason. My family is no prize and has its fair share of shit. But I didn't escape the frying pan just to jump into the fire. I can't believe how horribly this weekend has turned out."

"There's a much better reason for you to stay," he insists.

"Like what?" I ask impatiently.

"You love me. I belong to you," he whispers, and I close my eyes on a pathetic whimper. I want that to be true. I want to cry, and I want him to hold me. He runs the tip of his nose alongside mine. A tear rolls down my cheek.

"*You* belong to *me*," he says before he crashes his lips on top of mine. He snags my lower lip between his teeth and sucks it, bites it. My fingers slide into his hair, and his tongue slips into my mouth. I let him taste me while I drink as much as I can handle before my body throbs for more. And then I gather tufts of his hair into my hands and yank—hard.

"Fuuuuck!" he roars and breaks our kiss.

I scramble around the bed.

"I belong to *myself*," I snarl. "And yes, I kneeled in front of you and took what you gave me. But I will *never* kneel for you again."

He looks angry, but I still see that fear and I hate it. "You better not walk out of that door," he says.

"Or *what?*" I hiss.

We face each other. His bed is like a battlefield between us. I press my knuckles into the mattress and lean toward him so I can look him in the eye one more time. There's real distress in his that shakes my resolve. Damn him for making me love him so much.

"I am *not* afraid of you. How could I be? When you were so afraid of *me* that you needed a background check." I say.

His face is pained. "I'm sorry—"

"You should be," I snap. "But not for me. I've survived worse than a man who's too blind to see that I'm the best thing that will ever happen to him."

My heart tugs at the nearly gray pallor on his face when I turn to pick up my things. With each piece of clothing I throw into my bag, my resolve grows. I face him again. He's watching me, his face thunderous and his body perfectly still.

"I'm leaving," I tell him.

He shrugs. "You'll be back."

"In your dreams." I scoff dismissively and throw the last of my things into my suitcase.

"I'll be waiting," he adds.

I zip up my suitcase and stand up straight to meet his cold gaze with mine. "Don't hold your breath."

"You're *mine. My* queen. What do you have without your king?" he asks coldly.

"*All* the power," I say with an equally icy tone and smile.

Then I walk away from him.

Part 2

RIVERS WILDE
HOUSTON, TX

Chapter 15

THE RETURN

HAYES

I careen through the winding and nonsensically narrow street of the Rivers Estate. The rows of manicured shrubs are nothing more than blurs of dark green as I run yet another stop sign.

On a street without a single intersection.

In a subdivision with only one house.

It's just one example of the lack of planning and the sense of entitlement that's created the mess I've been cleaning up since I took control from Uncle Thomas.

It's been eighty-seven days of inconsistencies, complaints, and so much fucking disappointment that I'm starting to forget what it feels like to be satisfied.

A flock of baby geese step into the road just two hundred and fifty feet ahead of my speeding car. I slam hard on my breaks to stop in time. My high-performance Maserati protests with groans, shrieks, and sputters. I struggle to hold my steering wheel straight to stop the threatening spinout that's pulling my tires to the right. The acrid stench of burned rubber and the uncertainty of whether I had ten geese crushed beneath my car congeal like cooled grease in my stomach.

I peer out of my window and breathe a sigh of relief when the gaggle waddles past, completely oblivious to the havoc they nearly wrecked and how close their lives came to ending.

"Where's your sense of survival, you idiotic animals?" I chide them as I pull past them and hook a right up the dark, concrete tiled driveway. The rows of pink flowering bushes on either side were planted by my mother the year before she died.

I'm surprised Eliza didn't pull them up. She tore out the rose garden my mother planted within months of marrying my father. I pull up the drive and park under the huge carport that should have been knocked down years ago. I throw my car into park and give myself a minute to collect my thoughts before I walk into the house.

Built at the turn of the twentieth century by my great-great-grandfather, Jeb Rivers, it's one of Houston's oldest homes. As my uncle likes to remind anyone who will listen, at nearly twenty thousand square feet that sits on five and half acres of land, it's also one of the biggest and most expensive homes in the city.

Houston's nearly one-hundred-mile sprawl means that even as we get close to edging Chicago out of the number three spot on the list of America's largest cities, there's a seemingly endless supply of land that keeps home prices down. That forty-million-dollar price tag would buy a six thousand square foot penthouse apartment in New York City, max.

It's why Houston's wealthy can indulge in more cars, food, theater, and retail therapy than their wealthy counterparts in other cities. And indulge, we do. I stare out at the expanse of lawn that's bisected by a ground level fountain with a pool full of koi fish. The estate boasts a citrus grove, rose gardens, a tennis court, Olympic-sized infinity pool, and is surrounded by hundred-year-old trees. But after Confidence's visit, when I look at it, all I see is a tomb where our family's skeletons live. If I had my way, I would tear it all down.

A sharp rap on the passenger's side window of my car startles me out of my daydream. My uncle, the Crypt Keeper himself, is peering in at me. His thick silver eyebrows are drawn down over his thunderous dark eyes.

He doesn't look like an old man. He looks like an old villain. One that threatens to eat children when they make too much noise. His wide, thin-lipped mouth is moving, but my blissfully soundproof car keeps the assault from reaching my ears. I savor the quiet in my car long enough to take three deep breaths before I step out of the car into a jarringly different atmosphere.

"You're late. The team has been gathered for more than twenty minutes," he says. He's got the kind of voice that's powerful without being loud. But, the power of that is lost on me. I know that he's nothing more than an empty vessel for delusion and resentment.

"Well, since the meeting couldn't start without me, I'd say that I'm right on time," I tell him. "And if you had held this meeting in the office instead of here, it would have started twenty minutes ago," I tell him. We step in the gargantuan foyer and start up the stairs to the room that's always used for Kingdom business. Swish's old office.

"You forget that you're talking to your uncle, Hayes. I will have your respect," he says from behind me.

I stop and turn to find him standing on the bottom step, hands folded behind his back, an expectant look on his face.

I walk back down so I'm one step above him.

"*You* forget that you're talking to the head of your family," I remind him. "If you want my respect, you better set about trying to earn it." I turn and start back up the stairs. "The mess you've made of things has left us vulnerable on too many fronts and has lost you any built-in credibility I gave you because you're my uncle. You've done a piss-poor job," I say over my shoulder.

A lawsuit filed by a group of tenants whose homes were damaged in the flood last month is just the latest in a pile of shit that's been landing on my desk for the last three months. I've spent nearly all of my time as chairman of the board putting out fires. It's meant to be a figurehead position, but with an incompetent and corrupt executive team, I've been forced to take a more hands-on approach. None of them like it, but I don't care.

"The lawsuit is what we called you here to discuss," he says, still behind me as I push open the doors to the room that's decorated like a nineteenth century country club. Whatever traces of Swish there were in here are gone. I want to hurry and get out of here.

"Gentlemen, please have a seat," I say to the three men who stand when I walk in.

I sit down at the head of the table. "Tell me what's going on with this." I look at Rich Jones, the current head of operations.

He slides a folder over to me and opens the one in front of him.

"There are twenty-five thousand units that are included in the class; they represent an annual revenue of about three hundred million dollars to the Real Estate Investment Trust. Our investors expect those dividends and profit shares."

"What's this got to do with the flooded-out apartments?"

"Well…" He tugs at his collar and looks around the table at the other two eighty-year-old incompetents who had helped him and my uncle destroy Kingdom one bit at a time.

They all stare down at their laps.

Cowards.

"There are two main issues in their complaint. The first is that some of them were evicted without notice. The units took on water, but we disagreed with their complaints that there would be any significant problems with people living there once they dried out," he says.

"What was your disagreement based on?" I ask.

"Huh?" His eyes dart to his left again.

"You're on your own here, Rich. They're not going to jump in and save you." I hook my thumb at the two other men. "Tell me."

"It was just what we thought," he says in a high nasally whine that makes me wish hitting people wasn't illegal.

"But some of 'em left without notice, and we didn't know if they would be back. There were plenty of people looking for places to rent so we filled the vacated units right away." He shrugs his shoulders, eyes wide with complete bafflement at how what he's saying could be construed as fraud and theft.

"It says here you emptied occupied apartments and threw away personal belongings after residents were gone for less than seventy-two hours? Is that allegation true?"

"Yes, but we thought they were moved, and we needed to turn those units over to people who wanted to pay," he snaps defensively and wipes a drop of sweat from his forehead. I shake my head in disgust.

I reach into my pocket and pull out my phone and text my PA Muriel that I want her to find an executive search firm. It's time for me to build my own team. I've had enough indulging my uncle's ego and treading lightly.

"Well, we're going to settle this case. And we're going to make these people whole again. I want a report on the actual damage costs. They're suing us, seeking general and pecuniary damages. Our exposure at trial is unlimited. This isn't hard. Let's give them a little money for their troubles and send them on their way. On Monday, I want a list—a comprehensive one—of all other potential liabilities you're aware of. Even if it's just a repeated customer complaint. And I don't mean just in real estate, I mean throughout Kingdom. I also want a report of our philanthropic spending in the last ten years. I've received disturbing reports about our failure to support efforts that were pioneered by the Rivers family," I chastise them.

"The zoo doesn't need our help any longer. Why should we continue making such huge bequests?" Eugene Kinder, the CFO, chimes in from his chair.

I've never liked him.

"That's not for you to decide. I want those reports by the end of the week." I stand. The four men all stand and offer their disingenuous farewells.

"Uncle Thomas, will you walk me out?"

I wait for him outside the door. I scan the vaulted tray ceiling. The ivory-colored, intricately-carved crown molding runs along the perimeter of the room.

A huge crown sits in the middle of the letters R and K. Rivers Kingdom. That's what this used to be. That's how people have referred to us. But *we* have never called ourselves kings. Not until my uncle's reign.

He joins me in the corridor. "Yes, what would you like to discuss?" His tone is formal, his eyes wary as he waits for me to speak.

"Poppy refuses to remain on staff as long as you or Eliza reside in Rivers House," I inform him.

"Well, we'll be sad to see her go," he says and adjusts the cuffs on his shirtsleeves.

"She's not going anywhere. I've told her that you will be moving out," I inform him.

His eyes nearly bug out of his head. His lips pucker like he's sucked a lemon, and he seems incapable of speech. So, I continue. "In two months, members of Denmark's royal family will begin an extended occupancy at Rivers House. Poppy has arranged to have the house cleaned, and the rooms prepared, so you and Aunt Mai will need to make other arrangements for accommodation. Eliza has already been informed that she will need to vacate the house," I say.

He blinks at me, his face flushed red with embarrassment. But he manages to unstick his lips, and he fixes me with a judgmental stare.

"Aren't these sorts of details and message deliveries below your station, nephew? Or are you finding these more mundane and administrative tasks better suited to your capabilities?" he asks, smugness at his dig spreading across his withered face.

I shake my head in disappointment. "I'm not such a slave to my pride, *Uncle*, that I couldn't deliver a message that might have felt callous coming from someone who doesn't know your personal situation," I tell him.

He has the decency to look ashamed.

"Thomas, I'm not here to rub my leadership in your face," I say to the top of his bowed head.

"Why are you here? If not for the glory of it?" he snaps. His resentment is unmasked and fully evident in his eyes. I feel a pang of pity for him. He's never been happy with his position in the family.

"I'm here because it's my responsibility to make sure that the next heir receives a legacy that's worth preserving."

"As if it isn't now? I have been a wonderful steward of this family's interests," he protests.

"Ah, yes, the ever-growing pile of lawsuits from clients, customers, and partners alike says that," I retort.

"Of course they're unhappy. They want us to live like we're commoners. They want to pretend they're our equals. I stopped that. You want to settle with these people? Why don't they go find better jobs, so they can afford better than some flooded out apartment? We are not a charity. We are a business. If they think it's not fit for human occupation, fine. They should go find somewhere else to live."

"Those apartments are not fit for any human occupation. The reports are damning. Would you want to live there?"

"I would never be forced to make that kind of choice." He sniffs.

"How do you know? Don't you have the ability to put yourself in someone else's shoes and imagine what it would be like if you were in them?" I ask in muted outrage. I just don't understand where this man's heart is. How he and my father were both raised by my grandparents is a mystery.

"Why would I want to imagine being them? How vulgar," he says with a sniff of disgust.

He's a lost cause. I just need to completely declaw him and then I'll strip him of all his power and mandate his retirement from the board.

"You had fifteen years to do what you would. You sent me away. You made sure I stayed away. Perhaps you hoped I'd never come back. But here I am."

"Yes, here you are," he says with barely disguised malice.

"And here, I'll stay." I reinforce it with my own undisguised dislike. "You need to get used to it. Stop trying to undermine me; stop trying to make me feel like I have less right to be here than you do. I'm sorry you weren't born first. But you need to start thinking about what your life could be," I say with a heavy sigh.

He doesn't respond. He just stares straight ahead in stony silence, his face completely mottled with his pent-up anger.

"I've rented you a unit in the Ivy," I tell him weakly as I stand.

"No, we will not stay there. It would be an insult to the family's honor," he blurts through woodenly clenched teeth.

"How is it an insult?"

"They aren't fit to be our neighbors. They're commoners. That land was part of our dynasty," he spits.

Loathing floods me in a rush of heat, and I don't hide it when I look at him.

"We sold them that land. We took the money from it and made ourselves rich again. They even named it after us in a show of good faith. This one-sided feud is ridiculous. I'm not going to perpetuate it anymore."

"My father would shudder to see how you've degraded our dynasty," he says.

I've had enough of his shit. I step into his personal space and look him in the eye.

"It's a family, not a dynasty. *We* are commoners. Being richer than all of the monarchies combined doesn't make you one by de facto. And thanks to your inability to delegate or manage the business yourself, we're perilously close to being in debt. We're just regular people. We'll never reclaim any of the land we sold to the Wildes. If you'd had any real sense of what we needed, you would have embraced them."

His face mottles, and his already thin lips compress to leave what looks like a white gash where his mouth should be. He leans forward, as tall and straight at age eighty as he'd been at sixty.

"We are kings in our own right." His lips barely move. His eyes are hard and intense. "I will never embrace those bourgeoise hippies who don't know the meaning of the word 'empire.' The Riverses had assets on which the sun never set. The legacy you speak of is one that was built with my grandfather's bare hands. And now you're kicking me out so some royals can come and rent this house? Like it's a fucking hotel?"

"It's certainly not a home. And I'm done wasting resources to try and make it feel like one just so you have a free place to live. I've offered you an option. If you'd rather use your fixed income to rent a place elsewhere, you're welcome to do it. But, either way, you and Aunt Mai and Eliza will have to be out of here by the time the embassy tenants are moving in."

"I won't go," he says quietly.

"Yes, you will," I tell him.

"No, I won't. You'll have to have me forcibly removed," he says.

"Fine, if that's what you want," I say with a shrug.

"I'll call the press," he says, scrambling up to his feet when I start down the hall.

"You do that. I'll make sure to set my DVR to record your dramatic exit when Channel eleven airs the story." I give him a two-finger salute and walk around to get back in my car.

"You'll ruin the family's reputation," he calls.

I make my dispassion plain in my expression. "You've done a fine job of that yourself. Let me know what you'd like to do regarding leaving the house. I really have no problem being the bad guy. Everyone already thinks I'm a villain, why not get something in return for the headaches that come with that."

I drive down the winding road and watch the estate whiz by. When I was a boy growing up here, I never imagined I would come to think of it as a burden. A reminder of those ugly days after my father's death and the years I spent being a punching bag for self-important assholes and an ATM to any pretty girl who would give me the time of day.

I approach the private entrance to Rivers Wilde, and the tension I'm carrying starts to dissipate.

The gate lifts and I drive into the enclave, established by the Wildes before I was even born. This community, developed on land that was in my family for nearly one hundred years, is one of the most sought after addresses in Houston.

The huge golf course stretches for three miles on one side of Wildewood Parkway. The grand country club rises from behind its gates like a palace. I pause at the forked road and go right to the cluster of sky-scraping residential towers called the Ivy. The glass and brick struc-tures loom over the copse of trees planted around them. As I approach the four-lane circle drive, the guard who sits in the middle of it waves in greeting and the wrought iron gate starts its slow ascent.

"Evening, boss," Sammy, our valet, greets as he pulls my door open. "Your dinner's been delivered and is ready to bring up as soon as you call."

"Thank you." I grasp his outstretched hand, and he smiles when he feels the money in my hand.

"Will you be needing your car again, or should I park her for the night?"

I glance at the sky. It's clear and blue, but the orange tint of the clouds signals that it's dusk.

"No, leave her out. I'm going out before dinner," I tell him and head inside to change. On my way up, I call Remington Wilde. I haven't spoken to him since that day sixteen years ago. But from what I've heard, even from people who don't like him, he's a straight shooter. An honest man and a legendary attorney already. He's grown Wilde Law into one of the largest in the country and has made his name as Assistant Attorney General in the Civil Rights Division at the Department of Justice by the time he turned thirty. He's back home after his grandfather's death left him the head of the family. He's built the Civil Rights Division of Wilde Law incredibly fast. And his firm is representing the class that's suing us.

"Mr. Wilde's office," a crisp, British accented female voice answers after the first ring.

"Is Mr. Wilde there?"

"He's not available, may I take a message?" she asks immediately. Fucking gatekeepers.

"It's Hayes Rivers," I say.

There's a beat of silence, and she says, "Mr. Rivers, please hold for Mr. Wilde," and then there's a beep and Remington comes on the line.

"Who the fuck is this?" he says, just like he did that morning we met. I burst into unexpected laughter and he joins me.

"What's up, kid?" he asks.

"I'm going to give you that, because these days, I'm good with being younger than you, especially since we're playing at the same level now," I say.

"You can't even *see* my level." He laughs. "You just got back into town, and you're *already* talking shit," he says.

"Just telling you how it is," I say.

"You have no clue how it is. You need to come kiss the rings of the men who've been running Houston while you were eating pasta on a beach in Italy," he quips. I laugh. I'd forgotten that he was a cocky asshole. I haven't seen him again since that day we met in the clearing. But it looks like not much has changed.

"I got your letter," I say and don't take his bait.

"No hard feelings, man," he says unapologetically. "But you've got to know that what Kingdom is doing is very wrong."

"You're preaching to the choir. I'm not calling to give you shit. I'm about to do you a huge favor," I tell him.

He whistles low and long. "Well, shit. Maybe I should sue you more often." He laughs.

"You in the office early tomorrow?" I ask.

"Yes," he says.

"I'll come to you," I say.

"You better bring coffee," he says, then hangs up.

He's an asshole. But I like him. And I think he's going to be receptive to what I have to say tomorrow.

This lawsuit, since it landed on my desk, has been nothing but a headache. But now it's presenting me with a multitude of opportunities. I want to hold Kingdom accountable, but I know the board and executive committee will never back me on it. So, I'll find another way. This company is rotten from the inside out. If I've got to kill it to save the family name, I will. What's left isn't worth the paper its letterhead is printed on. And I want the family foundation that I control to be the source of the Rivers family influence.

And, I know just the lawyer to do it.

Confidence still isn't talking to me. She left my house that day and spent a couple of days with Cass's family in Rivers Wilde. She refused to see me before she left for Arkansas. I followed her home, and she made it very clear I wasn't welcome.

It's been a month, and she's returned every email and text I've sent with the same message, "I will never forgive you."

I know she thinks she means it.

I mean to make sure she has no choice. Because living without her isn't an option for me and this distance has only made that more apparent. It's time to take control of this situation.

Chapter 16

KINGS MEET

HAYES

"Can I have two coffees to go? One black. One with two creams and one sugar," I ask.

"Ah, you made up with Ms. Confidence," the man behind the counter says brightly as he rings up my order.

I'm in the middle of reading my email from Amelia, my new lawyer, and almost drop my phone at his words.

This is only my second time here. I peer at his name tag that says Lo. "How do you know Confidence?" I ask quizzically.

"Oh, that girl was in here making juju dolls out of stirring straws with her friend for a couple days after the storm. They were all named after you," he says and then laughs at whatever he sees on my face.

"What's a juju doll?"

"Ah, that's what we call them in Nigeria. Maybe here you call them voodoo? Like the Creoles?" He laughs.

"Oh. She made voodoo dolls and named them after me?" I ask and then glance behind me to see who was snickering.

The group of teenage girls all look away when I scowl at them.

"Yes, my man. My wife has been mad at me. But I've never had a doll made in my honor," he says and hands me back my credit card. I'm so dazed I don't even remember asking for it back.

"Thank you," I say absently and stick it back into my pocket.

"And she took her coffee just like that, two creams, one sugar. So, I thought maybe one of those was for her."

"No. Unfortunately, it's not." And I realize that I've been drinking my coffee like this since I met her. All of these subtle ways I've started to compensate for her absence in my life. I yearn for her in a way that claws at my insides.

"Well, we hope she forgives you soon and comes back. We liked having her around, and she loves my lattes," he says boisterously.

"Okay," I say, weirded out that he even cares.

I want to ask him to tell me more, but it's too pathetic. So, I just smile. "Well, if she comes back, I'll definitely make sure she has one every morning."

"Don't worry, son. It'll be okay," he says. I raise my brows to show that I'm not as confident as he is.

"Listen—in Rivers Wilde, we look out for each other. It's that small-town nosiness imported to Houston. You'll get used to it," he says.

"Lotanna, that line hasn't moved since I went back to get more scones. Let the man get on with his day, *cha,*" a petite, dark haired, very pretty woman whose name tag says Sweet calls as she walks through the swinging doors off the side of the bakery's main dining room.

Her accent is identical to his, so I assume that she's from Nigeria, too. "Sorry, Mr. Rivers. Lo loves gossip. He reads Ms. Regan's column every morning, and she wrote about you two a lot in the last month."

"Regan has a column?" Regan Wilde is Remi's twin sister, and as far as I know, is married with two kids and a journalist on a local channel.

"Well, we suspect it's her. We all just call it Regan's column. It's a sort of…"

"Poison pen," her husband provides the word she was searching for.

"Nasty, if you ask me," Sweet says.

"No one asked you. It's great," Lo says enthusiastically. "Our very own town crier. Anyway, we're all rooting for Ms. Confidence to forgive you, Mr. Rivers. Let us know," he says and hands me my drink.

I walk out of there and cross the small footbridge that leads to the office park of Rivers Wilde.

I thought moving to a big city would rid me of the curse of nosy Italian mamas that plagued the small village I had lived in with Gigi. But instead, I'd moved into what was essentially a small town and everyone is invested in what's happening with Confidence and me. I'm just glad my office is downtown, twenty minutes away, tucked safely in the old Chevron Tower. And far away from the constant questions that only remind me that my girl isn't talking to me and that I have no way of making her. Well, until yesterday.

"You're late," Remington Wilde says as soon as I step through the sliding glass doors of his office.

"This is all very man in the high castle, Wilde. Most executives work from home these days," I tease.

"Good for those motherfuckers. *They* can be executives. I'll continue being a leader and show up to the office every fucking day."

"Is everything a challenge?" I scoff.

"Yes. I'm addicted to winning. And *you're* late," he says.

"No, I'm just not early." I stick my hand out to shake his and we share a good-natured grin.

"So, you're finally back and in charge?" he asks, his dark eyes narrowed in naked skepticism.

"I'm back," I say before I unbutton my suit jacket and sit down across from him.

"I know you're not living in that old castle up there, are you?"

"No, I bought a place in Rivers Wilde. It's almost ready. Until then, I'm living in the Ivy," I tell him.

"How do you like it?" he asks.

"I like it fine," I say noncommittally.

"If by 'fine' you mean you like the good people, excellent food, world-class amenities, and being in the most convenient part of Houston, then I'm glad to hear it. Rivers Wilde is a tastemaker and so many have tried to replicate what we did. But there's not another community like it in Houston," he says.

"Cut the sales talk. I've already been brought down by one of your sales ninjas. And, *I'm* here to sell *you* something," I tell him.

He chuckles and quirks his lips proudly. "Our sales team is the best in the country. We still use my dad's training manual for our sales force. Almost thirty years later it's still turning out fucking soldiers on our sales team," he says and nods.

"You hungry?" he asks and nods at the menu.

"Nope, and I've got a chimichurri steak frites being delivered from Moxie's at twelve thirty. I'm saving myself for that baby," I joke.

"From what I heard, that's the only thing you're calling *baby* these days," he says and takes a sip of his drink. He grins at me mischievously from behind the lip of his cup. Confidence's hasty departure from my house and her decampment to Rivers Wilde for the remainder of her stay was clearly the subject of rampant gossip.

"I can't believe you have time to listen to gossip."

"Oh, I don't. But my twin, Regan, she lives for it and you two were the talk of the town after she was seen fleeing your house in the middle of a fucking hurricane. That sounded like some drama. And your step-mother sounds like a nut job," he says.

"Fuck off," I gripe.

He bursts out laughing. I watch him with a bored expression.

He wipes his eyes. "I'm done," he says.

"Good. Because it's actually a perfect segue about why I'm here. Your lawsuit, the flood victims? You need to hire them the best lawyer you can. Kingdom is pulling out all the stops because they don't want their other tenants to get any ideas." I get straight to the point.

"What? Are you turning traitor on your own company?" he asks and laughs.

"It's not my company. But the foundation has exposure. I'm trying to limit it," I say shortly.

"You live here. So, you know what my uncle has done. And I'm trying to find a way to work around his stooges on the executive committee. I think they'd be willing to settle. I want to make sure that my first act as chairman is to settle this case," I level with him.

He assesses me for a few seconds. "So, you're telling me you're not going to be Mr. Same Shit Different Day?"

"I'm telling you that there is shit I'm not willing to attach my name to," I say honestly.

"I'm listening," he says and leans back, confident that whatever I'm about to tell him, he's already got a stronger hand than I.

But he can't. Not when he doesn't know all of the cards in play.

"You need a *fucking good* lawyer. I saw that Jimenez asshole listed as the attorney of record. He's going to fuck it up for your clients," I say.

"He's one of the best litigators in the country." He swats away my comments with the shrug of one shoulder.

"Are you personally overseeing this matter?"

"No, but I am watching closely. I'm the one they came to. I just can't take it on right now," he says.

"Well, let me tell you that Jimenez doesn't give a shit about them. That's going to matter because he'll give them terrible advice and tell them to take whatever Kingdom's offering."

"Okay, I don't have time to launch a search right now, Rivers. But thanks for the advice." He rolls his eyes.

"I'm not here to give you advice. I said I have a favor," I reiterate slowly. "I know a lawyer. The one who won that huge insurance settlement for those people in the delta."

"Oh yeah, I've heard of her. Some weird-as-fuck first name, like Contracts or something, right?" he says.

"Her name is Confidence Ryan, asshole," I say.

"You know her?" he asks with an impressed, suggestive smile.

"Yeah, I know her. She's my girlfriend. The one you were teasing me about." I say it and ignore the flashback of her telling me she'd never forgive me.

"Oh, shit. Regan never said her name. I had no idea. You want me to hire your girlfriend to be the lawyer for a class action lawsuit against your company?"

"Yes, I'm trying to do what's right and what I know my father would want. But the board is going to fight me every step of the way. So, yeah. I want you to hire her. She's the best, and you'll need it." I say honestly.

"Her old firm put the word out about her, man. I heard she tried to fucking stab her last boss," he says with a laugh.

"If you believe that, then you're wasting my time," I say dismissively.

"Rivers, I don't want a PR nightmare on my hands by hiring some chick with a short fuse just 'cause you're pussy whipped," he says.

I ignore the jab and eye him impassively. "Why did you take this case, Remi?"

He shrugs. "Because this is *my* city. And some of the images I saw during the flood will haunt me for the rest of my life. It's been a month and we're still seeing stories of families trying to get back into the homes. But those are the people with good fucking insurance and savings. And Wilde Law is no different from any other Wilde World enterprise. We serve the Houstonians that a lot of people have forgotten about. Not because we're bleeding hearts, but because we're them. The underdogs."

"Your mother is a billionaire, and you're an underdog?" I chuckle.

"My grandfather was the son of Irish immigrants, my mother left Jamaica when she was sixteen with nothing more than her wit and her grit. They've had to overcome more than you can imagine to get to where they are. And Houston made all of that possible. The people who shop in our stores, the people who eat at our restaurants and buy gas from our stations. I took this case because I want to do something good for *my* people." His voice brims with passion.

"Then hire Confidence. That gossip about her is bullshit. You don't know me well, but if you think I'd let a woman who was less than incredible near my family or me, you're crazy," I tell him.

He eyes me with an enigmatic expression and then says, "Where is she?"

"Arkansas. "

"Your girl is in Arkansas? Why?" he asks with an annoying chuckle.

"She lives there," I say defensively. He raises an *I smell BS* eyebrow. "And I fucked up when she was here and she's not talking to me," I say and take a big gulp of coffee.

His chuckle turns into a guffaw.

I glower at him.

"Sorry, man," he says and doesn't sound sorry at all.

"Interview her. With hurricane season in Houston being an annual event, you'll never be short of work, and she'll draw clients for you," I say.

"And I could get her here for you, so you could try to win her back without going to Arkansas?"

"Yes. And I went to Arkansas. Two weeks ago. She pulled her shotgun out and trained it on me. I didn't get close enough to talk to her."

He bursts into raucous laughter and claps his hands together.

"Oh, *shit*. Does she have a sister?" he asks.

"No," I say, unamused.

"So, do you want me to tell her you asked me to interview her?"

"No. She won't take the job if you tell her that. And I don't want you to hire her unless you think she's the best person for the job."

"I'm too addicted to winning to hire losers. If I hire her, it's because I know she's going to deliver the best thing possible for the clients. And Barry is a shit. It would be nice to have someone more invested leading the case. So, yeah. I'll call her. Get her down here. But we'll have to disclose your relationship to the clients because they should know. "

"She's not talking to me. Nothing to disclose," I say.

"If she wants this job, she'll have to get over that and also talk to and about you in a professional manner. No domestic drama at the office," he says.

"Let me just tell you. When you meet her, you'll think she's the prettiest thing you've ever seen. And that's just the tip of the iceberg," I say.

He scoffs. "Lord, love is blind. No one is perfect, Hayes."

"You'll see when you meet her. Just remember that you will have to end my life to make her yours."

He does that annoying whistle of his. "Damn. It's like *that*?" he grimaces in sympathy. "Look, if that's your girl…you better get in there quick. Nothing more dangerous than a good woman experiencing the world without the aftertaste of whatever bullshit you made her put up with…if she gets too much of that…she'll never take you back," he taunts, but I detect the whiff of experience in his advice.

The idea of her getting over me makes me feel like I'm having an out-of-body experience. I can't let that happen. And yet, what does it say about how I've treated her if she prefers her world without me in it? I mean, she's not exactly a constant bundle of fun, but I can't imagine life without her. The thought of it makes me howl crazily at the moon.

"If she takes the interview, I'll let you know. You asked me not to say anything, so you better not tell her yourself. I'm not trying to have her hating *me* too."

"I won't say a word."

He eyes me, skeptically.

I sign a cross over my heart. "I swear."

"Okay. You better mean it. I like you. Ans since I have no clue what the feud is about—and my grandfather died before he could tell me—I think it's time we ended it," he says.

"Just like that?"

"It's stupid to hate each other when we're not even competitors. So yeah, just like that."

My respect for him doubles. I like how direct he is. And I like that he's not interested in a grudge for the sake of it. "Agreed," I say and extend my hand to shake his.

He takes it and grins. "I'm glad you're back. That family of yours needs new blood. Your uncle's a cold motherfucker. I was a kid when you were, so I don't remember much about your dad's time, but from what I understand, it was nothing like this."

He shakes his head, and I'm embarrassed that I can't say more than a noncommittal, "I know. I've got a lot to dig out of and no power; at least, not from the company. I'm just a figurehead. But I have money and discretion on how it's spent," I say.

"That's all the power you need. Where are your brothers?" His pivot is unexpected, but I don't mind. I've said everything I came to. Accomplished everything I needed to. So, I give him the rundown.

"Dare is raising hell in LA. Stone is saving lives in Medellin and Beau is probably high, sitting naked in a Mexican desert playing his guitar to the moon," I say.

He laughs.

"What about your siblings?" I ask.

"They're in Houston. Working for Wilde World. Except for Regan. Tyson manages operations for the grocery stores. We're all grinding. My mother is between here and her place in Montego Bay. We're good." he replies. "So, Italy? With your aunt? How was that?"

"It was good. I learned Italian. No pasta eating on a beach, but Positano is beautiful, and she was devoted to me and making sure I would be ready to come back. Even though, it turns out, there wasn't much to come back to."

"Well, make it count, kid. And I'll call your girl."

Chapter 17

TWIST

CONFIDENCE

"This is incredible," I say giddily to the very handsome, very charming man walking beside me. "What you described has me salivating. It's the case of a lifetime. There are so many questions with conflicting federal rulings. This could go to the Supreme Court," I say and then bite my tongue.

"Yeah, if it doesn't settle, it has that potential," Remington agrees.

"I shouldn't sound so happy at the sound of prolonged litigation, should I?" I ask him sheepishly.

"You wouldn't be worth the paper that Doctor of Jurisprudence is scrawled on if you weren't, counselor." He winks one of his twinkly, wide, lushly-lashed, Milky Way dark eyes at me, and I nearly trip over my feet. He smiles as if to say, *yeah, I get that all the time*. I bet he does. He told me his mother is Jamaican and his father is a second-generation Irish American. Well, Jamaica and Ireland should find a way to merge because their citizens clearly were born to procreate with each other. He is the definition of a heartthrob. He even smells good.

We step out onto the main street of Rivers Wilde, and I can't believe all of this is happening. "I didn't expect to be leaving here with a signed contract. I thought we'd have several interviews," I say.

"Well, *I* didn't want to let you leave here without a guarantee that you'd come back. You're everything these plaintiffs need, and I'm just glad you're in a position to start so quickly," he says, like I'm doing him a favor.

"Being unemployed for nine months finally pays off," I joke but make sure he hears the genuine gratitude in my voice.

The day he called had been a bad day. I'd gotten another letter of rejection from a firm in Nashville, and I was down to no more than a couple of months' living expenses. I needed a shoulder to cry on, and the only one I wanted was attached to the biggest asshole in the world.

I was on the verge of calling him to yell at him—again—when I got Remington's email. It was my first interview in months. The first application that had even garnered an email exchange. When they asked me to come to Houston for an in-face interview, I had fallen on my knees in my room and cried grateful tears.

And as mad as I was at Hayes, I couldn't pretend that all of my relief was due to the chance at this amazing great job. Some of it was that fate intervened to save me from my stubborn pride.

My heart had been blown to smithereens since I left his house that night.

I grieved in silence. I pretended I was okay. I hadn't been able to tell my mother what happened because I knew that she'd never forgive Hayes.

The thought of that knotted my stomach almost as much as what he did.

I want to forgive him. So badly.

I end every night with a prayer for the grace to let go of my anger. But it eludes me. And as much as I miss him, I can't forget what he'd said about me.

I've spent the last month licking my wounds and clutching my pillow.

Every night it smelled less and less like Hayes.

And the chasm between us grew wider and wider.

Except in one way, the way we always manage to find each other. And some nights, sleep has come only after I've called him, used his voice and my hands to make myself come and told him to fuck off before I hang up in his face. I'm still so hurt by him. Still so angry.

But I do miss him.

Fiercely.

I just don't know how to get over "fine to fuck, not enough breeding to bring home." Every time I think about it, it burns.

"So, what do you think of our cosmopolitan suburban version of small-town America?" Remington asks. I stare back at him and smile, grateful my staring off into the distance looked like me admiring the scene instead of me daydreaming about my boyfriend.

I let my eyes sweep the street and smile.

"It's incredible," I say simply and honestly. The enclave of Rivers Wilde, carved out of three square miles in southwest Houston, is the kind of place I used to dream about living when I was a kid.

We're walking across one of a dozen foot bridges that straddle the man-made shallow fountain that cuts a straight line through the community. The left northwest corner is a commercial district. It's a miniature of downtown Houston. Skyscrapers and shorter commercial buildings make up the ten blocks dedicated to the Wilde World Office Park.

On the other side of the bridge from where we are now, is the town square. It is the very center of the enclave. It's flanked by two residential communities. On the left is The Ivy. It's a golf course, country club, and a cluster of luxury condominiums in a cluster of sky-scraping high-rises.

On the left, The Oaks is a suburban prototype of single-family homes that range from starter homes to million-dollar mansions.

The Market runs along the southern border of the enclave, parallel from the Wilde office park. It's one huge indoor food market. There are greengrocers, spice markets, fishmongers, butchers, florists, cheese shops, the bakeries, everything has a kosher or halal options. The long lines that snake out of The Market's every day are due to the food counter. Over seven hundred feet of space dedicated to deliciousness highlights why Houston is one of the places where the phrase "melting pot" is not an exaggeration. From Afghanistan to South Africa and everything in between, the world's best cooks show off their cultural delights. And people line up to devour it. I had tamales today and they might be the most perfect thing I've ever eaten. They're only open for lunch during the week, but all day on the weekends, and I can't wait to visit.

"Irma's been here since Rivers Wilde opened its gates. And now she's a landmark in her own right," Remington says when I tell him I want to go back. "This is the dream at work. It's a community that's designed to encourage interactions between people who might otherwise see each other as foreign or different."

"That sounds amazing," I say and wish I could find a more eloquent response to his words. But I've never seen a place like this.

"You're actually in for a treat. Don, our resident Cajun, and Tommy, who owns the Vietnamese restaurant in the market, come together for a crawfish boil that the entire community turns out for."

"Crawfish?" I grimace.

"You haven't lived until you have these. Lemongrass and garlic meet Old Bay and jalapeños for the most delicious crawfish you've ever tasted." He groans dramatically and pats his washboard flat stomach.

"Well, I certainly hope you have a gym here, because it sounds like unless I plan on buying a whole new wardrobe, I'm going to need it." I laugh.

"Got that, too. Tae Kwon Do school, Barre, a dance school with classes that use everything from the ballet rail to a stripper pole. And if you just want to work out, there's a regular old sweat-it-out-on-the-treadmill gym, too."

"So basically, if you live here, you never have to leave?" I ask.

"Not if you didn't want to. And that's the point. To make home feel like enough. To create a real sense of community. One that doesn't exclude anyone who really wants to live here. Our housing runs the gamut, so whether you're making forty grand a year or four hundred thousand, there's a place in your budget in Rivers Wilde," he says with the same voice as the guy on the *Price is Right*.

"I'm taking a tour of a unit tonight, and I'm totally excited. This sounds like my kind of place," I gush. I know I sound like a fangirl, but I can't help it. It's out of a dream.

We walk down the wide, clean-enough-to-eat-off sidewalk. Sapling trees are planted in clusters every thirty feet or so. Baskets of flowers hang from the hooks that are fixed to ten feet of brick wall in between the glass-fronted stores that line the street. There's a healthy crowd of people strolling. They stop and speak to each other. I watch as two men shake hands and then sit down on a bench outside of the coffee shop, Sweet and Lo's.

"I had the best lattes I've ever had in my life there," I point it out to Remington.

"Yeah, it's the best in town. Did you meet Sweet or Lo?"

"Yes. Lo is a hoot, and Sweet wasn't sweet at all. But I love them," I recall happily.

"Here we are." He pulls open the door with the word TWIST scrawled in bright blue lettering on the glass door.

"So, we'll see you in the office tomorrow? We have a face-to-face with opposing counsel, clients will be present," he says and I find something unsettling in his voice and the way he's watching me.

"TB!" Cass shouts from behind me, and Remi's eyes widen in confusion.

I say, "Don't worry. She's not crazy. That's what she calls me." I give him an apologetic smile.

He raises his eyebrows in surprise. "Nickname?" he asks.

"More like an inside joke." I give him a halfhearted smile. His is more of a grimace.

"Okay," he says, and starts to back down the street. "See you bright and early tomorrow. We're really glad to have you on board," he says before he turns and dashes back up the street.

"Was that Remi Wilde? Oh my God. Do you know what his nickname is?" Cass asks just as I turn to face her. Her face is flushed and her hair is sticking to her face in sweaty strands.

"Yeah, that was Remi. And what was his nickname?" I ask when she doesn't offer it up.

"The Legend. His mind, his prowess on the basketball court, *between the sheets*," she chortles and waggles her eyebrows and then moves in for a hug.

I pull back. "I don't really want those visuals of my new boss, thanks. And let's just imagine that, hug, okay?" I eye her sweaty shirt. "Did you run from your office?" I ask her and give her a quick up and down.

"Don't look at me like that," she retorts, but desists in her attempt to hug me. "It's hot as fuck and I had to walk for ten minutes to get here," she says.

"You look like you've been walking for an hour," I quip and grin at her.

"You just wait until you've been standing without shade in the middle of the afternoon in Houston, TX for more than three minutes," she snaps and pulls at her shirt.

"I'll make sure to avoid that particular situation. Can't walk around looking like I work in a sauna," I tease her one more time and am rewarded with a scowl. "I'm hungry, let's get a table." I pull the brass handle of Twist's glass-paned double doors open.

"It's like a fancy saloon," she says as we step inside the restaurant. The cool air-conditioned, dark paneled room does look like something out of a western movie. But instead of sawdust littering the ground, there's a gleaming mahogany brand with the crowned horse logo of Rivers Wilde on the floor right under the wagon wheel chandelier in the center of the restaurant.

Instead of a bar that runs the length of the wall, there's a stage in the front of the room, complete with a red velvet curtain behind the wall of bottles. There are no seats in front of the gleaming countertop. It's just two bartenders, one man and one woman, making drinks and setting them on the bar where waitstaff picks them up. "Shut Up and Drink" is burned into the wood of the bar.

"Wow, I've never seen anything like this," I marvel.

"Hey, ladies, welcome to Twist," a small, dark-haired woman with a hugely pregnant belly approaches us when we step into the main dining room. "Your first time here?" she asks knowingly.

"Yes." I smile back.

"Yeah, your openmouthed, wide-eyed stare kinda gave it away." She laughs good-naturedly and then reaches for two menus that sit under a green chalkboard—"open secret" scrawled on it.

"That's our oxymoron of the day. Well, of the week or whenever someone thinks of one and changes it. Feel free to contribute. Every week, I pick my favorite and the author gets a free entrée," she says excitedly.

I pick up the chalk and scrawl "bittersweet" while she marks something down on her hostess stand.

"You want a booth or table?" she asks.

"Booth," we say at the same time.

"Awesome, come this way. And I'm Angie. My husband, Jackson, and I are the managers." Her soft brown eyes twinkle with pride. I can see why. It's a wonderfully unique place. Nearly everyone we pass looks up to greet her and tips their heads at us as we make our way through the wide aisle between the tables in the front of the huge space.

"If you need anything, just shout. But your server will take real good care of you," she says happily and puts the menus down on the stone tabletop of the booth she stops at.

"Actually, I need the ladies'," Cass says.

"Just walk past the bar and down the corridor. You'll see it on the left," Angie says.

"Be right back. Will you get me some water, please?" Cass says and drops her bag on the floor.

"Thank you," I say as I slide into the curved, butter-yellow leather covered seats of the booth and smile up at her. The high-backed seats wrap around the table and we can't see our neighbors on either side.

It gives us a view of the entire room. I admire how brightly decorated it is. The white brick walls are full of abstract artwork and broken up by large windows that face the picturesque strip of stores that line the street.

The artwork is all whites, blues, and yellows with splashes of red and purple that manage to look coordinated but somehow eclectic at the same time.

"It's so private," I say. Angie nods knowingly.

"You make yourselves comfortable and I'll get your waters and your basket of bread right out." She puts a hand on her pregnant belly and rubs it.

"Are you okay?" I ask, pointing with concern at her baby bump.

"Yeah, I'm fine. Why?" she asks sharply, peering at me with intense anticipation on her face.

"Uh—" I eyeball and wonder why she's acting like my answer is important. "Well, nothing…you keep rubbing your belly. I was just thinking maybe you were having some pregnancy-related difficulty," I explain cautiously.

She laughs at the joke she still hasn't bothered to explain to me.

"Oh. Thank goodness. I was only rubbing it 'cause I wanted to make sure you knew I was pregnant and didn't think this was a beer gut or something," she says and then gasps with embarrassment.

"I can't believe I said that out loud," she says apologetically. "Pregnancy has completely removed my already very porous filter. It's my fourth time; you'd think I'd be over this part. But I hate that I can't see my feet and this ass is as wide as the Houston Ship Channel," she blurts, a pained expression on her pretty face.

I want to laugh, but I don't think she's trying to be funny. I try to think of some sort of consolation to offer, but I have a feeling nothing I say would actually make her feel better.

"I'm sorry, you probably think I'm so vain," she says and shakes her head deprecatingly.

"You *are* vain. And nobody is thinking anything except how to get you to stop talking so they can get some food," a gruff but twangy woman's voice comes from the booth next to ours.

"Oh, Lord, I'm sorry." Angie smiles apologetically. "For talking, and for Henny's *rudeness*. Thank you for being nice." She rolls her eyes at the booth. "Your server will be right over. Glad to have you. Hope you'll come back." She makes an exaggerated scowling face at the hidden booth occupant and waddles off toward the front of the restaurant.

"As if anyone could mistake that belly for anything other than another one of your giant babies," the voice calls after Angie.

"Oh, Henny, be nice and introduce yourself," Angie calls back without looking over her shoulder.

A gnarled, arthritic hand with perfectly, French-manicured nails comes to rest on the shared top of our booths. Right over the side where Cass would have been sitting.

"You should be thanking me," the voice comes. I grin when a hand taps the top of our booth.

"Well, are you going to make me shift my ninety-year-old bones out of the chair, or are you going to get up and say hello?" she asks impatiently.

I giggle and slide out of the seat and step to her booth. The woman sitting there looks like she could be a fill-in for Sophia Petrillo on *Golden Girls*.

"Thank you," I say cheerily.

"You're welcome," she says tersely and then looks up at me with a pair of dark brown eyes that are set deep in a face that's got so many wrinkles, it's impossible to tell what she really looks like.

"Yes, I know," she says like she's bored. "I look like a bleached prune. You don't need to stare at me like you've never seen an old person," she says.

"Oh, I'm not staring 'cause you're old, I'm just waiting for you to tell me why I should be thanking you," I say good-humoredly. I come from a town full of crotchety old people whose bark is all lie. And I've never lived anywhere else where your elders 'spank you' even if you're not theirs.

"That girl never stops talking," Henny says. "She runs a tight ship, though. Once *she* gets out of the way." She raises her eyebrows knowingly and draws out that last word. "You'll enjoy every single meal you have here."

"I'm Confidence," I say and extend my hand.

She frowns and eyes me. "You look too young to have hippies for parents," she muses.

"Yeah. My grandparents' generation, I think," I say.

"You *think*?" She scoffs and gives me a disapproving frown. "You kids don't know your history. You should know what generation your elders belong to. Not just yours. I bet you're a millennial. You will be remembered for your selfishness," she chides. I throw my head back and laugh, the first real laugh I've managed in a while. She's awesome.

"Glad you think it's funny," she says dryly. "I'm here every day, if you want more."

Cass walks up just then, looks between Henny and me and says, "Of course, you've already made a friend."

I elbow her and say, "This is Henny."

Henny shakes her head and says, "Sorry, I have a one-new-person-a-day rule. Come back tomorrow." Then she picks up her fork and knife and digs into a huge baked potato that's bursting with what looks like brisket, cheese, sour cream, chives, and butter.

I stand there and watch her for nearly a full minute before I realize she's serious and isn't going to respond. Cass doesn't wait that long before she slides into her seat.

She's gripping a menu when I sit down. "Oh, this place has the nicest public bathroom I've ever seen. It's cleaner than mine. I wish I'd known about this neighborhood when I was moving back. It's like living in the suburbs but in walking distance from all the action. I totally would have bought a unit here."

"Yeah, it's really convenient. And apparently my new boss's family owns all of it," I tell her. She squeals and clutches her menu to her chest excitedly.

"I'm the worst friend. I didn't even ask how it went. I was so excited to see you! Tell me!" she exclaims and stares at me with googly eyes.

"Oh my God, it was amazing, Cass," I say dreamily.

"And you got the job!" she interjects excitedly.

I nod and let my grin have a moment of unfettered shine. "They want me to attend a meeting tomorrow before I leave for the case they're hiring me for. I've got some of the publicly available court records to review. So, I'm going to hole up in my hotel and study up so I can be ready. I want to make sure when I get on my flight tomorrow, he's not sorry he hired me," I tell her.

"So, you're going to leave here and not call Hayes?" she asks with surprise.

Hearing her say his name makes me flinch. Beneath the surface of my happiness for every amazing thing that has happened today has been the terrible sensation of how wrong it is that I'm here and not with him. How shallow my joy is without being able to celebrate it with him.

I forced myself to push him out of my thoughts whenever he entered them today.

"So, you're not here because you have a huge boner for Hayes

Rivers?"

"Of course not," I snap and look around the restaurant. There's a loud din. People speaking like they're in their living rooms instead of in a public place where anyone could overhear.

Just like home. God, I think I love this place.

"Hello? Are you listening?" Cass snaps her fingers in front of my eyes.

I turn startled eyes back to Cass. "Yes, I am. And that's not why," I lie.

"Yeah, right. He's worn you down, and you got a lucky break with this offer. Two weeks ago, you would have never accepted it," she pushes.

"Two weeks ago, I had enough money to live on for another month. Now, I don't. It's also right up my alley. This is a developing area of law that I kind of pioneered," I tell her. "But, I would have taken this job anywhere in the world."

"Aww, you should see your face. I don't know how the hell you managed it with him, of all people, after somehow avoiding it for so long." She shakes her head at me incredulously.

"Avoiding what?" I ask just as our server approaches with the water and bread baskets.

"Being completely head over heels in love. Wanting something more than your pride," she says.

"Welcome to Twist," our server interrupts as she bounces up to our table. Her wide mouth parts to reveal a perfectly straight smile that's contagious. She's slightly out of breath and leans on the table in mock exhaustion before she stands up again.

"I'm Kemi, I'll be your server today," she says and brushes a braid that's falling over her eye out of the way before she pulls a small spiral notebook out of her apron pocket. "What are you ladies drinking?" she asks.

"I'm fine with water," I tell her, wrinkling my nose at the menu. I hate having to decide what to eat.

"The hell she is. We're having champagne with lunch," Cass says, giving me a fierce scowl that dares me to argue. I don't. I want to be excited…I wish I didn't feel so heartsick at the same time.

"Wonderful," Kemi chirps and scribbles on her notepad. "What are we celebrating?" she asks as she writes.

"She got a job! A great one, and she's moving to Houston," she tells her and slides her eyes over to me and smiles proudly.

"Well, then, this calls for our special. It's a grilled Tilapia on top of a bed of the most delicious rice you'll ever have," she says.

"That sounds a little heavy for lunch," I say. I ignore how my mouth waters at the description. I've been eating my feelings, and it was not my imagination that my breasts are fighting with buttons in a battle for liberation that I think one more donut will tip in their favor.

"You should eat your heaviest meal for lunch, actually. So it's perfect," Cassie says.

I smile at her helplessly. "Well, my breakfast was pretty good, too," I admit.

"We'll have it," Cassie says to Kemi.

"You're in for such a treat. It's so good. The owners pick the week's special and announce it on Sunday night. It's always an amazing fusion of cuisines. I can't wait to hear what you think," she says.

Her enthusiasm is catching, and I wiggle my shoulders in excitement. "Can't wait, thanks." I smile at her.

"Awesome! Shout or wave if you need anything. Your food will be out in about fifteen minutes," she says and saunters off.

"You need to talk to Hayes," she says, and my heart thumps in my chest. I shake my head and look down at my hands.

The sounds of the restaurant clang around us, scrapes of forks on cutlery, bursts of laughter from the tables, the scrape of chairs being pushed away from tables. The dining room is devoid of any food smells. It smells nice, almost like a spa, but subtler. I'm sure if my stomach wasn't caught in my internal conflict, twisted by pangs of longing, churning from the fear that's become my constant companion, the at-mosphere would be soothing.

"You okay, TB?" she asks when I don't respond and don't look up.

"No," I admit, annoyed at myself. "I miss him. I hate him. I love him so much, I don't know what to do," I confess, still looking at my hands.

"I have a feeling he feels the same way," she says kindly.

"I know—" I whisper.

"Talk to him. Don't leave town without seeing him," she says.

"You don't understand. I don't *want* to forgive him because I miss him. I want to forgive him because I believe he sees my worth. And not just because we have great sex or he likes the way I look on his arm. I won't be another man's project or trophy. Or whatever I am to him," I tell her.

She quirks her lips in sympathy. "Oh, honey. You're the only one who doesn't see your worth," she says, and I rear back in surprise and hurt.

"What does that mean?" I eye her.

Her eyes soften, and her smile turns a little sad.

"It means if you did, you'd know that the only way anyone would look at you and see anything less than the amazing woman you are is if they're an idiot. And Hayes Rivers *isn't* an idiot. Yeah, he said something stupid to his brother. But he didn't know you from Sam when he said it," she reminds me, again.

I chafe at her defense of Hayes, of how right she is and how wrong she is. I rub a finger over the spot on my temple where a small headache is suddenly blooming.

"I would *never* ever insult him like that. I wouldn't look at him and see anything less than the human being he is. Yes, he's handsome. He's got a hot body. He's got pots of money and he's got power. I didn't look at him and wonder if he got rich by ripping people off or assume that because he's a big guy those things about him and his ex were true. I wondered if he would be tender and caring, constant, proud, honorable, determined, and convicted and smart. Those things have nothing to do with his money."

"You're deluding yourself," she says dismissively.

"How?" I chafe at the words.

"The wealth he was born into has shaped all of those things. Just like the poverty you were born into has shaped yours." She puts her hands up, palms facing me when I start to speak. "Hear me out, please."

"As if I could stop you," I grumble.

"I get it. You were raised to be proud of who you are. Not what you have. He was raised to believe the exact opposite. All of that honor, pride, conviction? They all fuel the need to protect the *things*—his name, his money, his position," she says.

"Yeah, but at what cost?"

"Whatever it takes, is what I'm sure he'd say," she shrugs. "You're such a hypocrite," she says.

"Excuse *me*? Is it Thursday or is it *Shit on Confidence Day*?" I ask.

"Isn't your whole career based on you wanting to preserve a way of life? What have you done to protect it? What wouldn't you do?" she asks.

I cradle my forehead in my hands and try to process what she's saying through a different filter.

"It's amazing that *he's* who you've fallen like this for. I always thought you'd need a man who would let you have your way. You're so stubborn. But you've met your match in him. I'm glad he's making you think. And I'm glad he's strong. I think it'll be good for you to not have to carry the whole world on your shoulders, TB," she says.

She covers my hand with hers to silence me.

"It's okay to be vulnerable," she says quietly. "It's okay to let him close enough to hurt you again. But you have to want him more than you want your pride, TB," she says.

"My *pride*?" I bristle at her characterization. "It's not pride. It's self-preservation. I didn't have anyone to stand between me and the bad guy. I have always stood in the breech myself. And I love him *so* much that if I let him, he could really ruin me." My confession pours out of me and I feel breathless having said it.

"I know… And I didn't mean to dismiss that. You just can't let fear lead you."

"What if he doesn't want me the same way? What if when he gets to see all of me, he finds me lacking?" I ask and reveal the real source of my anxiety.

"Ask him. Call him before you go."

"And say what? Can you help understand how I keep ending up with men who want me in bed, but don't think I'm fit to be on their arm in public?" I ask quietly. Tears of shame burn my eyes.

"First of all, he's *nothing* like Nigel. He respects you and he's crazy about you. It was so obvious when you were here even with all the madness that happened. And you should have seen him driving that *truck*, through all that water. He did that for *you*." She fans herself. "It was so… If you weren't my friend…" I give her a warning look and she winks.

"*Shiiit.* You need to spend some time in those Tinder streets and you'll know how lucky you are," she says.

"How's Tinder?" I ask. "I'm sorry I'm talking about myself non-stop," I apologize.

"You don't need to apologize, there's nothing to tell. I thought I met my soul mate, again. He showed up to our date in scrubs, told me he was a doctor and hadn't had time to get home before our date." She takes a long sip of her water.

"What kind of doctor?" I ask.

"The kind that also works the popcorn machine behind concession stand at Edwards Theatre in Greenway Plaza," she deadpans. I choke on the water in my throat. I cough and blow my nose, and she just shrugs.

"It's a jungle out there and you're over here hanging out with Remington Wilde, Hayes Rivers, and complaining."

"I'm not *complaining*," I croak out when I've recovered from my fit of laughter.

"I just hope you won't lump them together. Nigel and Hayes. They're not the same," she reiterates. Her expression is serious again.

"They're not," I admit. "I didn't love Nigel. Without Hayes… I'm just going through my daily motions. But inside, I feel like I'm falling to pieces," I confess.

"Oh, Confidence." Cass sighs, her voice soft and sympathetic now.

"I don't even know how it's possible to feel like this after three months." I put my face in my hands and groan. "And my family…"

"And I'm glad you've met someone who can help you so it doesn't swallow you whole. You have so much on your plate. You do a lot for your mother," she says. I frown at her.

"Of course I do. And I always will. It's just me and her. She's done so much for me. I owe her," I remind her.

"But you also owe yourself," she insists.

The waitress sails over, a huge tray on her shoulder and saves me from having to answer.

Chapter 18

NAKED

HAYES

"Can I come in?" I force myself to ask Confidence when what I really want is to shove past her and ask her what the fuck she thinks she's doing.

She stares at me, her hair hidden in the towel she's fashioned into a turban on her head. The rest of her isn't hidden at all. She's got on a light pink bathrobe that clings to her in all the right places and rubs me in all the wrong ones.

"Why the hell are you answering the door half-naked?" I demand.

She crosses her arms over her chest defensively and glares up at me. "Why are you banging on my door at ten o'clock at night?" she whispers furiously and glances down the empty hallways before she grabs my arm and tugs me forward. "Come inside. The last thing I need is a complaint for disturbing the peace."

I step into her hotel room and turn to face her.

"Why are you answering the door wet and nearly naked, *Tesoro?*" I ask again, my anger at the sight of her surpassing the initial insult that brought me here.

"I am not naked. I was getting out of the shower when you started pounding on the door. I wanted to stop you before you woke up my neighbors."

"You're very concerned about your neighbors." I look around the spare room of the extended stay hotel. "Why are you staying here anyway? Remi couldn't have put you up here. He has a block of suites at the Ivy's executive suites his firm uses for interviews."

"First of all, how did you know I'm here, and that I'm here for Remi? Secondly—not that it is *any* of your business—he let me choose my hotel and they're reimbursing me. This one is fine. And third, I'm concerned about my neighbors because I think the people right next door are a family who live here. I've seen them taking the kids to school every morning this week. They're asleep. So, keep it down," she scolds.

Of course, that's why. She's a fucking bleeding heart. It's why I love her.

"I'll keep my voice down," I concede right away. "And *everything* you do is my business. Because *you* are my business."

She rolls her eyes but doesn't say anything.

"Secondly, Remi's a friend. But he didn't tell me you were here. I ran into Gigi's friend, Henny. Apparently, you've been pining over me in public," I drawl and have to bite my lip to stop my smile when her nostrils flair.

"That old lady was eavesdropping?" she sputters.

"Don't let her hear you call her that, not if you want to live…and she did overhear and thought it would be such a shame if you left town without even telling me you were here," I say.

"How in the world did you know where I was staying?" she asks and tightens her belt.

"My assistant spent all day calling hotels near Rivers Wilde until she found you. And enough with the twenty questions," I snap.

"Fine, then you can leave." She pulls the lapels of her robe closed when my eyes drift to her throat.

"I'm not. And it's too bad about your G-rated neighbors. They put a dent in my plans," I tell her.

"What plans?" she snaps.

"The ones I had to fuck you so hard you'd see stars and scream my name loud enough that they'd hear you across the street," I say.

Her entire body flushes, and her hands drop from her neckline and rest on her hips. She leans forward and gives me her most disapproving glare.

"*Their* presence has nothing on the fact that my body is closed to you right now. There will be no fucking tonight. And don't call me *Tesoro*. We're not that anymore," she says angrily.

My anger spikes, too, but it's accompanied by a sting of pain at the way the words flow off her tongue. I know she's pissed, but it makes me feel like I've got a thorn stuck in my side when I hear her say we're not *that* anymore. I stalk toward her.

"Then what are we?" I ask and rake my eyes over her body. Her robe is damp and I can see the shadow of her nipples.

"I don't know, Hayes," she lies.

"Let me fuck you. You'll know, then," I whisper and her eyes widen and she tenses up again.

"That's not the answer to everything," she says.

"Take that off." I nod at her robe.

"No," she says and tosses her head in defiance. Her towel unravels and falls half off her head, exposing some of her hair. She reaches up to stop its slide and I take a step toward her.

"Don't, Hayes," she says, her voice low with warning, but her lips remain parted and her eyelids flutter.

My dick gets hard because I know what that look means. Her gown may be drying off, but her pussy is wetter than it was when she got out of the shower.

"Take it off, *Tesoro*," I say softly now, and take another step toward her. I'm close enough to grab the belt of her robe.

"I want to. But, I *can't*," she says, like the words ache when her tongue forms them. She gazes at me, her eyes limpid with need. Understanding dawns.

"You want *me* to take it off?" I ask.

She nods, two sharp tics of her head and I do an internal fist bump but keep my expression neutral.

I can see the need in her eyes.

Want is coming off her in *waves*. It's slamming into mine and envelops us in a haze of longing.

But my girl is proud and I'm desperate to break down this wall she's put between us.

I smile at her, a wolfish grin that says I know I'm going to have what I want. The flat of my hand cups the space right below her belly button and her shoulders lose the tension they've been holding.

I watch her face.

She watches my hand.

Her rapid breaths send my hand on a roller coaster of swells and dips as it glides up the center of her abdomen. Her muscles flex and ripple under my touch.

"Does that feel good, my little treasure?" I ask her quietly

She closes her eyes and nods. "Better than anything has ever felt in my life," she confesses.

I splay my fingers as they pass between her breasts and wrap them gently around her throat. Her pulse races under my fingers.

"*What* aren't we?" I ask again.

She opens her eyes and gazes at me. My tigress—her eyes are ablaze with intensity—and yet, I feel how vulnerable she is right now.

"We're not..." She licks her lips and her throat convulses against my hand.

I lean and press my lips to hers. Our eyes stay open and hers start to melt.

I taste everything I've been deprived of for the last month and groan.

"What aren't we?" I ask her again and tug the belt of her robe. The silk ribbon gives easily and her robe falls open. She gasps—a harsh, uneven breath—and sways forward. She still hasn't completed her sentence, but the look in her eyes tells me everything I need to know.

"We're everything, Confidence." I kiss her again; her lips cling to mine when I pull back.

Fuck yeah.

My need ratchets up at the small victory.

She's still mine.

"Tell me what we are," I command and place an openmouthed kiss on the hot, fresh, soap-scented skin of her neck. It's her spot, and she melts against me, ice turning liquid with every swipe of my tongue.

"We're lovers," she whispers, her breath hot in my ear. She threads a hand into my hair.

"We're fighters," she says and uses her other hand to unbuckle my belt.

"What else, Tesoro?" I growl, so hungry for her, my knees are weak.

"We're..." She breathes into my mouth as she unzips my fly.

My slacks slip down my hips and onto the floor and the rush of cool air on my rock hard dick snaps my patience.

"Let me remind you." I grab the full, lush cheeks of her ass and hoist her up.

Her legs wrap around my waist, and I lower her down onto my cock. "Oh my God." She gasps.

"We are each other's," I say and lift her off and lower her again.

"Yes. Mine." She groans and cups my ass, urging me deeper.

I walk us back to the huge window and press her back against it.

"Yes. Your god. Your king. Your man. Yours," I drive each point home with an upward thrust into her delicious pussy. "Say it."

She shakes her head. "You haven't earned it." She pants. I grin into the hollow at the base of her neck and fuck her harder.

"You feel that?" I ask and press as deep as I can.

"*Yesssssss,*" she cries and her fingers cling into my back, seeking purchase as she starts to come unglued.

I nod. "That's how deep I've buried myself in your heart. You love me. You can't turn that off, and I won't let you pretend you have."

I spin her around and lay her down on the bed. I pull out and kneel next to her.

"Suck me," I say and fist my hands in her hair. When she wraps a hand around the base of my cock, I hold her head in place and feed her slowly. She swirls her tongue around the tip and hollows her cheeks and sucks me off. My fingers loosen their grip and sift into her hair.

"You give the best fucking head, Confidence." I fuck her face, and she takes it like it's hers. She holds my gaze and starts to finger herself until her eyes flutter closed. I glance down her body and watch while her finger slips between the bare, fat lips of her pussy. She moans around my cock, and the back of her throat vibrates against my head.

"I'm going to come." I groan.

She sits up and grabs my ass, sucking harder. Her blond hair brushes the front of my thighs. The sight of her holding on, determined to take what I'm about to give her, sends me over the edge. She takes everything I shoot out, swallows, and sucks me until my knees buckle and it takes the concerted effort of every muscle in my body not to fall over.

"Fuck." I groan when she finally lets me slip from her mouth. I reach for her, but she rolls out from under me.

"What are you doing?" I peer at her frown.. My vision hasn't cleared yet, so I blink. Her frown is still there.

"That was a mistake. You should leave." She turns and rushes to and the bathroom, slamming the door behind her.

"Hey." I sit up and walk over to the door, turn the handle. But the door doesn't open.

"Open the door." I shake the locked handle.

"No, please, don't," she says, her voice breaking.

"Why are you crying? Please, open the door." I struggle to keep my frustration out of my voice.

"I'm so miserable without you, Hayes."

My heart aches at the hurt in her voice. "Baby, then come ba--"

"But, I am *so* mad at you," she interrupts in a voice broken by hiccuping sobs.

I bang my head on the door lightly. That night on the ledge, I made an unspoken promise to myself - that I'd make sure this queen never had a reason to cry again.

Fuck. "Confidence, I'm so sorry about everything."

"I don't believe you." Her voice is ragged with contempt that makes my heart skip a beat. She's angrier than she was a month ago.

"You walked in here thinking you'd fuck me until I felt better." Her voice gets clearer. losing the hurt and embracing her anger, with every word.

"Please, open the door, *Tesoro*. Let me explain." I'm ready to beg.

"No, Hayes. I *need* this job. I can't afford to be focused on you. I've got to keep my head together for tomorrow. Go home. I'll call you when I'm done."

"I'm not giving up on us," I tell her. "I know I've got a lot to learn, but I love you. And we are fucking worth it, Confidence."

Her silence is my answer.

It feels so wrong to walk away when she's hurting and conflicted on the bathroom floor of a shitty hotel room. But, I'm the reasons she's there and I don't want to upset her any more than I already have. And I know she can take care of herself.

So, I get up. "Call me tomorrow."

The door vibrates when, I assume, her head falls back or forward onto it. "I will, please…" She sounds tired and…distressed. She's right, I need to talk to her. To say words that scare, but that she deserves to hear. Once she knows how much of my heart she commands, she'll have power over me. And I swore I'd never give anyone that again.

But, right now, I'd do anything to show her that she can trust me. That I know her worth.

My feet feel like they're weighed down with one hundred pounds of resignation as I walk to the door and leave.

Chapter 19

EXPERT

CONFIDENCE

"What are you doing out here?" Remi's amused voice startles me. I look up from the paper I'm reviewing and shake my head. He's all the way at the end of the hall where the elevators are. I get up as he starts walking and try not to look like I've been pacing my bedroom all night and pulling my hair out the whole time.

After Hayes left, I calmed myself down, got dressed, and crawled into bed with my work. I've never been more grateful for a job in my life. But when I opened the case file and started to review it, my stomach had fallen to my toes. Hayes' company is the respondent. After my experience at Lancaster, I can't afford another bombshell about my love life. I know it'll mean I can't work on this case and that it might even cost me this job, but I knew I had to tell him. I'm so mad at myself for letting a man fuck up my career, yet again.

"Is the room locked?" Remi comes to stand in front of me. He looks like a taller, darker, more handsome Harvey Specter. Every single woman in this office looks at him like they all wished their name was Donna. Except for me. And not just because my heart, body, soul, and mind belonged to another, but because I would never even entertain the thought of being with a man who was in a position of authority over me. Not again.

"No. They're all in there. Ms. Swanson and Ms. Gauthier are in the room next door. I asked them to wait there for you, because I wanted to talk to you before we go in," I say.

Remi cocks an eyebrow at me and says, "You're talking really fast. And can your talk wait until after the meeting? "

"No. It can't," I say and then take a deep, calming breath.

"You okay?" Remi's hand rests on my shoulder and frowns down at me.

"I wanted to tell you… I don't know how to…" I say and cover my mouth when I realize my tongue is tied. I've been practicing what I'd say since the minute my alarm went off last night, but now the words are trapped by fatigue, humiliation, and anger.

"This case. I can't be part of it. The defendant, Kingdom. My boyfriend—" I shake my head in annoyance at myself. "It's…my ex-boyfriend," I force myself to say.

"*What* is your ex-boyfriend?" Remi asks and looks down at me, his expression mildly baffled, and I force the words out.

"Not what, who. It's Hayes Rivers. I see he's going to be here today. Your client won't want that kind of conflict in their attorney. I can't… and I understand if that means there's no position here for me. But I just—"

"I know about you and Hayes."

My jaw drops, and he chuckles. "I'm not running an amateur shop here, counselor. It was one of the first things personnel told me when we started checking your conflicts," he says.

I gawk. I've been bracing for him to rescind his offer. I spent the evening practicing my reaction and crying so that I would be all cried out when it actually happened.

"If you don't say something, I'm going to send you home. A tongue-tied litigator is worse than not having a lawyer at all."

My heart leaps in hope, but like I do with everything that feels too good to be true, I squash that feeling and pressure test it..

"Hayes and I are…unresolved. He's…determined."

Remi laughs. "That's his middle name."

Some of my skepticism wanes. "You *really* don't care about Hayes and—"

"I don't." His tone is uncharacteristically clipped. "Normally, I might. I avoid romantic drama in my own life, I certainly don't want to be a party to anyone else's. But this is an extraordinary case. Our clients deserve the benefit of your expertise and your very intimate knowledge of their circumstances. You're the best. And that's all I care about."

Relief floods me, and I expel a shaky breath. "Thank you for your faith in me," I say sincerely. He's a legend. A known taskmaster who doesn't accept anything but the very best from his associates, and exactly the kind of attorney I want to learn from. "I won't let you down."

He smiles and pats me on the shoulder. "I know. I've followed your career. I know you had a misstep, but you being so upfront about this just confirms what I saw when I looked past that stuff."

I return his smile despite the flare of pure, white-hot fucking hate in my chest when I think about how Nigel's cowardly, selfish actions will follow me for the rest of my career. But I guess it's best to go ahead and get this conversation out of the way, too. I steel myself and just say it.

"I know you've read a lot of things, but the way it was reported isn't even close to the truth." I hold his eyes, even though I wish the floor would open and swallow me whole.

He shakes his head. "You don't need to explain anything. I know Lancaster, and now that I've met you, I know you wouldn't throw your career away over some bullshit like that. And I can promise you that this firm doesn't punish people for speaking the truth and doesn't harbor predators, no matter who they are."

I don't trust myself not to sob, so I just nod my head.

He glances at his watch and down the hall toward the elevator and frowns. "I don't know where Barry is, I hoped we could put our heads together before the meeting, but he's late and we need to get started. I'll be honest and tell you he wasn't thrilled I hired you."

I grimace. "Yeah, honestly, after my round with him, I surprised you did."

"He's this office's hiring partner. But this is my firm. Today, he's going to try to show me *and* you that you're in over your head. So it might be best if you just observe today. Because I won't step in to rescue you if you stumble."

I straighten my posture and smile with appreciation. But my spine is tingling. I love being the underdog. It makes victory so much sweeter. "Thanks, Remi. I'll watch my step."

He reaches around me, unlocks the door, and pushes it open. "After you, counselor."

A woman, with the most luscious head of thick white hair I've ever seen in my life, is seated at the table with her laptop and finishes typing something before she looks up. Her face is breathtaking. High forehead, high cheekbones, almond-shaped, dark brown eyes framed by dark, swooping brows that are keen and intense. And her skin, the color of cinnamon, is completely unlined and belies the age her hair and expression attributes.

"Amelia Patel," she says in a light, pretty voice that makes me think she must have a beautiful singing voice. "Counsel for the defendant, partner at Harvey Brooks," she adds. I know who she is. She's the preeminent authority of mass torts, and I was less than generous when I wrote about her a few years ago. She smiles expectantly when I don't respond right away.

She has no idea who I am, but the minute I say my name, she will.

"I'm Confidence Ryan," I say. Her smile disappears, and she drops my hand as if she's realized she's petting a snake and turns to face Remi without saying another word.

I glance at him, and he gives me a wide-eyed *what was that about?* before he turns to address her.

"Confidence is our new Of Counsel. Ms. Ryan is just observing today. We just hired her yesterday and we're still in the on-boarding process, but all her conflicts cleared yesterday, so I wanted to bring her in on this conversation, since she wrote the jurisprudence on it," he says. I swell with pride.

I smile awkwardly because after his introduction, there's really not much for me to say.

"That's very impressive," Hayes says and swivels around in the chair with the abnormally high back that's been turned to face the window.

A rush of gooseflesh runs over my body and a cold dread blooms in my stomach. I bite back my gasp and smile, even though the effort makes my face ache. I knew he was going to be here, but it's still hard to feel comfortable given everything that's going on between us.

"Ah, I didn't see you, kid," Remi says good-naturedly and walks over to Hayes, who stands up. His eyes cut to mine and his expression is completely unreadable.

"Nice view, Wilde." He nods out the window. It overlooks the green of Rivers Wilde, and from here, with red and white awnings and sparkling clean streets, it looks like something out of a postcard.

"It is." Remi smiles, and I want to knock their heads together. "Glad you're here, actually. We have our new lawyer here today, it'll be good—" The door behind us opens and Barry, the partner who is acting as lead lawyer for the case, hurries into the room.

"I'm sorry I'm late, Remington," he says without addressing anyone else—not even the clients. They both stood up when he entered the room, and he dumps his briefcase, a box of files, and his coffee onto the table and mutters to no one in particular, "This fucking traffic is a killer," and they sit down. His toothy grin turns into a thin and insincere smile when he looks at me.

"Oh, I didn't realize *she* was joining us," he says to Remington without addressing me.

"Her conflicts cleared, and I figured this would be a great place to get her feet wet and maybe give her a chance to give input when she gets back," he says without any sign of irritation at Barry's barbed words.

"We don't need her input," Barry says dismissively.

"Why don't you need her input?" Hayes asks, and I stifle a groan at the tone in his voice. I wish he would look at me so I can give him a warning look. I don't want or need him fighting my battles for me.

"Because I think we should settle," Barry says easily, missing the thread of warning in Hayes's voice. The clients both gasp, "What?"

"Trust me," he says in a patronizing voice before he turns his wannabe megawatt smile on Hayes. "Mr. Rivers, I'm Barry Jimenez, the lead attorney for the class," he says and walks over, his beefy hand extended and his chest is puffed out like he's walking into a boxing ring.

Hayes eyes him and then his hand for a moment, just long enough to be awkward before he shakes it. "We're glad you made the time to come today and we're fully prepared to discuss settlement. I know that's what you want and I think it's in everyone's best interest."

"We haven't discussed this," Remi says.

"That's not unusual. I don't discuss case strategy on every case with you." He pushes a lock of his messy brown hair off his forehead, and I think he might be attractive if he wasn't such a jerk.

"I think we should go ahead and settle." He finally addresses his clients and reiterates with a little more deference in his voice.

"I know she's an '*expert.*'" He makes air quotes around the word, and I dislike him even more than I did yesterday. His dismissal of me sets my teeth on edge. "But like I've been saying since her interview, I'm sure she wrote a great paper in law school, but in actual practice, I just don't see how her contribution will be valuable." He waves a hand in my direction and Hayes's lips thin and curl upward in a menacing scowl.

Barry continues to jump on the thin ice he's standing on, oblivious that he's courting danger. Watching Hayes get offended on my behalf pisses me off, because no one has offended me more than he has. And unlike loving him, the world of big law is a jungle I feel perfectly capable of navigating and defending myself.

Remi looks down at the two clients and says, "Could you excuse us, please? I'd like the lawyers to have a chance to talk before we go on. I apologize, but if you two could just wait in the small room you were in before we came in, I'll come get you when we're ready."

One of the women crosses her arms over her chest and sets her chin. "Why doesn't *he* have to leave?" She points at Hayes. "Isn't he a client, too?" she asks. I like her. I'm glad she's not taking their shit.

"I'm leaving, too," Hayes responds. He walks over to the women and offers each of them an arm. His face is solemn, his smile sincere when he says, "Ladies, let me escort you out. Let's leave the dirty work to the lawyers." Ms. Gauthier, the older of the two, smiles prettily, her cheeks flush as she stands up and takes the proffered arm.

"Jo, he's trying to sweeten us up so they can do us wrong," Ms. Swanson says and grabs her friend's elbow and tugs her free of Hayes.

"But I want him to sweeten me up," Jo says and pulls free of her friend. She smiles up at Hayes and takes his arm and bats her eyelashes up at him.

"Your wish is my command," he says smoothly. He holds his elbow out to Ms. Swanson again and says jokingly, "Come on, I don't bite." His smile is so charming that it makes my fool heart flutter.

They walk out of the room, and when Hayes walks past the head of the table where I'm standing, our eyes meet. The air rushes from my lungs. There's unmistakable, naked desire in his eyes. It's territorial and so intense it feels like his hand is around my throat. I flush hot when I remember the way he had me last night.

He smiles and winks subtly before he continues walking.

When the door closes behind him, Barry pounces. "They're offering more money than most of these people will ever see in their lives. Litigation is going to be expensive, and this is a pro bono venture. There isn't much to discuss. I've got a trial coming up and I would like to focus. And maybe I could use Ms. Ryan for the document review there." He says this as if he's doing me a favor.

"Document review? You can't be serious." I gasp before I can stop myself.

Everyone's eyes fly to me, and I feel an immediate pang of regret and close my eyes briefly. But then, I open them and look him in his eyes. Because, truth be told, he's not wrong. I don't think I'm the smartest person in this room. About this topic, I know I am.

"I'm dead serious. I know Remi hired you. But, I made no secret of my opposition. You've got baggage, you think you're the smartest person in the room, and you clearly don't know how to be seen and not heard," he says in rapid fire succession like he's been holding it in.

I glance at Remi and he raises an eyebrow like he's asking *you gonna let him get away with that?*

I look around the room and wish I had a button to press pause. Inside, I'm fuming. But I won't let that show because this is how the best lawyers earn their stripes. Barry Jimenez is one of the best litigators in the country. He's won the Department of Justice's Silver Eagle Award twice. He's only one of a handful of people to ever do it. And he's doing to me what was done to him. I know if I back down, he'll lose any respect he has for me.

I remind myself that he's my boss. When I respond, I say, "I reviewed the settlement offer, and I disagree," I say simply.

"Thanks for your opinion," he says. "Let's get started," he says and pulls open the file folder.

"Gentlemen," he says to all of us and nods at the table. Lucky for me, I've never waited for an invitation to sit at any table and I won't start today.

I sit down, open my file, and start looking over the notes I made.

"So, we're giving everyone six months and a five-thousand-dollar voucher for furniture and clothes, right?" Barry ticks the broad terms off the list on his fingers.

"That's right." Amelia nods.

"I think that sounds very generous," Remi says, and my eyes fly to him. He meets my gaze, and challenges, "Tell me why I'm wrong."

"Yes, *Coincidence*, tell us why all of our years of experience should yield to your law review article," Barry says snidely.

I eye him and let the scorn I'm feeling show.

He's my boss, and I respect his career, and I don't give a shit about him making fun of my name. If anything, it shows how unoriginal he is. But damn if I'm going to sit here and be quiet while he screws our clients.

"My experience may be ten percent of yours when it comes to sitting at tables like this one. But when it comes to the way the law treats uninsured, non-property-owning survivors of natural disasters, you're not even a speck in my rearview mirror. I'm not going to sit here while you sell the people who entrusted their entire futures to you and this firm down the proverbial river. Excuse the pun," I add with a false conciliatory smile for Amelia's benefit.

"Tell us how giving them more money than they'll ever see is selling them short?" Barry says in a dismissive, condescending chuckle.

I have to clench my jaw to keep from growling at him. "I think giving them less than what they deserve and less than what makes them whole is selling them short. This flood will affect them for generations. Homes were lost. Valuable, irreplaceable things are gone. Their children are traumatized. They need some sort of therapy or something to help them work through some of the trauma we are supposed to be helping —"

"Therapy? Give me a fucking break, Remi," Barry cuts me off in a groan of exasperation.

"Remi, I have to agree. This feels like amateur hour," Amelia says and I flush. "You're putting a foal who doesn't know how to walk into a pasture full of hungry wolves," she says derisively.

"Amelia," Remi says in a warning tone.

She purses her lips. "My client and I are leaving. We will send a final settlement offer. You tell us what you think. We want to make people whole, but we're not paying for more than that," she says. She gathers her dark leather Gucci briefcase and strolls out.

Barry rounds on me. " Look *Conscience,* the kids in these communities are conditioned in way yours and mind aren't," he says, and this time I decide his intentional flubbing of my name is actually a Freudian slip. I'll happily be our collective conscience. Someone needs to be champion for the people who aren't here to make their voices heard.

"How, exactly are they *conditioned?*"

"They live in neighborhoods where crisis abounds," he says as if it's not a woefully insufficient answer.

I roll my eyes . "Have you been to their neighborhood?" I ask the question of everyone at the table.

Both of them shake their head no. Disappointment settles heavily around my shoulders that Remi hasn't either. "Why in the world not? How could you take this case without seeing what they were dealing with?"

"We've seen pictures; that's sufficient," Barry says.

"That is *not* sufficient," I snap. My voice is sharp, but I find it reprehensible that no one has even been there.

"Sorry, who the *fuck* are you, even? Why are you doing more than getting me coffee at this point?" Barry says suddenly. His temper has apparently broken free of whatever was caging it.

"*Coffee?* Who are you talking to?" I sputter. Propriety is forgotten; I am incensed

"You." He points at me, his teeth bared.

Remi stands up and comes between us.

"Listen, I'm not here to be a referee. Barry, this isn't a dictatorship. But, Confidence, I think we should at least entertain an offer. Let's see what they come back with," Remi says, and the stony glare on his face doesn't leave room for any push back.

The conference room doors open and hits the wall behind it so hard it bounces off.

"You're fired," Ms. Swanson says when she bursts into the room.

Barry glares daggers. "Look what she's done," he hisses and points at me accusingly.

"No, I'm talking to you," Ms. Swanson says to Barry. "You are fired. We want her. You don't care about us. We've been talking and we don't want to settle. We want someone who will do what's right and not what's easy. And if we can't get her, then we'll go somewhere else, and try to convince them to hire her over there. But either way, you're fired." Then she turns and storms out of the room, slamming the door behind her.

"You know what? Good luck," Barry snaps. "And Remi, just a heads-up since you're clearly too blind to see it, but Hayes Rivers is fucking her. Or at least, he wants to." His eyes rake over me with a lascivious, angry light in his dark eyes. "And maybe you do, too, because I don't know why the fuck you hired her." He gathers up his files and briefcase and storms out of the conference room.

Remi shakes his head and looks at me as he starts toward the door.

"I've got to leave for the day. I have a client to see. I've got some questions I need you to answer. And consider yourself the new lead counsel for this case."

"You're not going to fire me?" I breathe out in a rush before I can stop myself.

"No, I'm not," he says like he can't believe it himself. "You better be worth all this trouble."

Relief—rich and hot—floods through me, and I wonder if this is how people who receive a reprieve from death feel.

"I promise I—"

"I run at seven a.m. every morning," he says abruptly, and that shuts me up and brings my eyes to his face. He's frowning at me.

"Good…for you?" I say when he doesn't elaborate.

"Very good for me. And, while I'm running, I want to be reading your answers. I'll expect them in my inbox by then. You're down a team member, so plan on being here all night, Ryan," he says and then he's gone.

Chapter 20

SETTLING

HAYES

"You can't go in there, Mr. Rivers." The frantic voice of the woman sitting at the desk outside of Remington's office calls after me as I walk right past her into his office.

"Wilde, what the hell—" I stop in my tracks. He's not alone. Confidence, that asshole who'd talked to my woman like she was beneath him, and two men and one other woman are sitting huddled around the small conference table in front of the corner window of his office.

"Rivers, what the hell?" Remi stands up and looks over my shoulder.

"Mr. Wilde, he just walked right past me," the woman says from behind me.

"Rachel, it's fine. Just shut the door behind you," he says to her before he looks back at me.

Confidence is watching me like a deer caught in the headlights.

"What are you doing here?" Remi asks, and I look back at him.

"You rejected our settlement offer. Last week when we met you seemed ready to entertain it. Do you know how hard I had to lobby to get them to agree to the terms we presented? You will not get a single dime more out of us," I warn him.

"Oh, yes, we will," says Confidence as she stands up.

The other man slams his hand onto the table. "Remi, I am not going to sit here and watch this shit. You hired this person over my objection. You're letting her pilot this and she's decided to go full kamikaze."

"Barry, we've discussed this." Remington's voice is low, but it's got a thread of steel in it that raises my already high esteem of this guy even higher. It says more than the four words he spoke.

But Barry's rage has blinded him to the danger.

"No, she wants to stick it to her ex, so she's using this lawsuit as a weapon," he spits out.

"I'm not her fucking ex," I say.

"Okay, fine, her former fuck buddy, whatever," he spits. I turn to him and look at him more closely. Who the fuck is this guy?

"What the fu—"

"Barry, you're about to cross a line," Remi says and shoots me a warning glance.

"You've already crossed one, Remi. I know this is your firm, but I'm a partner, too. And I won't sit here and watch all of you be hypnotized by a nice ass and a smile," he says.

"You better shut the fuck up," I growl, and Confidence stands up, her shock apparently worn enough to loosen her tongue.

"Hayes, I don't need you to fight my battles—"

"Remi, this is highly inappropriate. You shouldn't have hired her in the first place. But to assign her to this case—it presents a clear conflict of interest." He cuts her off and rakes his eyes over her body in a way that nobody but me is allowed to look at her.

I walk over to him and get in his face. "You've got one more time to interrupt her, insult her, or look at her," I growl.

"Or what? You going to beat me up?" he asks. "I heard you like to do that," he says with a small smirk.

"All of you, stop it!" Confidence shouts angrily. Her fists are balled at her sides, her shoulders are hunched, and she's squeezed her eyes shut. "First of all, stop talking about me like I'm not here," she says. "You're arguing about who gets to have their way. Who gets to decide. And while you're doing that, people are living in limbo *at best*. At worst, they're sheltered in homes with walls breeding mildew. They are terrified that their children are breathing mold spores when they put them to sleep in the only home they can manage to find for them." She slaps her hands down on the table and leans forward. She looks between us.

"They're not greedy, grasping idiots that we should pay off so we can get back to defending white-collar criminals and helping banks find new ways to screw their customers," she hisses. She looks at Barry and shakes her head. "Do you think I want your job? I don't. There's a whole slew of things you know more about than I can ever hope to, but *this* is my specialty. And the size of my tits, the color of my hair, or the man I love, have nothing to do with any of it. This is not about you and how you feel about women or me," she snaps. She is vibrating with passion, and she's never been more breathtaking than she is right now.

I'm struck by the certainty of a few things. One, this woman loves me. She's trying to forgive me. But, I also know that if her clients end up with less than what they deserve, her estimation of me will always suffer for it. And my estimation of *myself*, as a man who is worthy of leading this family—with *her* by my side—into a future we can be proud of, will suffer too.

She looks at Remi, and her voice softens. "Thank you for taking a chance on me. Thank you for trusting me with this," she says and then glances at me.

"But I will not work in an office where you allow your employees to talk to people like he's been speaking with me. So, if this is the culture of your firm, then as soon as this case is over, I'll be resigning," she says gravely.

"Confidence—" Remi starts. But she's already turned to me.

"Hayes. What Kingdom offered is woefully insufficient to compensate the victims of the company's negligence and disregard. You have suits that cost more than what you're offering the individual families."

She casts her damning eye over me again. "If you can afford to buy clothes like *that*, you can afford to make those people truly whole. And that's not going to come with some cookie-cutter settlement in hopes that this will go away quickly. Because that's all that money is designed to do." She condemns me with her honesty. What I see in her eyes is much more than disappointment. It's disenchantment. Distance. I feel my first real pang of panic that she knows that I'm not good enough. That she really won't forgive me. The thought grips my gut in a fist of fear. My collar is suddenly too tight and I can't think of a single thing to say in my own defense.

She shakes her head at all of us. "None of you have even been to the sites. Or even talked to the people whose lives you're discussing. They're just some figment of your imagination right now," she chastises us.

"You know what, I've had about enough of this. This is a business," asshole says in a harsh dismissal of everything she just said.

But Confidence is not easily dismissed, and while on her soapbox, with her shield held up in protection of someone else, she is persistence personified. "You're *wrong*," she insists. Her voice is bolstered by her conviction.

Asshole's eyes narrow. His animosity for Confidence is rolling off him in waves. If she's concerned, she doesn't show it.

She keeps pushing.

"*This* is the practice of law. *We* are lawyers. Social engineers. Or least, we should be. We are here to ensure the best possible outcome for our clients. And you want to settle because you don't think they're worth the price of seeking justice on their behalf," she accuses him.

He leans toward her.

My chest tightens and my whole body tenses, but I don't move a muscle or take my eyes off him.

When he speaks, his voice is a snarl. "You're damn straight. I am not going to worry about people who, when they die, no one will care. We represent people who are captains of industries and who will be remembered forever. The fucking flood didn't go far enough, as far as I'm concerned."

The woman at the table, a thirty-something blonde in a nondescript black suit, gasps.

"Jimenez," Remi calls his name. That thread of steel is now a fully woven rope.

"Yeah?" Barry responds as if it's an imposition to do so.

"How long have you worked here?" Remi asks.

"Five years."

Remi actually looks surprised. "Already? Damn, time flies," he says.

"Yes, and I care about Wilde Law. I'm not going to stand by and watch the firm undermined by what amounts to some sort of affirmative action hire. I know we wanted more women at the table, but let's hire them for the size of their brains, not their breasts." He shoots a venomous glance at Confidence and a rush of anger pushes me to my feet.

Both Confidence and Remi say my name at the same time.

I look to find them both watching me. Confidence with a wary alertness, Remi with anger I know isn't directed at me.

"Then, one of you better do something about it," I say and sit down.

"Barry, we'll be sure to give you an excellent reference. You're fired. Effective today," Remi says.

Barry's jaw drops, but he doesn't make a sound.

No one does.

The room had been quiet before, but now, you could hear a pin drop.

Remi turns to look at the blonde. "Mila, can you take him down with you? I'm adjourning the meeting. We'll regroup later."

"Wait, you're fucking firing me? For what?" Barry sputters, regaining his composure.

"For violating conduct clauses in your contract," Remi says simply. His eyes hold the same steel as his voice.

Barry's face crumbles. "I just bought a fucking Porsche, and I put a deposit down for a pool," he says.

"Nice priorities," I say under my breath, and Remi shoots me a glare. I shrug unapologetically.

"I don't deserve to be fired!" he shouts, his eyes wide. He looks around the table for support, but everyone, except for Mila and me, has their face conveniently buried in a phone or iPad.

"You'll get a month's severance for every year you've worked here. With all of your experience and seniority, you'll have a job in no time. Mila will make every resource we have available to you in pursuit of that. But you can't work here any longer. It's just that simple. I'm sure you understand."

He lifts his head slowly and looks between the two of us wordlessly. His expression, completely blank.

"Barry? Are you okay?" Confidence asks. Her expression goes from concern to worry as she takes in the slack look on his face. Her voice triggers something in him because all of a sudden, his jaw tightens and his eyes focus their burning anger on her.

"Think you're so clever, don't you? Think you're going to win a fucking prize or something for your stupid case? I can't wait to see you fall flat on your face," he says with a voice so cold and vicious that Confidence flinches and takes a step back. It takes every ounce of restraint I possess not to walk over and throw him out of the window.

"Barry, please stop making threats," Mila says, sounding mildly bored. "I'd hate for you to leave with a police escort instead of on your

own. But you better believe I've got my finger on security's number."
She stands, folds her hands over her chest, and watches him impassively.

"Oh, I'm leaving. I wouldn't give you two femi-nazis the satisfaction
of seeing me really lose my cool," he sneers.

"And you keep your shitty severance. I'm calling a lawyer. I'm going
to take you to the cleaners, Remi," he spits as he starts walking.

When he slams the door behind him, the windows of the conference room rattle from the force.

"What an idiot," Mila says and walks over to where Confidence
slumps over in her chair. I start toward her. She looks at me and shakes
her head, no. Her blue eyes are glassy but unwavering.

"Are you okay?" Mila asks, peering down at her in concern.

"I'm fine," Confidence says and swallows hard. "Violent men and I
don't mix," she says with a nervous laugh. But I see the tremble in her
hand when she pushes an errant curl behind her ear.

I want to kill that man for putting that there. I hate that I can't walk
over and put an arm around her. I hate this distance. I'm done letting it
grow between us.

Chapter 21

UNEXPECTED

CONFIDENCE

"That line outside is incredible," I say, wide-eyed, to Remi as we stack the clothes that have been folded and sorted by gender and size into the bins lined along the five-hundred-yard-long convention center room. The volunteers are all busy at work setting up their stations for the doors to open at eight o'clock. "They did a great job getting the word out and there are shuttles all day for people who need it," I tell him.

"Yeah, the Rivers kid is putting his money where his mouth is, that's for sure," he says and reaches for another box of clothes the organizers just dropped off.

"Why do you call him 'kid'?" I ask a question that's been burning at the tip of my tongue.

"Because when I met him, that's what he was. And now, because it annoys him," he says with a laugh. I laugh along.

"You knew him when y'all were kids?" I ask, my curiosity about how his family's community is named after another family.

"No. Our families have been neighbors for thirty years now. When they bought the land from the Riverses in the oil bust in the eighties, the name of the development was one of the terms of the contract. And they hated having to sell part of their empire to a bunch of fresh-off-the-boat immigrants who made their money selling plantains in the hood," he says.

"Plantains in the hood?" I chortle.

He chuckles. "Yeah, we lived in one of the parts of the city that was like a food desert. No good grocery stores. Just corner stores—Popeyes, Church's Chicken, Shipley's Donut Shop, if you were lucky. So, my grandfather saved the money he made painting houses and opened Eat!. That was our first business. And who knew that grocery stores that catered to every single palette it could source for would be so popular?"

"Well, apparently your grandfather did," I say. They have three hundred and fifty stores in Texas and about two dozen in northeast Mexico.

"Yeah, and he and my dad founded Rivers Wilde. My mom's brainchild was Wilde Restaurants, Crick Crack being the very first," he says.

"Wow, it's amazing you've done all that in one generation."

"Yeah. We're kind of ambitious. And Houston is the most fertile ground for ideas that are all about the hustle. My mother's Jamaican, so she's got to have at least three jobs or she feels like she's being idle," he says.

"What about your dad?" I ask.

"He's dead," he answers in an uncharacteristically flat, hard voice.

"I'm sorry," I say.

"No worries, he has been for a long time," he says, with a dismissive wave of his hand. "Anyway, so I met Hayes once—because our families were enemies in a way that felt like a law. And then I ran into him in this little patch of land between our properties on the day of his dad's funeral. I called him kid. He didn't like it, so I did it repeatedly and now he's back and it's just stuck."

I laugh, but I don't feel like laughing. I miss Hayes. Like crazy. And I haven't seen him since that day in our office when I turned down his settlement offer. When this event was announced a week ago, I realized what he'd been busy doing.

"How are you guys doing?" he asks.

"We're not. But it's fine," I say, and wish that was true. Fine is the last thing I am.

"Does he know that?" Remi asks, and his eyes are trained over my shoulder. I turn and see Hayes walking in.

His scan of the room comes to a screeching halt when his eyes land on me. He smiles and starts toward me. My heart leaps in anticipation. I haven't seen him in two weeks.

A man steps in his way and starts to talk. The reluctance he shows to look away almost makes up for the fact that he had to stop.

"All right, folks. It's eight o'clock and the doors are opening. Man your stations!" a woman shouts over a bullhorn and I almost jump out of my skin in surprise.

"My brother Tyson will be here, and he's going to switch out with me at eleven a.m. And I'll be back at one o'clock. When you need someone to step in for you, let me know and I'll find a volunteer."

"Okay. But I think I'll be good. I brought snacks and I'm ready," I say and rub my hands together in anticipation. Today feels like the first time I'm actually doing anything meaningful for my clients.

After we rejected their settlement offer, the case was assigned a court date. In the meantime, I'm doing my interviews with my clients and preparing for our first hearing that's six weeks away.

Right now, it feels like we'll never get the mountains of records that we've requested. Kingdom, the corporation, is doing everything it can to stall. They asked for six weeks to even produce the documents we've asked for. So, we've filed for a continuation to give us time to review them. When I say *us*, I'm talking about my little team of four. One of whom hates my guts. And while all of this is happening, the people in the class are struggling to get their lives back together and are living in limbo.

The Kingdom Foundation, directed by Hayes, organized a clothing and book drive. The donations poured in. Today is shopping day for the families. I got here at 6:30 a.m. to help set up, and the line had already started forming. I catch a glimpse of Hayes disappearing in the direction of the picture section. But before I can call after him, the doors open and the people file in. We're in the boys' section, "Size twelve months to four years" in the store, and before we have the chance to speak to each other again, our first customers stand at our table. Instantly, I recognize the boy from Hayes's house the night of the flood. "Hey there," I say.

"Hi." He smiles brightly.

"Do you remember me?" I ask.

"Yeah. Of course. And thank you for volunteering today," he says like he's reciting something memorized and just remembered he needed to say.

"You're welcome. What nice manners," I respond.

"Well, this was all my idea," he beams.

"Was it?" I ask and look over his shoulder to make sure no one's waiting to actually be served. "You must be very proud of how it's all turned out then," I say jokingly.

He nods. "Yeah, the first time Mr. Hayes came to visit, he asked me what I thought folks needed, and I told him clothes for school," he says and my heart actually jumps.

"M-Mr. Hayes came to see you?" I ask, saying each word slowly, so that I can make sure he doesn't misunderstand me.

"Yeah, well, more than once—and not just me. We went around and met with lots of people," he says.

"What types of meetings?" I ask skeptically.

"Him asking questions about their living situation, families, and asking everyone to give him an idea of what they needed to feel comfortable. I took notes, and he even paid me for my time," he says proudly.

"Wow, well, that sounds awesome," I say and smile. And this time, there's not a well of pain behind it.

"Anyway, I just wanted to say hi. And thank you for being here and being the reason Mr. Hayes even came to visit us. He told us you suggested it," he says.

A peal of laughter propelled by relief bursts from my throat.

"Did he? That's awesome," I say.

"He's pretty cool." The young man nods.

"See you later." He waves and walks off.

I feel like crying at what I just heard, but I also feel completely giddy. For the last two weeks, my coffee order has been ready and waiting for me when I walk into Sweet and Lo's. I've had flowers on my desk every morning, my lunch delivered every afternoon. My car washed while it was parked in the garage of my office. Hayes has been relentless in his attempts to woo me.

But this…done not to woo me back, but because he's a good man trying to do right is the first thing he's done that makes me feel like maybe he sees me. That he's not just trying to convince me, but that he's doing it for himself, too. That thought makes me unbearably happy. I brush my tears away and turn around just in time to greet my very first customers.

Chapter 22

KNEEL

CONFIDENCE

"I'll have the meatloaf sandwich," I say to my waitress.

"Oh yeah, great choice." She smiles widely. "It's delicious."

"Everything here is delicious," Tyson says. His dark brown eyes twinkle with mischief, and he says, "including some of the diners." He grins and then winces. He glares at his older brother. "Remi, yo," he says in a comically, high-pitched voice while rubbing the side of his head that his brother just slapped.

"Stop talking to her like she's one of those THOTs in that little fan club of yours," Remi says without looking up from the menu.

"Yo, can I help it if they love me? I mean, maybe if you stopped and smelled the roses instead of trying to be some sort of superhuman legend, you'd get some of that love, too," he says.

I look back between the brothers and shake my head. "Can you guys please stop bickering? The car ride over was enough of that to last me a lifetime. I'd like to have some quiet with my air-conditioning and beer, please," I say.

"See, Remi, she likes me." He winks at me. "Can you stop getting in between us?" He drags his chair close to mine. "Excuse me, miss, but you've got some dust on your arm," he says and brushes the remnants of our afternoon off my arm.

"You're such a flirt, Ty," I say with mock disapproval.

"Only with the prettiest girls," he says and winks. His gaze drifts over my shoulder. I don't think anything of it until I see a gleam of mischief. He slings an arm over my shoulder, and I jump in surprise and then relax.

This is how he talks to everyone. All day, his contribution was keeping the people waiting in the incredibly long lines in a good mood. And he's good at it. Charming, funny, and very nice to look at. It made me feel better. Now that we've rejected the settlement offer, things with Kingdom are moving at a snail's pace. But this week there was a break in the clouds for our clients whose homes were beyond simple repairs. Remi took me to the land on the outer barrier of Rivers Wilde where Habitat for Humanity is going to be building homes for the residents.

A shiver passes over me and the hairs on the back of my neck stand up and I feel Hayes before I see him. Before I can turn around, I *hear* him.

"Remi," Hayes says in greeting, and his voice ricochets through me like a canon's boom.

My heart leaps into my throat. His proximity is frying my circuits, and I can't even remember what I was talking about or doing two minutes earlier.

"Ty." His voice is less friendly when he addresses Tyson.

Remi slides over and says, "Join us, Rivers."

He does and sits down right next to me.

"Confidence," he says quietly, and I shoot him a sidelong glance. I wish I hadn't.

The annoyed expression in his eyes is tinged with longing and it hits me in the center of my chest. His light gray T-shirt blends with the color of his eyes, and with the dim lighting of the restaurant, they look almost green today.

His gaze moves to Tyson, who has moved closer to me since Hayes sat down. He lifts his eyebrows in his classic *what the fuck do you think you're doing?* look.

I give him a *why do you think you have the right to ask?* glare.

"Rivers, I have to tell you, I think I'm in love with her, so I might need you to back off," Ty says good-naturedly. "You gotta watch out for him. He's the most committed bachelor in town," he whispers to me.

"Tyson, please remove your arm from my woman's shoulder,"

Hayes says in a deceptively calm voice. I bristle at that.

"I'm not his woman," I say.

His body tenses and he growls, "Like hell."

"Well, one of you is clearly very confused." Remi laughs.

"It's not me," I say.

The next second, Hayes's hand wraps around my bicep, and he's pulling me out of the booth.

"What in the world are you doing?" I yelp.

"You two don't break anything," Remington calls after us. I turn around and give him a look of complete bewilderment.

Why is he laughing?

Why isn't he calling the police?

"Hayes, let me go." I slap at his hand. He doesn't even look at me.

He pulls me down a long corridor, pushes open a door and switches on the bathroom light.

"What the fuck was that?" he asks.

"What the fuck was *what?* I'm not the one who just dragged me through a restaurant."

He crosses the small room in two strides and pushes me up against the sink. Not to intimidate or scare me. He's never been able to do either. Not since the night we met.

"You're not my woman? Are you fucking serious, Confidence?" he asks angrily.

"Hayes, what do you think——?"

"That was a rhetorical question," he growls and cuts me off and leans toward me.

"Not for me." I lean forward, too.

He shakes his head at me like he can't believe what he's hearing and takes a step back. He shoves his fingers through his hair.

"At least you're consistent," he mutters under his breath, but the bathroom has great acoustics and it bounces off the wall and hangs between us.

"What does that mean?"

"It means you know how to hold a grudge. And I've given you space to do it," he says.

"You've given me *space?*" I gape at him.

"Yes," he snarls and steps closer to me. "But there are fucking limits. And you clearly don't understand them."

"Oh, I understand *just* fine," I seethe.

"No, you don't," he says through gritted teeth. "Because if you did, you wouldn't be telling another man that you're not my woman. While his arm is around you." His eyes narrow, and his hands grip the sink on either side of me.

"Hayes—"

"You must have completely forgotten who I am." His eyes darken and he leans into me.

"How could I?" I snap.

"Then, did you forget who *we* are?" He leans against the door and turns the little knob in the handle. His eyes are blazing as he strides toward me. "I won't tell you how that felt. But trust me when I say you wouldn't have liked being in my shoes."

I flush and glance away from his eyes. I can see the hurt there, and as mad as I am at him, it's the very last thing I want to do to him. "I'm sorry. You're right."

"*Tesoro…*" He grips my chin and turns my head until he traps my eyes with his. They are full of determination, and they hold me in place. "I know you're pissed. You have every right to be. But don't get Tyson's ass kicked because you want to hurt me," he growls.

Worry tickles the back of my throat. "As if you'd go around beating up people because he was flirting with me." I dismiss his threat.

He leans in and puts us nose to nose, and then he rubs the tip of his against mine. "I absolutely fucking would," he whispers, and I'm caught between a swoon and pang of worry.

I pull my chin out of his grip. "This isn't a Kristen Ashley novel. You're not Dax Lahn. I'm not Circe," I snap.

He blinks and shakes his head in confusion. "I have no idea what that means."

"It's a book. And all I mean is that I want to stand on my own two feet so that no one can ever say different." My voice is stiff and lacks conviction. But it's just a reflection of what's happening inside of me. I don't even believe myself anymore.

"Is that why you didn't tell me about the interview at Wilde? You thought I'd use my connections to help you?"

"No, I thought you'd be pissed because they're your family's enemies."

"Not anymore. And I would have been happy that you found a job that felt worthy of your talents."

His expression is earnest and my heart starts to melt. "But he's representing the people who are suing you. I'm on his side."

"You and I are *always* going to be on the same side." He points between us. "They're not suing me, they are suing *Kingdom*."

His nonchalant demeanor is driving me crazy. "Hayes, we broke up and you haven't taken it seriously. You act like you're just waiting for this tantrum to stop. You've never acknowledged that you hurt me." I point an accusing finger at him. "And until you do, no matter how much I love you, I can't just act like it didn't happen. I'm moving here for this job, not you."

His eyes narrow and he exhales a long breath. "I think different. You took this job because you miss me and want to be where I am." he pushes back.

Bullseye. But I'm not ready to admit it. Not until I know he gets why this matters. "I took the job because I needed it, and it's perfect. If it had been in Alaska, that's where I'd be too."

He rakes his eyes down my body. My white blouse feels thin under his heated gaze. I shift in my shoes when he lingers on my hips.

"You've missed me," he says.

"I haven't," I lie.

"If I touched your pussy, what would I feel?" he asks.

"That's one question you won't be answering tonight."

"I want to touch you." He dips his head and kisses my cheek. His hand grips my hip.

"You'll feel better when I've made you come," he whispers against my cheek.

He moves so fast that my ass is up on the edge of the sink before I can protest.

"Do you want me to stop?" he asks. His finger trails up my leg and stops at my knee. Blood rushes in my ears, heat pools between my thighs.

"Of course not." I breathe.

His fingers slip under the hem of my shorts, and I grab his fingers.

"But I'm going to ask you to anyway." His eyes fly up to mine in surprise, but there's no anger there. In fact, I think what I see is respect.

"Why?" he asks and stands back up.

If it could speak, my vagina would be cursing me out.

"Because what I want isn't what I need, Hayes."

"Why are they mutually exclusive?"

"I don't want to just be your partner in bed," I admit.

"Oh, *Tesoro*." He sighs and drags his nose across my temple before he moves us back to facing each other. He cups my face in his hands and presses a soft kiss to my lips before he pulls back.

"There's not a pussy in this world I'd fall on my knees for. Not even yours," he says, the fierce love and tenderness in his eyes stealing my breath.

His eyes never leaving mine, he continues. "But for this, *Tesoro…*" His palms cover the space between my breasts and my heart kicks against the wall of my chest, desperate to find its way into the hand of the man it loves.

"For the love of the most brilliant woman I've ever met." He kisses me again. "I would spend the rest of my *life* on my fucking knees."

And then, my big, strong, beautiful man brings my entire world to a halt. He drops to his knees in front of me. On the floor of the public restroom.

"Hayes, get up." I tug his arm. "Please."

He grips my hips and presses his face in between my legs and inhales.

"Goddamn." His groan vibrates against me and moisture blooms beneath his mouth and nose. "I love the way your pussy smells. I fucking miss the way it tastes. I'm dying to feel it gripping my cock." He rubs his nose against my clit and pleasure skitters, like the kiss of butterfly wings, all over my body.

I thread my fingers into his thick, silky hair just as he leans away and stares up at me with that same fierceness.

But now, it's laced with need.

He has the look of a predator, and I wish he would hurry up and catch me.

"I want to plant my flag there so that everyone knows it's mine. But it's not even in the top five of my favorite things about you, Confidence. And it's certainly not the only thing I want." He looks up at me through his honest, smart eyes, and the rest of the world falls away.

"Oh, Hayes…" I trace the line of his strong brows and sweep down the slope of his nose.

"I want your fire. I want your courage; I want your loyalty. I want your anger, your disdain, your disappointment." I brush a lock of hair off his forehead. "I want your smiles. I want your laughter. I want you fighting for my team. And yes, I want your pussy. Every day." He squeezes my hips, and I want to give him everything he's just asked me for.

I grapple for what to say, caught between my fear and my love and neither one of them are serving me well.

"Stubborn, stubborn woman," he chides me gently, but with real reproach in his voice. "But I understand." He cuts off my protest. "You want to protect yourself. But you can't. Not from me. Not from us."

"Hayes…" I pull back slightly and shake my head. I don't know what to say.

"I know," he says with real regret in his eyes. "I fucked up. But I'm *not* that asshole who treated you like you were nothing. I'm not ashamed of anything except of what I said to my brother before I knew you. I'll never stop trying to make up for that," he says.

My hand comes to my chest and my fingers clutch the front of my blouse. "Oh, Hayes," is all I can manage.

His eyes go from pleading to demanding in a blink. "But, I need you to understand—"

"That you thought I was hiding something?" I interject.

"No," he says sharply. "That I'm responsible for my entire family. Not just the ones that are alive right now. But the ones who *will* be alive in a hundred years. I lost sight of that once and married someone who I barely knew."

"Well, *I'm* not *her*," I remind him.

"I know that… By the time the report came, I didn't care what it said."

"You didn't?" I ask, too overwhelmed to do more than parrot back his words.

"I already knew everything that I needed to know about you. You're the woman who leans in when most people lean away," he says. He cups my face. "I'm going to show you why us. *How* us."

I want so badly to throw my arms around his neck and tell him it's okay. That I see him, and that I'll always lean in. As if he can sense it, he adds a caveat.

"I'm asking for a lot. Your love. Your loyalty. Your body. Your children. Your life," he says. "But I'm offering you the same things in return."

Tears sting my eyes, and I search his. All I see reflects my own feelings.

"I want you to be my partner. I'm not taking no for an answer, not when I know you feel the same way," he says.

He reaches up and swipes a tear off my cheek with the pad of his thumb.

"I miss you," I admit.

His eyes flare. "It's about fucking time." Fierce need replaces the tenderness, and he surges to his feet. Without pausing, he steps between my legs and pushes my knees open. "And I'm going to let you go home without fucking you. Even though I know you want me to."

He chucks me under the chin. "But let me tell you, when we're right and we're back, I'm going to wreck your pussy. I'm not good with words, baby, but when I fuck you, I feel like you always know what I'm saying." He grinds into me. "But let me speak your language for a minute, so that when I tell you that I love you, you don't just hear it. You understand it. And you don't question it," he says.

"I know you love me. I do…"

He takes my hand in his and puts it to his lips. "Let me show you what you've shown me," he says softly.

"What's that?"

"What it's like to be part of a team that you can trust. That won't let you down," he says. "Give me a chance. Please." He comes as close to begging as I'd ever like to hear him again.

"Okay," I acquiesce. "But you better not fuck it up."

"Oh, I intend to fuck it up, but in the best way possible," he says and then he kisses my blues away.

Chapter 23

BIASED

HAYES

"You're early," Confidence groans, one eye open, but squinting. Her hair is tousled all over her head and her face is creased with the indentation from her pillow. She looks like every single fantasy I ever had as a boy and everything I thought I'd never have as a man.

I hold up the white wax bag full of pastries and wave them in front of her face.

"Breakfast," I say and drop a kiss on her warm, sleep plumped lips and step inside of her apartment.

"The place looks like nobody lives here," I say as I look around at the blandly and sparsely decorated space. "Where did you get this couch?" I ask as I drop onto the gray loveseat. Besides the glass coffee table, it's the only furniture in the entire space.

Well, except her bedroom. Not that she would let me in there. But the door is open, and I can see her sea of white comforters and pillows strewn all over the queen-sized bed in the center of the room.

"Ikea," she grumbles.

"Sleep well?" I ask and start unpacking the bag.

"Uh, not really," she says, and with a resigned sigh, she sits down next to me. She draws her knees to her chest and hugs them. Her pink tank top pulls tight across her back, and I watch her shoulder muscles flex when she rolls her neck as if trying to loosen it up. I slide my fingers under the drape of her hair and caress her nape until I find the knot of tension. I start to rub it, and she closes her eyes and moans.

"That feels so good," she whispers. I don't respond. I just watch her. The skin under her eyes is dark, little lines bracket her frowning mouth. She looks tired and stressed.

"Why aren't you sleeping well?" I ask. Her eyes open and she looks at me wearily.

"Because I'm afraid I've given my clients bad advice," she says and then jerks her head to the side. "Ugh, what am I doing?" she says in a harsh whisper to herself. "I can't be talking to you—of all people— about this." She sighs. "I'm losing my mind; I'm so tired. And Barry getting fired has turned into a nightmare. Word has gotten around, thanks to Barry spreading it, that I asked Remi to choose between him or me. And that's earned me a flock of…" She trails off, searching for the right word.

"Enemies?" I offer and press deeper against the muscle in her neck.

She lets her head loll backward, and her hair spills around my hand. It's warm and soft and my fingers immediately start to close into a fist to capture it. I want to yank her head back and kiss her like I should have when I walked in. But I relax my hand when she closes her eyes and groans.

"*Enemies* may be a little strong," she says and then chuckles ruefully. "But only a little." She shakes her head and sighs. "This is why I hated my last job. No one cares about anything but their careers, their egos, kissing the ass of the person they think can help them. And it's like everyone here has forgotten why we practice law," she says, her voice full of frustration.

"You're being awfully judgmental. They're practicing law, too. Everyone, even white-collar criminals and profit-driven, billion-dollar companies deserve a fair defense," I push back.

"I didn't say they didn't. Everyone is entitled to whatever protections and remedies the law affords. But working in areas of law where there's no money to be made is so disheartening," she says.

"Why? I thought you were doing some good?"

"Well, we would be if law firms like Wilde did it for more than the tax write-off. Our clients are too poor to even keep a roof over their head, much less pay for our very expensive, very well researched advice.

But that's what we promised them. I wouldn't want them to be worse off than they would have been if we hadn't brought the suit at all," she says and worries the inside of her lower lip.

"How's that possible? They've got you," I say.

"*I'm* not enough. Wilde is committing minimal resources to their pro bono cases. But this one is different. The implications of its outcomes are huge. Precedent setting potential, and it's barely staffed. So I'm doing the work of four people because I can't leave legal research that is going to determine what our brief argues to second year law students. This is too important. And no one else seems to think so," she snaps bitterly, and I feel the same guilt I felt when she challenged us the day Barry was fired.

It got me thinking about what I came home to do. What I wanted the legacy of my leadership for my family to be. Did I want to reaffirm our roles as society leaders, or did I want to do some good for the city that had made us rich? Did I want my name on a stadium? Or did I want to build schools? Affordable, quality housing, fill food deserts with grocery stores?

I've decided—and I wanted to show her, instead of tell her—what my plans were.

"What more ideal conditions would exist for it than with Wilde Law? They have deep pockets and nice office space and yeah, it's a tax write-off, but you didn't see other firms clamoring to take the case for free in the first place. They do good work. They have some of the world's best legal talent to choose from," I say and hand her one of the kolaches from Sweet and Lo's.

"Yeah, but they don't dedicate those resources, people, or money that the case deserves because they think their clients should just shut up and be grateful," she says resentfully.

"You've got a chip on your shoulder about this," I say and she nudges me with that shoulder.

"Hey, watch out—that thing is heavy," I tease her. That earns me a fierce little scowl.

"I do not."

"You do. And you tend to paint wealthy people into shapes that are distorted by your bias for, and dislike of, them," I challenge her.

She lets go of her legs and plants her feet on the ground. Her mouth opens in an affront, her eyes wide with offense at my word.

"I am not biased," she says in a high-pitched, loud voice.

I laugh. "Chill, it's okay. We're all biased. You just don't know it.

Because you're walking around thinking that you're being judged for being poor. You wear it like it's Joseph's multi-color cloak. Your suffering is not more valid because you didn't have money at the same time, Confidence," I say and her face turns red. "And yes, I agree that I have an obligation to the people whose money I've collected in the form of rent. But you're a lawyer, so you know that the way this plays out won't have anything to do with what my beliefs are. It's not a personal decision, it's a business one. And the business will do what is best for it. It's not going to pay them more money because we feel sorry for them," I tell her.

"They are not *them*. They are us. A country is only as strong as its poorest citizens, Hayes. So you should feel sorry for *us* as a nation because *we* are poor. And it *should* be a personal decision. This is not about contracts to rebuild. This is about Kingdom admitting that they have contributed heavily to the catastrophe their fellow Houstonians find themselves facing, and we will, in equal measure, contribute to the mitigation of the damage," she shouts at me.

"I agree," I say grimly.

"God, Hayes… I'm sorry," she says and covers her mouth with her hands. "This is inappropriate. For me to be discussing this case. And I understand about your hands being tied. I get it. You can't commit Kingdom to terms that are completely against its interests." She drops back down and rests her head on my shoulder. I wrap my arm around her and pull her into me.

"I wish I could snap my fingers and have them make different decisions. But I can't."

"No, I know…" she says as if she's trying to convince herself as much as me. "Maybe I'm being crazy. I'm committing career suicide by being the architect of a case that could change the way insurance companies, cities, governments, and banks treat people who have been the victims of natural disasters. I'll never find a job in this industry again," she says.

A lightbulb goes on in my head, and I sit up.

"What are you thinking?" she asks.

"You could always come work for me," I say.

"No way," she says with an incredulous laugh. She looks at me sideways. "And have *you* signing my paychecks?" She groans, but with a laugh, and right then, I know we're going to be okay. We always have this. Our ability to talk. Connect, argue, challenge each other and yet find humor in the midst of it all.

"Why not? Think about it. The foundation could create a legal defense fund that you could run," I say. She starts to cough.

I hop up to get her some water.

I pull open her fridge, and it's completely empty. "Where's all the fucking food?"

"I don't have any," she croaks defensively.

"Not even a bottle of water?" I ask, incredulous. She shakes her head, and her coughing subsides. "Who doesn't have water?" I ask and walk back to the couch.

"Me. I haven't had time, and I'm barely here. And when I am, it's just to sleep," she confesses.

I want to tell her that she should be sleeping in my bed, that she was supposed to be living with me. But I'm not going to ask her again. I want her to be the one to say it.

She yawns and eyes the pastries I've spread out. "Thanks for the…croissants, but can we go out for coffee? I want to get a latte from Sweet and Lo's. They're delicious, Hayes," she says brightly. I'm glad for the subject change because it was getting too heavy.

"Croissants? These aren't *croissants*. They don't even remotely resemble them," I say and pick up the eclair shaped like a piece of bread. "This," I say dramatically while I rip the dough in half, "is a kolache." I put the two halves under her nose. "Lo style," I add and her eyes light up and she sniffs the fragrant steam wafting under her nose.

"Who would give such a magical smelling miracle such a terrible name? What the heck is a coalatchee?"

"You're mispronouncing it. And it was brought here by the Czech immigrants who settled in Texas. I would say I'd take you to the Kolache Factory, because growing up that's all there was. But Sweet's in Rivers Wilde is next level."

"Mmm," she moans and licks her lips. "Gimme." She snatches half of mine. "What is this magic?" she drawls excitedly.

"It's grilled chicken, eggs, and potatoes wrapped in this dough and baked," I tell her, and she takes a huge bite and swallows greedily.

"Is this a Houston thing?" she asks.

"More like southeast Texas. No one else anywhere I've lived has ever heard of them," I tell her.

"Oh my God, that chicken. Does it have…curry or something on it?" She smacks her lips together, and I frown at her in mild disgust.

"What's all the smacking for?" I ask.

She smirks and smacks louder. "I'm country, Hayes. We smack our lips when something tastes this good. This is Czech food?"

"Well, the concept is. But Sweet's pastries are all made with a flavor of her home country, Senegal—that's in West Africa. And Lo, his real name is Lotanna, is her husband. He's from Nigeria, and he's the reason that Sweet doesn't give away everything she bakes and makes," I tell her.

"I love their coffee; can't wait to actually eat there. Let me get dressed and we can head out," she says and stands and hurries to her room. And instead of following her like I want, I pull out my phone and call Gigi.

Chapter 24

SWEET AND LOW

CONFIDENCE

Haye holds open the glass paned French doors of Sweet and Lo's. "After you."

"Thank you," I answer absently. I'm distracted by the sensory delights that started when we approached the bakery. I pass it every day on my way to work, but haven't had the time to stop. The smell of sugar, butter, and coffee that fills the air around it always makes my mouth water. But as I step around the glass window between the door and the dining room that reads, "We Bake the World" my foodie soul is dancing a jig at all the delicious promises the scene before me is making.

The cafe's abundance of windows, on both the front street facing side and the left wall that opens onto a small garden where people are seated reading and talking, give it a warm airy feel. It's packed with people, and the only thing louder than the concentrated murmur of conversation is the whirring of the coffee grinders, the hissing of steaming espresso makers, and the background music that's too low to make out clearly, but loud enough that you know it's there. I eye the huge chalkboard behind the small hostess stand ahead of us. The menu is written in neat cursive and lists everything from pastries and sandwiches to omelets and salads and specialty breads.

I crane my neck so I can see above the heads of the people clustered and waiting to be seated in the smaller-than-comfortable waiting area. My stomach tightens, as if to remind me how long it's been since I ate. Hayes is scanning the dining room, and I tug his arm to get his attention. "Think we can order and take it to go instead of waiting for a table?"

"Nope." He smiles and turns back to the dining room.

"Why not?" I complain and tug his arms until he looks down at me.

"My aunt is meeting us. She's here, already seated. Come on." He drops that bomb, then takes my hand and turns us toward the young woman smiling and waving at us from the hostess stand.

We take a few steps before I can gather my wits and pull my hand out of his and stop dead in my tracks.

The person behind me slams into my back and the sharp edge of his shoulders pokes my back and the toe of his rubber-soled shoes scrape against the backs of my heels. I spin around just in time to see a very old, frail looking woman falling backward.

I cry out, my hands over my mouth in horror. She sits right where she fell, flat on her ass, her spindly green floral-painted legging covered legs sprawled in front of her like a newborn foal.

I reach down to help her up and glare at Hayes, who's just made it back to my side. He looks between us with an expression of complete bewilderment on his face.

"I'm so sorry," I say and reach down to cup her elbow. She swats my hand away and says, "I can get myself up. I look old, but I bet you I could beat you in a race around the block." Her voice, thin and frail, says otherwise. But she hops up in one quick, acrobatic movement. "See? Right as rain," she says proudly.

"I'm Sally, Sally Turner." She says her name like it's a compliment. She's got to be eighty years old. Her face is covered in a spray of freckles that even kiss her eyelids and lips. Her eyes, a sparkling dark brown, are full of mischief and her smile is disarmingly youthful.

"Are you okay, Sally?" Hayes asks as if he's been saying her name his whole life as he puts a hand at the small of both of our backs and ushers us out of the way of the customers trying to get to the booth.

"Oh, I'm fine. I was just distracted by the specimen of man meat ahead of me." She nods at Hayes and winks. "You're Hayes Rivers. Nice that you finally came down from your tower to visit us," she says.

Hayes, as unflappable as ever, doesn't correct her and say that he's actually been spending a lot of time in town. Instead, he smiles roguishly. "I heard this was the place to come if I wanted to find a pretty girl to talk to. Of course, I came to see."

She throws her head back and laughs delightedly. "Oh, how wonderful, and you're charming, too. Those Wilde boys pretty things up nicely. I'd say you're about to add something better than pretty," she says and laughs again.

"I'll leave the prettying to the Wildes and my woman." He slips a hand around my waist. Her eyes roam Hayes's body like someone contemplating what part of their steak they'd like to eat first.

"Either way, we can always use another fine piece—"

"Uh, I'm so sorry I stopped like that; I'm glad you're okay." I interrupt her before she says any more.

"Oh, if I'd been looking where I was going, I would have seen ya," she says. "This your fella?" she asks.

I glance at Hayes; he's grinning from ear to ear. My heart flutters. He's a goddamn dangerous combination of overbearing and sweet.

I'm addicted to him.

I get near him, and I lose my mind. I miss being his woman and everything that comes with it, and I'm so close to giving him whatever he asks for. Close. But…

I smile serenely and say, "Not quite," to Sally. His hand tightens around my middle.

"Well, if you're not sure…" She gives Hayes a suggestive sidelong glance and wink.

I laugh.

She looks back at me with an indignant glare. "Honey, if I was just twenty years younger, you wouldn't be able to *fight* me for him. They don't make men like this anymore. I suggest you get *sure* real quick." She winks and strides off into the restaurant.

"Yeah. Get sure quick, *Tesoro*." Hayes's lips brush my ear, and his breath makes the hairs on the back of my neck stand up and my insides quiver. His hand slides along my waist and comes to rest on my abdomen. It takes up almost the entire space, and when he pulls me back into him, I feel like I'm melting.

"I miss you touching me, baby." I let my head fall back and rest on his shoulder.

"Hayes Garfield Rivers, you are in *public*!" An irate voice from ahead of us breaks the trance and we jump apart.

"Gigi," Hayes says and steps around me toward the dark-haired, hazel-eyed beauty, who but for the fact that he called her his aunt, I would never believe was old enough to be.

She glares at him. "Don't you dare use that voice on me, Hayes," she scolds even as she throws her arms open to welcome his hug. I watch as she embraces him, smacks his shoulders, and then wraps her arms around him. He lifts her off her feet. Her eyes, closed from the instant they touch, pop open, and they're assessing and shrewd as they run over me from head to toe. She's dressed in a navy skirt topped with a white tailored shirt with a patent-leather, nude-colored belt cinched around her Audrey Hepburnesque waist. Suddenly, my cut-off shorts feel both too casual and too short. My white camisole, too revealing, and my flip-flops, downright disrespectful.

When our eyes meet, I smile my best smile and thank God I tied my unruly hair back so that at least I don't look *completely* unkempt. My shoulders sag with relief when a smile—warm and real—blooms across her face.

She disengages herself from Hayes and comes toward me, arms outstretched. "Well, *Hayes,* look what you did. She's as pretty as a picture," she says to him as she wraps me in a hug that smells and feels like comfort and love. It makes me long for my mother. I wish she could see this place.

"I'm Gigi, Confidence," she says warmly. "I think we're going to be great friends." She hooks an arm through mine.

Hayes doesn't let go of my hand when I try to tug it free of his. He draws it into his lap and holds it there with the other one on top of it. I look at him to demand it back, but my words die on my lips.

He's laughing at something his aunt just said. His head is thrown back, his teeth gleaming, his eyes closed, and I can envision my future. What life could feel like if I spent it with him. Happy, holding hands, with family who fusses, but forgives. In nice suburban cafes that smell like bread and coffee. And where everyone is welcome, especially me. So, I don't pull my hand back. Instead, I squeeze his and rejoin the conversation just as our server comes and takes our orders.

Hayes jumps slightly and then lets go of my hand.

"What's wrong?" I ask. My hand feels cold without his sandwiching it. He fishes into the pocket of his jeans and pulls out his phone.

"I'm sorry, I've got to take this. I've been expecting this call for two days," he says. He slides out of the booth and strides toward the entrance.

I watch him go. His sky-blue polo neck T-shirt bunches across his broad shoulders as he turns to squeeze between the tightly packed tables. His jeans sit low on his hips and hug that fine ass of his.

"I don't blame you, sister," Sally calls from a couple of tables ahead of us.

I jump slightly and blush at being caught ogling. I look at Gigi and smile. She doesn't smile back. In fact, the friendly light in her eyes disappears completely. My throat convulses in surprise and dread.

"Is everything okay?" I ask.

"I need to ask you some things, right now before Hayes comes back," Gigi says the minute he's out of earshot.

"Okay…" I say and glance toward the door at Hayes.

"I have a check in my purse for one million dollars. If I gave it to you, would you leave and never bother Hayes again?" she asks.

Shock renders me paralyzed. I think if she whistled, the air she pushed out would knock me over.

"What?" I ask, offended, incredulous and for some reason, a little afraid.

"I could go up to three million. And I will. If you'll take it," she says.

Her expression is completely neutral. I can't believe she can be so calm after what she just said.

"Are you kidding me? Why would you even…?"

"Name your price," she says.

My heart slows to a hard, slow thud.

"What?"

"I'll give it to you. *If you'll take it*," she says slowly, like there's something she's trying to tell me without saying it directly. But my blood is boiling and I don't have the time or inclination for her games.

"I most certainly will not," I say and grab my phone from the table and reach to pick up my purse.

She puts a hand over mine to steady it.

"I'm sorry if that offended you. But it's not personal," she says.

"As if it could be anything but personal," I say without a thought for who I'm talking to.

"Confidence, Hayes is all that's left of my family. He's also, underneath that shell he wears, desperate for a place where he feels like he belongs. I will use my money, I will lie, I will offend, and I will do whatever to help him find it. After what he's gone through with that ex-wife—" she says unapologetically.

I lose my cool.

"I bet you never offered her money to leave him alone, did you? Why? Because she wasn't a nobody from nowhere, right?" I say angrily. I throw my napkin onto the table and lean in so that I can lower my voice. I am not going to let her bullshit ruin this lunch for Hayes. I glance over my shoulder and see him pacing in front of the restaurant, deep in conversation. I turn back to his aunt.

"That woman is criminally idiotic. I can assure you that *I* am not. Money is nice. But I don't want more of it than I need," I tell her.

"Yeah, right," she says dismissively.

"I know it's hard to imagine people not worshiping the same money god as you do," I say.

"How dare you?" she asks.

"How dare *you*?" I shoot right back. "You could have just asked me how I feel about him." I'm angry and surprised by the sting of tears in the back of my eyes.

"Oh, I don't need to ask to know it's obvious. But in my experience, love isn't ever enough, so I want to know what else you want from Hayes."

"I don't have to prove myself to you," I say indignantly.

"You're right," she says crisply, her eyes narrowing on me. "But let me tell you, If any of the things you think he's good for are comfort or financial security, then that will prove itself, too. I'm just trying to save us all a little time and a lot of heartbreak," she says coolly.

I don't know whether to storm off or hug her.

"Gigi?" Her eyebrows shoot up in surprise at the gentle deference in my voice. "May I call you that?" I ask.

"Of course, you may," she says archly.

I nod and smile politely. Then, I take off the gloves.

"You've known him his whole life and you're still putting a price tag on him. And I've only known him for four months, and I already know he's priceless," I snarl.

"How dare you?" She gasps.

"You're going to have to stop saying that. I dare because no one is in charge of me but me." I point at my chest. "Yes, I want him to spoil me," I say, and she smirks knowingly. I wipe it right back off. "With *respect, loyalty,* and free and exclusive access to his glorious body. But I can finance myself," I say through gritted teeth.

"Well then, why are you two doing this dance where you're not together? What are you holding out for?" she asks in frustration. I can see how much she loves Hayes; I can see how worried she really is for him. So, I decide to ignore her disrespectful questions and innuendos and put her mind at ease.

I sigh and search for the right words to describe Hayes and me right now.

"I love Hayes. More than I've ever loved another man. Ever. But, we're in a really weird place. He hurt me, and I'm trying to forgive him. Forgiveness doesn't come easily to me. But I'm trying," I tell her.

And I am. I know he said what he did before he knew me. But honestly, I'm bothered by the fact that he would say it at all. My parents didn't do a lot right by me. But they raised me in a place where I was surrounded by a lot of other people who did do right by me. I wouldn't be who I am today without those people. They are my family. Even though I'm not there, that town, its people, and its future is the wind beneath my wings. I love them. I take my role as their daughter, sister, friend seriously.

"What happened?" she asks.

"He insulted me," I say.

"So?" she asks.

"So, when someone insults me, I feel like they're insulting the people I love, too. And I won't let anyone do that. Not even the man I want to spend the rest of my life with," I say to her.

"The rest of your life?" She gasps. "Are you…?" Her throat bobs.

"No, not yet," I say. "But he loves me. I *will* forgive him because I can't live without him," I confess, and my heart flutters as I say it out loud for the first time. I am certain of those things, and they are the reason I'm here.

She grabs my hand across the table, and her eyes shine with tears.

"Oh, my dear," she says. I snatch my hand back.

"No." I shake my head. "I'm not your dear," I say plainly.

She pales a little.

"I know you were just trying to protect him. But have some faith in his judgment. And be honest with me. I hope this is just the beginning of our relationship. We should begin as we mean to go on. If you play games with me, we can be relatives, but never friends. I would much rather be friends, so please just say what you mean. And mean what you say," I ask.

I watch her face and wait for her to respond. I hold my breath, very aware that I may have just made an enemy out of the one relative Hayes seems to hold in high regard. Besides his brothers.

She stares at me in complete disbelief for a full minute. I start preparing to explain to Hayes why I made his aunt cry or storm off or throw water in my face. Then she lets out a hoot of laughter that sends several heads turning in our direction.

"Well, will you look at that," she says, tears in her eyes and a huge grin on her face.

"Look at what?" I ask.

"He found you," she says and digs into her food with gusto.

Chapter 25

LAID BARE

HAYES

"Tell me about your aunt," Confidence asks as soon as we've parted ways with Gigi. The question stumps me for a second. Not because I don't want to talk about her, but because I'd already moved on to what I wanted to show her.

"I want to hear more about her," Confidence says, and my heart warms because she sounds like she really means it.

"She's everything. The reason I don't have issues. The reason I can accept and give love. She took me in when no one else wanted me. And she put up with my shit and hasn't held it against me," I say and smile as I think about the way Gigi and I knocked heads when we first met.

"You love her," she says it like it's a question.

"Of course, I do," I say and pull her down one alley off Rivers Wilde's main street. "Come on, I want to show you something."

"What are we doing here?" she asks as we step out on the other side and onto a footpath that leads to The Oaks.

"I'm picking up my gate passes and my car. I want to show you my house."

"You bought this house?" Confidence gasps when we step inside the two-story foyer of the red brick house nestled in between a row of other two-story red brick houses that make up this picturesque cul-de-sac on Wildetree Lake.

"Yes, I bought *this* house," I respond and take her hand and start for the stairs. "When you see the view from the master bedroom upstairs, you'll see why," I tell her, and my excitement builds with each step up the staircase.

"This is beautiful, Hayes," she says and glances around the house. I follow her gaze, and I have to agree. About a tenth of the size of Rivers House, this is a house that already feels like home.

"I like it," I say, intentionally noncommittal.

"Like? How can you just like it?" she screeches and pulls her hand out of mine. She runs it up the cherrywood stair rails and sighs. "It's like the dream house on my Pinterest board," she says.

"Is it?" I ask.

But I know it is. She showed me the first time I went to visit her. When I saw the pictures of this place on my realtor's site, I knew I was going to buy it. When I came to visit for the first time, I knew right away that this would be my home. Now, I hope she's going to feel the same way.

"I want to show you something and then I want to tell you something and then I want you to be as mad as you want about it. But when you're done, I'm fucking you. And when we leave this house later, we're going to be back together."

Her eyes widen, and her jaw drops before she composes herself. "Hayes…" she starts, her voice full of fight. I yank her to me and kiss her quiet. Her lips soften and her arms slip around my neck and she kisses me back like she's been missing it as much as I have.

It feels so good, but I force myself to stop kissing her.

Her eyes are glazed with desire; her plump lips pout when I pull back. "I've told you about that caveman shit," she grumbles, but nestles into me.

"Yeah, you told me." I press a kiss to the top of her head and wrap my arms around her.

"But that's what I become when I think about you. You're mine and I'm not going to act like you're not. Not for one more day." I breathe in a good whiff of her hair that's tickling my nose. She smells like sun-flowers and rain. So clean and bright and strong.

"Come on." I put an arm around her waist and lead her to the bedroom.

It, along with the rest of the house, is fully furnished and decorated.

"This room is kind of..." Confidence looks around and searches for the right word to describe the explosion of white, yellow, and peach that is my bedroom. "I would say feminine, but that feels like a massive understatement." She laughs and looks around. "Do you really sleep in that bed?" She points at the white, four-poster bed with yellow drapes flowing from the top of it.

"Gigi took my 'do whatever you want' too literally," I explain. "But don't worry, baby, I plan on getting rid of it before you move in," I say.

"Hayes, give you an inch..." she says.

"Oh, *Tesoro*, by the time we leave this house tonight..." I look at my watch and note that it says eleven a.m. "I would have taken ten miles and put in a request for another hundred. You can say no, but I want you to look me in the eye and tell me you don't love me. Because that is the only way I'll let you go," I tell her.

She dips her head and hides her face, but I know my girl. She always puts a lock of hair between her lips and presses them together when she's happy but doesn't want to show it. She's holding the end of her ponytail between her fingers and is holding it to her mouth for a moment before she looks up.

"And you need to stop telling me what's going to happen and how I'm going to feel and what you're going to do with me," she says irri-tably.

I've pushed enough for now, and in a few minutes, I'm going to have a real battle on my hands, so I change the subject and steer us to the big bay window at the back of the bedroom.

"Look." I point over her shoulder into the distance.

"Oh wow, we can see all the way to the Habitat for Humanity project site." She puts her hand on her throat.

"Have you been out there yet?" I ask.

"Yeah, once. Just this week. I think it's awesome that Wilde World is giving up that parcel of land for its development," she says, and I smile.

"That's not Wilde World's land," I say as nonchalantly as I can.

"Yes, it is. It shares the wall with Rivers Wilde," she argues.

"I know. You know that the land Rivers Wilde is built on all used to belong to my family, right?" I ask.

"All of it?" she asks.

"Yes, all of it. That land beyond the wall," I say and point to the short stone wall that was built to divide the land. "All of that still belongs to us," I inform her.

"What?" she turns around to face me. "You own all of that? Habitat for Humanity is building on your land?" she asks.

"No, they're building on *their* land. I donated it to them. Nearly fifty percent of what's left. One thousand acres for their project," I say.

"You…*gave* it to them?" she squeaks. Her head swings wildly back and forth between the expanse of green pasture land that's one of the most unique things about Houston. Urban and rural blend within feet of each other. And it's self-contained, but with easy ingress and egress to streets that are the major traffic arteries of the city make the location ideal for commuters going to all of the major commercial centers in Houston. The Galleria, downtown, Greenway, Katy, Sugar Land, The Medical Center. She stares at me for a few minutes, her face tight with concentration as if she's looking at a puzzle that makes no sense.

"What?" I ask.

She frowns. "It's just that there's a dissonance between your actions and words, Hayes. Last time we talked about this, you were shocked that we wouldn't accept a settlement. Now, you've committed your family's resources to doing exactly what you refused to do last week."

"Well, it was actually almost two weeks ago, and then, I hadn't been to see any of the properties. I hadn't met Matt and Jasmine and their ten-month-old who couldn't go anywhere without the machine they use to treat his asthma," I say.

"I heard about your visits," she says. "Your little notetaker was very proud of himself."

"He's a good kid. And after those visits, I decided to make that donation. Some of those units should have been condemned before the flood." I shake my head as I remember the rubble and debris that still lay strewn in the parking lots of these units. It's a disgrace and I couldn't sit by while they suffered.

"Does Remi know that? Why wouldn't he tell me that?" I ask.

"Because I asked him not to. I wanted to tell you myself, and I didn't want you to know until I thought you were ready to hear it," I tell her.

Her eyes narrow slightly. "Why do you get to decide what I'm ready for?" she asks.

"Because I'm the decider," I say, mimicking George W. Bush's infamous words.

"Oh, really?" she asks and crosses her arms over her chest.

"Yes. That's what I do. I make decisions that I think are best for myself and my family. Sometimes they mean I will have to hurt the people I love. Not be candid with them. Move them around like pawns," I say.

"How do *you* feel about that?" she asks, surprising me with how soft her voice is.

"I feel fine about it. I'm not impulsive, Confidence. When I act, it's after long deliberation. There have been moments in my life where I didn't think, where I just acted, and I hurt people without any really good reason. The ends didn't justify the means."

"You should hear yourself, Hayes. You're a stage five control freak," she says, but her voice is completely devoid of recrimination. In fact, I hear shades of pity, and I don't fucking like it.

"I have to be," I say tightly.

She holds her hand out to me, and I step forward and take it.

She brings it to her lips and brushes the back of them in a sweeping motion. She looks up at me through her lashes, and I'm struck by how every time she looks at me, her eyes nearly lay me flat.

"You can't control people, Hayes," she whispers, and a knot tightens in my chest at the distress in her voice.

"I'm not trying to control anyone. I just take opportunities when I see them," I say, and before she can cut me off, I tell her what I've been dreading. "Like when I realized that Kingdom wasn't going to do anything they weren't forced to when it came to the tenants, I knew Remi would need the best lawyer on his team."

"What do you mean?" she asks and then her eyes widen and her mouth falls open.

She drops my hand. "You didn't," she says quietly.

I'm shocked she hasn't guessed already.

She jumps to her feet. "If you say that you asked Remi to hire me, I am going to walk out of this room, and if you try to stop me, I will scream at the top of my lungs until someone calls the police," she yells.

Fuck.

"I didn't *ask* Remi to hire you," I hedge.

"But?" she bites out between her clenched jaw.

"But… I *did* bring you to his attention," I say.

She growls and balls her fists. "Why, Hayes? Because you wanted me here so badly that you'd persuade your friend to give me a job I wouldn't be considered for otherwise? How do you think that makes me feel? After everything I shared with you, you know that is the very last thing I would want," she says and starts for the door.

My arm whips out like a lasso and I draw her to me.

"No, you aren't leaving," I say. "And scream because the closest house is three empty lots away. And you'll be screaming for nothing because you know I will not hurt a hair on your head to keep you from leaving," I say.

She looks pointedly at her arm, where my hand is cuffed around it.

I let go.

"I'm not holding you, but you're not walking out of here over *that*. You needed a job. This one was perfect for you, and Remington already had your résumé. He just needed someone to vouch for you. And I did," I say. "But you know him now. Do you think he would have hired you because his friend asked him to? His twin sister works somewhere else because he won't hire her," I remind her.

Some of the fight flows out of her.

"Why didn't you tell me, then?" she questions. Her voice is raised to a near shout, her eyes are pools of conflict. She's angry, hurt, but she also…understands.

"Because you are so fucking stubborn, *Tesoro*," I say in exasperation. "You would have cut off your nose to spite your face and spit in Remi's the minute you knew I was involved," I say.

"I would not have," she says.

"Liar," I taunt her.

"I would not have. Not everything is about you," she says.

"Liar," I say again.

"Stop saying that," she says angrily.

"Stop lying," I say.

"You are not a mind reader!" she yells now. She's practically vibrating, but with something much more potent, vibrant, and transformative than anger. It is relief and acquiescence. She's relenting.

I press my advantage.

"You and I are cut from the same cloth, molded from the same earth, sky, water, and fire. I *can* read you." I trace a line down her forearm.

"Did you do this because you wanted me to take you back?" she asks and points out at the development.

"Partly, yes. But not just because I want you on my arm and in my bed, but because I need you by my side," I say.

"You do?" she asks, and I laugh at the surprise in her voice.

I nod over at the window, at the land. "I could have sold it. It's some of the most valuable land in Texas. But, what's the point of enriching my family and living in a walled off castle when the rest of the world is burning or in Houston's case, drowning. But I wouldn't have considered it if I hadn't met you. At least, not as quickly," I admit.

"So, you did it because—"

"Because I *knew* it was the right thing to do. The only thing I *could* do. You said this should be a personal problem. And you're right. When I think about what I want the legacy of my times as head of this family to be, I find that preserving it isn't enough—not just for the sake of it, anyway. That land has sat empty for two hundred years. It doesn't flood, the only real expense of it is the property taxes, and because it was a donation and they're a 501(c) (3), it's a nice tax holiday for all of us. So, win-win," I say with a shrug.

"My brother is on death row. He killed my father during one of their drunken rages," she blurts out suddenly and I freeze.

"What?" I say because I don't know how else to respond.

"Yeah, the one named Fortune," she says.

"What happened?" I ask her.

"There was a terrible storm that night. Otherwise, I wouldn't have been home," she says, her tone a little wistful. "When they were both drunk, I couldn't bear to be under the same roof. But the river was already swollen from rain a few days before, so it was flooding. I was trapped in the house, and they were fighting. Over the last beer. Fortune had opened it and Daddy snatched it from him. The bottle broke, and Fortune stuck the edge of it into Daddy's neck and he bled to death right there while my mother and I hid under the dinner table," she says dimly.

I convulse in horror. That's unimaginable.

"I love where I come from, but I could never live there again. I was trapped between two terrors and it was only when one was gone that I was able to escape the other," she says, her eyes distant and dull.

She's drawn her knees up to her chest, her heels rest on the edge of the window seat cushion and her feet are dangling off the edge. Just then, I can see her as a young girl, sitting on the edge of a river bank, her long hair hanging off one shoulder as she looks over it at the danger behind her. Her toes being tickled by the water while she listened for the danger at her front.

"Did he hurt you?" I ask, even though I absolutely do not want to know if he did. I know that if she says yes, I will never rest well. Knowing someone hurt this woman, and I will never be able to make them pay.

"Of course, but he also made me stronger. I always fought back. I never took my beating lying down," she says, and I want to go and find her brother and spare him the comfort of that needle.

"Well, am I free to go?" she asks quietly.

"Free to go where?" I ask, truly confused.

"Don't you want me to leave? Isn't this exactly the kind of thing you'd wanted to know and avoid when you ordered the background check?" she asks.

"For a smart woman, you're pretty damn obtuse," I say. "I told you why I ordered it, and that by the time it came through, I didn't care what it said," I remind her.

"And you care now?" she asks quietly.

"Did you not hear me earlier?" I ask and place my hands on her shoulders.

"Which part?" she says. Her smile is small, but it's there for the first time all day. I skim her arms and the sweep of all of that unbelievably soft skin at my fingers makes me want to take her clothes off and pull her supple body against mine and show her what my words have failed to.

That I need her constantly.

That she owns me as completely as I own her.

That I love her endlessly.

"The part about you and me being made from the same combination of elements. About you being mine?"

"Still?"

"*Tesoro*, knowing, doesn't change anything. In fact, it just shows me how alike we are."

"Why? Are your relatives murderers, too?" she asks, and shoves her hands through her hair and looks up to the ceiling in despair.

"Maybe?" I shrug and think about it quickly. "I don't know," I say.

"Well, then, they're not. If you had a murderer in your family, you would know it, trust me," she says.

"Then, I don't know that I would care. You've been shaped by the river, learned more from it than you did from the man who spawned you. You are not him. You have shaped me," I tell her.

"Ha, right!" She laughs. I ignore her and press on. "You know the Mississippi River starts in Minnesota, right?" I ask her.

"Of course, I do," she says.

"Well, at its mouth, it's narrow enough that you can walk across it in less than a dozen steps," I say.

She looks at me, eyebrows raised in question.

"You're like that river. At least in the way you've affected me," I say.

"How? Easy to cross?" she says morosely.

"Stop pouting." I chuck her under the chin. "I mean that you *started* like that for me. A pinprick sized drop of water on the very still waters of my life. And the minute you touched me, you caused a ripple that blurred everything I thought I was certain of. The way I saw myself, my obligations, my future. And now, just like that river you love so much does, it winds its way south, you rush through me, and I'm *drowning* in you." I kiss her quickly.

"I'm all for you loving me, but it's not worth your life." She uses the very same joke I made that night in the hot tub and I laugh.

"Actually, I can breathe deeply for the first time in a long time. I know we're from totally different worlds, but I feel like we're also from the very same one. We love our family—not just the ones who were born of our blood. My brothers, Stone and Beau, aren't biologically related to me at all," I tell her. "You're not the daughter of a sadistic drunk and the sister of a killer. I'm not the scion of a line of philanthropic, but short-sighted men and faithless women. Our legacies—what we choose to leave of ourselves in this world—is up to us."

She sighs…

"Why didn't you tell me sooner?" I ask her.

She purses her lips, and then she blows out a breath. "I don't talk about it. No one in Amorel does. It's our collective secret. We all like to pretend that Merle—that's my dad—never existed and that Fortune is already dead," she says quietly. "And I'm ashamed of what they did *and* how I deny them. But to acknowledge them is to remind everyone not just that my brother killed my father, but about the blood that runs in my veins. It means something that it's part of my history. And, in a way, that's more than just a random moment. That it shaped me. Reduced me. Just like the river. Just like I thought Nigel had done. Just like I was afraid you'd do if I gave you another chance," she says.

I grasp her chin a little more forcefully than I need to and turn her face toward mine. "There is nothing that could reduce you. You wear your name like a crown, and it's one of the truest things about you," I tell her.

She sniffs dismissively. "It *feels* like a joke. And I'm afraid sometimes that it is. My brother Fortune is going to die on a table with a state-sanctioned, poison-filled needle in his arm. My brother, Happiness, ran away before he was thirteen. I can't imagine that his life has brought him much of his name's meaning." She shakes her head.

"Well, first, I think you're giving your parents a lot of credit. Your mother, I will say, seems lovely. But fortune teller didn't seem to be one of her skills. They gave you a name they liked. You've made it your own. You can decide that what you've done with your life is worth less than some whim by your parents twenty-seven years ago. But you would be lying to yourself," I tell her.

She looks up at me through her long lashes and smiles.

"You *believe* in yourself. Enough to see beyond your current situation and reach for more. That's more than I can say for myself. I didn't consider that your interest in me could be more than all of the things that I've used to define myself. But I swear, by the time we left Italy, I knew I didn't care what it said, and I knew that I could trust you," I say. And then I add the part that has been a more recent revelation. "I know that one of the reasons that people think of my money when they look at me is because that's what I show them. I started changing that after your visit. If I wanted more from people, I had to give more," I say. "You asked me about wanting more from my experiences than money could buy."

"Oh, Hayes," she says wistfully.

"What?"

"Thank you for speaking so my heart could hear. I don't want to be bought. I don't want to be wooed with flowers or nice trips. I want to be wowed by you living your best life. Because I want to live mine, too," she says.

"Let's do it together." I pull her off the window seat and carry her toward the bed.

"What are you doing?" she cries. "I'm still talking…"

"Well, when you're done, you're going to put your pussy on my dick and make it dance," I say. "I just want to get you in position."

"Aren't you mad that I didn't tell you sooner? How do you not have any more reaction than this?" she asks.

"I already knew," I admit and then brace for her reaction. Her body tenses and I just hold on tighter.

"You knew?"

"Yeah. After you left that day, I read it. I wanted to know what spooked you so badly," I say.

She glares at me.

I smile at her.

Her glare falls apart, and her mouth trembles before she covers it with her hands.

"You have the heart, spirit, and courage of a queen. I'm proud to know you. Proud that you love me. You've taken something and made it into nothing," I say.

She rolls her eyes. "You've got it backward," she says exasperatedly.

"No. I don't. I'm telling you that you have taken something that *should* have reduced you, changed you, trapped you, maybe even erased you, and you have made it something so insignificant that you can leave it out of your life story and no one will know it's missing," I explain.

The light in her eyes changes. It softens, becomes more luminous, and she relaxes in my hold.

"You really don't care?" she asks.

"Of course, I care. But not in the way you think. I'm sorry you lived through that. I care that you think it's something you should be ashamed of."

"I worry sometimes that it's in my blood," she whispers and clouds roll into her eyes. So, I sit down on the bed with her still in my arms.

"What is?"

"That violence. Not because I feel inclined to it. But because I always know when it's coming. Will I pass it on? Will it suddenly rear its head?" She sounds dejected.

I squeeze her a little.

"My grandfather was a cruel man. Everyone acts like he walked on water because he donated money for a hospital and because his name was Rivers. But I know what he was. My father, for all of his failings, raised me to believe I am my own man. He sent me to Gigi to make sure Thomas wouldn't ruin that. And as much as I resented it then, I'm very grateful for it now as an adult. Because I can see that left to Thomas, I'd probably be just like him. Forgetting that my name is more than an access card for us. It can also be one for others. There is no such thing as a generational curse. There's intent and action."

"Then why do you feel responsible for what Kingdom has done? Why are you spending this money and time on the flood victims?"

"Because I can. Because it's a chance to correct the course, and I'm taking it. I'm not trying to raise people from the dead, *Tesoro*. Just trying to fix things going forward."

"What if I make the same mistakes they did?" she asks.

"I hate to break it to you, *Tesoro*. But, you have your own flaws to worry about. You're stubborn, impulsive, and for all your instincts about violence, you seem to walk into danger all the time. Like falling off cliffs that you go walking down at night." I tap the tip of her nose with my finger.

"Don't touch my nose; it'll make me sneeze. And thanks for the praise." She shoves my shoulder lightly.

"Tell me mine," I ask.

"Your flaws?"

"I know…you probably have to think really hard about it," I joke.

"You're possessive, cynical, and suspicious," she says without missing a beat.

I let out a bark of surprised laughter, and then I kiss her softly.

"And you're perfect. And mine," she adds.

A cloud breaks over us. Sun streams in, and it feels like the return from a long march, and I'm so glad to be home.

When I break the kiss, she cups my face and sighs my name.

"Yeah, that's better. Next time you say my name, though, I want you to scream it," I say, then stand up and throw her onto the bed.

Chapter 26

THUNDER

CONFIDENCE

I land on Hayes's mattress with a small bounce and little shriek. My heart is thudding as I push my hair out of my eyes and see him looking at me like I'm the very last meal he'll ever eat.

His nostrils flared, his eyes hot with desire, and his lips are flushed. Mine tingle, sending signals to him that they want to feel him. All of him. I've missed him more than I can say. Sex was one of the ways we communicated.

We would say "I love you," "I hate you," "I'm scared," "I'm angry" when we fuck. And now, I'm hungry to know everything he's kept from me in the time we haven't touched each other.

"*Tesoro,*" he says huskily and pulls his shirt off. I can't believe all of that is mine. He pulls his jeans off, too, and the most beautiful cock in the world peeks out of the top of his boxers.

"Come here." I crook my finger and he lies down next to me. He slides one of his strong, warm hands up my thigh and cups my pussy.

"Fuck, you can never ever keep this from me again," he says and pinches my clit. I gasp loudly, sharply, and I rock into his hand as heat and wetness fill my panties and I press against the warmth of his palm.

He dips his head and takes my lips with his, and I sob at how perfectly right it feels to have my lips in the sacred embrace of his.

"I love you so much," he whispers into my mouth. "I never want to be away from you, *Tesoro*. Never." He grabs the front of my blouse and yanks until the straps give…the fabric sliding down my body sends a rush of anticipation across my skin like a river of electric shocks.

"I love you, too," I say urgently, desperate to get these words out of the way so that I fall into his kiss and drown in the river of emotion he's swept me away on. He gives me what we both need. He cups the back of my neck and rolls us until he's lying on top of me, and then he slams his mouth onto mine and pushes past my lips and sweeps my mouth with his tongue. He kisses me like that and I can't breathe. I don't want to. I want to die with him stealing the breath from my lungs. I want to drown in him.

When he drags his lips off my mouth, he takes my lower lip with him and holds on to it with his teeth. The sting of his bite feels so good. Just like everything he gives me. Even when it hurts.

He drops his forehead onto mine. Our chests heave in unison, we breathe nose to nose, open mouth to open mouth. His eyes are shining and they hold me in a trap so exquisitely loving that I feel like I'm floating.

"I would cross galaxies for you, swim every ocean, fight dragons," he says and his hands push my skirt up around my waist. He pushes my panties aside, wets his fingers by pressing them into my mouth and then slips his hand between us. He skims my clit with the edge of his blunt finger nail and then slides three of his big fingers into me.

I cry out at the sharp bite of my flesh stretching. He pushes them in, pulls them back out, and bends his head to my breast.

"I love seeing you like this. Your pussy is so goddamn tight, *Tesoro*." He captures my nipple through the lace of my bra. He bites it and flicks the sensitive flat of it with the firm tip of his tongue.

I'm chanting his name and he finger fucks me harder, bites my swollen nipple, and tears leak from the corner of my eyes as my orgasm breaks with no warning.

"*Ti amo tanto*," he says against my chest, and I feel the reverberation of his words in my heart.

"I love you, too," I respond.

He kisses his way upward. His mouth is wet, his breath hot as his breathing grows more ragged.

"*Sei la mia anima gemella*," he says as he parts my thighs.

"And you are mine," I respond.

"*Non posso vivere senza te*," he says and slides into me with one, deep, powerful thrust forward of his hips.

"You'll never have to live without me," I assure him

He grips the headboard.

"*Ti fotterò così forte*," he growls.

"I don't know what that means." I moan when he pulls back out.

"It means I'm going to fuck you so hard…" He bites his lip and tightens his grip on the headboard. I'm mesmerized by the flex and bulge of his big biceps over my head.

"So hard that what?"

"Let me show you," he says, and he thrusts up into me so hard my whole body slides up the mattress and the headboard rattles.

"Let me ride that wave, *Tesoro*." He pulls back out of me and I smile wide, lick my dry lips, and gaze up at my god of sin, my Duke of Midnight, my Renaissance man, my heartbreaker, my heart fixer, my everything.

I'll never stop falling in love with him. We make *magic t*ogether.

I want to hold my breath and stop time. The feeling I have, of being enough, of being loved for all that I am, with no desire to change anything about me. With more than acceptance of the baggage I bring—with pride. I want him and this forever. Right now though, even that wouldn't be long enough for me.

"You make me so fucking crazy." He puts one hand on my hip and thrusts short, deep, hard, fast, and my eyes roll to the top of my head at the intensity of his fucking. I feel like I'm being consumed.

"*Sei il tesoro più prezioso che ho trovato e che vorrei custodire per sempre.*"

I have no idea what that means, but I remember the first time he called me *Tesoro*, and my heart swells. I flash back to the moment I fell in love with him. It was that night on the ledge when I was sure that I was going to die.

And my heart, facing its potential demise, made a decision. If he hadn't been there, I wouldn't have made it off that cliff. And since that night, he's owned my heart. That river will roll over the delta whenever nature commands her to without any regard for the best laid plans of mice and men. And Hayes, *my* river, will roll over me. And I will love him through it all because my heart has chosen him.

"I would rearrange the universe to have you," he says, and his body flexes over me. The muscles in his shoulders and arms flex under the smooth, golden-hued skin that covers his beautiful body, and his thrust is so deep and hard that I'm sure he'll split me in half.

His chest heaves and he thrusts up again.

"Rearrange *me*." I sigh and he thrusts even harder.

"Shatter *me*," I beg and he fucks me hard, his arms and chest flex and ripple over my head, and when I come in the most spectacular explosion of tension I've ever felt, my whole world distills to the moment that would make this act between us a covenant—a promise.

He grunts into my neck and drills me into the mattress.

Yes, I will never get enough of this.

He lifts onto his knees and grips the headboard, his lower lip trapped between his teeth, his body moving like a machine between my thighs—fast, hard, and unrelenting—until he throws his head and shouts my name between grunts.

He pulls out and spurts on my stomach and thighs. "I claim you." He pants before he slides back into me.

Our come mingles and smears between our sweaty bodies. I lift my hips and press us together. My orgasm's aftershocks are still sending dancing, shimmering shivers of electricity through me.

Then Hayes drops his big body onto the bed next to me, and a huge cracking sound is our only warning before the entire bed collapses beneath us.

We lie on the sunken mattress and stare at each other before we burst out into laughter.

Then, as if in response to our mirth, the splatter of rain starts to beat on the window.

"It was raining during our first time in Italy," I remind him.

"'Because thunder only happens when it's raining,'" he croons the hook to the Fleetwood Mac classic in my ear. "And I promise you, this is the only place where we'll make this kind of noise. In our home, there will always be peace. You'll always be safe," he whispers and pulls me into his arms.

And then he rolls me over, slides back into me, and we make a storm of our own.

Chapter 27

SURPRISE

CONFIDENCE
Two Weeks Later

"Hey, I'm heading to Sweet and Lo's after my appointment at Blush. Want to meet me for coffee?" I whisper in Hayes's ear. His eyes are closed, but he's been awake for at least five minutes. I heard the change in his breathing when I stepped out of my bathroom. I let him pretend, though, so he could watch me. I got dressed right in front of him. His broad, sun-darkened, muscular shoulders twitched when I slipped my panties on, but otherwise, he hasn't moved.

I inhale the scent of his sleep and sweat and our sex, and I want to get back into bed with him. But I have an appointment at Blush where it's very hard to get an appointment. It's one of Houston's premier hair salons. The hair stylist, Tanaka, is one of the most sought-after stylists and colorists in the country, and she had a cancellation four weeks ago that bumped me up on the waitlist. And no way am I missing it, not even for a morning ride on Hayes's gloriously thick dick.

"Yeah, I'll meet you." His sleep-roughened voice is sexy, and the way his mouth moves as he forms his words is something I could sit and watch all day.

"What time?" he asks sleepily into his pillow.

I glance at my watch and do some quick math. "Maybe around eleven a.m.?" I say.

One of his eyes pops open and he peers at the alarm clock by my bed and flips over, wide-eyed, to stare at me.

"Are you having a quadruple bypass? Why does it take four hours to get your hair done?" he asks. I smack his shoulders, and then my hand goes back for a more tender caress of the skin that's wrapped around the love of my life.

"I don't have time to explain. Go back to sleep. You put in some good work last night. You must be tired." I stand to leave.

His long, sculpted arm darts out, and he wraps his fingers around my wrist. I lean in for a kiss and think if I skip my stop for coffee, I'll have time for a quick little something—not that there's ever been anything quick and little about sex with Hayes.

The thought of coffee turns my stomach so violently that I pull back right before our lips touch and sit back down.

"You okay?" he asks. His eyes are only half open, and those beautiful wild hazel eyes are full of real concern.

"Yeah, I'm fine. I don't know what the hell, I just felt a little sick when I thought about coffee, which is crazy 'cause I can't imagine how I'd get through the day without it."

"Get back into bed, and I'll give you the other thing you can't get through the day without." He tugs me back to him.

"No. If I don't get this appointment, I'll be in a bad mood until I get my hair done by her, and that's at least a month away, if I'm lucky," I tell him grouchily, but only because his offer is so tempting.

"I think your hair looks amazing," he says.

"Because you're a man and you're fucking me. You probably don't remember what color the hair on my head is unless I'm standing in front of you," I joke and stand up again.

"I'm insulted. You have no idea how much time I spend thinking about your hair. Wrapped around my fists when you're on your knees in front of me. Draped around my hips when your lips are wrapped around my cock. Falling down around me when you're riding me…"

"Not when it's blowing in the wind while we stroll?" I ask and shake my head in feigned disappointment.

"What fun would that be?" he asks. His grin is so wide and happy. I snap a picture of him with my phone and stare at it a beat before I look back at him. His eyes are sparkling, his morning stubble is dark and heavy, and his smile is full of contentment that I put there.

"No fun at all," I agree before I turn to leave.

"Come back to bed," he calls after.

"Now way. I can't be late for this. I'll see you soon. Bye." I chuck a peace sign at him and then walk happily out the door.

"Well, well, well," the dark-haired, olive skinned, handsome man behind the reception desk at Blush drawls in the most beautiful baritone I've ever heard.

I stop and look over my shoulder to find who he could be talking to. Because it can't be me. There's nothing interesting enough about me to warrant that intrigued look on his face. There's no one there. I turn back to face him and plaster a confused smile on my face. "Are you talking to me?" I ask.

His jaw drops. His eyes bug out of his head, he slaps his cheeks and then he shrieks.

Loudly.

I spin on my heel to get the hell out of there.

"Wait, wait, wait," he calls in that baritone again and in a display of super human speed, he's behind me with a hand on my shoulder, stopping me.

"Where are you going?" he asks with an amused chuckle.

"Why'd you scream?" I ask him angrily and fold my arms across my chest while I wait for him to respond.

"Because you look like Jayne Mansfield, who is like, my favorite actress of *all* time, and then you open your mouth and sound like Dolly Parton, who is my favorite *singer* of all time," he explains.

"I love and respect Dolly like any good Southerner, but I do *not* sound like her and I don't know who Jayne is."

He actually steps back, grips his chin thoughtfully, and studies my chest. "Hmm, I'm telling you. If we brightened up that blond all over and gave you one more bra cup, you'd be a dead ringer," he says.

"This is probably the strangest conversation I've ever had in my life," I say.

"It's not strange." He pouts. "They're my idols. It's like Dolly Parton and Jayne Mansfield had a baby and sent her to deliver me from an ordinary existence." He claps his hands together repeatedly in my face.

I smile and step around him.

"Oh, I *see*. You're crazy." I point at him with a knowing smile.

"Totally, sister, and I ain't afraid to show it." He winks, and then we both laugh.

"I'm Noé." He sticks out his hand to introduce himself.

I shake his big, warm, very soft hand. "What hand lotion do you use and where can I get some?"

"Oh, it's my own special blend," he says with a wink, and I pull my hand out of his.

"Are you making a sexual innuendo that implies that your special blend is your spunk? 'Cause, if so, that is so nasty," I say.

"Nasty? Oh, sweet baby Jesus. You said *nasty* and you sound just like Dolly! Please tell me you're a customer and you're going to come in at least once a week." He throws his head back dramatically.

"I might come back once a week if this is the reception I get. I feel special," I say with a cheeky smile.

"You *are* special. And hot to trot, too. But, we can't stand here gabbing all day. Tanaka is a stickler for time, even for too-hot-to-trot blonde bombshells with great tits." He gives me an exaggerated wink and grin, grabs me by the elbow, and leads me to the receptionist desk.

I'm totally charmed by him. People who can talk to anyone amaze me.

"What time is your appointment?" he asks as he leads me back to the reception desk.

"It's at seven thirty. Color, cut, and blowout," I say, excitedly.

"Okay. I'm going to need you to fill out all the paperwork again," he says and hands me a clipboard.

I look down at the stack of papers and recognize the first one. "I filled these out online when I made my appointment. Why did you have me do it if I was going to have to do it again?" I say and look at him quizzically. This is one of my biggest pet peeves, so my good humor fizzles.

He frowns sympathetically, either ignoring or missing my irritation. "I'm sorry. But your submission was all messed up. Your name was off, so we thought there might be other errors. I made the executive decision to delete it and have you do it again." He pats my hand in more misguided sympathy. "Since we're worried about the time, just fill out that top form, okay? You can do the rest while you're under the dryer with your foils." He winks.

I purse my lips but fill out the form quickly. "Filling out redundant forms will not get between me and the magician who's going to be like the miller's daughter in *Rumpelstiltskin* and turn this hay into gold," I say and then cringe at the high-pitched fangirl tone in my voice. "Sorry," I mutter to Noé without looking up at him.

"No problem, Dolly. She's a legend and we get people in here acting like they're about to be baptized. You're tame. For now. Wait till you get done with your hair, you'll be like one of those television pastors. It's why our advertising budget is zero," he says proudly.

I hand him the paper, and he frowns. He blinks up at me and then looks back at the paper and says, "Your name is Confidence?" he asks.

"Yes. I know it's unusual, weird, whatever. But it's mine," I say.

"I erased your e-submission because I thought it was an error. What a fucking fabulous name," he says.

"Thank you." I grin.

"But, I'm still calling you Dolly 'cause that is how I'll always think of you," he says.

"Fair enough. There are a lot worse things than being named after an idol," I agree.

"Okay, come on back. Let me get you settled in Tanaka's chair. We book our clients so everyone has thirty minutes where they have her exclusive attention. Since it's your first time, she'll have a lot of questions. I'll get you some champagne to sip while you're chatting," he says.

"I was thinking more like coffee," I say and then swallow down the saliva that floods my mouth at the word. "Or maybe something that's more suitable for morning consumption," I say.

"I'll add orange juice to your mimosa," he says and walks me back to the room where one chair sits facing a full-wall mirror. Next to it is a small stand cluttered with flat irons, brushes, and bottles of product.

"Have a seat. Tanaka will be here in less than a minute." He pats my shoulder lightly and turns to leave. "I'll be back with your mimosa. I squeeze the juice fresh, so it will be a few," and then he disappears through a door in the back of the room.

I stare at myself in the mirror. Do I really look like Dolly Parton? I mean, I'm blond, short, bigger-than-average breasts, bigger-than-average ass, tiny waist that I inherited from my father. My hair is unruly, but that's because I haven't washed it in two days and haven't brushed it in a day. My bare shorts-clad legs dangle several inches off the floor, the toes of my Top-Siders barely skim it when I try to reach. My stomach grumbles, and I put a hand over it. I should have eaten breakfast. I wonder if I could bribe someone to run across to Sweet and Lo's for one of their ridiculously perfect almond croissants.

"Hey, I am Tanaka," a loud, lyrical voice sings, yes, sings at me just before a very tall, very beautiful woman steps through the same door Noé had left through. She looks like Tara from *True Blood*, even down to the black leather jeans hugging her endlessly long legs.

"Hello…" I do my best Adele impersonation.

"Tsk, tsk, tsk." She shakes her head. "Only I sing," she says pleasantly, but firmly.

"As it should be," I admit.

"Your hair is a disaster," she scolds. "What a waste of beautiful cuticles. You do not take care of it," she says and picks up a few strands of my hair. She pulls a little magnifying glass out of her pocket and holds my hair under it.

"What is this color at the end?" she demands, dropping the lock of hair unceremoniously before taking a step back to eye me closely.

"That's my color. I've just got through growing out a terrible brown I got from some online company that has since disappeared."

"Are you saying that's your natural color?" she asks, disbelief plain in her voice.

"Yes, it is. Why?"

"I've been trying to mix a blond just this shade for the last six years, and I've never managed to get it quite like this." She picks the hair up again and strokes it. She slides her hand closer to my roots and says, "*This* color, though, it needs some help. I saw you want a color, cut, blowout?"

"Yes," I say.

"Okay, well, you've got such heavy hair, I think we should cut about five inches from the back and maybe seven from the front," she says casually.

"Um, no. I was thinking maybe half an inch off the ends," I say.

"Well, if that's what you want, there are about eight chain hair salons within two miles of here. Go there. *They* can do that. You do not need *me* for that," she says, and I jump out of my seat.

"No, I don't want to go there. But I don't want to cut all my hair off," I say.

"Why not?" she asks like it's a true puzzle.

"Because that's not what I had in mind, and you can't expect me to just say okay when you're talking about cutting my hair up to shoulders," I say.

"Trust me. If you do not like it, I will do your hair for you every single week for a year and not charge you a single cent," she says.

"Really?" I ask in surprise.

"You will love it. But yes, in case you're truly an idiot, I will abide by my word and put up with having a person with bad taste in my chair every week for a year without getting paid a penny," she says.

"Okay, although somehow that doesn't sound like it would be very much fun," I say.

"Oh, it would be a lot of fun. I do *not* take orders. I style what I see. The heads of hair that lead you here are all my vision—not what those men and women walked in and demanded. So, if you want to keep this long towel of hair on your head, you can go find someone else to help you with that. But I will never give you another appointment, so think carefully before you leave," she says.

"God, you're ruthless," I say. I look in the mirror. I lift my hair off my neck and turn my head to look at my profile.

"It wouldn't be that short. Your neck isn't long enough to make that flattering," she says.

"Please think nothing for my tender feelings, pick me apart, I can take it," I say.

"Did you come for flattery or because you want to walk out of here looking like the very best version of yourself?"

"The latter. I'm ready. Do what you will."

"You'll be happy. My motto is if you leave pretty, you'll come often. And I've only had two clients in twenty years leave here unhappy. And they were both insane." She says this with a straight face.

"I'm ready. Do what you will," I say in resignation.

"Excellent." She claps her bejeweled hands together. I look past her into the mirror and say a silent goodbye to my hair.

"Let me ask you some questions before we go ahead with the color," she says and pulls a small piece of paper out of her pocket. "DOB, April 25, 1990." She glances up at me. "You need to start using eye cream. You've got the beginnings of fine lines that no twenty-eight-year-old should have," she says and then glances back down.

"Yeah, just have at my ego, I wasn't going to use it today, anyway," I say.

"That was just advice from woman to woman. I've got melanin on my side, but I've been using eye cream since I was fifteen. I'm forty-five and look the same age as you," she says with a shrug. "If you want to age terribly, feel free to ignore me," she says.

I smile stiffly and make a mental note to visit Sephora before the weekend is out.

"When was your last period?" she asks. "You left that blank." She points at the paper when I don't answer.

"I didn't realize that was a required question." I frown.

"Well, there's all this hysteria about pregnancy and hair dye, so I always ask to make sure you're not possibly pregnant because there's a general consensus that you don't dye your hair until the second trimester," she says.

"Well, I'm on the pill, so…" I say.

"Okay, great, so when was your last period?"

"Hmm, let me see. I keep track of it, so let me go see when I last wrote it in," I say, and I pull my phone out of my purse and look at my calendar. And start scrolling.

I scroll back to September, scan the calendar and realize there's no entry for the week my period usually shows up.

"Huh," I say and go back to August and see the same. I look back at July and see the dates.

"Um, July 28th," I say. And when she just stares at me, I throw my head back against the chair.

"No. I'm *not*," I say unequivocally.

"Why? Are you celibate?" she asks.

"No, but I'm on birth control," I say, and it sounds more like a plea than a statement.

"Then that baby really wanted you to be its mama." She points at my very flat stomach and shrugs.

"How can you sound so cheery?" I snap.

"'Cause I'm not the one who's unexpectedly pregnant," she says.

"I'm not pregnant," I insist.

"Well, one way to find out." She turns around and yanks open a drawer on her little stand of tools. She turns around and holds up a pregnancy test.

"Why in the world do you have pregnancy tests in your drawer?" I ask and stare at her wild-eyed.

"Ain't I a hairdresser?" she asks impatiently. "Do you know how many times a week I see that deer-in-the-headlights look that's on your face right now? I ask this ten times a day. Just go back to the bathroom and get it done."

"No. I am not taking a pregnancy test just because I forgot to write down my period last month," I say and put my hands up to ward her off. How is it possible for my stomach to feel heavy and flutter at the same time? My heart is racing, and my skin is tingling. I can't even think straight.

"Okay, but I can't color your hair today," I say.

"Of course, you can," I cry in desperation. This can't be happening.

She sighs. "Let me be more deliberate with my word choice," she says slowly. "I *won't* color your hair today. Not unless you pee on that stick, and it's negative," she announces.

"Okay, fine. Don't color my hair. I'll get the cut and the blowout," I say and watch her drop the test back in the drawer. I have a moment of regret where I think I should have just taken it, but I can't do it.

Noé walks in with the mimosa on a small silver tray he's carrying like it's a tray of crown jewels.

"Good Lord, did you grow the oranges yourself?" she asks.

"So sorry, I had to run out to Randall's to get the oranges. We were out," he says, and he drops the mimosa down in front of me. I pick it up and start to take a sip, and my stomach grumbles. And I know I'm not pregnant. But I put it down because if I am, it would be very irresponsible to drink it without having proof. The thought of a baby— Hayes's baby—inside of me makes me dizzy. But, at the trailing tip of the whirlwind of disbelief, panic, worry, doubt, and surprise is a bolt of joy.

Hayes.

His baby. I close my eyes and see a bundle with silky chocolate curls and glittering topaz hazel eyes.

"Come, let's go back to the bowl," she says and starts to stand me up.

"I've changed my mind," I say before I can talk myself out of it. "I want to take it," I say and stick my hand out.

"Okay, here you go," she says and then points me in the direction of the bathroom.

Chapter 28

DISTRACTED

HAYES

"Hayes, good morning." Amelia's graver-than-normal voice makes me wish I had ignored her call. I finish tying the laces of my sneakers and sit down on the bed.

"Your voice makes me think there's nothing good about this particular Saturday morning, so let's just cut straight to the chase," I tell her.

"Your uncle and stepmother are mounting a petition to have you ousted as chairman of the board," she says.

"You're kidding," I say and drop my forehead into my hand. That rat faced motherfucker. I've been treating him with kid gloves. But they're about to come off.

"Hayes?" Amelia calls my name when I don't say anything more.

"Can they do it?" I ask.

"Well, yes. Clearly, because they have," she says.

"No, I mean, is there a way to remove me? I thought it was a position I held until death," I said.

"Normally, that is the case. But there's a clause for removal if you are unfit to hold the role. That is the clause they have evoked," she says.

"Unfit?" I breathe into the phone in complete indignation. "In what way? By what measure?" I demand.

"By reason of illegitimacy," she says slowly. Meaningfully.

"Illegitimacy?" I ask.

"Yes. Hayes. They're demanding a DNA test and I would suggest you comply without any protest."

"I don't understand," I say. "A DNA test for what? That would only help them if I wasn't my father's son," I say angrily.

Amelia is silent.

"Are they implying I'm not my father's son?" I demand an answer, but my throat is dry and my heart is beating faster now.

"That's *exactly* what they're implying," she says.

"Based on what?"

"Based on what they say is a discrepancy between your mother's medical records and death certificate. I don't know what that means, do you?" she asks pointedly.

"Of course not. That's ridiculous. I'll take the DNA test today. Shut this shit down now and then I'm done playing nice with him," I say.

"Okay. You can be done playing nice with him. But Hayes, is there any way at all, that the paternity test could come back anything other than what you expect? This is an extraordinary move they've made. If it's a Hail Mary, it's a hell of a gamble."

"I have a birth certificate with my parents' names on it. I have the same blood type. I look just like my father and my grandfather. This is ridiculous. It's an attempt to embarrass me. Send me the details on when and where I can take the test. The sooner the better and I want those results expedited." I glance down at my watch. I'm late meeting Confidence, and I almost want to text her and ask her to meet me back at her place, but I'm not going to let this asshole ruin more than he's already tried to.

"I'll send you the court order. I advise you to go to a random lab instead of your doctor for the test. Just to avoid any questions about tampering or manipulation of their process."

"Fine. I'll be looking for it. I've gotta go," I say before I hang up.

I should have thanked her. That couldn't have been an easy call to make. My mind is reeling. My uncle must really hate me to have done this. A paternity test. It's ridiculous.

And yet…my mind is not easy. I have a kernel of dread in my gut that I will ignore until I don't have to. But it's burrowed itself into the lining of my life; its sharp, thorn-like tip burns as it embeds itself into the story of my life. And with every step I take, it burrows deeper, and it feeds on years of being denied my rightful place at the head of this family. I've been too soft. And I should have seen something like this coming.

I let a woman pull me off course once, and I lost pieces of my legacy that my father scarified for. And I'm letting it happen again. Nothing is more important than the family legacy.

"Fuck that," I mutter. If anything Confidence will help my find my way through this. She makes me stronger, better.

I need to talk to her. I'm running late by the time I leave her apartment, but I walk slowly. I think of what my uncle's shit is about to cost me... I'm not going to let him cost me my future, too.

Chapter 29

TOO LATE

CONFIDENCE

I glance at my phone for the third time. Hayes is never late. But it's Saturday. I was a little nebulous about the time, he just erred on the other side of eleven o'clock. I turn around and look at my hair again. She didn't do a permanent color, but she rinsed it with a golden blond that makes it look like spun gold in the light. She cut it so it skims my shoulders. I feel naked and cold. But my face looks more…I don't know…visible.

I'm pregnant.

I stare at my reflection and try to see how I'm different. I must be different. Right?

Hayes and I blended our cells together to create a miracle. I think I'm in love already and all I've seen is a blue line. Hayes's DNA has coalesced with mine. That little amalgamation of us has burrowed into my womb and will take from me, blood and marrow. Teeth and bone. And a life will grow from it. I'm falling in love at the speed of light with a blue line. I do what I have been too afraid to since I took four pregnancy tests in the bathroom of Blush. I laugh.

I want to wait and get a blood test before I tell Hayes, but I'm not sure that I can. There's not a single solitary cell in my body that expects him to be anything less than jubilant when I tell him. We are in such a good place. The litigation with Kingdom is moving along, but so are his side-by-side efforts to help alleviate the suffering of his tenants while they're in legal limbo. I've watched him write checks from his personal account this week that, no matter how much money he has, must have stung a little. But he's smiled every time he's paid for something that makes their lives easier. And he's doing it all anonymously. He doesn't want the attention, and he doesn't want to cause any friction with Kingdom's board. It has just been one more thing about this man who makes me feel like he would move mountains to be with me. I feel the same way.

I can't wait to tell him what we've done together.

"Well, look what we have here," a voice from beside me calls, and my blood freezes in my veins. I turn my head slowly and take in the tall, dark blond, handsome man whose beautiful smile hides a black, devious heart.

"Barry," I say flatly and curl my lip in disgust.

"Confidence," he drawls like he's making a joke.

"What are you doing here?" I ask.

"It's a public place. Or did you have the entire town blacklist me?" He glowers at me.

"I didn't have anyone do anything. You running around ranting about feminazis and conspiracies did that."

"That mouth of yours is only good for one thing. And talking isn't it," he says.

I roll my eyes at him. "Was that supposed to offend me? Make me cry? Make me care?" I ask with contempt and malice and disgust. "You're pathetic," I spit at him.

His expression loses any pretense of charm, and he pushes himself off the window he was leaning on and walks over to me, clearly thinking he can intimidate me.

"You didn't think I was pathetic when you worked for me," he says.

"No, I didn't. But I was also clearly suffering from a clear case of extreme slumming. I'm all better now and I see you for exactly what you are," I say with a smile. I turn and start down the narrow alley that runs between Blush and Twist. I stop as soon as I realize I'm walking away from people. Away from the light and out of sight. I can hear him rushing to catch up with me. It takes everything I have to not run. I try to reach into my purse for my phone so I can call Hayes, or 9-1-1. But my hands are trembling.

I smell it on him like I did my dad. He's in the mood to hurt someone, and I just walked down a fucking alley. His hand closes on my arm and spins me around to face him.

"Let me go, Barry!" I yell, and he hustles me farther down the alley.

"I'm just getting started." He leans forward and puts his face in mine. "And maybe if you ask nicely, once he's done with you, I'd be willing to give you a—" My hand flies out and up before I can stop to think. The crack of my palm against his cheek and the burst of white-hot pain at the contact make me feel like I detonated a bomb.

He grabs my wrist with one hand and my chin with the other. "You fucking bitch," he grinds out into my ear. He presses his body into the back of mine, and I hate myself for the sob that escapes me when his erection presses into my back. He presses his lips to my ear and whispers, "You're lucky you've got that body. Why don't you show me what you showed Wilde and Rivers that's got them so hot and bothered over you?" He grinds into me, and I scream. Loudly enough that it bounces off the dark stone walls. He covers my mouth with his hand, but not before I can bare my teeth and bite down on his palm. I almost gag at the musty, salty taste of his skin in my mouth. But it does the trick. He lets go and I break into a run. I only get two feet before he's got me back in his iron tight grip.

The skin on my arm burns as he struggles to hold on to me. I kick him and scream at the top of my lungs, "Hayes!" before his hand is back over my mouth and his hot breath all over my face. "You think he'll care what happens to you?" He throws me against the wall and steps between my legs. "I'm going to fuck that cockiness right out of you," he says and starts unbuckling his pants.

And I start fighting for my life. His hand is still pressed to my face, and now he's pressing so hard that I can't open my mouth to bite him or breathe.

I kick, punch, fight, slap. I might as well be fighting an eight-foot wave. He completely overwhelms me. I close my eyes and wail in my throat and beg God to make it stop. I feel his penis, hard and heavy, pressing against the bare skin of my inner thigh, and I think about Hayes and my baby and I want to die. I sob helplessly into his hand and hope he kills me when he's done. I left Arkansas to escape violent men, and he's managed to find me anyway.

A loud roar comes out of nowhere and cuts through the ringing in my head, and then, I'm falling. His body is yanked free of mine, and I land with a thud on my ass and look over to see Hayes on top of Barry. His fists are flying and making contact with sickening thuds and crunches of skin and bone. "You motherfucking piece of shit!" he yells in between his arm's wild swings.

I run to him to try and make him stop. I'm afraid he'll kill him. But he's in a rage and doesn't hear me. I run back to the top of the alley and scream for help at the top of my lungs before the tsunami of emotions overwhelms me and I faint.

Chapter 30

HELPLESS

HAYES

"I wanted to talk to you before you went out there. Confidence is waiting," Amelia says.

"What is it?" I ask and finish buttoning my shirt. I'm being released from the courthouse jail where I've spent most of the day.

She sighs and leans back against the wall. "Well, I have good news and bad news. What do you want first?" she asks.

"The good, please," I say. "Maybe the sun will explode as soon as you're done with the good news, killing us all in the process. And you'll never get a chance to tell me the bad news."

"Are you *drunk*?" she asks after a beat of silence.

"I've been in jail. The only thing I've had to get drunk on is the clusterfuck juice of my life. Give me the good news first," I repeat.

"The DA isn't pressing charges against you."

"I wish he would," I snap.

"Hayes, that is your anger talking," she says like I'm being tedious.

"I want as many opportunities to tell the world what a piece of shit Barry Jimenez is. And if standing trial for defending my woman would give me just one more chance to tell everyone, I'd do it."

"A trial would be a disaster for you right now. All of the rebuilding of the Rivers name will go down the drain," she reminds me.

"I don't care," I say.

"You should," she snaps. "Here's the bad news. Your uncle has petitioned the board for your removal, without regard for the DNA results," she says.

"The fuck he did!" I shout and spin around to face her. "What? How? Can they do that?" I ask in alarm.

"Yes. They can. There's a clause added by your grandfather about thirty years ago that gives them the right to do this."

"What does it say? This clause?"

"In the event that the actions of the chairman materially damage the social standing of the organization or cause a negative light to be cast on the family's reputation that their ability to lead the board could be questioned or challenged. Your uncle and stepmother are doing that."

"Is this about that asshole who attacked my girlfriend?" I ask angrily.

"This is about you having to be pulled off him after breaking his ribs, his nose, and knocking out one of his teeth," she explains.

"Well, the DA hasn't pressed charges," I say.

"But Mr. Jimenez is suing you civilly, Hayes. For a lot of money," she says.

"I don't really give a shit about the money. You think I was going to stand there, watch him put his hands on my woman, try to rape her, and just kindly ask him to stop? You're out of your mind, and he's lucky I didn't fucking kill him. If I ever see his ass again, I might," I tell her.

"Don't say that out loud. Because if he ends up dead, whether he had a heart attack or died in a plane crash, you won't be able to stop the rumor from suggesting you had something to do with it. You have extraordinary power. Access to an almost limitless amount of money. It wouldn't be far-fetched to think you'd dispose of an enemy and try to make it look like natural causes. So, do not talk like that to *anyone*," she says.

"Fuck that motherfucker and the law that allows him to turn himself into the victim here," I spit out.

"Well, now he's cooperating with your uncle. And they are coming for you hard. I'm going to file for a temporary restraining order on the action to remove you. I don't expect it will be granted, but at the very least, it will force them to present whatever evidence they have against you in their little coup d'état. That is what this is. It is full out war. They want you gone, and they'll do it by any means necessary," she says.

"I think you're overreacting. They want money, not my life," I brush her off.

"Don't dismiss it. It's not just money. It's control of the entire Rivers family line and future. They want it. I want you to keep your head down. And you're going to like what I have to say next even less," she says.

"That is a very high bar you just set. What could be worse?"

"I want you to put some distance between you and Confidence," she says.

"Fuck. No," I say immediately. I feel a flush of guilt when I remember that I had even considered the same thing myself. I close my eyes to push down the rage that threatens to consume me when I remember the scene I walked in on. Her against the wall. Him between her legs. Hurting her. My stomach roils.

"No way. Are you kidding? You want me to stay away from my woman so that punk-ass uncle of mine can have what he wants? No fucking way," I say.

"No, I want you to stay away from her, so he can't use her to get to you. He knows she matters to you, and that makes her a target. Make him think you've broken up. Just until it goes away. The petition he filed has rules. I'm filing the TRO today. It'll be denied. We'll have seven days to respond. Just think about it," she urges me in that intense whisper she does when she's trying to be persuasive. But I don't need persuading.

"I'm sick of this, and I'm ready for it to be over," I tell her.

"Good. We're going to need to spend all week getting our response together. Now, the DNA results will come back before then, and depending on their outcome—"

"Why do I get the impression, Amelia, that you're worried about the results?" I cut her off.

She stares at the floor. Her silence is alarming.

I press her.

"Tell me. Now," I say. "What do you know?"

"Nothing, Hayes. I don't know anything. But I'm worried because Swish told me something before he died—*right* before he died."

"What?"

"He said, 'Hayes is his...' and that was all. I don't know what 'his' meant. I didn't even make anything of it because he was so close to the end, and he'd been in and out of consciousness for two days. I have always thought they were the words of his dying mind. Until..."

"Until my uncle brought this up." Understanding dawns. "Shit. You think somehow, he raised me as his own, but I'm not?" I ask her.

"Honestly, until today, I did think just that. I was sure that the test would come back proving you were not your father's son. But him filing this second motion, to have you removed, says he's not one hundred percent sure of his position. Otherwise, he would just let the DNA test results take you out. That's why I want to try and buy you as much good will as possible. If you are his son, then I want you to be able to fight the other charges. It's important that you maintain an unimpeachable public reputation."

"No, I need to focus on maintaining my unimpeachable *private* reputation. The woman I love and who I plan on asking to spend the rest of my life with was almost raped today. I don't care if I get to be the chairman of the board of a company that would turn its back on people who have been harmed by its negligence. I don't. That will not be my legacy. I have my own money. I have my own fucking name. And I have a woman who I love more than anything that I need to keep safe. I need to focus on that right now," I tell her.

"I think distance could keep her safe. And you, too." I dismiss her and decide to end the conversation because I'm desperate to get to Confidence and see how she's feeling. I take my keys, phone, and wallet from the small envelope they brought in with my clothes.

"Let me know what the DNA test says, Amelia. But honestly, I am about done with this family and its shit. I'm not the head of it. I'm just the next in a line of men who have been puppets controlled by the whims of a man who has been dead for a hundred years. That doesn't make me a ruler or king or leader. I'm just filler."

"Hayes, don't make hasty decisions."

"I'm not making any decisions. For once in my life, I just really don't give a shit," I tell her and walk out.

She's waiting on a bench by the back door that leads to the exit. She's curled up, her legs tucked underneath her, her hands wedged between her thighs. Her head is bent. She looks so small, and as I get closer, the bruises he left on her become visible.

My gut knots. The door slams shut behind me and she looks up in my direction, her eyes wide at first and then softening with relief when she sees me.

"Hey, baby," I say as I start toward her. She jumps off the bench and runs toward me. Her arms are pumping, her hair flies behind her, and her face is a mask of determination as she launches herself into my open arms.

"Hayes," she breathes my name into my neck. She's trembling and squeezing my neck so tightly that I almost can't breathe. But I would rather die than let her go. My heart is in my throat as I stand there with her in my arms. Her heart thuds against my chest, and she cries quietly. Her tears soak my T-shirt and I feel frustrated at my powerlessness.

"I've been so scared, Hayes," she whispers against my neck.

"I'm so sorry, *Tesoro*." My ribs feel two sizes too small for my body.

She's been alone all day. I hate that she felt a moment of fear. I hate that she had to worry about me on top of all of that.

I walk us out just like that to the SUV that Amelia ordered for me. It's nearly two in the morning and the few reporters who are still hanging around waiting for me to be released are snoozing when we step out. They all wake up when the door closes, but the driver has the door to my car open and we're inside before more than a few camera flashes catch us.

As soon as the door closes, I raise the privacy screen. I try to put her down on the seat next to me, but she won't let go. She's trembling. I cup her face and find her cheeks wet with tears.

Cold dread fills me. I thought I'd gotten there in time.

"Baby, did he…?" I can't bring myself to finish the question.

"No." She shakes her head. In the dark of the car, I can't see her face, so I reach up to turn on the overhead lights. She puts a hand on mine and says, "Please, don't."

"Why?" I bring my arm down and cup her cheek. She nestles her face and her breath brushes my skin in warm puffs. "I'm just so happy to be with you. That you came for me. It was fucking awful. I haven't been that scared in a very long time," she whispers.

"Oh, baby." I feel so fucking useless.

"So, thank you, Hayes. You've saved me twice now," she says and then climbs down from my lap. She rests her head on my shoulder and by the time we're pulling up to the valet at The Ivy, she's fast asleep. I carry her up to her apartment.

She doesn't stir as I put her in bed. I lock her door behind me and tell the doorman that no one should be allowed up without her okay. Then, I get into the back of my waiting car.

In the dark of the car, I cry. Like I haven't since I was a boy. Not a sobbing cry, but hitched breaths and watery, greedy gulps of air, while my chest heaves under the weight of everything that has happened in the last twenty-four hours. By the time I get home, I'm spent.

Chapter 31

WOUNDED

CONFIDENCE

Since the terrible incident in Rivers Wilde, my life has been lived in hectic, noisy spaces that fall between crying jags, snatches of fitful sleep, police interviews, and worry. I went to work that Monday, despite my bruises and aches. I had nothing to be ashamed of, and I had a lot of work to do.

The pro-Barry movement has lost most of its members. But the few loyal ones who don't seem to care that he tried to rape me in broad daylight don't try to hide their contempt. On top of that, we hit a real roadblock in the class-action suit against Kingdom. The class is divided. A lot of them want to settle. And there's talk about them breaking away to form their own suit.

Oh, and I'm officially pregnant. I went to see my doctor after getting slammed up against that wall and they did a blood test. It's official. I'm due on the 28th of May. I'm ten weeks along and I have an ultrasound picture tucked into my purse. Hayes and I have been talking every day, but that's it. He's been busy every time I've tried to see him. I thought he needed some space like I did. But now, I'm worried that he's avoiding me.

While he had been in custody after his arrest, Amelia had filled me in on what happened that morning and why he'd been late to meet me in the first place.

The memory of that night, knowing that he's alone while dealing with what happened in the alley, as well as the prospect that he is not his father's son, has torn at me and kept me awake every night since I saw him.

I was starting to feel frustrated because I had been through an ordeal, too—a big one, and I didn't have my best friend's shoulder to cry on. I'm pregnant and haven't told him because I hadn't had the chance to. He hasn't answered his phone all day.

Amelia called me this evening to say she had the DNA results but couldn't reach Hayes. She said she was headed to his house, so I asked her to bring me with her. And here we are.

"This isn't a good idea," Amelia says for the fourth time in the last two minutes.

"Maybe not. But if things go wrong, I'll handle it," I tell her.

"You can't handle a man that size. What if he loses it again?" she asks.

I reach up and punch on the overhead light in her car.

"If you make one more comment about Hayes that implies he's a danger to me or dangerous at all, I will make sure he fires you," I tell her.

Her eyes narrow, and she leans forward. "I've served this family for years. Swish himself trained me. I'd like to see you try to get rid of me," she says coldly.

"No. You *wouldn't*," I tell her honestly. "I don't hold back when it comes to him. And if you believe any of that shit his ex-wife spewed about him, you don't deserve to lick his boots, much less to be on his payroll," I growl at her.

Her eyes widen, and she leans back. "I'm glad you've got so much backbone. You're going to need it. I don't know what's in that envelope, but if it's not good, things could get ugly," she says somberly. Her eyes are so grave and my heart sinks.

I glance up at Hayes's house. There are no signs of life inside. But I know he's there and I need to get to him.

"Let me just say this—since you don't seem to know—he would never touch me or anyone who couldn't defend themselves against him. He's not a bully or an abusive man. Sure, he's an asshole sometimes, but that's how he's managed to survive in this cesspool of humanity he was born into. I'm his second chance. He's mine. No matter what the results say, we'll be fine because that's what we do. I've been preparing myself, it'll be okay. You can leave."

"Okay," she says quickly, easily, and with a touch of relief.

"Okay. Give me the envelope and then get out of here. I'll find my way back or Hayes will bring me. Either way, tomorrow we get to work on taking that uncle of his down," I say and wait for her to nod.

"God help the person who comes up against the two of you. You're like two sides of the same coin," she says, her voice full of marvel.

"That's right," I affirm, glad that she finally sees it. "God help them."

I open the car door, turn around to give her one last reassuring smile and say, "I'll see you tomorrow."

I decide to knock first. But after three knocks, with two minutes between each, there is still no answer. So I use the key and let myself in.

The house is quiet. The ticking of a wall clock, the hum of a sub-zero fridge, the whir and click of the air-conditioning coming on and the chirp of what sounds like hundreds of cicadas fill the otherwise still, dark house.

"Hayes," I call. There's no resounding echo, none of the certainty that comes from knowing that you're heard, even if you're not seen. I feel my first real prick of worry for him. I should have come sooner.

"Hayes," I call out again and start up the stairs. The carpeted runner silences my footfalls, but the wooden steps still creak every other step. It's silent upstairs, too. There's a light peeking around the frame of the door that leads to his master bedroom. As I get closer, I hear his snores. I push the door open and my anger spikes.

Lined up along the foot of the bed are four empty bottles of Jack Daniels. I watch him. Even in his sleep, he's strong and powerful.

His brows are relaxed, his stubble-covered jaw is still strong, but not so rigid. His lips are parted and soft. For the first time, I see the little boy who grew up without his mother in a house that was managed like a chessboard. Manipulations, lies, and death blows.

I spend a few minutes watching him and then pick up the glass of water by his bed and throw it at him. His eyes pop open in surprise. I step back when he starts to shake his head back and forth to get the water off and wipes the water out of his eyes before he looks up at me. His eyes are murderous.

"What the hell?" he yells at me.

"You tell me!" I give him the full force of my anger, too. "I've been trying to reach you for *days*," I seethe.

"I told you I needed a few days," he grumbled.

"I knew you needed some time to think. And I walk in here to find you living like you're a frat boy on spring break." I point at the bottles lined up on the floor.

"Stop screaming," he moans and cradles his head.

"I'm not screaming. Even though I should be. You fucking abandoned me, Hayes!" *Now,* I raise my voice.

"I didn't," he groans.

"And you abandoned yourself. We have shit to do. Shit to discuss."

He covers his face and groans into his hands.

"You threw water at me, *Tesoro,*" he grumbles.

"Yeah, I know. Because I'm the one who did it," I say with dry sarcasm. He scowls, completely unamused.

"I just needed a couple of days," he says miserably.

"Hayes, what the hell have you been doing in here? Are you high?" I ask him.

He sits up straight and shakes his head. "I don't know where my phone is. I haven't seen it since the…" He winces as if he's in pain and says, "since the fight."

"How did Amelia reach you then?" I ask,

"The house line, like she always does. It's an encrypted line, and she's unduly paranoid, so she always uses it to talk to me when it's urgent," he says. And then he shakes his head and looks at me with real confusion in his eyes. "What the fuck is wrong with my family?" His voice is etched with pain and my heart aches for him because I don't have any answers to that question.

"I don't know. But, we need to talk."

He sighs.

"I know that you have more shit going on right now than most people deal with their whole lives. But you've also got more power, privilege, and wealth than those same people can dream about. And with all of that comes all the obligation. More money, more problems, right?"

He nods.

"So, get off your ass and put on your streetwise hat, because your uncle is playing dirty," I tell him.

"No kidding." He sighs and rubs his hands tiredly over his face.

"We have to think like desperate people who don't have safety nets or moral compasses," I tell him.

"You sound like Amelia," he grumbles.

"You should do whatever she tells you to do," I say.

"You've changed your tune. I thought she was a 'vulture,'" he says.

"The board meeting is in *two* days. No atheists in foxholes," I say.

"Do you mean *my enemy's enemy is my friend?*" he asks.

"Whatever. We have a lot of work to do!" I snap impatiently.

His expression has morphed from slightly annoyed to happy.

"Why are you smiling? Do you like getting chewed out by me?" I ask.

"I don't know what *chewed out* means, but it sounds like it could be hot," he says.

"Hayes," I huff.

"That morning, when he attacked you. I was coming to break up with you," he says.

I freeze and stare at him. Tears, hot and unbidden, fill my eyes. My breath is trapped in my lungs, and I can't speak.

"I wouldn't have done it," he says quickly and rushes to stand by me. When he puts his hands on my shoulders, I lean into him.

"But why?" I hear myself say in a voice that I don't recognize. It's thick with hurt.

"I had just gotten the call about the DNA test. I was angry and thought I had let Thomas get away with too much because I'd been distracted," he says, not quite meeting my eyes now.

"By me?" I ask.

"Yes. But by the time I got there, I knew there was no way I could give you up. The sun rises and sets in your eyes, Confidence," he says.

My heart starts kicking again and my tears dry.

"But walking into that, seeing him on you. I thought…" He swallows thickly. "I'm sorry. So sorry that I wasn't there. I'm so fucking sorry that he put his hands on you. That I was late." He sounds so distressed.

"Hayes, why didn't you just talk to me? Is that why you haven't left your house? You've been avoiding me?" I ask.

He laughs darkly. "No. I was afraid I wouldn't be able to stop myself from going to that fucker's house and setting it on fire," he says. I grab his hand and squeeze.

"I *was* scared that day. But I'm okay now," I tell him. "I just want us to focus on what we can control. And we have to get ready for this meeting. It's only two days away." I feel desperate suddenly to lighten the mood. I've spent four days in a state of complete anxiety and it's taken its toll. As much as I'm dreading the rest of our conversation, I'm glad we have it to talk about.

I lean back on the windowsill and he sits on the bed watching me with a smile on his face.

"What are you smiling at?"

"You," he says, his gaze growing more intense. "You're my everything. And I want to be your everything," he says intently.

"You *are* my everything, baby," I assure him.

My heart is in my throat.

And in his eyes.

"I'm thinking about myself, my future, my responsibilities so differently because of you," he says and my heart swells. "So, yeah, I'm worried about the DNA test. But that's not what has given me nightmares. It's that I've done anything to hurt you or *allowed* anything to hurt you." His eyes are glittering with fire that speaks of loyalty, constancy, and forever.

"I know, baby…" I say and want so badly to put him in my pocket and protect him from everything that's coming this week. "I feel the same way."

"You're my priority. Because you are my future. You have a view of the world that I want to use as my lens for the rest of my fucking life. Even when it feels like it's do or die, I know that you and I are a sure thing."

"Never doubt that," I say.

He runs his hands through his hair. "Everything feels so complicated, except for us. I don't care if I'm not the heir. I don't care if they remove me. The only thing I need is you."

He stands up, naked as the day he was born. Even soft, his penis is beautiful and thick. His whole body is beautiful and thick. I let my eyes feast on him, and when I get to those eyes—those fucking eyes—I blurt out, "I'm pregnant."

Chapter 32

TRUTH

HAYES

"You're what?" I ask and sit back down on the bed, only briefly registering the cold, wet sheets bunching under my bare ass. I'm dazed and a million questions and emotions flood me as I try to recover from the curve ball she just threw at me.

"Hayes." She walks over to me, her blue eyes crinkled in concern. "Are you okay?" she asks and then lays a hesitant hand on my shoulder.

"Did you say you're pregnant?" I ask, dazed, but fuck me, also praying to God I wasn't hearing things.

She nods, her eyes wide, her blond brows raised in uncertainty.

Relief, joy, gratitude rush through me like a current and washes away my hangover, my dread, and my regret.

I jump off the bed and sweep her into my arms. "Marry me," I growl in her ear.

She throws her arms around my neck. "Of course I'm going to marry you." She laughs happily and presses a kiss to my cheek.

I pull back and stare at her. "When did you find out?" I ask.

"Today," she beams. "I had a blood test."

"How far along?"

"Ten weeks," she says, and I squeeze tight before I remember myself and let her go.

"You can hug me," she says.

"I don't want to hurt *el bambino*." I put her down and kneel in front of her and press my cheek to her stomach. "There's a baby in there," I say in complete wonder and awe.

She runs her fingers through my hair and says, "Hayes, we have so much we need to talk about. I wasn't going to tell you about the baby until later, when all of this was over, but then you said all of that romantic stuff and it just came out," I say.

"So, what you're saying is that you'd like to table this conversation?" I ask and stand back up. I lean in to kiss her, and she leans back.

"Nah, you need a shower and a toothbrush," she says and jumps out of my grasp. "Go do that and then come down and let's talk."

I walk into the kitchen to find her sitting at the table, two mugs on the table. A white envelope sits on the table in front of her. It has my name and social security number on it. My stomach plummets to my knees. I know right away it's the DNA test results. But I ask anyway.

"Is that it?" I ask and nod toward the envelope.

"Yeah, Amelia gave it to me. You have to be the one to open it," she says, her eyes dry and firm, but full of concern as she watches me closely.

"I'm okay," I say, and I find that I am. My future is set, because Confidence and I are set. This is just a hurdle I've got to clear on my road to where we're going together.

"You want coffee?" she asks and pads on her bare feet across the travertine tiled floors into the kitchen. "Were you at work?" I ask, noticing her skirt and blouse for the first time. "Yeah, this morning, but then I went to the doctor and then came here."

I pick up the envelope, rip it open, and pull the paper out.

"Hayes, don't you want to sit down?" Confidence sounds alarmed. I hear her hurried footfalls as she rushes back to the table, but I just stare at the paper and gather my resolve.

"No, let's not make an event of it. I just want to know." I unfold and read what it says out loud. "With regard to the DNA of Hayes Rivers, when compared to the DNA sample obtained from Jason Rivers, twelve of the fifteen DNA markers were a match. This indicated sanguinity but does not indicate paternity. The matching markers follow the patterns we see between nephews and uncles and grandsons and grandfathers." I finish and look up at Confidence. Her face is pale, and her hand is squeezing her lips together.

"How is that possible? He couldn't have been my grandfather. He didn't have any children besides me. So, if he's my uncle.... Then what does that mean? Uncle Thomas is my father? How?" I ask. Her eyes widen and take up almost the entire first half of her face. She's shaking her head back and forth and her eyes start to fill with tears.

I stand up and walk over to her and yank her hand down. "What does it mean? Say it," I demand, irrational in my fear and anger. I'm demanding she answer a question she couldn't possibly. And yet, because she's so much braver than me, she does.

"Gigi," she croaks like it hurts for the words to pass her lips.

"No." I shake my head.

"Who else? Does your father have other siblings?" I ask.

"I don't fucking know. I didn't even know Gigi existed until I was fourteen. Anything is possible." As it starts to sink in, other realities rear their heads. I start to pace. If he wasn't my father, then his dead wife wasn't my mother, either. I don't know the name for what I'm feeling. I've grieved for people I don't know. Who aren't my parents.

"So, I'm a Rivers, but not my father's son. Who are my parents?" I ask.

"I don't...I don't know," she says and I want to shake her.

Or shake this house.

Or shake the world.

I want everyone to feel what I'm feeling. The ground beneath my feet has shifted in a way that's permanent. I will never be the same.

"Confidence. Who am I? Who is my family? *What* is my family?" I shout these questions at her. The horror on her face is too much for me. I turn away from her. I'm talking to the wrong person, anyway.

I pick up the receiver of my landline and hit the second preprogrammed button and press the phone to my ear.

"*Prego?*" Gigi's voice is husky with sleep and I look down at the alarm clock by my bed and realize it must be one or two in the morning in Positano. I haven't called her during any of this. I didn't want to worry her, and now I realize she's the only person who can answer my questions.

"Gigi, I took a paternity test," I say.

"Who's pregnant?" she asks.

"To determine *my* paternity," I clarify. I'm met with silence. I look up at Confidence who still looks like she's seen a ghost.

You okay? I mouth and walk to the fridge to get her a bottle of water.

She's carrying my fucking kid.

I crack it open and put it down in front of her and realize that Gigi hasn't made a sound.

My heart sinks.

"You knew," I say and Confidence's hand pauses in midair on its way to put her water to her lips.

"Hayes, I—"

"You what? Whose son am I?" I ask her slowly. My heart thuds wildly. My entire body is tingling, and my head is swimming.

"Hayes, it's not that simple—" she starts.

"Yes. It is." My hand slams down on the table before I even realize it's in motion. Confidence jumps up and comes to stand beside me. She puts a hand on my shoulder and I want to shake it off.

I don't want comfort. I want answers.

Gigi starts to cry softly.

"Whose child am I?" I ask her again.

"Hayes…" She's weeping loudly now.

So is my queen. I watch her. Want to go to her. But not until I have answers.

"Gigi, tell me. Now," I ask, and the words taste like ash in my mouth.

"Mine," she sobs, and I drop the phone.

I don't remember sitting down, but I must have.

"Okay, Gigi, okay," I hear Confidence saying, and then I hear the phone clatter into its cradle on the counter.

"My life is a lie. All of it. I'm a lie. I'm…" Bombs are exploding somewhere inside me. My memories are imploding. My father disappears from the memory of learning to ride a bike. He vanishes from the conversations we had about the birds and the bees.

"You are Hayes Rivers. You're a brother, a son, a friend, a lover, a father." She takes my hand and puts it over her stomach.

"A father." I pull her to me and press my face into the soft, tiny swell in her abdomen. "I'm going to be okay," I say. She's like a shot of valium, and my pulse starts to slow.

"Hayes, the worst is over," she says, and like the fool I am, I believe her.

Chapter 33

HISTORY

GIGI

"I will begin by saying that I am only sorry for the deceit and the fact that I had to live my life pretending that you weren't mine," I say slowly and force my eyes to stay on Hayes's face. I want to look away so badly.

Those green eyes are shuttered and as cold as chips of emerald. Except, those are his father's eyes and they have never been able to hide the fire that is always burning inside of him. The curiosity, the feeling, the passion, the thirst for better, the compassion, and right now, the anger.

"So, you suffered?" he asks.

I nod.

"Good," he snaps, and I smile. Because there I am. That cold, unforgiving streak that makes me a Rivers *and* him my son.

He's been a mirror to everything I've lost and yet has reminded me how lucky I was to have had any of it in the first place.

"I did what I did for you," I continue.

He laughs and my patience snaps. I stand up and walk over to him, plant my feet, and stare down at him.

"I know I owe you a lifetime of explanations and apologies, but no matter what I have done, I have loved you first," I say through lips that are barely moving, and a jaw that is so tightly clenched that I know I'm probably doing some real damage to my teeth.

"Yes, so much that you let someone else raise me for the first half of my life and then lived with me for the second half but lied the entire time," he says sullenly.

"Hayes, there are some things that are more important than our individual needs or wants. Now, please, I'm here because I wanted to tell you this face-to-face. Will you let me?"

He opens his mouth to speak and Confidence's hand slides over his and she says, "Yes, he will," and squeezes his hand when he starts to contradict her.

I misjudged this woman, and I'm so glad that Hayes has better judgment than I do because she is exactly what he and this family needs. And she loves him something fierce.

I smile gratefully at her and sit back down.

"The Riverses founded this city. With our carpetbagging money we came and bought land, financed cotton gins, and gave the Allens money to buy the land that this city is sitting on. And then, we settled here. And in this city we are titans. Power covets power. Above all. Money and fame were never the goal. Power was how you survived. Power was what gave you the ability to execute your vision. And with it came the money, the fame, the access to anything you could ever want.

"Once you've tasted it, you never want anything else. That's how we were raised. When I was eighteen, I had my coming out. It was a silly thing, but a tradition that the ruling families of Houston had started to make sure that the next generation was shaped by the best and bright-est."

"According to whom?" Confidence asks.

"According to the men who saw themselves as masters of the uni-verse. The rules of entry were steep and enforced to the letter. Number one was no new money, which—to the founding families of Houston— was a dirty word. Either way, that was how they kept people from buying their way into the elite club they'd made. This group of people produced governors, presidents, titans. They didn't want to share that.

"And girls like me? We went to college not to get an education but to find a husband. My parents sent me to the East Coast to Wellesley College."

"Isn't that all girls?" Confidence cuts in again. I smile at her and think that for all her hard-earned street smarts, this girl has a lot to learn about the family she's joining.

No matter how much she's grounded Hayes, he's still got the blood of ambitious, ruthless titans in his veins. He's not chasing a win in the moment. He will always think about his place in history. Like all of the men who came before him that have dreamed about the eternal sunlight of their glorious time as rulers among men.

"Yes, it is. And all of the men at Harvard, MIT, BU, Brandies, and Tufts knew it. So on the weekends, our parties were packed with men. And that's when I met and fell in love with your father." I look at Hayes "At a party where neither of us were having a particularly good time. I tripped, he caught me, we sat down to talk, found out we were both from Houston and spent the rest of the night falling in love. When we went home that summer, we found out that my family was opposed to the match," I said.

"Is that really a thing?" she asks.

"Oh, yes. In fact, the boys in my vintage would say—"

"Vintage?" Confidence says with a scowl of confusion.

"That's stuck-up speak for 'in the same year at school,'" Hayes tells her quickly. I frown at him before I continue.

"Yes, in my year at school, they would say 'heiress or above only,' and it wasn't something they said behind closed doors. It was a rule. And for heiresses like me, the same applied. My love—he had money, but not the kind that they liked. And there was someone else they wanted for me.

"His family was offended. They decided I wasn't what they wanted for their son. And family, to both of us, was everything. We went our separate ways.

"He married someone else. I moved back East. But then, after my father got sick, I came home. We ran into each other at a fundraiser." I can't help my smile as I remember that night. Seeing him again.

"We made a choice. When we got married, your grandfather disinherited me. Made your fath—" I stop when Hayes blanches. "I'm sorry, Jason, his heir. He was a newlywed, home from Cornell with his pretty, Beacon Hill heiress on his arm. He married the right girl, from the right family, and she had good childbearing hips—as my father called them," I recall.

"You moved to Italy?"

"Not then. Your father and I bought a farm out in Brenham. We were raising steer, and I was three months pregnant when he just… *disappeared*."

"What does that mean?" Hayes asks in a sharp voice.

"He left early one morning to go into town and just never came back home. It took me a week to call the police because I was sure he'd come back with a story about how his car ran off a cliff and he'd had to camp in the woods and wait for rescue. But after a week, I realized I couldn't hide anymore. I went to his family. They had no idea where he was and accused me of having something to do with it. They had money of their own; they were smart and they wanted revenge. So, I hid you. Right under their noses. James's wife's hips weren't so childbearing and she was ill. My father had disinherited me, and Thomas was on the verge of being expelled from West Point. We were all such a disappointment to him. The only thing he saw value in was you.

"He refused to reinstate my inheritance. But he would give it to you. If I let James and his wife raise you as theirs. At the time, I thought it was a good idea. I was beside myself with grief and without two coins to rub together. And despite everything, I still believed in the Rivers name and I wanted my son—the true oldest child—to take his rightful place. And Thomas didn't know. By the time he came home at the end of that term, I was in Italy. James and Ann had their brand-new baby boy in their arms, and he was none the wiser. I don't know how Thomas found out." I shake my head dismally.

"Well, Amelia has a clue. They obtained a copy of Anne's autopsy. It says that she'd never given birth. And so, their hope is to prove that I'm illegitimate. They have no idea of the truth," Hayes says in a low, dark voice that gives me the chills. I want to rewind, and I want to kill my little brother. He's always been such a selfish pain in the ass.

"I don't know what is wrong with Thomas. He is so resentful of everything and I don't understand it. He says he loves his family, but he's forgotten, just like our father did, that family is the people who make it up. And the name is only as good as the people who bear it. I'm worried about him. That he would do this. Power is all he's ever wanted. But he's going to be sorry. This is going to open up another can of worms that none of us wants to revisit," I say.

"What? What could be worse than playing musical parents with me?" Hayes asks.

"Nothing could be worse than that," I say quietly. My heart is breaking that this is how he has to find out. But it's time.

"So…"

"Your father. His name was Lucas Wilde," I say and wait for the light to go on. His head draws back and his eyebrows shoot into his brow line. He shoots out of his seat and stalks over to the huge mantle over the fireplace in his living room.

Confidence's hand slams over her mouth, and her eyes dart between Hayes and me like she doesn't know where to look.

"Do you mean, the *late* Lucas Wilde?" Hayes asks without turning around to face me. He braces his hands on the mantle.

"Yes. Him," I say.

"The father of Remington, Regan, Tyson? *Him*?" Hayes repeats.

"Yes," I say.

"I thought he died when Remi was a kid," Hayes says slowly.

"No, that's when he divorced Remington's mother and ran off and married me. He was declared dead years later," I answer and find that my defensiveness is still there.

Hayes turns around then. His eyes are dark, red-rimmed and so angry that my heart convulses with the knowledge that it's all directed at me.

"You ran off with a married man who had three children?" he asks me the question I ask myself every single day.

"Yes," I answer, and when he turns back around, as if the sight of me is too much, I look at Confidence who is staring ahead blankly, unseeingly.

I get up and walk over to stand behind him. "We were in love. And he married *me*," I plead. "I know it sounds so wrong. I know we shouldn't have been, but these things happen—"

He turns around again, his eyes narrow slits now. I flinch at the ex- pression in them.

"You know what *doesn't* happen? You don't give your kid away and pass him off as someone else's," he rages.

"I didn't give you away," I cry. I look at Confidence for help, but she's watching Hayes intently, her eyes reflecting the ache of sympathy inside of her.

Hayes stands up. "Wait. Remington Wilde is my older *brother*?" he asks in abject horror and shock. My stomach sinks and my panic rises. This could be a disaster. But I don't dare ask Hayes for his discretion. Instead, I give him the truth.

"Your *half*-brother, but yes. You have the same father. Or you did," I respond, and my heart constricts at the thought of Lucas and how much I loved him. How much he loved me, how badly he wanted to raise Hayes and Remi together, even though, in the end, he chose me over the possibility of being with his oldest son.

"And Remi's mother, grandmother, they all know this?"

"Well. They know Lucas left me. They know I was pregnant. *This* is why they hate us so much. But they don't know who you are. *Everybody* thinks you're James and Anne's child. I told them and everyone else that I lost the baby," I say and feel like vomiting at the look on Hayes' face.

"So, let me get this straight. I am a Wilde and a Rivers. *You* are my mother. I am the true heir because I am the true oldest of the oldest child. *You* are my *mother*," he repeats.

I nod.

"I want you to call Amelia and make an official statement. Sign it, notarize it, and we'll deliver it to Thomas's attorneys. And then, I want you to leave and never come back," he says quietly. Then he stands and walks out of the room. His back is ramrod straight, just like his father's had been. I watch helplessly as he walks up the stairs, his back straight, without a glance back in my direction.

I look at Confidence, unsure what to say. "He doesn't mean it," she says softly. Her eyes are full of pity. I didn't expect that, not after how I had treated her and what I've done to Hayes.

"He does," I say tearfully.

"You don't know him well at all," she says sadly and shakes her head.

I'm offended and want to be mad. But I know she's right. I just nod. This lie has precluded a real intimacy with my child because I was always afraid of slipping up. I love him. I have been a shoulder to lean on and supportive of all his endeavors. But I also pushed him into marriage with a woman who proved to be treacherous, and I tried to run a good one away.

"Give him some time and some space, but don't you dare walk out and never come back," she says.

I give her a watery smile.

"And that statement, please. Send it to Amelia today. The hearing is tomorrow. We'll want to kill this question now. And deal with the question of fitness alone…"

She stands there, uncertain a little, and I ask, "Did you have something to say?"

"Does Remington know?" she asks.

"I don't know, but I don't think so. No one knew. They were just told to stay away from each other. You know? The dispute over the land was real, but what really put the wedge between us was Lucas leaving his family."

"Was it worth it?" she asks without elaborating.

"Yes," I answer without asking for clarification, because it was all worth it. "For the year I had with the love of my life. For the son we made together. For the life our son got to lead. I would do it all again. Hindsight is easy, but it's what I did, and it was hard. And it took me a long time to recover. When you're a mother, you'll know. Doing what your child needs instead of what you or they want is hard."

"I can only imagine," she says, and I can't read whatever's really in her eyes. "We'll see you tomorrow."

And only because I know he's in good hands do I let myself out of their house.

HAYES

Confidence slides into bed with me, and she doesn't say a word. She lies down so we're face-to-face.

"Hey," she says and takes my hands in hers. She lays them on the soft swell of her lower stomach and whispers, "Here we are. We're safe in here."

I close my eyes and make promises to that little life growing inside of *my* life. My love. My everything.

That as long as I draw breath, he will know only love—the tough but yielding kind—from me. That no one would be able to convince me to walk away from him.

That I'm ready to be his father.

That I'm the man his mother needs.

That I know that his inheritance is more than just money and name. It's our values; it's the synchronicity between who we are in private and who we are when the world is watching.

"Do you think less of me?" I ask.

"No. Never," she says. Of course.

"Still want to marry me?" I ask.

"Yes, and before I start to show, please," she says.

"Your wish is my command," I say. They're the last words we speak before we fall asleep.

Chapter 34

JUDGMENT

HAYES
Two Weeks Later

"Thank God, that's over," Confidence says. She steps into my side and slips her arms around my waist. We step out of Kingdom's office building and out into the bright afternoon sun. The building is casting a shadow onto the big granite courtyard where overworked employees come to escape the air-conditioning and their computers for a few minutes.

"Yes, it was ugly for a second at the end, but it's done," I agree.

"Will your uncle be okay?" she asks. Bleeding heart.

"He's going to be just fine. I think retirement in exile on his ranch in the beautiful Texas countryside hardly amounts to hard time for all of the shit he's pulled over the last year," I say.

We settled the case today. Kingdom paid damages that were negotiated by Amelia and Wilde Law. The Foundation established a Project School Bell that will deploy mobile classrooms to neighborhoods that are recovering from the flood so their children can continue to go to school close to home while their schools are being renovated. It's the first in a string of programs that the foundation will fund over the next few months as part of its commitment to the city of Houston. Some of them are being done in conjunction with Wilde Law. When I think about Wilde—and Remi—my stomach contracts painfully. I still don't know how to tell him that his father is my father. And that his father may not be dead after all.

"Hayes?" Confidence calls my name and bumps me with her hip. I look down at her, and she's got a concerned look on her face.

"Yes, my love?"

"You okay? You blanked out for a minute," she says.

"Yeah." I shake my head to clear it. "Just thinking that we've got a lot of work to do. But at least now, I can do it without Thomas around."

"Looking for ways to undermine you," she adds. We start toward my car that's idling on the curb. "The car will take you back to work, if you want," I tell her.

"Yeah, that would be great." She rocks up on her heels and presses a kiss to my mouth.

"Thanks for being here today. For being here every day." I circle my arm around her waist and kiss her back.

"Hayes," Gigi says from in front of us. She stands up from the bench she's been sitting on. My heart hurts to see her. I haven't let myself think too much about her. Last night when Confidence asked me to talk to her, I'd said no. I had nothing to say. She gave birth to me, but that didn't make her my mother.

I'd said it so flippantly last night, but when I see her standing in front of me, I know it's not that simple. Like a reel of film on a screen, flashes of our life together in Positano run through my mind. Our fights. The first time we picked figs from the tree we planted together. How she slept in my bed with me the night before I left for college and talked to me all night about growing up in Rivers House.

My stomach churns, and I slide my eyes to Confidence who has gone very still beside me.

"Gigi, why are you here?" I ask her. I don't want to do this in public.

"Because *you* are," she says simply. She looks tired. And for the first time, I can see age creeping along her pale, drawn face. Her hands are clenched in front of her and she looks so frail. "Listen, can we talk—"

"You're dead, Rivers." A loud voice booms over the courtyard, and we all turn back to Smith Street to see Barry Jimenez walking toward me, a pistol in his trembling hand pointed in my general direction.

"Oh my God, it's Barry," Confidence calls just as the first shot rings out. I grab both women to put them behind me and hustle them into the building. The armed security man is already rushing out, and after a second shot, Barry is tackled to the ground.

But something happens, and Gigi doesn't end up behind me. Instead, she slumps against me and cries out in pain.

"Gigi," I call out and let go of Confidence to lay Gigi on the ground. Her light blue dress is soaked with blood that's gushing out of a small wound in her shoulder. I pull my tie off and knot it around her arm and press my hand to the wound. She winces.

"We need an ambulance!" I hear Confidence screaming in the background, but it's muted by the sound of the blood that's rushing through my ears.

Gigi grabs my hand and pulls me down to her. "Hayes." She groans, and her eyelids flutter.

"Oh, no you fucking don't." I shake her, and her eyes open.

"Don't use that kind of language, Hayes, especially not in public," she says weakly.

"Well, don't you fucking close your eyes after you've been shot!" I shout at her.

She laughs weakly. Now I can see how much I look like her.

"God, Gigi." I shake my head in denial that this is happening.

"Listen to me, Hayes. I know I wasn't your mother in your heart, but in mine, it's all I've ever been. You have been my every prayer, every dream, every hope. All of my love has always been yours. All I want is for you to be the man you were born to be," she says.

"Don't talk like you're going to die. I'm still pissed at you," I say.

She reaches up to pat my cheek. Her bloody hand is sticky against my face. "Of course you are. You're a Rivers." And then her eyes close.

Epilogue 1

GIGI

"Just rest, Gigi," Hayes whispers down at me. His big hand smooths the hair off my face and I have to stop myself from nestling into his touch. I haven't earned that. It's too soon. I know that what happened outside his office is why he's here. I hope it means that I'll be able to persuade him to stay. To give me a chance to earn it.

"I—" My throat is parched. I had a tube inserted while I was in surgery and the words I want to say are caught there.

"Save your voice, we'll have time to talk when you're better," he says in a voice that's more soothing than I can stand.

His eyes, so like mine, search my face, and I know he's looking for clues that he missed. That downward tilt on my right eye that mirrors his. The way my ears curve close and then pull away from my head. Maybe he's even imagining how he'll age. Will his jawline hold as firmly as mine? I lift my free hand and circle his wrist. I want to tell him that he gets this loving tenderness from his father. I want to tell him that he's the greatest love of my life. That I only let them have him because I wanted more for him than I thought myself capable of giving. Instead, I just hold on to my son's arm and let him look into his mother's face properly, for the first time.

The creak of the door opening behind us startles both of us. He turns and from the way his posture changes, I know it's Confidence. He deflates a little because he knows that he can lean on her. I love that he's found someone strong enough to help him carry the burden of holding our family together. I think that together, they'll do a better job than my generation did.

She comes to stand beside Hayes and wraps an arm around his waist. She squeezes him and he wraps an arm around her and holds her close. If I died, this would go down as one of the happiest moments of my life. My son is grown up, and even though I didn't do everything right, I've helped him grow into a man who is capable of love and who's not afraid to stake a claim on something he wants and then do the hard work it takes to make it his.

"Gigi, how are you feeling?" she asks.

I nod.

"Remi's here," she says. My heart plunges to my toes and my lungs constrict. But I nod.

"Are you sure you want to give it to him?" she asks. I let go of Hayes and pick up the letter I have tucked into my side of the bed. I rub the worn paper in between my fingers and nod again.

She smiles, a pained but encouraging smile. "I'll send him in. We'll be outside."

She takes Hayes's hand and they turn to leave. Just before they step through the door, Hayes looks back over his shoulder and says, "I love you, Gigi." Then he's gone.

I watch the door. My heart threatens to burst out of my chest so that everyone can see what a cowardly muscle it is. I clutch the letter that Lucas wrote Remi a few days before he disappeared. I know that this will change everything. That peace will probably never be my companion, but it's time.

Epilogue 2

CONFIDENCE

My phone buzzes from its perch on my bedside table. I fling an arm out in the dark and fumble for it. A text message from Hayes flashes, and I open it.

"*Press Play*" And then the next message is a video.

"*Where are you?*" I type back.

"*Press Play*" is his response.

"Not exactly how I imagined our wedding night," I grumble and sit up. I've been waiting in our room for an hour.

By myself.

Hayes left to get something he forgot downstairs. I spent the first half an hour getting myself ready. When I draped myself across the bed, I looked like everything I knew Hayes loved. My lingerie is a confection of ice-blue lace and satin. My hair smelled like roses and my lips were smeared with cherry flavored lip balm. Now, my hair is a tangled mess, I have sleep in my eyes and I'll probably want to brush my teeth again before I kiss Hayes.

If I ever kiss Hayes again.

"*You haven't pressed play, have you? Stop being mad and watch,*" his text says and so I push aside my annoyance and comply.

The video starts and my heart lodges in my throat. I clutch my chest and every drop of irritation I felt seconds ago disappears.

On my screen, my mother and I are dancing at the wedding. We're wrapped in each other's arms. Our heads resting on each other's shoulders. The look on my mother's face steals my breath. She's smiling. Her eyes are closed and she looks like she's having the very best dream. We've been fine since Daddy and Fortune left. But she hasn't smiled like this since long before that horrific night. We'd held each other then, too. But we'd been fused together by terror. Tonight, it had been nothing but pure love.

The song, "The Rose" by Bette Midler was her choice. And the slow, repetitive melody on piano and the gently joyous strains of the violins wrap me in the same tender embrace my mother's arms gave me while we danced. The camera zooms onto our faces for the last ninety seconds of the song and I watch as the tears run down her face and drop onto my shoulder. I hadn't felt her tears then and I watch as she composes her face and a bright smile spreads just as the song ends. The scene cuts to a white wall and I blink to clear my vision at the abrupt change in background.

Then Hayes sits down in front of the camera. "So, this is where I've been," he says into the camera. He sweeps his hand over the parts of himself that are visible in the camera. His hair is tamed into waves of chocolate silk again. The broad, bold angles of his cheekbones are more prominent than normal because he's completely freshly shaven. His tuxedo looks crisp and stiff again. When we'd stumbled up to our room after the reception, we'd been sweaty from dancing, and his collar had several smudges of my lipstick on it.

"I was watching that video while you were in the bathroom and it finally hit me what I should give you for a wedding gift. I wanted it to be something that money couldn't buy." He gives me one of his closed mouth, sexy as fuck smiles. His intelligent, oh so beautiful hazel eyes search my face as if he knew exactly where it would be when he was making the video.

"The two of you are what every mother and child should be." He runs a hand through his hair and exhales a breath. "The gesture of you dancing with your mother on what would normally be the father-daughter dance is everything I love about you. Your loyalty, your pride, you love, the respect you have for where you come from and your refusal to let anyone dictate what's possible. I can't believe that you're my fucking *wife*. And I wanted to make you something that *you* could want to watch over and over again, too. Especially in the moments when I've pissed you off and you're wondering how I talked you into spending the rest of your life with me. I'm not the best with words. Especially not soft ones. But for today, I want to record some. Especially since I'm about to fuck you until you can't walk for a week." He grins mischievously.

"You are more than my little treasure, *Tesoro*, you are my big magic. My forever wonder. The Russian doll that never stops surprising me with the depth of your brilliance. And you're the reason I'll never doubt that love *is* power." His eyes pierce through the screen and wrap themselves around me.

I clutch my chest as my heart riots against it and my throat constricts against the tears that are blooming.

"Your love has changed me. You've rewritten my future. Because of you, I know that my legacy will be whatever I choose. If people look at me and see a king, it's because I'm standing next to a queen." His firm, full lips purse around the last word.

"*You* are my reason," he says with a fierce conviction that feels like wind beneath my wings. His eyes soften and his shoulders relax. "The baby that's growing inside of you is just the first of many masterpieces we'll make together. You are *my* river. You've been the making of me. And I hope that one day I'll feel like I've earned the gift of your love. It's my privilege and honor to be your husband. I love you so much. More than I'll ever be capable of expressing. Now, lie back and get ready for me. I'm walking in now."

The door opens, and the screen goes blank at the same time. Hayes walks into the room. His bow tie is gone, his shirt unbuttoned completely, and his lightly-haired chest and the smooth tanned skin of his muscle carved torso peek out between the gap in the stark white fabric.

"Hey, wife." His eyes are alight with a heat that singes every part of me it lands on. His eyes drag up my body and he pulls his shirt off completely. The flex of the muscles in his powerful shoulders and arms distracts me. When I look back at his face, he's standing right in front of me.

"Hey, husband," I mimic him. I sit up on my knees so I can slip my arms around his neck. His warm hands slide along the swell of my abdomen before they slip behind my waist. He pulls me into his chest and presses his forehead to mine. He closes his eyes and hums low in his throat.

"That was so beautiful," I whisper against his lips and his eyes open and his gaze tangles with mine.

"You like it?" he asks with a satisfied smile.

I nod my answer when I find that my throat won't release my answer.

"Good," he says gruffly and squeezes me close. He buries his face in my neck and nuzzles it with his lips. I tighten my hold on his neck and think I might die from the intensity of the love that I feel for him. And what a way to go. I kiss the side of his face.

"I'll watch it again. Forever. And not just when you've managed to piss me off." I peck his mouth with a quick kiss to stop him from interrupting me. "I love it. And I love you. I'm the lucky one. I'm the one whose future has been rewritten. I hope you never regret letting me stand next to you. I hope you're always proud of me."

"Until my last breath," he whispers before he kisses me.

Finally.

And what a kiss it is.

His lips are impatient, his tongue insistent, and I open for him. Warmth rushes through me when his tongue sweeps my mouth and I press into him as tightly as my protruding belly will let me.

We get lost in the current of love, triumph, and togetherness that has become the river of our life.

I hope you loved that. I made a free ebook out of a short story I wrote for these two. You'll be signing up to my newsletter to think you'll love If you are reading the print version, email me at:
dylanallenwrites@gmail.com to receive it.

Read *The Legend*, Remi's story, next.

Acknowledgments

This small note cannot possibly convey the depth of my gratitude, it is fathomless.

To all of my colleagues who walk this very unique path along side me, I'm glad to have you in my life and am grateful for your constant support.

To my Day Dreamers and my DREAM TEAM I LOVE you guys! You make my day, every single day! You inspire me to keep writing and I am so thankful for the parts of your day that you spend with me.

To all of the blogs who have tirelessly and graciously read and then promoted my work— you are my heroes. I couldn't do this without you.

To the readers who buy my books, who email, message and tweet me! Thank you SO much for everything. You're amazing and I write with your wind at my back every day!

To my family—my parents, my sisters, my brothers-in-law and my cousins—you are my TRIBE! Thank you for being wonderful and loving.

And to my husband and my children. You are the heartbeats of my life. Thank you for inspiring me, loving me and supporting me. I love you all more than anything else in the universe!

Love,
Me

Also by Dylan Allen

RIVERS WILDE SERIES

The Legacy
Book one of the Rivers Wilde Series. An opposites attract, enemies to lovers stand-alone that kicks off this brand new series.

The Legend
This is a second chance at love story. Remington Wilde has loved one woman in his life and even though timing and family manipulations keep pulling them apart, it's a love worth fighting for.

The Jezebel
Regan Wilde and Stone Rivers were born enemies. But love has other ideas.

The Gathering
A delicious holiday novella with points of view from all six main characters including a scene from Tina and Tyson Wilde's point of view for the first time

The Daredevil: A Rivers Wilde/1001 Nights Novella
Tyson Wilde laughs in the face of danger and has yet to face a challenge he's not up to. Until Dina Lu walks into his life and threatens to turn it upside down.

The Mastermind: A Rivers Wilde/1001 Nights Novella
He lives under a golden spotlight. She's shackled to a past that must stay hidden. A fire-burning, second-chance romance novella.

THE SYMBOLS SERIES.

Then Came You
Set in London this is a workplace romance that features two people who are trying to outrun their pasts and protect their cynical hearts from more pain. But when their lives collide and their hearts and bodies yearn for each other, they'll have to decide if they are brave enough to fight for their love.

Still The One

This second chance romance features high school sweethearts who were torn apart by tragedy and treachery. Years later, when they realize that their feelings haven't changed, they embark on a mission to unravel the mystery surrounding her father's disappearance. But what they discover about their past might make a future together impossible.

Best for Last

This emotional, enemies to lovers, second chance romance features two people on a collision course with destiny. He's the heir to a British Dukedom, she's trying to find her place in this world. Opposites attract and sparks fly when they meet in a lush coastal city in Ghana. When serendipity reunites them, they'll have to reckon with their pasts to have the future they want.

STANDALONES

The Sun and Her Star

A friends to lovers, second chance at story. Angsty, emotional, sexy, and unforgettable. Graham and Apollo are two people who find each other just when they need to. What starts as a deep, abiding friendship grows into the kind of love that can move mountains. This story is a reader favorite.

Thicker Than Water

A friends to lovers and workplace romance that follows the love story between an undocumented writer and the movie executive who changes her life. This story is hopeful, honest, and achingly relevant. Go in with an open mind and prepare to fall in love.

The Sound of Temptation

A second chance forbidden romance that follows star-crossed lovers, a talented musician and the artist who becomes his muse. It spans nearly ten years and is a turbulent, exhilarating, heart pounding, and deeply intimate love story you will never forget.

If you've read my books and haven't already, please leave a review. Nothing fancy, but a line or two helps so much!

I love to hear from readers! Stay in touch with me at
Dylan@dylanallenbooks.com

About the Author

Dylan Allen is a Texas girl with a serious case of wanderlust.

A self-proclaimed happily ever junkie, she loves creating stories where her characters chase their own happy endings.

When she isn't writing or reading, eating, or cooking, she and her family are planning their next adventure.

I love talking to you guys! Feel free to send me an email at Dylan@dylanallenbooks.com

Are you on Facebook? If you are, then PLEASE join my private reader group, Dylan's Day Dreamer.

It's where I spend most of my time online. My Day Dreamers get exclusive giveaways, sneak peaks, glimpses into my every day, and lots of other fun bookish things! It's fantastic and my favorite place on the internet.

Discover More Blue Box Press Authors

Go to www.TheBlueBoxPress.com for more information.

Dylan Allen
Jennifer L. Armentrout
Kristen Ashley
Xio Axelrod
Steve Berry
Lexi Blake
Audrey Carlan
Marie Force
C. W. Gortner
Heather Graham
Donna Grant
Larissa Ione
Suzanne M. Johnson
J. Kenner
Randy Susan Meyers
Jennifer Probst
Kristen Proby
Christopher Rice
M.J. Rose
Kennedy Ryan
J.R. Ward

On Behalf of 1001 Dark Nights,

Liz Berry and Jillian Stein would like to thank ~

Steve Berry
Benjamin Stein
Kim Guidroz
Chelle Olson
Asha Hossain
Chris Graham
Tanaka Kangara
Jessica Saunders
Stacey Tardif
Suzy Baldwin
Grace Wenk
Dylan Stockton
Peggy Boulos Smith
Richard Blake
and Simon Lipskar